FALSE POSITIVES

Kim Aleksander

PHAROS BOOKS

COPYRIGHT

DEDICATION

$$\frac{J^3 + G}{F \times 4} = h^2$$

What a wonderful power the machine gives you!
But is it going to dominate you? This statement of
what the need and want is must come from you—
not the machine. And not from the government
that's teaching you; or not even from the clergy.
It has to come from one's own inside. And the
minute you let that drop and take the dictation of
what the time is instead of the dictation of your
own eternity, you have capitulated to the devil.
And you are in hell.

Joseph Campbell – *The Hero's Journey*

And I looked, and behold a pale horse; and his
name that sat on him was Death, and Hell
followed with him. And power was given unto
them over the fourth part of the earth, to kill with
sword, and with hunger, and with death, and with
the beasts of the earth.

Revelation 6:8

PROLOGUE

ON THE DESK BEFORE HIM lay an HP-35 hand-held calculator. Its crimson digits emitted an aura that formed a blood-red, translucent sphere in the air. The glowing ball of light hovered before him and pulsed in rhythm to the beat of his heart. It was well past midnight, and the effects of the mind candy showed no signs of relenting. A gift from his father, the machine was a modern wonder of the new electronic age that had rendered the engineer's slide rule obsolete with one fell swoop. Diabetes had done the same to his father, he reflected, but he was way too high to dive into those murky waters tonight.

Crumpled wads of computer punch cards were strewn across the floor. They were miniature tumbleweeds, littering a ghost town constructed from books pulled from the stacks of the campus library. It was an eclectic inventory of esoteric reference material. Volumes on the world's religions were scattered like toppled tombstones in a long forgotten graveyard. Other works covered topics that ranged from computer programming to transcendental enlightenment. A bible rested peacefully beside his foot opened to the Book of Revelation. The Qur'an lay beside it.

The instant Zen he'd dropped earlier in the evening had fine-tuned his senses to a state beyond the real. He was experiencing sensory super-saturation with even the smallest of movements. Everything was crystal clear.

He poked the perforated holes through the thick data cards and felt the fibers tear one by one. As spent slugs piled up on the desk in confetti snowdrifts, he blew them off the edge in slow, deliberate breaths and delighted in his man-made blizzards. A thoughtfully singed draft card was in there somewhere amidst the flotsam, and that brought a sad smile to his face.

The code he punched was the sublimated result of a restless mind in search of an outlet. Physics didn't thrill him. Philosophy seemed like the ranting of madmen, yet mathematics came as naturally as the English language for him. Apart from the rest, however, the field of computer programming was akin to being master of the universe. He could create. He could destroy. And he could do this all within the safety of his own mind without anyone being showered with Agent Orange in a jungle somewhere in Southeast Asia.

While others were out and about organizing acts of civil disobedience, he was expanding his mind. He had no intention of spending even one night in jail, even if that might bring him somehow closer to Henry David Thoreau. No, this project would be his little secret. He preferred to fly under the radar. Besides, there was no beating the system by ranting from a soapbox. That's how you got shot these days, and that would suck, he imagined, rubber bullets or not.

He referred to his notes often as he methodically poked hole after hole. After completing each card, he held it against the nearby lampshade and marveled at the kaleidoscopic pointillism that shined through. He gazed at the patterns as if they were some new form of Rorschach test. Several times he saw God, but that was the acid working its magic. Through the night he fried, tripping the light fantastic. He plugged away like a moonstruck maestro obsessed with weaving the tapestry of time.

※ ※ ※

THINGS WERE COMING to life on campus. He could sense it though the walls of his dorm room where he'd holed up to perform his magic through the night. His fingers were sore, and his hands were cramping. There had to be an easier way, he thought, but he was nearly through with it. He steeled himself to the task. A dog barked in the distance, and the deep, red glow of the sunrise announced the dawn. He looked at his calculator. The batteries had died. Remembering his father, he held the final card up to the lamp for inspection. It was beautiful—flawless. He had finished.

"I need a shower," he said to himself and pushed back from his magnum opus.

Twelve stacks stood at attention, each precisely five hundred cards tall and wrapped snugly together by the hundred with a crisscross of rubber bands. The code was neat. It was precise, and he knew it was perfect.

He sloughed off his clothes, dropping them along the hallway on his way to the shower. Deftly avoiding the bathroom mirror—he'd made that mistake before and wasted four hours once—he turned on the taps and braced himself against the initial chill factor. The water felt thick as oil as it warmed. He was coming down, he knew, and did his best not to freak himself out. Grabbing a gritty, green bar of Lava, he made a respectable attempt to scrub away the drug-induced film that covered his body. Five minutes later, he was staring at his face in the mirror.

When he finally emerged from his inner journey, it was 10:30am. His clothes had miraculously vanished from the hallway, and he heard conversation in the living room. "Damn!" he cursed. His roommate was back.

He walked to the common room and found his roommate sharing a joint with a couple of friends.

"Hey, man! You all right?" his friend asked. "You were in there a while."

"Ya, I guess. I got a bit of the flu," he lied.

"It looks like you were burning the midnight oil last night."

He looked to the desk and noticed that his punch cards were gone.

"Where are my punch cards?" he asked.

"Oh, those. I figured you were, um, incapacitated so I thought I'd help you out. I gave 'em to my girlfriend. She's dropping them off at the computer center on her way back to her dorm."

"You what?" he practically shrieked at his friend who towered over him. His friend was tall but rangy.

"Take it easy, man. She's cool; smart too," his friend said. "She won't lose them or nothin'."

"What does she look like?" he demanded.

"Tall, red hair, athletic. You've seen her before."

"Fuck!" was all he could say. "Fuck, fuck, fuck!" he screamed and tore for the door, wearing only a towel around his waist.

"Geez, what's his problem?" asked one of the guys, as he re-lit a very large marijuana cigarette.

"Not sure. Probably stoned. That would be my guess."

Stoned themselves, they all found this enormously funny and fell into a giggling fit.

⌘ ⌘ ⌘

THE COMPUTER CENTER was located in the basement of the new math building. He'd crossed the campus towel-clad and barefoot in possibly the fastest four hundred meter dash the school had ever seen. Luckily, he wasn't picked up for streaking, he thought, as he re-tied his towel around his waist and entered the building. Security consisted of a bell that hung above the door and a computer operator named Ted. Things had changed since the anti-war sit-ins that closed the place a couple years back when demonstrators had claimed that the school's computers were being used towards the war effort. The students had run amok for a bit, damaging some equipment and destroying a few tape reels. Fortunately, no one really knew where to start with twin CDC 6400 mainframes, thus damage was trivial.

"Hey, Ted," he said.

"Hey, nice outfit," Ted replied.

"Did someone just come over here and drop off six thousand punch cards?"

"Uh, ya. Some chick came by here a couple hours ago. She was way cute."

"Ya, well those were my cards. What did you do with them?"

"I fed them to Seymour."

"Please, tell me you're joking."

"Nope."

"What happened?"

"You know, that's the weird thing. It was trippy. I fed the cards through the card reader like I've done a million times before. It took me almost a freakin' hour, and you know what happened?"

"Tell me."

"Absolutely nothing."

"You're serious?"

"Ya, six thousand cards without a single error; and then, when I run the program, the system blinks at me with that seductive green eye of hers. And then, *poof*."

"*Poof* what?"

"*Poof* nothin', that's what. It just did nothin'. I never seen that before, man, ever."

"Whoa."

"Ya, I can imagine that would be a major bummer for someone would just punched a bazillion holes. Hey, why *are* you wearing a towel? Did I miss another party?"

"Where are they now?"

"Who?"

"The cards!"

"Dude, mellow out. They're in the machine room. It has to be a glitch or something, so I was going to run them again after the suits are done."

"Suits?" he asked.

"Ya, you know, the *federales*—G-men. They'll be here any minute. They take the afternoons these days. Time sharing with the man. That's what we do."

"It helps with the grant money, I'm sure."

"Here they are now. Right on time, these boys. You want the cards back when I'm done?"

"Nah, that thing's a flop. Go ahead and trash 'em."

"You sure?"

"I'm sure." A subtle look of guilt and paranoia flashed across his face as he said this.

"Okay, man. Whatever. Milas, you gotta go. Like now."

The door's bell tinkled behind him. He turned and saw three very clean-cut men in suits standing in the doorway holding oversized brief cases. He offered them a mock salute and a grin as they held the door open for him. He marched past with his chest puffed out and his towel swishing at his legs. His pupils were as large as flying saucers.

"Hippie," he heard one of them say to his back. But he kept on truckin'.

Chapter 1

THE ROAR OF A HARD RAIN on the rooftop awoke Marnie before her alarm at 5:50am. This was a bad sign. She'd now be forced to trudge through her daily constitutional on a treadmill instead of breathing in the fresh air of the morning and absorbing the infinite activities of nature along the Donaldson Run Trail and Military Road. Marnie loved this run where she tramped through some of the more swank areas of McLean with its immaculately manicured yards near the Washington Country Club Golf Course and through the trees at Potomac Overlook Park. Instead, she'd be stuck indoors on account of inclement weather.

She spun herself around in bed and dropped her feet on the Pergo laminate floor of her apartment. It was cold. She paced to the bathroom naked with a lithe grace and splashed some water on her face. She looked at herself in the mirror. Marnie was thirty now. A thick mane of rich, red hair the color of burnished copper framed the face of a girl from another time. A time before the lines of age would change it one way or another as it does to everyone eventually. She tied her hair back into a ponytail that reached to the middle of her back and pulled on a semi-used sweatshirt from the floor. It read, "MARYMOUNT" in dark-blue capital letters across her chest. She'd been a star pitcher on the varsity softball team and the fastest girl on the track team back then. Looking back at a slightly different person now, she smiled to reveal the crows-feet of easy laughter that she'd already learned to live with for years now. She didn't mind them because for one thing, she wasn't about to give up laughing any time soon.

Navigating through what some might call a kitchenette, she pulled a two-liter, recycled plastic Coke bottle filled with chilled water from the fridge and drank nearly a quarter of it in the four short steps to her living room. It wasn't much of a living room.

Marnie called it her "living room slash study slash gym." Actually, it would be more accurately described as a gym and dirty laundry gathering area; there were several stacks of overdue library books haphazardly piled around a laptop computer and a TV bolted to the wall in front of a treadmill. She searched through a mountain of laundry on the floor—some of it clean, some not—working in a few key stretching moves during the process. After locating some grey sweat pants with holes in them and a pair of fresh white socks, she laced herself into a pair of Air Nikes that had seen better days.

She reached down in front of the treadmill and flicked on the power. The machine responded with an electronic beep and an array of red lights on its front panel. She deftly plotted a virtual running course into the machine, pressed start, and felt the heavy rubber belt begin to move beneath her feet. The machine's program began what would methodically build up momentum from warm-up to flat-out sprint. Marnie grabbed the heart monitor that dangled on the machine's railing and strapped it around her waistline. She cinched it up snugly beneath her breasts. Checking the monitor, it read a normal eighty-five beats per minute and would soon be getting into the one-fifties. Marnie reached for the remote and switched on the television for a bit of distraction during her warm up.

"Morning talk shows and crap, that's all that's ever on at six in the morning," she thought aloud. She inevitably found herself on FOX watching breaking news. The sensationalist commentary that accompanied the news today never ceased to amaze her.

She switched the channel to CNN.

Her attention was abruptly grabbed by what at first seemed to be yet another suicide bomber having taken himself out along with several innocents in an outdoor market in the Baghdad. She quickly realized, however, that this was not your average martyr. Christine Amanpour was reporting live. They cut to footage showing a young woman wearing a billowing, head-to-toe *abaya*, the customary dress worn by Iraqi women. She was being interviewed before the camera. White text crawled across the red marquee below the image. It read, "Teenage girl kills nine in suicide bombing." The camera cut to a scene of horrific devastation where the girl had apparently detonated herself.

Marnie grabbed for the remote. At first she was stunned, but she didn't quite understand why. She'd never imagined these people—these terrorists—to be anyone other than men. By the time Marnie got the volume up, the segment had ended. She asked herself the question to which she'd never quite learned an answer: "What pisses these people off so much that would cause them to do this? And even more perplexing," she thought, "why were those who filled these young minds with visions of martyrdom hell bent on doing so?" It frustrated her that the news rarely gave the whole story. She wanted to know *why* this girl had done what she'd done, but the news rarely told you that.

Beep. The treadmill's computer kicked it up a notch. The machine changed from a flat grade to a ten percent incline with a growling whir, increasing the pace. The sounds were now completely second nature to Marnie. She stepped into a jog without giving it a second thought. Each of her footfalls gave off a synthetic chirp so very unlike the birds she'd be listening to if not for this morning's weather. She shut off the TV and dug into her ritual. Fifty minutes later she was showered and out the door.

⌘ ⌘ ⌘

THE TRIP TO SOLUTIONS DRIVE in McLean was not a far one, but this morning it seemed to take forever. Marnie could not see a thing through the fogged up windshield of her near-ancient Mustang convertible. With the top up and her body still radiating heat, she stuck to the slow lane on the Capital Beltway, constantly wiping the condensation off the inside of the glass. She should have known better by now, she thought, or at least have developed a system more advanced than using her sleeve to cope with the Virginia rains and her feeble defroster. The ironic reality was that though she was a veritable whiz with technology, she was not at all interested in mechanics. She'd much rather ride with the top down than fix anything as mundane at her car. So much so, that by the time she stepped into her office at Burns and Lynch Consulting, she'd already forgotten about it completely. There were many things that captured her problem-solving spirit, but her Mustang was not one of them.

Marnie's office didn't amount to much. It was almost a mirror image of her apartment, save the kitchenette, gym, and television. Small hills of books and documents had annexed the majority of her desk; she'd run out of space on her bookshelf some time ago. There was just enough room for a computer and a phone, though to answer the thing she had to stand up whenever it rang due to the barricade before her. This usually resulted in a raft of voice mail messages that she rarely listened to and a blinking red light that she mostly ignored. Besides, if anyone really needed to contact her it would be through email, knowing she couldn't be off the Net for more than a few hours at a time.

Logging in, she opened her email program, scanned through the headers, and found three emails from her boss with the same subject. "Call me ASAP! Urgent!!!" they read. When using email, Mark Harmann was a man of few words and many exclamation points, and this drove Marnie absolutely mad—so mad that she'd told him off on more than one occasion. "For God's sake," she'd admonished. "The least you could do is enlighten me to the topic, so I know what we'll be talking about." She vowed to intentionally ignore emails like this until he learned to put in some detail. This drove Mark Harmann reciprocally mad, causing him to add even more exclamation points to his ever-nebulous subject lines.

It wasn't that Mark Harmann wasn't a good boss. He was a great boss. He was a man with whom she'd been intimately involved at one time and was now her mentor. He had a mind that thought in ways she could barely comprehend, which—somewhat sadly—was the reason for their breakup, although Mark called their romantic demise the direct effect of the natural selection of relationships. That was nearly ten years ago, and though their youthful twenty-something passion may have waned, their professional respect for each other had blossomed into something unparalleled among their colleagues within the circle of their expertise.

Marnie sighed, got up, and made her way to Mark's office. The words, Mark Harmann – VP, were etched into the opaque glass of the door. She could see his blurry image pacing in circles around his desk like a shark. Entering without a knock, she gave him a half-assed salute and a sardonic grin before plopping herself onto a sumptuously oiled leather sofa set.

On the coffee table sat an elegant chess service cut from mahogany and oak. It was set well into the middle game from their previous unfinished match. Her black pieces were on equal footing with his white. She studied the board, recalling how the pieces had made it to their positions. She could also see the possibilities several moves out that would change her positional advantage into a material advantage heading into the end game. Her planning was apt to be in vain, however, as she'd never once been able to deliver the *coup de grâce* of checkmate in the hundreds of war-games she and Mark had waged against each other. Mark was unbeatable, which stood to reason knowing his years of experience designing and developing war-games for the U.S. Department of Defense—not to mention his love for the game of chess.

"I'll call you back. Bye," he said and cut the connection without waiting for a response.

"Typically Mark," she muttered to herself.

"Marnie! Where have you been? I've been trying to reach you since last night."

"You know I hate phones and arcane subject lines," she said with a wry smile.

"If you weren't so damn smart, I'd fire you."

"You've been saying that for five years, Mark."

"Seven and a half actually, but you've gotten away with murder because you were too cute."

"Were? Like was? As in past tense?"

"Yes, were. Now you're utterly pulchritudinous."

"Whatever that means." She rolled her eyes, yet felt herself blush slightly.

"Ya, whatever."

Mark was never that great with flattery. The more passionate he was, the more he was compelled to use sophisticated vocabulary with which to convey his emotions. This often rendered him unintelligible and eventually led to a wedge being driven between the woman who only wished to hear three special words and the man who spoke in tomes.

"Anyhow, enough of that, we got it! We got it Marno!" He was practically levitating in his excitement.

"Got what?"

"The big one!"

"You mean *the* big one? You are kidding me!"

"I can't tell you any more than that. What's your security clearance with the Feds?" he asked.

"You know damn well it's secret! Tell me more!"

"Can't," he said and walked over to his speakerphone, jabbing the well-worn three buttons of his secretary.

"Melanie, bring me Marnie's DHS docket," he said and hung up.

"Homeland Security? You've just told me something," Marnie pointed out.

"Marnie this project is TS, and I'm not leaking any more until you're cleared."

"How much?"

"Thirty-two point seven mil. I was trying to track you down to get your signatures last night."

"What do they want us to do for them?"

"Oh, prevent another 9/11, basically. And possibly end the Iraq war."

"Iraq is not Homeland Security," she said with suspicion in her voice.

Mark sat down on the couch across the chessboard from Marnie and mimed the zipping of his lips with two fingers. He then wagged a forefinger at her. "Not another word!" he said.

"Here you are, Mr. Harmann," Melanie said as she entered Mark's office with a polite knock. She handed him a manila folder about an inch thick.

"Hello, Miss McCloud. Are you well?" she asked.

"Well and fine, Mel. You?"

"Couldn't be better, thank you," she replied. "Mr. Harmann, I've taken the liberty of refreshing Miss McCloud's resume with her most recent projects and have enclosed a complete set of her professional history and educational references as well as her current proof of security status. Everything is in order, and all of the signature lines are marked with a red sticky. There are nineteen in total. Please leave them signed upon my desk when they are ready, and I'll have them sent by courier to Washington this afternoon. Will there be anything else?"

"Nope, thanks," Mark said.

At this, Melanie smiled with a demure nod and left the room.

"You really should work on your social skills, especially with her. She's a gem. You want to keep this one," Marnie told Mark.

"She's paid to put up with me and paid well."

"Aren't we all?" Marnie sighed.

The big one was something that Mark and Marnie had been working on since before they'd even joined Burns and Lynch. It began with the simple concept that computers, if powerful enough, could process information faster than the human brain. And if these computers were fed enough information regarding a particular subject, they would be able to process it with precision and in multiple permutations with more efficiency than any human being and, furthermore, any team of experts.

This concept was applied to a tangible subject as early as 1952 when Allen Turing demonstrated the first computer chess program. Over the years since the 1950's, technology advanced exponentially. At Los Alamos in '57, experiments on a Univac MANIAC 1, processing eleven thousand operations per second, proved that a computer could play chess, determining the best move by thinking four moves ahead. MANIAC 1 took three hours per move to analyze a chess position without bishops and was easily beaten by even the most amateur chess players, though few had the patience to wait for such an opponent to make up its mind. This included chimpanzees, though they tended to want to bite or throw their pieces rather than play them.

Over the course of thirty years, some of the most able minds from M.I.T, Carnegie-Mellon, Stanford University, and most notably IBM had honed computer chess into a fearsome adversary named DEEP BLUE. On May 11, 1997, DEEP BLUE defeated chess Grand Master Gary Kasparov in a six game match held in New York. This was the first time a computer had ever beaten a reigning world champion in a classical chess match. DEEP BLUE was configured to use thirty of IBM's most advanced processors coupled with four hundred eighty specialized chess chips. It could evaluate two hundred million moves per second. Gary Kasparov had one brain and could calculate ten positions every three minutes. It just wasn't fair.

It was this triumph of technology over man that had inspired both Marnie and Mark to pursue the arcane field of artificial intelligence during their post-graduate work. It was their passion for applying computer-assisted logic to real-world problem solving that led them to become the most sought after consultants in the burgeoning field of strategic computer modeling and simulation.

"Do you know what this means?" Her words came out in a dreamy tone as the cogs of her mind began to churn at the possibilities.

"Indeed I do and more," he said. "I believe it's my move. Your pawns have been eating me alive." He used a single finger to scoot one of his own pawns to where it threatened Marnie's queen. "Have some of your own medicine. Your queen is in check."

"Obviously. And there's no such thing as checking a queen," she said and continued her pawn march, intentionally sacrificing her queen. "Take her. She's yours. Do what you will with her."

"Tut tut. Let's be civil. I will ravish her though," he said in a lecherous tone while calmly capturing her queen.

Marnie's next move captured a pawn, effectively forking Mark's rook and king.

"Check," she said.

"Hmm, interesting," was all that Mark said, as he captured the pawn with his king.

Looming at the end of the board was Marnie's rook, which she now moved into position to attack Mark's white queen. "Take that, you ravisher."

"Sadly for you, I won't." He moved his threatened queen to safety. "I've seen that look in your eyes before."

"Coward," she said, jumping her knight to a center square, revealing her well-laid plan. "Bet you haven't seen this before."

"From you? No. From others? Yes. Spassky vs. Fischer. Reykjavik 1972," he said and slid a singular pawn to the sixth rank, attacking her bishop.

"A mere distraction. Is this a Fischer tactic?" She removed the bishop from harm's way.

"Actually, I'm playing Spassky, but that's irrelevant. Fischer lost—a rare event, considering his mastery of the poisoned pawn variation of the Najdorf Sicilian." He took her king's pawn without hesitation, revealing her imminent defeat. "And so will you, my dear. That's mate in three."

"What the—? Damn it! How the hell can you remember all that?" she exclaimed.

"I'm a genius you seem to forget," he smiled. "Plus, I cheat."

"Bastard!" she laughed and toppled her king to its demise upon the board.

Mark stood up and stretched. He looked more like a stock trader in his custom tailored shirt, flamboyantly patterned Escher print tie, and ever-present suspenders. His suspenders were a fashion throwback that Marnie always joked were a necessary device required to keep his pants on at work. It was hard for her to imagine that they might soon be playing out their war-games on a much, much bigger scale, however vicariously that would be.

"Come, let's go tell the dynamic duo what's in store for them."

Chapter 2

Salome Kahn was clearing her desk and preparing to leave work. Her office at the Martyr's Foundation was always tidy and well organized, but the habit of straightening things at the end of the day was a satisfying ritual and bought her some time to think.

She'd just finished a brutally emotional session with the Sadeghi family. Salome had the unfortunate duty of informing the Sadeghis that their daughter would not be coming home. The daughter, Fatima, was barely nineteen years old and had run away just over two months ago. She had left only a note behind that told her parents that she had been chosen to do God's will. She'd not been heard from since. The Sadeghis were blindsided by Fatima's abrupt departure. They were busy but loving parents who, like almost everyone, had no training or experience to allow them to detect the textbook changes in their daughter's behavior. If they'd noticed anything different about Fatima, it was chalked up as a phase of becoming a woman. That she was descending upon the slippery slope of extremism had never crossed their minds.

The all-too-short story of what actually happened to Fatima Sadeghi was tragic. Late last year, she'd fallen in with a new circle of friends she'd been introduced to through her boyfriend. This group of young men and women were brought together by the fact that each of the men had recently volunteered as suicide commandos. Volunteering was a straightforward process these days. Registration forms had appeared on Tehran's streets and university campuses with no apparent signs that the government had any plans to stop this all-out recruitment movement. In fact, Tehran was home to many ostensibly charitable organizations that fronted as recruiting centers where registrants were given a number of options in how they could volunteer. One could select suicide attacks against Israel or U.S. forces in Iraq. Other options included training for the assassination of Salman Rushdie or any of the Danish cartoonists whose work was condemned as denigrating the image of Muhammad. Volunteers were estimated in the tens of thousands, an estimated twenty thousand had been chosen for training.

As the men of Fatima's newfound group slipped away from society to begin their training, the women were left alone. Rather than being saddened by the loss of the men they loved, they became emboldened. Determined to make their mark against the crusaders and infidels in the name of God, they too began volunteering. While the majority of volunteers remained men and boys, the planners of these attacks against the West could not deny the disarming effectiveness of putting women into play. They knew that women drew less attention than men and were less apt to be subject to rigorous security checks. Security procedures still had trouble dealing with searches on women, as it was considered indecent and violated Islamic laws that required women to remain traditionally clothed in public. The recruiters had no qualms when Fatima Sadeghi and the rest of her girl gang willingly offered their services.

On Monday, the fifth of March, a woman wearing an explosive vest loaded with acetone peroxide entered an open market in Baghdad. Over the vest was strapped a fragmentation jacket that held a lethal payload of 7-millimeter steel ball bearings. The entire apparatus weighed fifteen kilos and was fashioned under her *abaya* as a ruse to make her look pregnant. Waddling slowly through the crowd, she used her arms to protect her explosive, unborn child.

During her training she'd learned that acetone peroxide, or TATP, had earned the nickname of The Mother of Satan for its renowned instability. Cautiously, she navigated her way beneath the camouflage of her *abaya* like a black raven, a harbinger of death. She was weary from hauling her heavy load, but wanted her act of martyrdom to cause maximum impact and thus pushed deeper into the crowd.

As she approached the market's center, she recognized the kill-zone from the photographs she had studied. The time was nigh. She was trembling with fear yet overcome with anticipation for the rewards she expected to receive in paradise. At that moment, as her thumb twitched above the vest's detonator, a large basket of pistachios fell from a vendor's stall on to the ground behind her. Someone shouted. Startled and on edge, she spun around, seeking the source of the commotion. The weight of her suicide vest coupled with the fatigue of carrying it and the carpet of pistachios beneath her feet proved a combination of elements that toppled her. She fell face first to the ground. The Mother of Satan did the rest. Due to the position of the explosives centered around her stomach, the ground absorbed the brunt of the explosion while her body was torn in half and hurtled in opposite directions. Fortunately for many, the collateral damage was minimized because the detonation occurred while she was prone; however, nine people were ravaged by the discharge of shrapnel and several others were seriously wounded. While this martyr did not go out in the blaze of glory she had hoped, her actions still had the intended effect of striking terror in the hearts and minds of those who bore witness to the traumatic event both locally and globally via the world's news networks.

The pregnant martyr had been Fatima Sadeghi. Salome had broken the news as gently as she knew how, but when the Sadeghis demanded evidence—not believing that their daughter was capable of such a heinous act—she was obligated to show them a photograph of Fatima's disembodied torso that had been taken by a security clean-up team in the aftermath of the suicide bombing. Upon seeing their daughter's mutilated remains, Mrs. Sadeghi wailed aloud, while the father simply wept.

Salome found it terribly difficult to console the Sadeghis. After all, there was not much she could offer beside her compassion and sympathy. She could not in all honestly tell them their daughter was in a better place. Nor would she ever admit that Fatima's attack was in any way an act that would be condoned by God. Fatima was a girl who had been seduced by the lure of a religion misrepresented by men with ulterior motives that were decidedly unholy. Salome, of course, had not shared these sentiments with the mourning Sadeghis and mainly sat with them in silence as they processed this harsh reality in their own way. Eventually, they mustered the courage to return home with the knowledge that they would never see Fatima again.

Salome said she would be available anytime for them if they needed someone to talk to and recommended that they join one of the many support groups the Foundation helped organize. There they would meet families who were fighting to recover from similar tragedies. The Sadeghis thanked Salome for her kindness. She gathered her things and escorted them to the building's main entrance. She watched them leave and couldn't help but feel their pain as they walked away overcome by the shared grief of their loss.

As she turned and reentered the Foundation, Salome caught a glimpse of a disheveled young man staring anxiously at the building's façade. She observed him through the door's mirrored glass and thought there was something vaguely familiar about him, but she couldn't place it. Salome was about go back outside to ask what he wanted, when the young man darted out of sight around the corner.

"Well, so much for that," she thought. It had been a long day. Salome dismissed the young man from her mind and returned to her office.

Chapter 3

For servicemen in Vietnam, Thailand was like a little slice of heaven in the middle of hell. During the war, the U.S. military was granted the use of airbases located around Thailand for Air Force operations. Soldiers were garrisoned at these bases in Korat, Udon, Ubon, Nakhon Phanom, Takhli, and U-Tapao, while those on R&R mainly stayed in Bangkok if they didn't leave for other places like Hawaii, the Philippines, or home. While off-duty, soldiers enjoyed free beer donated to the troops by American beverage manufacturers and their rations of whiskey and cigarettes from the PX. The Thais realized quickly that there was money to be made in providing comfort services for these foreign soldiers. Brothels sprung up near the bases, and in some of the more organized establishments, female companionship was offered on contract by the week.

Milas's time at the Defence Attaché Office in Saigon did not include a lot of fraternizing. He was comfortable with the fact that he was a bit of a loner and mainly kept to himself; however, this didn't prevent him from hearing the stories that soldiers returning from Thailand had brought back with them. He'd had his share of sorties into the red-light district of Saigon, but when the tales of Thailand were sung in the barracks, they had an air of seduction he found compellingly more exotic than his admittedly tawdry experiences in Vietnam.

On April 28th, 1975, three A-37 Dragonflies dropped six two hundred and fifty pound Mark 81 bombs on the runway at Tan Son Nhut. The fall of Saigon had begun. The DAO came abuzz and evacuation preparations began. It was a form of organized chaos as sixty C-130s were scheduled to arrive and take an estimated ten thousand people out of Vietnam.

Milas found Colonel Ray amidst the mayhem and was briskly ordered to collect every scrap of data he was working on and sit on it until the colonel came and found him. Milas did as he was told.

At 3:30am, Milas was roused from sleep by the sharp crack of an explosion. He sat up from his bed of tape-reel canisters that held the data of the Phoenix Project. He was dazed and was considering running when Colonel Ray walked in. The colonel gestured at the canisters under Milas's rear end and said, "Is that all of it?"

"What was that explosion, sir?"

"Rocket attack. Just killed two Marines," he said. "Is that all of it, Lieutenant Milas?"

"Yes, sir."

"Can you carry it?"

"Sir?"

"I said, can you carry those tapes, Lieutenant!"

"Yes, sir!"

"Good, because you're going to haul that pile to somewhere safe. You're on the first herky bird out of here at oh-four-hundred hours. Now get your ass ready to board that plane. I'll find you later," he said and quick-stepped from the room.

Milas had just enough time to find a rucksack that would fit the tapes and gather his few possessions from the barracks before four o'clock. He lugged his load across the DAO and took a jeep to the airfield, where he found the colonel waiting for him.

Colonel Ray had to shout to be heard over the roar of the C-130E Hercules aircraft engines. "That's your plane!" he yelled, pointing at one of the giants taxiing on the near runway. An instant later the plane's tail section was engulfed in a ball of fire, having been hit by a North Vietnamese rocket.

The colonel frowned at this, contemplated for a moment, and then shouted, "That's your plane!" pointing at a second C-130 that was holding on the far runway. "Get in!" he said and got behind the wheel of the jeep. Milas tossed his bag in the back and jumped in. The colonel sped in the direction of the plane as they passed the other that was burning. Milas watched as the crew climbed down a rope ladder from the cockpit window and a fire team raced to control the flames.

Colonel Ray skidded the jeep to a halt at the bottom of the C-130's ramp and leapt out, approaching one of the ground crew who was looking warily into the sky. He pointed at Milas and then the Hercules. Milas grabbed his bundle and dragged it to the ramp. The colonel met him there and shouted, "This is your lucky day, son! You're going to Thailand! Don't you fucking lose those!" He pointed at the at Milas's rucksack.

"What am I supposed to do with them, sir?" shouted Milas.

"Don't worry, I'll find you! Now get your ass in there before they blow the shit out of this one too!"

Milas dropped his bags and gave Colonel Ray a salute. He would never see him again.

The Hercules carrying Milas and one hundred twenty other evacuees, touched down with surprising grace at the U-Tapao Royal Thai Navy Airfield just before dawn. When the behemoth taxied to a stop and the massive ramp was lowered, Milas felt a wash of sea air fill the cargo hold. It smelled like paradise and jet fuel.

CHAPTER 4

JAMES HAWK AND PATTRAPONG SANPAKDEE (a.k.a. Phet, with a hard P) were deeply engrossed in a computer game as Marnie and Mark entered the lair. The lair was an immense data center that housed the core systems of the Burns and Lynch McLean Facility. Located sixty feet underground and protected by cement reinforcements, it was more like a bunker than anything else, except for the several million dollars' worth of technology that hummed the monotonous tune of two hundred some-odd fans whirring. Oddly, they all whirred in the key of B-flat, sometimes major sometimes minor, Phet had pointed out one day as he strummed chords on the electric guitar that rarely left his side. Phet was a tactile thinker. He played guitar while he worked. It was part of his process and a queerly impressive quirk that added to his image of being somewhat of a savant.

"Alright, guys. Take a break for a minute, I've got an announcement," Mark said, emerging from the elevator with Marnie at his side. He pulled a pair of wheeled chairs around and rolled them towards the boys, as Hawk and Phet were affectionately known around the office. While they were both well past boyhood, they often didn't act it.

"Pause," said Hawk.

"You first," said Phet.

"Both of you, c'mon. Now!" Mark said a little louder than usual.

The boys each hovered a finger over their keyboards and counted down from three, watching each other with a wary eye. Finally, they paused the game, both letting out a reflexive sigh of relief.

"There's a flaw in your latest," said Hawk. "An exploit. He's acquiring resources at an unnatural rate."

"Leave it to Phet to find a bug and use it against you," Mark said. "Send it to Jennifer in development. She'll get it patched."

"Not bug! Tactical advantage leveraged against inferior adversary," Phet jabbed through a thick Asian accent that usually never included irrelevant things like the article, 'A'.

"Inferior my ass! I was just kicking yours," Hawk spat.

Hawk and Phet were Mark's most trusted testers for his war games, a sideline Mark continued as a means to enhance his income while allowing a playful outlet to test his theories regarding war craft on the American game-playing demographic. He trusted these two more than the people he paid to do this because of the simple fact that he didn't pay them to do this. These guys were true aficionados of computer games, especially war simulations. Actually, they were holders of much loftier titles than game tester. Hawk was a Technical Architect and Phet was a Senior Security Analyst. Each held enough credentials to fill two of Melanie's folders and, having worked on hundreds of Burns and Lynch projects as consultants, they were formidable captains of their industry. But that was work. Games were fun.

"Guys, we have a surprise for you," Mark began. "You'll need to go up and see Melanie and sign a bunch of papers before I can tell you much, but you two gents will be on exclusive rental to the United States Government for the next twelve months or more."

"The Feds? That's nothing new," said Hawk. "Any branch in particular?"

"Does the name Frances Townsend ring a bell?" Marnie asked.

Hawk and Phet looked at each other then back at Mark and shrugged.

"Charles E. Allen?" she asked.

They shook their heads as a collective "No."

"I'm barking up the wrong tree, here," Marnie thought aloud. "How about Wilson P. Dizzard the Third?"

"Oh, he wants to barcode people," said Hawk with obvious distaste.

"Human RFID!" exclaimed Phet. "Mexican laser virus!"

"That's Mexican laser visa, you nitwit," said Hawk.

"Wow! That struck a chord," Mark observed with interest.

"It's a privacy thing," explained Marnie. "Actually, gentlemen, you'll be happy to know that The Department of Homeland Security—the agency you'll be working for, or should I say billing hours to—has practically condemned radio identification in their report, *The Use of RFID for Human Identification.*"

"So they say," said Phet in a tone that would have sent a wicked chill down Orson Wells's long-dead spine.

"Actually, Marnie, DHS isn't the whole picture. You boys ever heard of ALIEN?" Mark asked.

Marnie looked at Hawk and Phet who in turn both looked at each other.

"ALIEN," Hawk said with an ominous tone. "This is deep."

ALIEN was an acronym for All Source Intelligence Environment. In its strictest sense, it was the system used for sharing classified information across defense department intelligence offices. It encompassed a great deal more than that, however. In fact, since its inception DHS had been pushing, with executive backing, for the standardization of systems to facilitate interconnection and the transfer of disparate data to a unified knowledge base.

"And wide!" piped Phet. His eyes gleamed behind a pair of ridiculously thick eyeglasses.

"Indeed," said Mark. "Now go up and see Melanie and get your stuff signed before I tell you more than I should. Hawk, you first. We need to talk to Phet about something."

Hawk raised his eyebrows, gave a shrug, and lifted his lanky frame from the ergonomically designed chair that had been made especially for him. Hawk was six foot four and wiry as a desert gunslinger. He flashed a look at Phet and said, "Don't touch that game 'til I come back, young'un, or there'll be hell to pay."

Phet looked him straight in the eye and said, "Your mother wears army boots!"

Everyone laughed at this as Hawk made his way to the elevator for his impromptu signature session with Melanie.

"Phet, we've got a small problem," Mark said.

"What problem?" It sounded more like *pom-pem* when he said it, but Mark and the rest of Phet's friends understood that Phet had no intention of correcting his accent. Everyone knew that he could speak flawless English when he wanted to—on first dates, for example, or job interviews, neither of which had occurred in anyone's recent memory—but he chose not to most of the time. Those who knew him also knew that his accent was part of his charm, which tended to temper a simmering intellect that often put people on the defensive when talking with him. This was probably the reason why he didn't get very many second dates.

"We can't get you local site access for security reasons," Mark continued. "I'll put it bluntly. You don't have the security clearance you need due to your dual citizenship, so they won't let you on site."

"What? I am American!" Phet said. His tone raised and his cheeks flushed. "I play rock n' roll! My mother work ass off running Bangkok go-go bar. She take money from sex tourists to send me to here for education! What more American than that?"

Mark could not suppress the smile that came to his lips, while Marnie had to stifle an out-loud laugh of her own.

"Not funny," Phet fumed.

"Relax, Phet. You are on the project in a role that you are perfect for," Mark explained. "You're the outside man. A system with internetworking connections as complex as ALIEN requires that intrusion is a proven impossibility. If anyone can find a vulnerability, you can. Besides, they wouldn't let you bring your guitar in anyhow."

"So, I am ALIEN hacker?" Phet beamed, relishing in his double entendre. He stroked his guitar and played a short riff to punctuate his cleverness.

"That is a fact. You okay with that?" Mark asked.

"Yes, I like this. I play guitar and hack federal fascists! We finished, right? Phet go see Ms. Melanie now," he said, using his name in the third-person as Thais often do when speaking to someone of respect. Phet swung his guitar to attention like a rifleman and goose-stepped to the elevator.

"He doesn't mince words, that boy," Mark commented.

"I don't think I could have said it better myself," said Marnie.

"You can see why he's best kept at a distance?"

"You do have a point."

"When was the last time you and I had lunch?" Mark asked.

"Umm, about seven and a half years ago."

"Want to break that trend?"

"It's only ten o'clock."

"You'll need what, about an hour to get everything square with Melanie?"

"Thirty minutes, I guess. That is, if I'm actually going to read any of it."

"Fine, get it done. Then we'll go. I know a place where we can celebrate. It's a ways away."

"Just where and what are you thinking, Mr. Harmann?"

"Phoenix," Mark said, as they walked side by side towards the elevator. "You won't need to pack. You'll be wearing a uniform and living on-site. No personal effects allowed. Don't worry; they have a place you can jog there. I've insisted they give you a selection of Nike army boots to choose from."

"Underwear?" she joked, as the elevator door slid open and they walked in together.

"Strictly forbidden."

"You're incorrigible," she said, punching him hard in the arm.

"Bring your ID."

The elevator doors slid together, and they left the lair below them.

Chapter 5

When she finally left the offices of the Foundation, Salome was approached by a young man on the street. She immediately recognized him as the person she'd seen lurking outside earlier. It was still daylight, and there were plenty of people milling about. Salome felt perfectly safe. She was more curious than startled that this stranger would be stalking her.

"Miss Kahn," said the young man. "You may not remember me. I am Ashad Alizadeh. I was one of your students at the University last year." He spoke clearly and calmly, but his appearance told Salome another story. His hair was disheveled, and he looked as if he had not slept in days. The clothes he wore, while apparently clean and not threadbare, were wrinkled and didn't fit him properly. Both his pants and shirtsleeves were inches shorter than they should be.

"Ashad Alizadeh," Salome said aloud as if trying to remember the name. The fact was that she knew quite well who this young man was. It was easy enough to remember considering that she'd not had that many students over the course of a single semester. It was impossible for her not to remember that Ashad was possibly one of the best and brightest students she had taught. She was shocked at the transformation of the handsome young man to whom she'd given deservedly excellent marks. The person standing before her was but a ghost of the Ashad she remembered. "Ah yes, Ashad. Yes, I remember you. Are you well? You are looking a bit… rough," she managed.

"I am troubled, and please forgive my appearance Miss Kahn. I was hoping that I might be able to speak with you. It is a matter of great importance."

Salome briefly considered dismissing him and telling him to make an appointment through The Foundation, but she sensed an undercurrent of urgency in Ashad and changed her mind.

"Well, Ashad, The Foundation's offices have just closed, and I was about to go home and have some dinner." She thought about what that meant, which was eating alone and avoiding her brothers if they were there. Her father had been on a business trip and wasn't to return until tomorrow. Salome weighed her options and made a decision. "I know a restaurant near here. It is called Safa. Do you know of it?"

Ashad shook his head, looking moderately ashamed.

"I guess I should not expect you to. It is a woman's place really. The food is good, the owners are wonderful people, and best of all it is quiet. Would you like to join me?"

Ashad seemed not at all taken aback by Salome's offer. In fact, he was grateful for her take-charge attitude, as his plan had not gone further than the sidewalk where they now stood. Reflexively, he reached for his pockets and felt around realizing he hadn't enough money for street food let alone a meal in a restaurant. Salome was adept enough to pick up on Ashad's body language and graciously offered him a proposition.

"Please, let this be my treat. It is the least I can do for a former student. Would you allow me the honor, Ashad?" she asked to his obvious relief. "How did you get here? Did you drive?" She caught herself before he could respond, and said, "Come, I shall drive. My car is just around the corner."

They drove to Safa located on Mirzaye Shirazi Avenue just below Motahari Avenue. The restaurant's owner, Maryam, was a matronly-looking woman with large, red cheeks; she welcomed Ashad and Salome into an empty restaurant. She was dressed in a flamboyantly modern *manteau*. It was a type of dress that usually resembled a shoulder–padded trench coat when styled traditionally. This had earned it its universal nickname of "the uniform" by Iranian woman who have been subject to the Islamic dress code imposed since the 1979 revolution. Maryam, however, and many modern Iranian women persisted in expressing their individuality in various ways by altering the uniform. Some went for more color, some added embroidery and beads, while others wore more form fitting versions as opposed to the drab, shapeless traditional *manteau*. Maryam's dress was complemented with a colorful *rusari*, the headscarf worn by Persian woman who in spite of pushing the fashion envelope would not want to be considered badly veiled and attract the attention of the morality police, resulting in potentially serious consequences.

"You look lovely, Maryam," Salome complimented her. Her own dress could be considered risqué, though it was severely toned down in comparison with the wardrobe accumulated during her time as a student that now remained stowed away in suitcases never to see the light of the Iranian sun. "How is business?" she asked.

"Lunches are busy, but look around. The place is yours. We don't really have any rushes in the evening as you can see." Maryam was eyeing Ashad and was about to say something when Salome intervened.

"Please excuse my manners," she said. "Ashad, this is Maryam. Maryam, Ashad is a student of mine from the University. We bumped into each other at The Foundation, and we have come here to catch up over some of your delicious cuisine."

Ashad and Maryam exchanged polite nods, and Maryam ushered them to a table in the corner.

"But you are too kind. I would hardly call it cuisine," said Maryam. "We do offer excellent home cooked food, however. I make it myself, so I should know. You, my son, are looking too skinny. I have seen more meat on a butcher's pencil. May I prescribe my *khoresht gheymey?* It is sure to please."

Ashad salivated at the thought of the rich, succulent split pea and lamb stew, slow-cooked with onions, turmeric, tomatoes, dried limes, and served with basmati rice. He couldn't remember the last decent meal he'd had. He thought of home, his mother, father and brother, and a time that seemed much further away than it really was.

"I will take that look on your face to be a yes," Maryam smiled at which Ashad nodded dumbly. "Alright then, will you be having your usual, Salome?"

"Yes, thank you."

"Okay, that will be a spinach salad with Parmesan and pomegranate seeds for you and my best stew for the quiet one. I'll be back with some water unless you'd like some *doogh.*"

"Bring both, please," said Salome, and Maryam disappeared into the kitchen.

The drinks and food came and went, but the awkward silence remained. Ashad had devoured his food like a starved animal, forgetting any table manners he may have known. Salome had watched politely, but grew more uneasy as her thoughts explored the possibilities of what he could be going through. Finally caving in to her concerned curiosity, Salome decided it was time for Ashad to talk.

"Ashad, you came to me this evening and have said that you are troubled, yet you have not uttered a word for nearly two hours. I do not know how I can help you if you do not tell me what is going on."

Ashad looked around the empty restaurant and then worriedly toward the kitchen.

"You have nothing to fear from Maryam," she said. "She is a friend of mine."

"I am sorry, Miss Kahn. When I sought you out at The Foundation, I had so many things to say that were running through my head."

"You had thoughts, or you have them?" she prodded.

"I have much to say, but I do not know how to say it. Frankly, I am embarrassed by your hospitality and how I must look. I am like a derelict compared to your grace."

Salome found his eloquent phrasing a complete juxtaposition to his shabby appearance. She was confused by his self-effacing comment yet admired how well spoken he was. This was a glimmer of the Ashad she once knew. She smiled patiently and said, "Let us just start with the facts. What has happened to you to cause you to become like this?"

Ashad sighed heavily, revealing a burden that Salome could not yet fathom. "My brother," he began. "He has joined the *jihad*."

Salome nodded and said, "Go on."

"Well, before Javid—that is my younger brother—left us, he had grown distant, spending more time alone or away from home. My family became concerned obviously when he began lecturing us on religious ideologies, speaking of defending Islam against its invaders and slaying its enemies. We listened and tried to steer him away from such thinking, but our efforts only seemed to make him turn away from us more, as if we'd betrayed him. And then, one day, he disappeared. He was just gone."

Salome recognized the pattern that she had heard about more than enough from the families she had counseled. Isolation combined with a powerful ideology is a dangerous admixture. She knew that when the thoughts of would-be extremists percolate to the surface that the process of differentiation from the rest of society begins. The questioning of social norms is accompanied by the vocalization of their new found beliefs, and when their ideas of extremism and violence are eschewed by friends and family who are not indulgent to their thoughts and ideation, so begins the process of withdrawal and isolation.

Isolation provides a cocoon within which the activist can indulge their ideology without the restrictive routine of having to act normally among those who do not share their views. As they continue to distill their passions, they reach out to others while still deciding what to do. If there is no successful intervention by friends, family, or even law enforcement, they inevitably reach out and are often taken in by other "true believers." This is usually the point of no return, where the neo-terrorist will in all likelihood go forth and meet the violent expectations of the group. The psychological effects and dynamics of the collective are simply too powerful for one impressionable mind to reason against.

Salome knew the impact that losing a loved one had on families, but in her mind she was seeing something darker in Ashad. She could feel that there was something more that was haunting him. Rather than questioning him directly on this she asked, "Are you looking for my help in finding your brother, Ashad?"

"No. I have already done that, Miss Kahn," he said.

"I do not understand."

"So tormented was I by the loss of my brother and the effect I saw that it had on my mother and father, I left the university and joined the *jihad* in search of him."

"You stupid boy!" she thought but was immediately overcome by empathy. No matter how dangerous or reckless it was to go chasing after his brother, Salome could not deny that if she were in a similar situation she would probably at least consider doing the same. But to actually go through with it, that took more than stupidity. It took courage.

"Were—or are—your parents aware of this?" she asked.

Ashad began to answer, but croaked on his own words. He cleared his throat, tried again, and failed. He began to cry.

"You stay here," Salome said, rising from the table. She went into the kitchen, settled the bill with Maryam, and returned a few moments later.

She nearly had to lift Ashad from the chair, but when he got to his feet, she was able to walk him out of the restaurant and to her car. He fell into the passenger seat like a lifeless mannequin. Salome closed the car door, first making sure that he was all the way in. As she got into the driver's side, she noticed Ashad's tears had been replaced by a vacant stare.

"Ashad, let's get you home," she said.

Ashad did not break down again. He simply continued his blank stare that was obviously looking inward, seeing nothing before him. "They are gone," he said. "They are all gone."

Chapter 6

THE SIGNIFICANCE OF MILAS'S PARCEL was cause for his near immediate departure upon landing at U-Tapao. He was met on the runway and escorted to a room where he was given a sandwich, a Coke, and a pack of unfiltered Pall Malls. Nobody talked to him. There was a guard posted at the door. Having eaten and halfway through his third cigarette, he was ushered onto a helicopter and flown to the Military Assistance Command, Thailand at Don Muang in Bangkok.

Upon finally delivering the Phoenix tapes, he was told to stay put and that he was to await further orders from Colonel Ray. In the meanwhile, he was setup in the Winsor Hotel, the R&R center for American forces located on Sukumvhit Soi 20.

A day passed with no word except for the fact that he was now officially on extended R&R. With nothing else to do, Milas toured the city. He was enchanted by the architectural pastiche of modern concrete and ancient teakwood. There were gilded temples and palaces. He marveled at the magnificent structures with ornate, curving roofs that reached into the cerulean blue heavens. Everything he looked at had a surreal quality to him. While he knew that his mind was still digesting the abrupt yank from Saigon, he also knew that he had arrived in a very mystical place.

It was not long before he was sucked into the pull of fellow servicemen at the Winsor. As he began to run with them, he was soon enmeshed in different kind of mystique altogether. His nights became a haze of alcohol, marijuana, and sex. Two years of suppressed emotions surged to the fore and were released in a tidal wave of manic behavior.

Milas awoke one morning after a binge that had lasted nearly a week. His hand hurt more than his head, which was not normal. It was swollen and his knuckles were cut. He flexed his fingers and tried to remember what he'd done. He concentrated, but his mind was a complete blank. He stared at the ceiling fan, watching it whirl.

Something stirred in his bed beside him. Slowly, he pulled down the bed sheet to reveal the form of a sleeping girl. Her long, black hair was splayed across her back as she lay prone with her face in the pillow. It was not the first time he'd woken up next to a naked girl since arriving in Thailand, but it was the first time he'd done it with zero recollection of how it came to happen. His alcohol-induced amnesia worried him as he studied her and his damaged hand. He slid from the bed and went to the bathroom, thinking a cold shower might help to revive his forgetful brain-cells.

After showering, he found her on the bed with the sheets wrapped around her. She was sitting with her legs pulled up against her chest. Milas watched as she considered him with curiosity, her chin perched on her knees. He found some clean clothes and proceeded to get dressed. She was watching him. He was feeling his hangover and became irritated by her silent stare.

"What?" he said with mild annoyance.

She didn't say a word.

"Oh no," he thought. "Another one who can't speak a lick of English."

"Who are you?" he asked the girl, sounding not unlike the caterpillar from Disney's *Alice in Wonderland*.

She made a strange gesture with her hands but refused to speak.

He sighed in frustration. Pointing to his chest, he said, "My name is Andy." Pointing at her, he repeated, "Who are you?"

The girl repeated her hand gesture. She then pointed at him and then to her head, giving a quick a twirl of her finger.

"Did you just call me crazy?"

This produced a beam of delight from the girl. She clapped her hands, and gave him the thumbs up sign. Her smile was beautiful.

"How did you get here?" he asked.

She gave him a melodramatic expression of disapproval and then commenced a series of gestures that included her hitting her open palm with her fist.

This girl was definitely different. An idea occurred to him. He placed his hand in front of his mouth and said, "Can you hear what I'm saying?"

She responded with a confused look.

He removed his hand and said, "Are you deaf?"

She nodded.

"Wow, this adds a whole new element to the language barrier," he thought to himself. "You can lip read English?" he asked with surprise.

She gestured by holding her thumb against her pinky.

"A little bit," he said for her. "Okay. How did you get here?"

She sighed and repeated the same series that included the punch.

He looked at his hand. "I learned sign-language in the Boy Scouts, but I have no idea what you're saying." Andy went to the nightstand near the bed and rummaged around in the drawer to find a pad of paper and a pencil. "Who did I hit?" he asked.

She very carefully wrote the name, Hank, on the pad.

"You can write English," he said, again surprised. She showed him her pinky again.

"I punched Hank Strauss?" he asked now somewhat amazed because Hank was six foot two and built like a tank.

She nodded and wrote, "Hank no good. You take care me."

Andy looked at the bed and asked, "Did we...?"

The girl shook her head. She then made a fist and extended her thumb, using this to pour imaginary liquor down her throat. Her drunkard impression made him laugh.

"What's your name?" he asked again, this time pointing to the paper.

She wrote, "Fon."

"Like telephone?" he asked, using his hand to mime holding a phone to his ear.

The girl rolled her eyes at him playfully and then gestured with both hands. He watched as her long and elegant fingers floated in a downward motion.

Her name was Rain.

❀ ❀ ❀

THEY SPENT THE MORNING together performing their pantomime until they got hungry. They spent the day together and then the night and every night after that. Andy learned that Fon had been born deaf. She'd learned signing from her mother who was also deaf and spoke the old sign language of the markets. She had learned English and American signing from the missionaries who had setup a Christian school for the deaf in Bangkok. Her dream was to go to a university, which was why she was working as a freelance prostitute. Andy came to realize that prostitution was viewed differently here than in the West, and though he didn't like the thought of it when considering Fon, he began to understand it from a different perspective.

Having met Fon, Andy instantly lost interest in the soldier party scene. He found much more pleasure in being with her and watching her expressions than drinking himself into oblivion every night or frequenting massage parlors and go-go bars where young women could be chosen by the numbers they wore on their uniforms.

Andy became even more captivated with Bangkok as he saw it through her eyes. They prayed at temples and gave offerings to the monks who dwelled there. They rode on river taxis. Fon introduced him to places he'd never have seen on his own. Some of these would have been normally accosting to the senses, such as the open air markets that smelled like morgues—their tables of open meat covered with flies, pig faces on display, and buckets of eels that sloshed at their feet; but Andy soaked it all in, reveling in the experience. They went to kung fu movies that starred Ho Chung-Tao, who would very soon become the legendary Bruce Lee. The movies were in Chinese with Thai subtitles, but following the plot was not all that hard for Andy. Besides, he was more interested in Fon's company than anything else. They shared food together that had enough chilies to burn a hole straight through his body, but all of it was made sweet by the fact that he was falling in love.

Chapter 7

THE SUN MADE AN APPEARANCE, replacing the morning's storm clouds to make for a glorious, albeit chilly, late winter's day. The rain-filled thunderheads had moved eastward resembling colossal kernels of brilliant white popcorn with flattened bottoms floating in the distant sky. Marnie eased back into the comfortably heated seats of Mark's Lexus SC 07 convertible and stared skyward. She was intentionally trying to ignore the fact that she was sure Mark's defroster worked with luxurious precision.

"This isn't Phoenix," she said, sitting up straighter as they approached the grey colored building at 1500 Tyson McLean Drive, otherwise known as Liberty Crossing. Roughly fifteen minutes from Solutions Drive by car, 1500 Tyson McLean Drive was once known as PRC Drive. That was before Congress handed forty-billion dollars to George W. Bush four days after 9/11 and some of that money was put to use to create what was initially called the Terrorist Threat Integration Center. In 2003, the organization cut its teeth on the first combined inter-agency intelligence databases out of their temporary location located on the fourth floor of the Central Intelligence Agency's Original Headquarters Building. A lot of things had changed or were still in the process of changing since that infamous day when the Twin Towers fell. The creation of the DHS apparatus was unarguably the most extensive reorganization the U.S. government had seen in over fifty years. Here in McLean, only a few years later, stood the National Counterterrorism Center, an intimidating structure conjuring images of stealth and secrecy; to Marnie it actually looked like a building where one would expect to find government agents busy at work thwarting enemies of the state. Muted images of human figures could be barely spotted within, deftly obscured by the mirrored and deeply tinted windows that covered the building's façade.

Mark caught a glance of Marnie staring contemplatively over the top of her sunglasses as he slowed the convertible before the security gate at the building's side entrance to the lower level parking lot.

"Those windows are both bullet and blast proof. Each office is a security vault in and of itself. This place was built to post-Oklahoma City bombing standards," he said.

Marnie said nothing.

The security guard at the gate wore an indistinguishable uniform, but was easily identified as a man of seriousness by his military bearing and the menacing .45 caliber automatic pistol that hung at his right side.

"Identification please, Mr. Harmann," said the stoic sentry. "And Ms. McCloud's."

"They know me here," he whispered with a sly wink to Marnie, "and apparently you too." He bounced his eyebrows at her with puckish aplomb.

Mark unclipped a small, black leather holder from the car's sun visor and held out his hand to Marnie. She reached down on the floorboard for her purse, but not without noticing the guard's hand move to the butt of his firearm. Instinctively, she moved with exaggerated slowness. She carefully opened her purse, extracted her wallet, removed her driver's license, and placed it into Mark's open palm.

The guard examined their identification thoroughly, looking from each card both held in his left hand to each of their faces; his other hand still on the gun. Apparently satisfied, he returned their IDs.

"Open the hood and trunk please, Mr. Harmann," said the guard.

Seemingly from nowhere, two other guards of equal seriousness appeared beside the Lexus. They circled the car in an eerily graceful dance, each holding convex mirrors attached to short pole lengths that allowed them to see beneath the vehicle's chassis without having to stoop or crawl on the ground. Mark reached down with his left hand and released the hood then popped the trunk with his right. The serious twins made their way to the front and rear of the vehicle and performed a thorough inspection, presumably for anything explosive. The rear twin closed the trunk and gave a curt nod to the guard in the booth, which Marnie saw reflected in the rear-view mirror. In what seemed longer than it should have, the front twin completed his business and dropped the hood from a professional distance, sealing it with an elegant *thunk*. He flashed a thumbs-up sign to the booth guard and departed with the other as stealthily as they had appeared.

"You are clear to enter, sir," said the booth guard. He used his gun hand to pick up a hand-held radio.

He muttered what seemed like gibberish to an unseen party and gestured for Mark to drive forward towards the security gate that was slowly rolling upward to reveal a tunnel that led beneath the building.

"Did you hear that guard speak in tongues? That was a shibboleth," said Mark. "Warring tribes in ancient Israel used a person's dialect as a form of security screening. When the Gileadites defeated the Ephraimites sometime around thirteen hundred B.C., they secured the fords along the river Jordan in a measure to identify and kill any Ephraimites who would be attempting to escape homeward incognito. Forty-two thousand refugees were caught and slain by this tactic."

Marnie cut him off. "This isn't Phoenix."

Mark ignored her, took a breath, and continued. "You see the trick was that Ephraimites couldn't say the *sh* sound. So when they had to say something like shoe, for example—though I doubt they ever wore anything but sandals—it came out *soo*. It's kind of like when Phet says *pom-pem*, except Phet could probably fake it to pass security. Americans employed this technique in World War II, to identify American Japanese from the baddies. Lollapalooza is still a bit of a tongue twister for most Japanese who weren't raised in the States. Not state of the art, but definitely effective."

Mark had maneuvered the car through the parking garage as he'd talked and parked in a stall clearly marked VISITORS. He didn't bother to put the top up, as he figured security was most likely pretty good around here. He assumed that there were several CCTV cameras and possibly even a riflescope trained on them now.

"This isn't Phoenix." Marnie repeated, looking more than a little miffed now.

"Look," Mark said with an exaggerated look of exasperation. "A little misinformation never hurt anyone. Besides, I'm not actually misinforming you, which you'll figure out in about six months on your own. Trust me. The best is yet to come."

He walked around the car and opened Marnie's door for her. She sat there, obviously in a mood.

"Are we really having lunch?" she asked. "You know how I get when I'm hungry."

"Believe me, I know. Yes, we are having lunch, and let me just say this will be one you'll not soon forget."

Grudgingly she joined him, and they made their way to a red-painted door clearly marked ENTRANCE, behind which Marnie would be subjected to thirty minutes of further security screening that would allow her swifter access on future visits, including: retina detection scanning, electronic fingerprinting, and voice recognition.

By the time they emerged, she was starving and well beyond grumpy.

Chapter 8

Unsure of what she should do, Salome pondered the helpless Ashad in her passenger seat. Finally, she settled on the only thing she could think of and decided to bring him back to her family's home. She ignored the imagined scenes of her brothers berating her as best she could and drove to her father's mansion.

Salome was relieved to find the house dark as she pulled into the driveway. She pressed the button that closed the wrought-iron security gate, shut off the engine, and coaxed Ashad to the front door. He removed his shoes automatically as she let him in, which she assumed meant he was at least no longer catatonic.

"There are plenty of guest rooms, so not to worry," she said. "And here we can talk in private." She led them through the foyer and toward a sitting area, turning on lights along the way.

Ashad, having recovered somewhat from his emotional stupor, took in these surroundings with a sense of awe. Never before had he seen such luxurious trappings of wealth. He began to succumb to the feelings of inferiority that went well beyond the fit of his clothing. Salome noticed him staring at everything and said, "My father is a very wealthy man. Do not let this intimidate you. You are my guest, and I do not judge people by the money they have or do not have. I judge them for the people that they are. Please sit down. I am going to make some tea for us, and then we shall talk."

The sitting room was used for formally entertaining guests but also served as a family room. Layers of plush and intricately patterned Isfahan rugs blanketed the floor. Ashad felt his bare feet caressed by their sumptuousness. Surely, he thought, they were mind-bogglingly expensive—worth more than all the money many would see in a lifetime. As he padded across the room, his eyes fell upon a collection of the Kahn's family photos. He found it interesting that among so many brothers there were seemed to be more pictures of Salome than any one of them. He focused on these, and soon it dawned on him that roughly half of them were much older pictures and that the woman in these must be Salome's mother. The resemblance was uncanny.

"Oh, don't be looking at those," said Salome, entering the room and carrying a tray with their tea. "I told you to sit," she said and kicked a few pillows in his direction. He followed her orders and gathered the pillows, bringing them to where she now sat on the floor beside a low table. She set out a cup of tea for him.

As he sat, he gave one more look around the room and said, "I shudder to think of what would happen if one of your brothers or father were to come home."

"My father is on a business trip and won't be returning until tomorrow; otherwise, I do not think I would have had the nerve to bring you here—although I still may have with you in the condition you were in. My brothers—those that still live here—are either out or upstairs asleep. I did not realize how late it was, but that is probably a good thing. Regardless, I will handle them. You are obviously in need, and I am helping you. As I have said, you are my guest here."

"Thank you very much, Miss Kahn. Your kindness is truly a blessing."

"Now, Ashad," she said equally politely but with a bit more seriousness in her voice, "I do not wish to upset you, but again, I do need to know what is going on if I am to be able to help you. What did you mean, when you said, they are gone?"

"My family, Miss Kahn. They are gone." Ashad managed to control his emotions and continued, "They are gone because of me. I have told you that I had joined the *jihad*. In doing this, I thought that I would be able to bring my family back together, but I was so very wrong."

Ashad told Salome of how he registered as a volunteer through the same organization that his brother had. He had done this by discovering papers that Javid had inexpertly hidden within his room. Ashad deduced where his brother had applied and followed suit, pretending to be a willing new volunteer. All of this was done against the will of his parents, who pleaded with him not to embark on such a foolhardy and perilous undertaking.

"Do not cause us to lose another son," Ashad echoed their pleading for Salome.

In order to play the fanatic, one had to become a fanatic, and thus Ashad Alizadeh became immersed in the world of Islamic extremism. While these organizations recruited thousands of volunteers, not all of them were seen fit for tasks that required the taking of life, including one's own. He attended meetings and other gatherings, eventually surviving the weeding-out process, having gone through a series of initiation tests and hazing rituals designed to separate the wheat from the chaff. Those who were determined unworthy were either offered administrative duties or turned away in the end. If one survived the recruitment process, one then entered an inner realm. When this happened for Ashad, he became privy to more detailed information, as he continued his charade of becoming a martyr.

As time went on, he ever so subtly he began to inquire about his brother. At first, it seemed his search would be fruitless until he finally met someone who claimed to have known Javid. Heartened by this news, he stepped up his own personal propaganda campaign. "I have come to fight alongside my brother. He is an inspiration for everyone," Ashad lied to all.

Ultimately, he could only learn that Javid's last known whereabouts were at a training camp forty-five kilometers outside of the city of Nahavand, in western Iran. Having gained this knowledge and that the camp was one of the final staging areas for *jihadists* who were preparing for attacks within Iraq, Ashad did everything he could to get himself transferred there. The problem was that his training was not yet complete, and thus he was still located in the northeastern Eshrat-Abad district of Tehran at the Mostafa Khomeini garrison.

When his efforts to relocate proved ineffective, he took it upon himself to apply the little training he did have to fabricate a number of pipe bombs that he fashioned into an improvised explosive device. He detonated the roadside bomb as a bus carrying a regiment of Iran's Revolutionary Guard passed by. While the construction was crude, Ashad had intentionally made the device as non-lethal as possible. In effect, it was simply a very loud firecracker that caused no damage but to the car in which it was hidden and the eardrums of those unlucky enough to be near when it went off.

The attack was immediately blamed on Sunni rebels in the media; however, Ashad told his commanders that he was the one responsible and that he was ready to do it again in the heart of the American presence in Iraq. While they didn't necessarily believe he had actually tried to blow up a bus full of Revolutionary Guardsmen, they took note of that certain fervor in his eyes and knew the time was ripe for this recruit to serve his purpose. His training program was immediately accelerated, and he was shipped off to Nahavand within days.

The Navahand training camp was small, housing fewer than a hundred troops and located in the middle of nowhere. Due to its remote locale, security was not overly meticulous. Upon his arrival, it was easy for Ashad to determine if Javid was still there. And he was. He soon found that Javid was in the final phases of preparing for his attack. As part of the final process of executing a terrorist operation, Javid was isolated from the rest of the troops. He was at the stage of mental preparation, readying his weaponry, and rehearsing his final actions. And there was praying—lots of praying.

Come dark on the second night after his arrival, Ashad had helped himself to a few supplies that were easy to carry and stole into the tent where Javid was located. It was easy to bypass the guard who had left his post to urinate. This would be quick, he thought. He would rush in, and Javid would recognize his older brother and come to his senses. They would escape into the night, leaving this nightmare behind them and return home to their mother and father.

Ashad was mistaken. Javid turned and laid eyes on his brother, but there was not a trace of recognition behind them. His crazed gaze was that of a madman. Ashad realized at that moment that he had truly lost Javid, yet he could not force himself to fully admit to the fact. While Ashad was frozen with indecision, Javid screamed for the guard. When no one responded, Javid lunged at the intruder trying to gouge at his face with his bare hands. Ashad pushed him away. When Javid attacked again, Ashad leveled him with a devastating blow to the solar plexus. Ashad whirled at the sound of voices just outside the tent then stood paralyzed, looking at his brother's curled form that writhed on the ground. Javid let out a hoarse wail. Ashad knew if he waited another second, he would be caught or more likely shot by the guard. It was now or never, he thought. He leapt to the back of the tent, opposite the voices at the entrance and carefully slit an opening through the canvas with a knife he'd stolen earlier for just this purpose. He pushed through the hole in the tent and ran for his life, leaving what was left of his brother behind.

▓ ▓ ▓

"THIS PERSON WAS NOT MY BROTHER," Ashad bemoaned, "It was like an evil spirit had possessed him. I left him there and fled into the desert, hiding from the patrols they sent after me. I was able to reach the old city of Navahand on foot by morning, where I managed to take a bus back to Tehran unnoticed by any watchers they may have posted. I was home-free, or so I thought, though leaving Javid still weighed heavily upon me."

Salome had listened to Ashad's tale with rapt attention as if experiencing his adventure first hand. She imagined the pain and horror he must have suffered when after all he had endured to find his brother, Ashad found Javid supplanted by a deranged stranger.

"Please continue, Ashad," she encouraged him to go on.

"I returned home," Ashad gave another heavy sigh as if he was finally coming to terms with the reality of his plight. "Again, I was wrong. I was a fool to think that I could escape their web and the tentacles they have spread across this country. Once you join this group and get passed a certain point, there is no leaving. They knew who I was and learned whatever else they required from Javid. I am sure of this now, as when I walked down the neighborhood streets where Javid and I had grown up and played together as boys, I saw the column of smoke. They had set my home afire as my parents slept. And now, because of me, they are gone."

"Monsters!" Salome cried out horrorstruck by the malevolence of such an act.

A voice startled both of them, "Who is this man in our home, and what is he doing here?" It was Salome's youngest brother. He stood arms akimbo, sneering with an air of arrogance. Being ten years her younger, she was not about to take any abuse from him, especially after hearing the shocking story of brutality that Ashad had endured. It also helped that he was alone.

"Firouz!" she snapped. "You will address our guest with courtesy."

"I shall not," he spat in return.

Salome got to her feet and was in his face in the blink of an eye. Her actions were so swift they startled not only her brother but also herself.

"Then you shall leave us alone," she said with surprising menace. She looked down upon Firouz, who stood an inch or two shorter than she. Her expression told him that she was not to be toyed with.

"Father will hear of this," Firouz answered lamely and cast a venomous stare at Ashad. His glare remained fixated on Ashad, as he ascended the staircase, moving slowly to the upper floor.

"Yes, he will," Salome called after him. "But from me!" She put her hand to her chest and felt her heart beating fiercely. She took a deep breath to calm herself and returned to Ashad, who sat with a look of terror on his face.

"What is it, Ashad?"

He seemed to be thinking of what to say.

"Ashad?"

"Miss Kahn, I am astonished. You moved like a lioness and practically man-handled your brother." His words belied his expression, but this was lost on Salome.

"Yes, well, I suspect we should retire for the evening so as to avoid any more conflict, although tomorrow will be a challenge. We will worry about that in the morning. For now, your problems are far worse than I imagined. I do not know how I personally could help you, but I know my father will know what to do."

"Again, Miss Kahn, your kindness knows no bounds."

Salome escorted Ashad to one of the guest rooms on the ground floor, who immediately noticed it was far grander than any room in his old home. It was large enough to accommodate not only what Ashad considered to be one of the largest beds he had ever seen but also a beautiful, antique writing desk. He marveled at the bookshelves that covered two walls and were filled with hundreds of texts.

"I used to do my studies in here. Now, it is somewhat of a home office for me." Salome made a cursory inspection to ensure that it was clean and suitable and showed him the attached bathroom, making sure there were fresh towels for him. "Perhaps, I shall raid one of my brother's closets to find you some new clothes," she said with a mischievous grin. "In the morning, please remain here in this room. I shall retrieve you when I think it is best so as to avoid any unnecessary issues with my family."

"Do not worry. I will stay put. I have nowhere to go, Miss Kahn." Ashad gave the room an appreciative look. "May I use one of your notepads," he asked, motioning toward the desk. "I like to write poetry. I find it helps me to get to sleep."

Salome thought this a slightly odd request, but was done questioning things for the night. It had been a very emotional day for the both of them. "Of course, Ashad. Please be my guest. Good night."

As she was closing the door, Ashad said something that she didn't quite catch. She thought she heard him say, "Fourteen eight."

"Excuse me?"

"Fortunate, Miss Kahn. I am very fortunate to be helped by a person like you.

"It is nothing," she said. "Please try to get some sleep."

"I will, thank you," he said. "Good night, Miss Kahn."

CHAPTER 9

THE INEVITABLE CAME when Milas reported back to MACT. The orders had come through. He was going home. Colonel Ray's hand was involved in insuring that Milas was stationed at Fort Meade in Maryland. It was not a coincidence that this was where the NSA was located. The colonel knew it was where Milas's skills could be best applied, but Milas didn't know what to feel. He knew he had to go home, but he was now distraught due to his feelings for Fon. If he left her, he knew she would go straight back to earning money from the soldiers who stayed behind. He had no real money to speak of himself, so staying was not a realistic option. If he did stay, he'd soon become destitute and unable to take care of himself, let alone Fon. The best he could hope for was to return to the States and figure out a way to get transferred back to Thailand as soon as he could.

He broke the news to Fon, who seemed to take it matter-of-factly. Milas made sure she understood that he didn't have control over his life at the moment, but that he was going to do everything he could to come back and be with her. He taught her how to address a letter to the APO address that would allow him to receive mail from her and got an address from her in exchange. They spent their remaining days together trying their best to ignore the fact that they would soon be apart. That Milas would be leaving intensified their emotions. They spent a great deal of time in bed together, making love and simply holding each other. On their last night together Milas lay with Fon. She slept with her arm around him and her leg draped over his body in the afterglow of their emotionally charged sex. He lay there feeling her warmth and the rhythmic pulse of her breathing. A rainstorm lashed upon the window and a crack of thunder pealed over the city. He kissed the top of her head, breathing in the scent of her hair, and he cried.

WHEN MILAS FIRST RETURNED to the States he was tortured by
the thought of having left Fon. He wrote her constantly and was
always on edge if he didn't hear back from her soon enough,
which was always. Then one day, the letters from Fon just
stopped. He redoubled his efforts, writing letter after letter but
received not a single reply. He became angry when his friends
told him to forget about her, but he eventually came to realize
that they were probably right. She'd found some other soldier to
take his place. Time passed, and she slowly faded from his heart,
except for the times when he lay in bed alone and listened to the
rain.

In the years between 1975 and 1982, Milas had a stellar career
in the military and was able to attain both a Master's degree and a
PhD thanks to Uncle Sam. During his time at Caltech, he'd met
plenty of girls, but there was one who stood out among the rest.
Daphne Cole Porter was studying to be a physicist and had the
sexiest brain Milas ever met. An elaborate courtship ensued and
at the end of their final school year they were married. It rained
on their wedding day. Fon never crossed his mind.

Due to the nature of military secrecy, Milas was never able to
discuss the details of his work with Daphne, though he wasn't
one to hesitate bouncing an opinion off her on regular occasion.
She was a thoughtful woman who was an astute advisor. She
became his trusted confidant. While they didn't agree on
everything, they argued well and respected each other, never
letting a difference of opinion be a thing that could come
between them.

When Milas retired from his post, Daphne gave him her full
support. She was aghast at what her husband described when he
told her of the reasons he'd decided to leave the military. She
backed him on his decision to deliver his message to the people,
and they crossed the country together as he embarked on his
speaking tour against a government that was seeking to survive a
nuclear holocaust instead of preventing it. It was to both of their
dismay that America wasn't interested in the ideas he was
preaching, but this only inspired them further. When Milas
became disillusioned by the reaction of the congressmen and

senators who he spoke with, it was Daphne that pushed him to try harder.

Then came the anonymous warnings and the death threats, which Daphne told her husband to ignore. "The truth will set you free!" she would tell him. Although he didn't quite understand how it would, he was spurred on by her encouragement. The truth, however, would eventually condemn them both.

CHAPTER 10

THE BURNS AND LYNCH CONSULTANTS were escorted from the basement security check through several secured passageways to a conference room on the sixth floor by a sharply featured and punctilious woman named Rose. Marnie had sized up Rose during her security screening as someone who never made mistakes and was quick to point out when someone else had. She imagined that Rose was a person who rarely laughed, and in this environment, who could blame her?

The conference room was surprisingly stately, which seemed in discord to the sterile passageways they'd been routed through. Its centerpiece was a magnificent table that looked as if it were hewn from a singular piece of cherry wood—the preferred material of decorators in the Washington area—though its size made that impossible. The table's finish was an example of superb craftsmanship and matched the paneling that covered three of the room's walls, the fourth being impenetrable glass. Marnie caressed the intricate natural grain patterns, finding them somehow sensual to her touch.

Rose cleared her throat with a not so subtle *ahem* and said, "Please make yourselves comfortable. Coffee is there. Restrooms are there." She indicated these with her arms and the lackluster zeal of a zombie flight attendant and left the room. The door closed behind her. An audible click was heard a moment later.

Mark was already sitting with a blue mug of coffee watching Marnie pace like a caged tiger when a telephone resembling a plastic starfish chimed with a soothing, low warble from the center of the table.

"Mr. Harmann. It's Rose. The chief is en route. ETA is two minutes. He's brought lunch." Rose ended the connection before Mark could reply.

"That's a first." Marnie smirked and made her way to the coffee pot; beside it she found a kettle from which she poured herself a mug of hot water. She squeezed a wedge of lemon into it, tossing the rind into the nearby dustbin.

Mark was quiet, and she didn't like it when he was quiet. It irritated her, as she knew it meant he was up to something. The thing was that he was always up to something, which meant that when he was quiet, he was being downright devious.

"What are you up to?" she asked. At this, he merely bobbed his eyebrows and offered his patented "who me?" face, which goaded her to a new level of vexation.

She spun when the door opened with an abrupt knock and a pair of efficient looking men in dark suits filed into the room, each taking a post in opposing corners where they stood hands folded before them. Marnie had just enough time to notice the clear plastic coil dangling from the nearest one's ear when an unmistakable voice just outside the door caught her attention.

"Hell no, I didn't speak French with him. I can barely speak English!" said the voice to an unseen party. Laughter filtered into the room from the hallway, as the man behind the voice entered.

"Mark Harmann! How are you doin', son?" he said. "Long time no see. What's it been, about a month?"

Mark rose from his chair and said, "That's about right Mr. President. It's a pleasure to see you again."

"You don't need to kiss my butt just because you're in front of a lady, Mark. Now, who's this? Is this the Marnie McCloud you've been bending my ear about?

"Indeed it is, Mr. President."

The look of utter shock on Marnie's face was one for *Candid Camera's* hall of fame. Her jaw fell then closed then fell again in a peculiarly accurate portrayal of a fish out of water.

"You didn't tell her, did ya?" asked the POTUS.

Mark shook his head with a devilish smile on his face.

"You rascal! You are one shifty critter. Young lady, you must be in shock by the look of it. Don't worry; I have that effect on people. I believe it to be my looks." The president adjusted his trademark red tie with mock swagger. "I've got just the cure for you though."

"You're... You're..." Marnie stammered.

"That's right, Missy. He is I, and I am he. Hungry's what I am! How 'bout you?"

The president poked his head out the door and hollered, "Blaine! Bring in the dogs!"

Blaine Grosvenor was a 26-year old college dropout who'd acted as the president's aide for nearly four years and was nearly famous for it. When G-dub wanted a peanut butter and jelly sandwich, Blaine got him a PB&J. When Jr. Bush needed a breath mint, Blaine was Johnny on the spot with a Tic-Tac or two.

Blaine entered the room with a brown paper bag in each hand that read Liberty Café. He immediately set about emptying the contents onto the elegant table, setting table places for three out of paper napkins and plastic cutlery with a competent flair.

"I took the liberty—pardon the pun—of ordering Cokes for everyone," Blaine said as he inserted straws into their drinks. "Apologies in advance for being presumptuous."

"Cut the crap, Blaine. This ain't the Harvard admissions board," said the POTUS. "Coke's fine. Besides, that diet stuff tastes like horse pucky anyhow."

The president walked over to Marnie and took her by the hand. Gently placing another hand at her back, he led her to her place at the table across from Mark where her lunch awaited.

Taking the chair at the head of the table, their host declared, "An all-American lunch: one kosher foot-long with everything on it. Fully-loaded! Just the thing you need. Roll up your sleeves. This here's a workin' lunch, and things might get messy."

Marnie stared at the tube of processed meat heaped with a mountain of onions, ketchup, mustard, and relish before her. She then regarded the two men at the table waiting for her to take the first bite, both smiling like wolves. Hot dogs had always grossed her out completely. She didn't know whether to smile back or take the plastic knife in front of her and lunge across the table at Mark's throat for not preparing her for such a consequential introduction. Her mind raced from her shoes to her clothes, her face, and her hair in the span of a second. She tried to quell the flood of uncertainty and emotions that came from being blindsided as she'd been just now. Marnie was about to snap and possibly might have even used the plastic knife when something clicked in her mind.

"This is a test," she thought. Mark had set this whole thing up intentionally to show the customer—and what a customer he was—how she'd react under the pressure of a surprise attack. She'd seen him do this to others during interviews. He'd done it to her before. It was formulaic and one of his routine tactics. "Why didn't I catch on sooner!" she fumed inwardly.

She took a deep breath and remembered that she was looking at the most powerful man to have nearly died from a peanut. The thought calmed her, and she actually let out a small laugh under her breath. Marnie smiled, held up her Coke cup and said, "*Bon appétit*, Mr. President."

The POTUS let out a cackle.

"Hot damn!" he said. "For a second, I thought we were both gonna need Secret Service to save our asses. Miss McCloud, you are cool as a cucumber." At this, he dug into his hot-dog with gusto, smiling at Marnie as he chomped away.

"Well done, Marno," Mark said and took a bite as well.

Marnie, Mark, and the president sat quietly eating for a moment. The president then casually turned to Rose, who had somehow appeared in the room without Marnie noticing.

"Is she clear?" he asked Rose through full cheeks, waving a mustard stained napkin in Marnie's direction.

"Yes, Mr. President. As of 11:30am today she's been granted top secret clearance on a need-to-know basis."

"Well, then. I guess it's time we got to work, as there's plenty she needs to know."

CHAPTER 11

SALOME AWOKE and hastily made herself presentable, making her way downstairs with the hope of averting any trouble with her brothers. She expected to find them congregated around the large table in the kitchen and arguing about how they would deal with Salome's indiscretion, while they drank coffee, ate their breakfast, and waited for their father to return. Their mothers had thankfully joined Mohammad Kahn on his trip and would be something she'd not have to face first thing this morning. Her life in Iran truly was a Cinderella story, she thought, but somehow the happy ending had eluded her thus far.

She entered the kitchen, steeled against the verbal onslaught she'd prepared for and found the room empty but for a maidservant who was tidying up. This was odd, thought Salome. The kitchen was rarely empty on a Saturday morning. She made her way down the hallway to check on Ashad. The door was open. The servant staff had already eliminated any evidence that there may have been a guest at all. Salome walked to the desk and found that her copy of the Qur'an had been removed from the bookcase and lay closed upon the desktop. She also noticed that a few sheets had been torn from a notepad. Otherwise, there was no sign of Ashad. She checked the washroom then surveyed the entire mansion, but there was no trace of him to be found.

An idea sprang into her mind, and she rushed to the front door. Ashad's shoes were no longer there. Puzzled, Salome returned to the guest room and studied the desk. She ran her fingers across the surface of the notepad and felt it smooth. She then took a pencil and rubbed it lightly edgeways across the page as she'd seen detectives do on American TV shows. There was nothing there as far as she could tell. "Where had he gone with nowhere to go?" she thought. "Had he left in the night? Did her brothers chase him out?" She tossed herself on the bed in frustration and let out an exasperated sigh.

"Is everything alright, my dear?"

Salome hit the ceiling. "Oh, Father, you nearly frightened me to death!" she gasped, quickly rising from the bed to greet him.

"You know this house. It is so big that you think you are alone sometimes when you are not."

"Yes, but that gives you no right to appear from nothing like a *djinn*!" she pouted then ran into his arms. "I have missed you, Father." Salome could not help but feel better now that he was home.

"And I you, my Mooshi," he said, hugging her and calling her by her childhood nickname, Little Mouse. "Firouz tells me you had company last night?"

"Oh, that little snitch! I told him that I would tell you myself. Where is he? No one is here this morning."

"I am not sure where he is. He called me on my mobile last night, sounding rather upset."

"Well, he has no reason to be, although I was rather abrupt with him," she said in reflection. "But he deserved it! If he had an ounce of pity, rather than that contemptible personality of his, he would have realized that Ashad was a good person in need of help. I brought him here because it seemed he had nowhere to go, and I thought if anyone would be able to see a way out of the dreadful mess he was in, it would be you, Father."

"Ashad?" he asked. "And where is this Ashad now?"

"Gone! He has vanished into thin air." She threw her arms about her as if demonstrating the fact.

"I think you better tell me about Ashad," he said with some concern. "Come, let us go sit in the kitchen. I am hungry."

They sat at the large table and Kahn called for a servant to prepare some food. Salome recounted last night's encounter with Ashad, telling her father as much as she could remember from what he had told her. She told Ashad's story with passion and became even more emotional when she concluded by describing the murder of his parents.

"That is a sad and tragic tale," he consoled her. "How is it that he came to you for assistance?"

"He was a student of mine at the University—a very intelligent and dedicated young man. I believe that he had no one else to turn to. He had so much going for him, and now his life has been destroyed!"

"What did he tell you of this organization? Where was he recruited? Did he give you the name of the place or of anyone he met there?"

"No," she said, and racked her brain to remember anything like that. "No, I do not remember him saying any names. Why, Father? Is there something that you can do to help him?"

"I am not certain of this at all. To me, this story seems overly fantastical and also vague. If there were more detail—some names—I would find it more plausible."

"Father, you should have seen him! He was so afraid and terribly affected. He looked like a shell of the person I knew as a student!"

"I believe you. It is this Ashad that I am unsure of. Are you absolutely sure he did not mention anyone or anyplace other than this supposed training camp in Nahavand and the garrison?"

"I am sure of it," she said with a sigh of frustration.

"And he has just left in the night after you so boldly and graciously took him in to our home. Did he have the courtesy of leaving you a thank you note?" asked Kahn.

"A note?" Salome thought of the pages torn from the pad upon her desk. "No, Father, there was no note, but he appeared to have written something. He said he liked to write poetry. I assume he took whatever it was with him."

"No note, no names, nothing," said Kahn. "Well then, unfortunately there is not much that I can do. He has, as you said, disappeared into thin air. It is not like I can go knock on the door of the garrison and inquire about the boy. I am afraid that we will have to wait until he shows up again. If he does, he may be able to provide us with something tangible that I can work with. Only then might I be able to help him. Let us hope he can remain hidden from these supposed terrorists long enough to stay alive."

Salome was forlorn at the thought that Ashad was somewhere out there hiding from these terrible people. The servant came, bringing hot tea, cheese, and a plate of fresh baked bread.

"Father," she said, and looked at the food. "I am not hungry. I cannot eat."

"Oh, come now. You must eat something."

"I know, thank you. I will, but later. I am going to take a long, hot bath and rest my mind."

"You do that then. I do hope you feel better after. Perhaps we can play a game of chess later?"

"Will you let me win?" her voice reflected the ease at which her father could soothe her troubled emotions.

"Of course not!" he laughed.

"Then I shall have to beat you once and for all!" Salome reached up and hugged him then left for the bath. Her father always had the remarkable talent of cheering her, and she loved him dearly for it.

Kahn sat and listened to the sounds of the house. He heard the bathwater begin to run and the door close. He waited, taking some bread and cheese while biding his time. When he heard Salome shut off the tap, he knew that she was already in the bath and would be staying there a while. "My Mooshi," he sighed to himself.

He removed his mobile phone from his trouser pocket and took a sip of tea as he selected a number from his contact list.

"God is great," the voice on the other end of the line spoke.

"She knows nothing," said Kahn.

"And the boy?"

"Keep him alive. I will deal with him personally."

"As you wish."

Kahn disconnected the line.

CHAPTER 12

IN THE WINTER OF 1982, Andy and Daphne were headed back to Richmond after a briefing he had given to a senator's chief of staff on Capitol Hill. It was snowing lightly but the roads were safe—nothing to prevent their hitting the Interstate in their old but trusty Ford Bronco. It wasn't until they'd got off I-95 that the light snow had evolved into a blizzard. It was late, and Milas was tired from the two-hour drive. He noticed with annoyance a tail-gaiter who was shining his brights in through the rear window. Milas took a turn onto the Richmond Henrico Turnpike and accelerated, leaving the discourteous driver behind. They were almost home.

Milas sped along the turnpike surrounded by a dense copse of snow-covered trees. He knew this stretch of road well. It was one of his favorite drives during the day, but now he just wanted to get home. He reached over, found Daphne's knee, and gave it a squeeze. "You know I love your knees, right?" he said. It was an old joke they shared. They were Daphne's least favorite feature about herself. And if he loved her knees, things only got better from there.

"Indeed I do," she replied.

Without warning, something rammed the Bronco from behind. It was a hard tap on the back-left corner of the vehicle and was perfectly executed, causing them to slide out of control. The old Bronco handled terribly and Milas overcompensated by cranking the steering wheel in the opposite direction of their slide. They both watched helplessly as the Bronco left the road and hurtled into the trees. The car came to a brutal halt as it struck solid, immoveable wood. The force of the impact drove Milas's head into the steering wheel. Stunned, he looked over at Daphne. Her body had been thrown halfway through the windshield. Milas struggled to get out of the car. When he managed to free himself from his seatbelt, he leapt out and fell to the ground. His leg was severely injured, and he cried out in pain. As he lay in the snow, Milas saw a car up on the road. Its lights were off. He shouted for help, but it slowly drove away. Crawling back to Daphne, he managed to pull himself upright and level with the Bronco's hood. He called her name and received no response. He hopped around the tree that had crumpled the front of the car and came around to reach Daphne. Her eyes were open, but her body was still and her head lay at a grotesque angle. Daphne's neck was broken. Milas howled with grief. His love was dead.

⌘ ⌘ ⌘

NOTHING COULD HAVE PREPARED Milas for the loss of Daphne. Without her he felt as if he were nothing. There was no way he could continue on his quest with the vacuum of her absence haunting him. In addition to that, his memory of that cold night on the turnpike with that car up on the road put him in a state of arrant paranoia.

Milas fled the country, running from his pain and his fear. He returned to Bangkok, thinking it the farthest place in the world from where he didn't want to be. His attempts to lose himself resulted in a drinking marathon that ran for forty days straight. His rampage proved too much for his body to handle. He blacked out in a bar within the popular veteran's stomping grounds of Washington Square. When he couldn't be revived, the owner who'd seen his share of overdoses called an ambulance. Milas slept for over twenty-four hours before he regained consciousness. He awoke to the sound of a thunderstorm outside his hospital window. Embarrassed and feeling like he'd drunk hemlock, he checked himself out and headed home.

Milas returned to his rented room at the guesthouse he was staying at and trashed the place. He was angry with himself. He was angry at the world. He was angry at Fon. In his twisted state of mind, he concluded that if Fon hadn't run off with the next soldier to come along, Daphne would still be alive. He accessed the part of his brain where he stored information like the first phone number he'd ever had. Within the same mental file, he located the address Fon had given him so many years ago and set out to find her.

The green and yellow taxi stopped at the address, and Milas asked the driver to wait, handing him a hundred baht note. There were children quietly running around in a playground in front of a large house. Milas approached a pair of large double doors that were wide open. As he entered he found the foyer to have been retrofitted into a reception area. He asked for anyone who could speak English and was requested to wait while they summoned the pastor.

After a brief wait, Milas heard soft footsteps padding their approach down the marbled hallway. The pastor had arrived.

"I am Santana," said the slight man in a friendly voice. "What can I do for you, Mr.—"

"Milas. Colonel Andrew Milas." He reached out to shake the pastor's hand. Santana simply nodded. "I'm looking for someone," said Milas. "In 1975, this was the address of a friend of mine. Her name was Fon."

"You are a veteran of the Vietnam war," said the pastor. "You met a girl here in Thailand, and now you have come to find her."

"I'm not here for a confessional, Father."

"I am sorry. It is just a story I have heard many times before," said Santana. "Regrettably, these stories rarely end happily ever after."

Milas thought about that, realizing how very true it was, especially for him. "Her full name is Anong Sanpakdee. She's deaf. Can you help me, Father?"

"Beautiful girl," said Santana.

"Excuse me?" said Milas.

"Anong. It means beautiful girl, Colonel," explained Santana. "Deaf, you say? Interesting. Prior to becoming an orphanage our mission here was running a school for the hearing impaired. It's quite possible that she was here at some point, but it has been what, seven years?"

"She was here. We exchanged letters through this address," said Milas.

"Recently?" asked Santana, his interest piqued.

"No. She stopped writing in June 1975."

"I see. And what makes you think that this, er, Fon wishes to be found?"

"Are you going to help me or not, Father?" Milas was beginning to lose his temper with the man.

"Colonel Milas," Santana spoke calmly. "You are not looking very well. Are you feeling all right?"

"No, I'm not. I've been sick. Look, I'd really appreciate some help here."

Santana considered this and said, "Of course I will do what I can, but these things take time. I do not wish for you to get your hopes up. Our efforts these days are spent looking after the children who have been left behind by parents unable or unwilling to care for them. We are not a detective service."

"My hopes are not up, Father."

"Very well. How may I contact you, Colonel, should I discover any information that may shed some light on the whereabouts of Miss Fon?"

Andy asked for some paper and wrote down the address and phone number of his guesthouse. He handed Santana the note, thanked him, and left. Walking back past the playground, he noticed the children had stopped playing. He felt their eyes on him. The orphans' hope-filled stares evoked a feeling of melancholy in him.

Santana watched as Milas's taxi drove away. He stepped down the hallway and entered a small classroom where a woman was standing tiptoed upon a chair to erase a blackboard. He walked to where he could be seen in her peripheral vision. When she noticed Santana and turned to face him, he said, "We need to talk."

Chapter 13

"MARNIE, I CAN CALL YOU MARNIE CAN'T I?" the POTUS asked and continued without waiting for an answer. "You don't know why you're here, and I'm sure Mark's told you a whole sack of lies to throw you off the trail just to put you on the spot here today. But I know why you're here, and I'm going to tell you why you're here."

It was somewhat disturbing for Marnie to witness how seamlessly the president shifted from unstudied Texan bonhomie to the grave sobriety of a man with the weight of the nation on his shoulders. She felt that the air had become heavy and the room had grown smaller, but she opted to pin these feelings on her imagination. Mark sat up straighter in his chair, seemingly tuned into this unannounced change in the president's aura, and she followed suit.

"We are at a turning point. The world is at a turning point. The country is at a turning point. America is not only surrounded by people that hate us, hate our way of life, hate the way we live our lives, but our nation is now host to enemies within. There are people right out there on these streets who, when their orders are called in, will cause murder and mayhem on American soil. People are suspicious of their own neighbors and strangers in the park. Heck, we don't even know if the guy selling Lotto tickets at the local 7/11 is going to turn a city block into a crater during the next World Series. There are bad people out there, and we don't know Tom from Larry."

Marnie sat politely at attention, not feeling overly informed by the president's words. After all, she'd heard most of what he'd just said in his last State of the Union address if not the one prior, or on some radio show or news program. Over the past few years, Americans had grown accustomed to a new state of fear. During the eighties, Marnie lived under the specter of a modern cold war where nuclear missiles could be sent raining down from above, launched from submarines or sent through space. The brinksmanship between America and the USSR was portrayed as regularly as a sit-com by a before-her-time actor who was spending billions on a weapons program named after a sci-fi movie phenomenon, where the villains were dubbed an evil empire.

Psychologically, it could have become debilitating, and it was for many. She recalled a short story her high-school sweetheart had once written and let her read. The story's climax found him and Marnie making love in the moments before an imminent nuclear holocaust. Writing was her boyfriend's way of dealing with heavy issues, as well as trying to get into her mind and subsequently her pants; however, Marnie had her own methods. She could somehow transcend the constant undercurrent of apprehensive solicitude by compartmentalizing her fears, pushing them down to the point where she could get on with her life of simply being a girl going to school.

That threat seemed to have vanished overnight when the Iron Curtain came down. Mark had told Marnie years ago that most military analysts agree that it was the Star Wars budget itself along with Reagan's brinksmanship that changed the USSR. However, that didn't do much for her state of mind or the nation's. What should have been a global sigh of relief and the beginning of a long holiday from the anxiety of being vaporized by some godless Russian turned out to be only a brief recess until a new fear was ready to take its place. Ballistic missiles carrying nuclear warheads had been replaced by hijacked commercial airliners, suicide bombers, and only Allah knew what next. Ivan and his evil empire had been replaced by Osama bin Laden and al-Qaida, only this time the world was not dealing with atheists.

Islamic fanaticism and its Allah-endorsed *jihads* promised paradise to its martyrs. This was now, and although she had become somewhat blasé when it came to the yellow, orange, and red that measured the country's daily threat matrix, it was still terrifying when she let herself think about it. Didn't she just watch a teenage girl blow herself to bits this morning on CNN? Marnie felt, as did many Americans, that it was only a matter of time before she either turned on the television to some new horror, or worse, was one of the unfortunates in the wrong place at the wrong time. But this was nothing new to her. What she was trying to figure out was what the president wanted from her.

"You've heard me say this before, and I'll say it again," Bush said. "You're either with us or against us. Now some people think this is because I'm colorblind or because I can't count past two. Well, Michael Moore can go fuck himself."

Marnie's eyes opened as wide as an owl's.

"What?" he said at her surprised expression. "The First Amendment still existed the last time I checked. If that fat bastard can say all the unsubstantiated crap that flies from his cake-hole, let alone bitch me out at the Oscars, I can call him whatever I like. He acts like an expert when he barely knows a fraction of what's really goin' on. Give that asshole a day in my shoes, and he'd crumble like dried cow shit. Hell, he'd cry like a fat little girl."

The president took a moment to compose himself and took a sip of his soda before continuing. He tugged at his suit jacket and straightened his tie again. He had reverted to a cowboy again in the blink of an eye.

"Got my ire up, he did. Anyhow, Marnie, why I'm here talking to you right now is because I take great personal pride and interest in what we're accomplishing in this here building. I've personally met most of the people who work here, and I spend a great deal of time keeping tabs on things. Intel from this place goes straight into my daily brief. Never before have we seen this level of cooperation between agencies that have historically been rivals, or at the least very territorial.

"Now, here's the kicker. All our little kids are finally ready to play in the same sand-box, and our toys aren't talking to each other—at least not the way we want them to and certainly not fast enough. I'll admit that I'm a complete Eskimo when it comes to computers, but you see, that's why we hire the experts. That is, in fact, why you are here.

"Mark here is privy to whole raft of things that until now you've been off-limits to. Well, that's gonna change as of ten minutes ago. He's told me enough about you to make me think you can be a valuable asset to our team here. Mark says it, and I trust Mark. And that's good enough for me. Of course, the extensive back-ground check we've run on you is an added level of comfort."

Marnie shot Mark an indignant look as sharp as a hot lancet.

Mark shrugged and gave a face that read, "What can I say?"

The POTUS continued. "Apparently, you and he have cooked up some program, system, or whatever you call it that can out-think an army of geniuses. Better, faster, smarter—that's what I'm lookin' for. You see, the bad guys are getting smarter by the minute, and we're sittin' on more intelligence data than you can shake a stick at. We just can't get through it all fast enough to react most of the time, and when we do it's a crapshoot half the time. You're here to bring it all together."

Marnie let out an audible gulp and grabbed at her soda.

"Ah, that's the hot-dog talkin'. Now, don't misunderstand. You aren't doing this alone. Believe me; you'll be dealing with the best and brightest from all over the place. Mark knows 'em all. You'll be working with spooks, kooks, earls, and dukes. We got people so smart you can't tell what they're talkin' about. Well, maybe *you* could. Anyhow, we all have one mission: terrorists. We're gonna hunt 'em, we're gonna find 'em, and we're gonna stop 'em, if it's the last thing we do."

President Bush paused and took in his audience of one. Mark had obviously heard this pitch before. Marnie instinctively reached for her drink again, buying her time in case she actually had to say something. It was bizarre. She'd somehow overcome being star-struck at having actually met the President of the United States in the flesh; however, she couldn't utter a word because his last comment—all the more the way he said it—had categorically terrified her.

The president gracefully saved her.

"Well, Marnie, that's about all the time I got for a pep talk. I'm a busy man. I hope you consider this project with all the seriousness it merits. I'll be looking for good things from you."

With this, the president rose and gave a nod to Mark. He then offered a smile and quick wave to Marnie. One of the Secret Service agents already had the door open for him and the other followed directly behind him, leaving them in a presidential wake of silence. Slowly, Marnie reached for the plastic knife and turned her gaze toward Mark.

"Why, I oughta..." she hissed.

"Sorry, I know. The food wasn't all that great, but you have to admit the company was entertaining." Mark couldn't suppress laughing aloud.

"He called me Missy!"

"Take a breath. Calm down."

Marnie sat silent for nearly a minute, mentally assessing what had just occurred. She took in slow, deep almost melodramatic breaths through her nose like a yoga novice. Mark simply watched with smug satisfaction and curious interest while she went through the motions of digesting what had just occurred.

At last she said, "Mark Harmann. That was the most surreal experience of my life. It was beyond anything I could have imagined, and I thank you for that. Now, I've got one question."

"Shoot," said Mark.

"Just what the fuck am I supposed to be doing anyhow?"

Chapter 14

MARNIE WAS RUNNING AT FULL STRIDE in the final stretch of her morning regimen. She found herself near the Potomac River, sprinting along a path that was blanketed in cherry blossoms. Plumes of petals sprang up in her wake like a vapor trail as she ran. Her arms pumped in rhythm with her legs and her breathing was strong and steady. Her mind was elsewhere.

For nearly two months, Marnie had undergone the biggest brain-dump of her life. Nothing in her academic life or her professional career had prepared her for the overload she'd experienced after joining Project X. At times, she felt it was like trying to fit the ocean into a teacup—the ocean being a fathomless body of information; the teacup her brain. Other times she was just too plain tired to think. The work was mentally exhausting, and she knew it would take a toll on the body if she weren't careful. The only thing that was keeping her sane were her runs of splendid isolation where she could let her mind work on things in a detached mode as she loped like a gazelle along her well-trodden nature paths.

One of her favorite things about the job was the schedule. People at this IQ level were often misfits, non-conformists, or prima donnas who weren't necessarily good at dressing up for the part or showing up at eight o'clock on the dot every morning. Hours were from "ten-ish" to whenever, which was usually late, but only as necessary. Meetings were convened as needed as opposed to on a weekly recurring schedule. She resented having meetings for the sake of having meetings and felt that they were leftover relics of an ineffective management style from days gone by. She was thoroughly impressed with how well this system worked and was convinced that it did work because it was superior to the conventional eight-to-five Dilbert world she'd previously had to endure. She'd often wondered who'd slipped in that extra hour from when Dolly Parton starred in *9 to 5* and now. Marnie fantasized about bad things happening to them, preferably with something as mundane as a rusty paperclip.

What she found exceptional was how incredibly *not* boring the work was. Mark had always told her that she possessed the attention span of a gnat because she bored so easily. In truth, she couldn't recall the last long-term assignment when she hadn't pondered either slitting her wrists due to outright ennui or murdering someone just to break the monotony of her day. This was different. She was immersed in a team of certifiable geniuses from a multitude of backgrounds. This forced her mind to keep pace with the variety of perspectives and the depth of understanding into arcane and classified subject matter that was well beyond her experience. But if Marnie had one thing going for her it was her ability to learn fast and adapt quickly. With Project X, she had hit the ground running.

❇ ❇ ❇

PROJECT X WAS BORN when the Washington brass realized they had a lot to learn after 9/11. One of these key realizations was the connection between computer simulation and the entertainment industry.

It was not lost on many that the plane attacks on the World Trade Center and the Pentagon were strikingly reminiscent of a Tom Clancy novel. In the immediate aftermath of September 11, 2001, the federal government had brought together a team of imaginative thinkers that included big screen Hollywood movie directors and screenwriters. They were tasked with a project ideally suited for their creative mindset. Their job was to imagine scenarios in which terrorists could attack the United States. Stephen E. de Souza was one of a handful of screenwriters selected for the team. His plot for the screenplay, *Die Hard*, had centered upon terrorism on American soil. The imaginations of de Souza & Co. were perfect for the job. Having been flown in by helicopter to the NCTC, one of the directors noted the unique, X-like shape of the edifice as seen from above and dubbed their secret assignment Project X. It wasn't that clever, but the name had stuck.

Letting their Hollywood imaginations run wild, Team-X conjured possibilities and drafted scenarios from remotely plausible—like the majority of Hollywood action thrillers—to genuinely grisly. These scenarios eventually led to the creation of groups such as the Institute of Digital Innovation, or IDI, a research center at the University of Southern California in Los Angeles.

Roughly a hundred million taxpayer dollars were poured yearly into entities such as IDI that specialized in developing military simulations. Marnie had learned that IDI produced studies that were concerned not so much with incidents that have occurred, such as airliners careening into the World Trade Center and the Pentagon, but more so with what else could possibly happen next. She also learned that IDI's simulation designers had created "virtual humans" that could be programmed with a multitude of personalities and varying emotions just like characters in a movie. Leveraging the latest in state-of-the-art computer technology, they'd created virtual realities where one could pluck a rose, get pricked by a thorn, and even smell the blossom with uncanny realism. However, it was usually bomb detonations, the smell of cordite, and hell-fire that the design teams strived to emulate with authenticity.

It came as no surprise to Marnie that her very own Mark Harmann was good friends with the founder of IDI and knew practically everyone that worked there. All of Mark's computer war-games over the past few years were produced in conjunction with IDI and at least one branch of the U.S. armed forces.

Through Mark, Marnie had come to understand that simulations and virtual war-games were not merely for entertainment. The money invested in these virtual simulations actually saved the government millions in reality. By harnessing the application of computer modeling to simulate war and terrorism, analysis could be performed at pennies to the dollar while the risk associated with carrying out expensive real-life war-games and mock terrorist attacks was practically eliminated. Going one step further, these simulations could become predictive in nature, allowing analysts to foresee potential outcome scenarios of projected events. Armed with this foreknowledge, military commanders were now able to formulate strategies with devastating effectiveness, while agencies such as the National Counterterrorism Center strived to use similar techniques to avert terrorist plots.

Marnie was really in her element now after six solid weeks of immersion. Predictive analytics and artificial intelligence were her forte. Groups like IDI produced a staggering amount of data. The Department of Defense had its own think tanks, including the U.S. Army Simulation, Training, and Instrumentation Command, known as SRICOM. Several private defense contractors such as Boeing, Lockheed Martin and Raytheon also contributed virtual mountains of information, as did quite a number of private think tanks scattered about nation's East Coast. The National Counterterrorism Center itself was an information glutton that could steal from the plates of twenty-six separate government and law enforcement agencies by peering into their networks. The problem was that someone had to analyze all this information and there were not enough hours in the day or people employable that could keep up with the torrents of intelligence data that found its way to the databanks of the NCTC.

While Marnie knew that data mining was a fairly new term, she was keenly aware that data mining technology was far from new. Companies selling consumer products had been able to produce market research reports based on the vast number of barcoded items scanned through supermarket and department store cash registers for years. Recently, data mining had become a buzzword bandied about by executives delving into the esoteric sphere of business intelligence, which was aimed toward making better-informed "data-based" decisions as opposed to relying on corporate management guesswork.

As Marnie boned up on the applications of data mining, she found they were far more numerous than she'd ever imagined. One application that she found very relevant to her task at hand was a military program known as Able Danger. In October of 1999, Able Danger was begat from a directive by the Joint Chiefs of Staff in order to face the simmering threat of al-Qaida. The program employed data mining techniques to correlate publicly available information with classified intelligence in an effort to identify affiliations among individuals known to have ties with terrorist organizations. Able Danger had supposedly identified the September 11th attack leader, Mohamed Atta, as well as three of the 9/11 plot's other nineteen hijackers as possible members of an al-Qaida cell linked to the 1993 World Trade Center bombing.

It was also alleged that Able Danger had identified Mohamed Atta thirteen separate times prior to 9/11 as well as a potential problem in Yemen two weeks before the October 12, 2000, attack on the USS Cole. Although several theories were run through the media, much of it rebuffed by the 9/11 commission report, it was a concept known as stove-piping that prevented this crucial information passing from one agency to another and getting in front of the right people who could do something about it. Able Danger's intelligence was suppressed by a policy informally known as "the wall" that forbade agencies such as the CIA and the FBI to share intelligence.

As Marnie saw it, the wall hadn't come down, but it now had specific bricks removed that allowed the flow of intelligence into a massive, centralized data store larger than any she'd ever seen attempted. What the NCTC needed was an expert system that could sift through this vast, seemingly incomprehensible volume of data, perform the wizardry necessary to make sense of it, and make suggestions for a course of action in certain events and situations. Of course, this was all easier said than done and much, much harder to do well.

Expert systems involved complex inference rules that employed various methods of logical reasoning. They required problem domain experts who were subject matter specialists responsible for creating the knowledge base that actually contained the expertise. Fortunately for Marnie, there was no shortage of experts on her team. And then there were the knowledge engineers who helped the experts figure out how to represent the collective body of expert knowledge and then somehow cram this information into a super-computer and build the necessary rules. These inference rules were what made computer problem solving possible.

Marnie was considered one the foremost knowledge engineers presently in the market, which was why she was now the lead knowledge engineer for Project X. One of her biggest challenges in this role was explaining the limitations of the computer thought process to the lay people who would be using the systems to make decisions.

Many expected computers to serve in the role of an omniscient oracle, magically seeing into the future and offering portents to the seekers of higher knowledge. It was a common desire, fantasized and written about across the history of time. Unfortunately, this was material best suited to stay in Hollywood, as things really didn't work like that. At least not yet they didn't.

That computers could think was something Marnie understood to be a common misconception. The simple fact was that they couldn't. Computers compute; people think. In all of her years working with artificial intelligence, there had been some remarkable achievements, but Marnie still knew that computers couldn't think for themselves. Ironically, the reasoning behind even the most complex computer systems still relied on logic that dated back to the likes of Socrates and Aristotle. The problem was that computers were number crunchers, but they weren't philosophers.

It was this realization that spurred her work towards harnessing technology to enhance the human thought process instead of working towards the vision of one day relying on computers to do all the thinking or even philosophizing. The latter was a quixotic dream that would probably never be actualized in her lifetime. At least the former would pay the bills until such time she could afford to trade in her Mustang for a horse and go into the sunset chasing windmills.

Being Lead Knowledge Engineer meant that Marnie served as a liaison between the fecund minds that analyzed intelligence, providing the expert knowledge and the computer developers who actually programmed the expertise into the system. She and her team were responsible for the knowledge-base; they spent a great deal of time digesting the information from the experts and hand feeding it in a form more palatable to the developers, not unlike a mother bird feeding her young. After only a week on the job, the developers had come to call her Mom and were so bold as to cheep at her with gaping mouths when she brought them anything they could sink their teeth into. She found it weirdly comforting in a way that she couldn't quite put her finger on. Regardless, she dismissed this with the knowledge of just how eccentric the members of Project X actually were.

Marnie downshifted out of her reverie as her run ended. Pacing in circles for a bit, she panted and felt the sweat drip down her lean frame. She bent over and placed her hands on her knees, taking in deep gasps of air and feeling her pulse gradually slow. Taking one last look at the stunning bursts of cherry blossoms that regally adorned the landscape with their delicate garlands of the palest pinks and white, she made for her rattletrap of a Mustang and headed towards Liberty Crossing for another day at the office.

CHAPTER 15

SIX PEOPLE SAT around the elegant table of Conference Room 4-D. It was the room where Marnie first met the president and the location of all subsequent project meetings involving bigwigs from Washington. Mark and Marnie were positioned with their backs to the glass wall, while two men in military uniforms inhabited the territory on the other side of the table. The ends of the table were flanked by Retired Vice Admiral Ephraim Chase, director of the NCTC and Rose, who was armed with a laptop and poised to take notes with an expeditious fervor.

"We've got a problem," General Patrick Sharp spoke first. Sharp sat with an upright posture as if a wooden plank had been stuffed down the back of his shirt. His features were severe though not entirely uninviting to Marnie. His lantern-jaw, coupled with his military style brush-cut, made his head look intriguingly box-like.

"What's that?" Mark asked.

Rose slid a sheet of paper over to Mark, who picked it up and immediately started reading. The document read:

> For the President only
>
> Recommendation for Middle East peace and regional stability:
>
> Eliminate Islam with extreme prejudice.

"Yes, I can see how that might be a problem," Mark said.

"I think that might just qualify for understatement of the year, sir," barked the general. "The system has also provided a list of specific targets. The majority of this list is a virtual who's who of Muslim leadership both abroad and on American soil. But there are also some very alarming entries, including a U.S. senator. There's one name, Warden Islam, on the list that we cannot identify as anyone of known importance. It would seem your system has a thing for Muslims, but all in all something is definitely off kilter here."

Marnie kicked Mark under the table.

"Marnie?" he said, suppressing a groan. He slid the document in front of her.

Marnie read it and laughed aloud.

"Is this some sort of joke?" the general reddened slightly.

"Not at all, sir," Mark said and attempted a reciprocal foot attack that Marnie deftly parried with a dexterous crossing of her legs.

"May I ask a question?" Marnie asked.

"By all means, ma'am," said Sharp.

"Where'd this come from?" Marnie asked, tapping the memo before her.

"It was generated over the weekend during a trial run," said Sharp.

"And I didn't know about it." Marnie let this comment soak in for a moment. "Well, I'm the lead knowledge engineer, aren't I?" she asked.

Her question drew a pregnant pause.

After a moment Mark said, "Yes."

"Well, I can say with authority that there are several factors that would prevent this type of recommendation from being generated," said Marnie. "There are safeguards optioned on by default. However, with the safeguards off, Junior could in fact conclude a radical course of action such as this. But ultimately, the reason for such a result would be traced back to the data within the knowledge base. Depending on how you look at it, this could be the mother of all false positives or Junior's way of playing Machiavelli given the data he's been fed and the questions he's been asked."

"Excuse me. Junior? Machiavelli? I'm lost," said Admiral Chase.

The admiral was an avuncular looking man whose hair had gone white some years back. He wore glasses that he had the habit of looking over when asking a question. A salt-and-pepper mustache perched on his lip like a caterpillar.

"No one's come up with a name for the system, so we've been calling it Junior," she explained.

The admiral let out a chuckle of his own.

"And," Marnie continued, "I can tell you that the system could not possibly produce the recommendation contained in that memo through forward chaining. Someone has turned on Machiavellian mode, and if they're thinking of feeding this tripe to the president, we definitely do have a problem here."

"What exactly is Machiavellian mode?" It was the admiral again.

"Sorry, has anyone read *The Prince?*" Mark interjected.

"Yes, the ends justify the means." This was Major Ron Ray, who'd been quiet up to this point. The young major was fortyish and unfortunately blessed with swine-like facial features. He was lean in stature but looked as hard as an anvil. To Marnie, however, he looked a little too much like Kevin Bacon in a uniform for her liking.

"Correct. Although that is a common misnomer, it is perfectly relevant here," Mark continued. "As Marnie indicated, the system runs in several modes. The default mode is based on what we call forward chaining. You know, basic IF-THEN statements. These statements are put together to help the system infer conclusions based upon the information contained in the knowledge base, a computer's means of reasoning. This is obviously an oversimplification, as we have to deal with uncertainty, confidence, heuristics, and rationalization. In short, given a set of rules and a chunk of information, the system can conclude the probability of events. You with me so far?"

Vacant stares met Mark eyes from across the table.

"Okay, part of the problem-solving paradigm is the explanation of the line of reasoning. It's pretty simple. I'll give you an example. I've got a friend who's a complete oenophile."

"If you're going to give an example, please speak in a language we can all understand." General Sharp was getting perturbed.

Another kick from Marnie caught Mark square on the anklebone.

"Alright, point taken. The guy loves his wine. So much so, that he's become somewhat fanatical about it. He considers buying good wine to be an investment, though not a financial one particularly. In his own words, it's more a mélange of Bacchanalia and hedonism tempered with a bit of patience. You see, the longer one waits for a good wine the better it might become and the greater one's gratification may be. The catch is that you never know until you pop the cork what you're going to get or so one might think.

"The remarkable thing is that he's come to the conclusion after an enormous amount of data analysis that Bordeaux grapes produce the best wine in hot, dry weather. In short: the hotter the weather, the riper the grape. And the dryer the season, the more concentrated the juice. Taking these two factors into account, he's crunched several decades' worth of historical weather data from the Bordeaux region, and the results substantiate his theory *in toto*. He's even become so audacious that he's boiled it down to an equation. This equation really has some professional wine quaffers' noses out of joint. In spite of this, he's used his formula to predict what years will produce the best Bordeaux. Not just the best Bordeaux, but those that will make the best investment. In fact, his formula revolves around auction prices, and he's successfully predicted the two best-selling vintages in the past fifty years. You can check it out on his website. It's amazing, really."

"And what, may I ask, has any of this to do with going to war with Islam?" asked Chase.

"I'm getting there, sir. I've just illustrated that from two factors a simple wine lover has been able to actually predict the future by looking at data across a few decades in a very specific locale. Now, multiply everything by like a gazillion. That's the amount of data stored in Junior's knowledge base. Take electronic communications, for example. First, you have to know what you're looking for. Let's say, potential terrorist activity. We could perform link analysis to make connections between seemingly unconnected people or events. Spikes in email correspondence or phone calls might seem innocuous at first glance; however, if one of the parties involved happens to be a suspected terrorist, data mining could expose an entire chain of events not previously revealed, and furthermore, evidence of future events about to happen."

Mark paused to take a visual temperature of his audience and nearly caught pneumonia.

"Moving right along," he continued. "So we've got gobs of data on terrorist activity, and we've asked the system about a suspected terrorist, 'What is this guy going to do next?' The system reasons with its inference engine using the expert data in its knowledge base, which includes, for example, data based on the use of various credit cards. He may have purchased a six-pack of baby bottles at Target, some lighter fluid at Home Depot, and a plane ticket to London. Junior takes that pattern and applies it across the knowledge base to discover that five other people made similar purchases. They just happened to all be Muslims with no known children under the age of five. Imagine that! Funnily enough, all of these people were booked on the same trans-Atlantic flight on the same day. Forward chaining presumes they're going to try to blow up the plane. In fact, this is in nearly every respect how the plot was discovered and subsequently prevented at Heathrow earlier this year. From the data in hand, it seemed entirely possible that something bad was about to happen. We also knew the who, where, and when. Fine, that's plausible; so you accept the conclusion, act towards a remedy, and arrest the bastards."

Marnie twirled her index finger in a gesture that said, "Get on with it."

"Now, the system is telling you to kill all Muslims. Are you going to accept this on blind faith? Probably not. You more than likely want to know the rationale behind this determination, right? Well, the system will allow you to ask it, 'Why kill all Muslims?' Junior will allow you to trace the line of reasoning used by the inference engine. Heck, maybe Junior thinks there's a good reason for it. I don't know. I would very be interested to find out. Everybody with me so far?"

Mark had a better chance interpreting body language at Madame Tussauds.

"Okay, enter *The Prince*. What I've just described about baby bottles to bombs is an example of forward-chaining inference. We concluded—assuming our data is accurate—that there was potentially a problem with mixing liquid explosives and air travel.

"Now, as some have interpreted Machiavelli, the ends justify the means. These days, we have taken this into our vocabulary and use the word Machiavellian in a pejorative sense. It's not correct, but the use has become so common that many think of it as such and misuse the term often."

Marnie stifled a yawn. Mark glanced at her and caught her actually twiddling her thumbs in her lap below the table.

He continued. "Now, the system has another mode called backward-chaining inference mode, or as Marnie has named it, Machiavellian mode. With backward chaining, you start with an end result. This is a target goal. The system will basically tell you what events could occur in order to attain the goal. Where Machiavellian mode can become dangerous is when someone puts in a target goal and follows the backward-chaining steps forward to attain this goal without moral or pragmatic reasoning. Both of these concepts are completely foreign to computer logic and easily perverted by differing opinions. Both concepts are also purveying factors in *The Prince* that are used to temper so-called evil actions by the state so that the use of extreme force against an unruly populace, for example, is done in moderation and only when absolutely necessary to maintain control within the kingdom.

"So, if the president got a memo on his desk that said, 'How to Take Over the World for Dummies – A Step by Step Guide,' first, we'd have to conclude that someone asked the system, 'How do you take over the world?' From this, that same someone could have simply typed up a nifty little doctrine based on the system's results. If the document was acted upon, it could spell major trouble, especially if these steps toward world domination were extreme in nature, ignoring both morality and pragmatism. This is obviously a ridiculous notion, but it allows you to see the potential impact of a misused and misunderstood theory.

"Now, having said all that, I'd like to point out that this memo before us could be the result of a combination of three things. One, Machiavellian Mode is turned on; two, the knowledge base is flawed; and three, elimination of Islam is not the target goal. If you ask me, I'd say it's all of the above."

Marnie was roused by this and sat straight as a bolt in her chair.

"You're saying that Junior has been tricked into manifesting some sort of political agenda to take control of the world?" she asked. "What kind of idiot would possibly think that could work?"

Mark had no answer for that.

Marnie knew that the misuse of the system was a disaster in the making. An expert system's power depended on high-quality knowledge about specific subjects. An inherent problem was that knowledge acquisition was a slow and laborious effort. With the amount of intelligence data that the NCTC worked with from several differing systems, Marnie saw it as crucial to break this bottleneck. With this in mind and the brightest minds at her disposal, she created a programming interface that drew information from these interconnected systems and codified it to automatically populate a massive, unified knowledge base upon which the system could apply its reasoning. It was impossible for anyone—any team of people for that matter—to keep on top of the daily influx of data and keep the knowledge base current. Her interface, the Nexus, did just that. The Nexus pulled intelligence from the databases of a multitude of disparate systems and crunched it into a palpable form at well-nigh the speed of light. It was a breakthrough for the project team. It was a work of art, really, and a testament to Marnie's uncanny ability to deliver an elegant solution for a seemingly Herculean task. But there was a fly in the ointment somewhere, and she was determined to root it out.

"That, people, would be a complete fuck fest," she said and slumped back in her chair, tossing her arms up with a sigh of exasperation.

The men at the table were used to such language but usually from sergeants and captains, not from a civilian and especially not from a woman. Marnie was both. Rose blushed and looked at her hands as she performed dictation on that last sentence.

The admiral cleared his throat and spoke. "Miss McCloud, I must admit that ninety-nine percent of what's just been said has gone straight over my head. You seem have a succinct way of putting things and a thorough grasp of the problem. No offense to Mr. Harmann, but do you think you could translate all this techno-babble into words that we can understand?"

Marnie looked to Mark with a barely veiled smirk. Mark gave her a nod.

"I'll try," said Marnie. "Our system is designed to predict the probability of events based on all information available. It does this through forward chaining. This is how, like Mark said, we are able to identify and hopefully prevent potential terrorist attacks.   When the system uses backward chaining, or Machiavellian mode, it takes a desired end result and provides the necessary actions to arrive there. Am I making sense?"

"Very clear, thank you," said Chase, smiling.   "There's nothing inherently wrong with this Machiavellian mode is there? I mean this is potentially a very valuable tool in our arsenal. And we are paying a lot of money for it."

"The system's logic and algorithms are near perfect, sir." Marnie replied.   "Any problem with backward chaining would more than likely have to do with what scenario Junior is being asked to solve for and who interprets the plan of action. Computers don't have morals.   They're just dumb machines when it comes down to it. Depending on the desired result, the system could determine that killing a bunch of people is the most effective means to achieve its goal. It's up to human beings to determine if the ends justify the means. This is why we call it Machiavellian mode."

"I understand." Chase nodded thoughtfully.

"There's one more thing, sir," added Marnie.   "Even in Machiavellian mode, a recommendation such as what is in this memo should not have come forth. Ethnic cleansing, genocide, murder—call it what you will—is generally never good for business. Using logic and knowing human history, the system would simply not determine such actions toward a winning strategy. It knows that regimes that employ such methods never last long regardless of the short, swift gains they achieve. There's something else happening here. There's something wrong with Junior, but I can't tell you what, where, or why yet."

Chase exchange glances with Major Ray.

"Well then," said the admiral. "It seems Miss McCloud has summed it up nicely for us. I suggest we have Major Ray spend some quality time with your team to gain a thorough understanding of what is before us and how to remedy the situation.   Major Ray is an experienced technology expert.   I believe he will provide significant value to the project. Rose will give you a copy of his CV.

"Considering that our go-live with this system is on the near horizon, we best have all our ducks in a row before we start shoveling shit into the president's briefs."   Chase let his joke linger for a moment. No one bit. "Hmm, tough crowd," he said.

"Well, if we're all agreed on this, let's break this session and meet again say, two weeks from today?"

Marnie couldn't help but notice a faint smile on Major Ray's face. He really did look like Kevin Bacon, she thought. Not the *Footloose* one either, but the sinister one that was cast in a multitude of other not-that-great films over the years. It was unsettling.

Everyone agreed on the next meeting date, and all stood up to shake hands and say goodbye. Major Ray confirmed that he would commence involvement with her team at o-eight-hundred hours the next day. Marnie corrected him and told him ten o'clock would work better. She needed time to prepare for her new team member, she explained. Rose typed a few last things into her laptop, shut the lid, and escorted the men out of the room, leaving Mark and Marnie alone together.

"Is it my imagination or was that just totally weird?" Marnie blurted out as the door clicked shut.

"I'm not sure, really," said Mark.

"I mean ignoring the fact that they're running trials without my involvement, don't you think it strange that they're adding this Major Ray to the project? Have you even heard of him before today?"

"Nope," said Mark. "But adding the major doesn't seem like it's a result of that memo we just saw. It seems to be part of a plan that we've not been let in on. What I find extraordinary is that the memo isn't a total train wreck for us. They're acting like this is a minor blip, and they're ready to take the system if we can make sure Junior doesn't recommend we go on a killing spree."

"So, it's not my imagination then. That was weird," said Marnie.

Chapter 16

KAHN AND HIS DAUGHTER were in the sitting room of the mansion. They were enjoying a rare moment of time together when they had the house all to themselves. Each was aware that they were not completely alone, as they both imagined Salome's mother watching over them from the pictures on the mantle. She was an invisible link whose absence catalyzed the love they had for each other. Surrounded by this love and the warm comforts of home, they sat quietly delighted, playing a game of chess.

"I have been thinking, Mooshi," Kahn said to his daughter as she was intently studying the chessboard.

"That is precisely what I am doing right now!" she said and made a move.

"I can see that you are not very happy these days," he said softly.

She looked up at him from her position, kneeling on the floor.

"Ever since you have returned from school you have seemed down," he explained. I know the whole business with the university was very unfair and stressful for you. And although I think you are doing wonderful work helping people through the Foundation, I just don't see you smiling and laughing as much as you should. You have made it quite clear that you are not about to let me find you a husband. It seems that you have no interest in getting married at all. I cannot think of any of your friends who remain single. You know, you are heading for the life of a spinster."

"How dare you!" she said, with mock anger. She could never really be angry with him. "What are you saying, Father?"

"Well, to be frank, I think you were happiest in America. I know we spent so much time apart, but I could tell from your emails, letters, and the time you came back that you were filled with passion and truly experiencing life there. You talked with such enthusiasm about your friends, teachers, and the people you met. And now that you have come back…" he paused in search of the right phrasing, "you have not been able to find your place."

"My place is here with you."

"Oh, Mooshi, you know that cannot be forever. I am an old man now."

"Are you ill, Father?" she said with concern. "Is there something you are not telling me?"

"No, no, no; nothing like that, dear. It is just that I feel that it is time that you become your own person or at least get back to that person I used to know and your happiness again. You know I will always love you and watch over you, but you cannot live forever under my wing. You need to lead your own life, and I am just not sure that you can do that here anymore."

Salome contemplated her father's words. She was so fortunate in how he treated her—never telling her what she should be doing or what a woman's role was. "He is right," she thought. "He is always right." She realized that she really had not had much of a life since she'd returned from school. She'd had such high hopes for a career teaching at the university, but that was squashed almost before it had even started. She really had no true friends to speak of. Now, she was just kind of going through the motions. Her job at the Foundation was, for the most part, simply being a pain absorber. Yes, it was fulfilling to help those in need, but there was no real passion in it for her.

"What is it that you have been thinking about?" she asked.

"I was thinking that I am going to win!" he exclaimed. "Checkmate."

"Oh, I could not care less! I saw that coming from miles away."

"Yes, well most people use that kind of foresight to win."

"When have I ever beaten you, Father?"

"Never."

"Exactly. So tell me what you are really thinking."

"Very well, Mooshi," he said lovingly. "I was thinking that you might be interested in going back to America. You know that I have setup up some satellite extensions of the Foundation there, and then there is that professor you always talked about who said that if you ever wanted a job he would make one for you."

"Oh, I couldn't leave now. Not with Ashad having disappeared."

"Let's be realistic. Ashad was mostly a stranger to you until just recently. He was your pupil at the most."

Salome gave her father a look that conveyed she was not about to dismiss Ashad so readily.

"Besides," Kahn continued. "If you decide America is what you want, there will be months of preparations and arrangements. By that time I am sure we will know the fate of this young man."

"You are serious about this?" she asked.

"I want you to be happy, Mooshi."

"Let me think about this, Father."

"Of course, it is your decision."

Kahn was a seasoned expert at manipulating people. He'd learned over the years that while violence was brutally effective, there were situations that required more finesse. He had the ability to understand a person and begin pulling their strings within minutes of meeting them. It was second nature for him, and most people were all too ready to let down their guard and provide valuable insight to an active listener. For Kahn, this was information that he could use to feed a person an idea and let them believe it was their own.

Ironically, while he applied the same technique upon Salome, he did not do this with the intention of receiving benefit. Well, not entirely. There would be much to lose if Salome were to learn certain things that she should never know about. But he also did this because he cared. He knew his daughter better than anyone. He knew why she wasn't happy, even if she didn't know this herself. And he did love her. She was the only connection that remained of his one true love, Salome, his wife who died the day his daughter was born.

Kahn had died a little himself that day. He had not experienced loss like that before in his life or since. He mourned, but eventually he became harder, burying the sadness deep within. He compensated for this emotional suppression by projecting savagery upon those unfortunate enough to cross his path in the line of business. He also compensated for this with a fierce love for Salome.

He had named Salome after her mother, and as she grew he could see his Salome in his daughter. Now that she was a woman, she was the spitting image of her mother. Even her voice shared the same tenor, and Kahn heard this in every word she spoke. Salome's personality, intelligence, and contagious optimism were constant signs that the woman he loved lived on in his daughter. For all the pain and cruelty Kahn had dealt out to others, Salome was his Achilles' heel—the one chink in his otherwise invincible armor. He would never let any harm ever come to her. And now, in order to protect her, he had to send her away again.

Chapter 17

At the heart of the NCTC was the operations nerve center called the war room. In a grand departure from the dowdy stereotype of government office décor, the war room designers had verged on voguish. Over eighty miles of cabling connected cutting-edge equipment that was custom fitted for the operation. Sleek, organically shaped modular desks fanned out across the open-plan floor, also known as the pit to those who worked there. The pit workers had a bevy of incredibly sophisticated and expensive tools at their fingertips. Each desk was furnished with three flat screen LCD monitors that connected to separate systems, which in turn could connect to virtually anything. Separate phone systems with discrete physical cabling provided both secure and super-secure connections on black and red colored phones respectively. All desks were arranged to have a clear view of the stage, essentially one entire wall of the war room covered with three projection screens, each larger than those found in the local multiplex.

Marnie paused along the catwalk that encircled the war room while on her way to a meeting with Major Ray. The pit buzzed with activity. The lights were dimmed and a kaleidoscope of smaller lights flashed and reflected like constellations across the surfaces of a thousand smoothly polished glass and plastic facets. The pit looked like a professionally lit stage where the latest techno-thriller was about to be filmed. After nearly three years of silence and just days before sixth anniversary of the 9/11 attacks, Osama bin Laden had released another videotape.

She'd already seen the tape and read the subtitles of the translation twice, but the pit crew was running this one through the rigors. She overheard snippets from the analysts.

"Is that beard real, or is that a dye job?"

"He's had a trim, that's for sure."

"You think that's a sign?"

"How should I know? Do I look like a frickin' terrorist to you?"

Snickers wafted up from the darkened pit. Something was afoot. One of the techs on the floor, Jack, had ported his work-monitor onto one of the massive projection screens on the stage. It was still lunchtime for some and everyone was ready for a small bit of fun. Trolling for anti-U.S., insurgent attack videos—part of his daily routine—Jack had discovered a cartoon clip on You-Tube. You-Tube, an angel-funded, Internet sharing phenomenon, allowed people all over the world to upload videos to a global audience. Though revolutionary in concept, true artistry was rare on You-Tube and copyright abuse rife. The clip was a riotous parody of Osama bin Laden, depicting blooper out-takes from his video releases complete with a rubber chicken that squawked, "Death to Americans!" This particular video was taken from an animated TV comedy, *Family Guy*, which had become practically a legend in office lore around water-coolers everywhere due to these wacky bin Laden burlesque cameos. Peals of laughter erupted from the pit followed by a round of applause as the clip finished. American entertainment had effectively marginalized bin Laden to a comedy routine. The pit got back to work.

Marnie laughed aloud at the bin Laden blooper reel. It couldn't be helped. And she was charmed by the ease in which her compatriots could use humor as an effective bonding glue of camaraderie in the face of undeniable treachery. The words of bin Laden's actual video, however, still lingered in her mind and had obviously bothered her more than it had her co-workers, or so it seemed to her. Sure, there was your obligatory anti-capitalist vitriol and impassioned Islamic evangelism, she thought. And there were odd references to the anniversary of the bombing of Hiroshima, global warming, and even the sub-prime mortgage crisis presently affecting the United States. But what was nagging at her was bin Laden's twisted attempt toward denouement. In one breath, he had stated that his fighters were duty bound to escalate the fighting and killing of Americans, and in the next breath, he announced that the solution to this bloodshed was for Americans to embrace Islam.

While others simply dismissed this as Osama's same old ranting, Marnie saw this as an ultimatum and one that was not readily swallowed by the greatest superpower in the past two hundred years, not to mention one united under God, not Allah. Bin Laden had basically just told America, "Join us or we'll kill you," and Marnie couldn't wrap her mind around it. He was either brilliant or mad, or more likely both, she thought. She found herself compelled to understand more about a religion that was breeding fanatics faster than rabbits—fanatics who were getting in line to kill those who didn't agree with them. "Wasn't religion about tolerance, understanding, peace, and love?" she thought. This was not how she was brought up to understand religion. She needed to know more.

⊞ ⊞ ⊞

THE INITIAL REVULSION Marnie had felt for Major Ron Ray was short lived. During the time since Ray had joined the team, they'd spent countless hours together searching for bugs in Junior's knowledge base. He learned quickly and could think on his feet. Marnie found his experience vast and his demeanor engaging. She was surprised to learn that Ray even had a sense of humor concealed behind his hardened exterior. Major Ray had turned out to be completely respectable and very likable.

Marnie had learned that the major was a lifetime soldier, or at least he planned to be. He had at least twenty more years before he thought of retiring. He'd served in the Middle East for most of his career with the Army. He saw action during Desert Shield in 1991 when he was a twenty-six year old E-4 Specialist, and served his country in both Operation Enduring Freedom in Afghanistan and the invasion and subsequent, ongoing war in Iraq.

Major Ray was recognized early on by his commanding officers for his knack with technology, which quickly made him an invaluable asset during these modern computer wars, where his skill set could be leveraged for maximum effect. The military had found another application for the major in more recent years, using advanced systems to protect American interests at DARPA, the Defense Advanced Research Projects Agency. DARPA, a unique organization within the Department of Defense, supplied technological options for the entire Defense Department. Its charter was to be the technical engine towards the transformation of the DoD through radical innovation. Through DARPA, Ray had been collaborating on projects with certain government entities on and off since 2003. One of the most noteworthy projects was known as the Total Information Awareness, or TIA, a program developed by the U.S. Information Awareness Office.

The TIA program underwent several transformations since its inception. Beleaguered by public scrutiny over its alleged violations of personal privacy, the Information Awareness Office head, Admiral John Poindexter, gave TIA a name change by changing the word, Total, to Terrorism. This was an effort to give the program a more publicly palatable counterterrorism façade that was more acceptable media-wise in a world where counterterrorism had become stylish thanks to the likes of TV's Jack Bauer. Unfortunately for the Information Awareness Office, the facelift on TIA did not have the desired effect, and to the cheers of civil libertarians the IAO was defunded. The fact that Poindexter was a convicted Iran-Contra liar didn't help much either with those who held the purse strings and had images to maintain on Capitol Hill.

Regardless, TIA survived its grounding and avoided the scrap pile. The fact was that the government still needed a system that could detect, classify, and identify potential terrorists with the hope of preempting attacks against America and its interests. Saved by a classified annex drafted by legislators obviously sympathetic to avoiding further terrorist attacks on American soil, TIA found a new home at the National Security Agency in Fort Meade, Maryland. The location was also known as Crypto City, and Major Ray was presently overseeing two projects there with the innocuous code-names of Baseball and TopSail. He'd overseen the development of both from their infancy back at the IAO. It was because of these that he now found himself on Project X working with Marnie McCloud.

"So tell my why again we've been busting our asses on Project X, when you've already got Baseball and TopSail?" Marnie asked.

"Been there; done that," said Ray. "You know full well that I can't tell you everything, but what we're doing at the NSA is different in several ways from what you've accomplished here; and I must say, I'm impressed."

"Well, I guess I should be flattered, but I'm still confused."

"Let's just say that Crypto City has been developing similar tools for information extraction, analysis, and dissemination. We too have the same goal of anticipating and preempting terrorist attacks, but your algorithms are both new and very, very good."

"Please tell me something I don't already know," she pleaded.

"Okay. I knew I'd have to let you in on this at some point, so it might as well be now. We've been feeding data from our systems into Junior to see if we can get a new perspective on things based on the advanced algorithms your team has developed, and I think I know where your bug is."

"Run that by me again?"

"There's a ghost in the machine. For years, the government has relied upon data analysis for deterministic purposes, and the systems have never churned out one hundred percent accurate information. I mean, sure, there's solid stuff there—stuff that's been acted upon with excellent results—but every once in a while, we get something that makes us scratch our heads."

"Like terminate all Muslims?" she asked.

"Bingo. You win a kewpie doll."

"Gee, thanks. So what is it?"

"They're these little plastic—"

"The bug, for Christ's sake." She cut him off.

"Oh, right. We see this happening whenever we loop data through a particular system at the NSA, but we don't know why. Everything has been used to debug this from Chaos Theory to Freakonomics. Nothing can tell us what causes this to happen. There are some of the best analysts in the free and not-so-free world looking at this, and they're stumped."

"Does it usually recommend wiping out an entire religion?" Marnie asked.

"Usually, it only gives us a name," he replied.

"And what do you usually do when you get a name?"

"Ah, well, they usually end up dead a hundred percent of the time."

"You're letting a system put hits out on people?" she nearly shouted. "Are you insane?"

"It's been going on for a while," he said without a trace of remorse.

"Did you ever think of *not* using a system that's telling you to kill innocent people? I mean that's what any normal person would do, right?"

"It's not that simple. The system in question has been highly effective in serving our interests for many years. We just need to control it better, and I'm hoping you can help with that."

"And how exactly do you see that happening?"

"I think you might know the bug man."

"The bug man? Do tell."

"First, you'll have to promise that this will be between you and me."

"Or what?" she asked.

"Or you might wind up dead."

Marnie studied his face for a good five seconds.

"You're not joking are you?" she asked.

Major Ron Ray's smile was a flat line across his face.

"From whom do you get your orders, Major?" she asked.

"From very, very high up," he replied.

"I see," she said and thought of Kevin Bacon again.

Chapter 18

WHEN MARNIE ARRIVED at Burns and Lynch Headquarters, she bypassed her office and made straight for the lair. As the doors of the lift opened, her ears were assaulted by possibly the loudest electric guitar rendition of *The Star Spangled Banner* since Hendrix played it at Woodstock. Phet had supplemented his work area with a Mesa Boogie amplifier that produced an impenetrable wall of sound. If it wasn't so loud, Marnie thought she might actually have appreciated his artistic solos skillfully wrapped around the song's melody. She put a finger in each ear and pushed her way through the sound waves.

"... And the home of the brave!" Phet finished his performance *a cappella* in a voice Marnie didn't know he had.

She stood behind him and offered him a polite, personal round of applause.

"It's a good thing this room is sound proof," she said.

"Miss Marnie! Long time no see," Phet said, reverting to his more familiar voice.

"Yes, it has been a long time. How's it going?"

"I'm lonely," he moaned. "No one here to thrash about the head and shoulders with my rapier wit."

"I'll be sure to tell Hawk you send your love."

"That dusty, old cow-poker is no help at all. I am nowhere with infiltrating hallowed ground of racist pigs," Phet sighed.

"Ya, about that. Phet, we've known each other a long time, right?"

"Six years, four months, and twenty-two days, Miss Marnie."

"Phet, that's a little bit freaky," she said.

"I remember perfectly. You interviewed me for job. It was my birthday. I pray to Buddha: please let red-lady give me job. And you did! How Phet can forget that?"

"I didn't realize I had such a lasting impression on you."

Phet strummed his guitar and sang a horrific rendition of *Nothing Compares to You.* It was worse than if Mickey Rooney had the karaoke mic as Mr. Yunioshi.

"You're creeping me out."

"Sorry, Miss Marnie. Why you here? What you want?" he asked.

"This is going to seem a bit strange, Phet. It's kind of personal."

"Personal? How so?" he asked.

"It's about your father."

"My father? What about my father?" His voice raised nearly an octave.

"Do you know where he is?" she asked.

"Father left mother with nothing but big belly and heartache. He's no good G.I. coward who run away and leave my mother like slippery eel."

"How do you know this?"

"I just know."

"Do you know where he is, Phet?"

"He stay in Thailand. He is philandering drunkard."

"Hmm, he sounds like a real piece of work."

"Piece of shit, Miss Marnie. Big stinky piece of shit."

Major Ray had told Marnie of a man who just might have the answer to Junior's hiccups. In one of the more intriguing stories she'd ever heard, Ray spoke of a brilliant young student at Berkeley who was drafted into the Vietnam War in the seventies. He'd excelled in his studies but not fast enough to escape the draft. Upon landing in Saigon, he'd been cherry-picked for a role in military intelligence and swiftly rose through the ranks.

When the war ended, he returned to the United States and held several important positions for over a decade until—according to the major—he cracked. He abruptly retired and began touring the country, giving speeches that railed against the government. And then, in 1982, he simply vanished.

Ray claimed that this man had a connection with the NSA's elusive system ghost, though he would not explain how. The man, by some bizarre twist of fate, was Phet's estranged father.

"Phet, I need to speak to him. It's important."

"He in trouble?" he asked.

"I'm not sure," she admitted.

"I help you find him, but only if for good. Not bad."

"I can only give you my word that I'll try for the former."

"I trust you, Miss Marnie. Phet find yellow-bellied dog of father for you. Come, I show Miss Marnie now."

Phet walked over to his computer workstation and logged in with a dexterous display of incredibly fast finger work. He opened his email program and then a folder labeled Loser. It was filled with hundreds of emails. One sender's email address made up the entirety of the messages within.

"This is my fink father, son of bitch, dead-beat Dad," he said.

"You're in contact with him?" she asked, making a mental note of the address.

"No, Miss Marnie. He send email for years. I never read."

"Why do you keep them then?"

"My business. Not yours, Miss Marnie."

"Understood," she said. "So how do you find him?"

"Oh, that's easy," he said, and his fingers danced across the keyboard again.

Phet opened the five most recent email entries from his father and displayed the Internet headers of each message. He purposefully ignored the message body, refusing to acknowledge the words from his father.

"You see this number? That is his IP address from the machine that sent the email. He has two actually. This one is his computer's address. It stays same. This one here, changes in each email. You see only last section changes. First three stay same. This is the address from his internet service provider."

Phet entered a few rapid-fire keystrokes to bring up a black-screened command line window. He then typed in a command, and said, "There you are, my pretty."

He followed this with a series of hurried finger strokes while saying, "Who is Thai net dot com," as he typed. He pressed enter and after a couple seconds, a long listing of information was displayed on the screen.

"You see this? This is information on an Internet company in Thailand. Address is Bangkok. This domain is Class B subnet. That is sixty-five thousand five hundred thirty-four possibilities. They are subnetting—"

"—Phet," she interrupted his hyper-technical spiel. "We're trying to find a person, not a computer."

"Moment, Miss Marnie" he said as he scanned the data. The screen reflected mirror images upon the lenses of his bulky spectacles. "Ah ha!" he announced. "I have clever subterfuge. Responsible person for this domain name is Mr. Wichai Putiwongpantip. This is his email address."

Phet opened a different email program, apparently his personal account, and composed an email in speedy, staccato clicks in the Thai language to Mr. Wichai. The text was completely undecipherable to Marnie. He clicked send with a flourish, delivering the message into the Ether.

"Ta da!" he exclaimed.

"What did you just send?" she asked.

"I tell Khun Wichai my father is hopeless halfwit and need my help to wipe his own buttocks. I say father lost password and cannot pay his bill online. I ask him to send new password and copy of the latest bill. He will balk at new password for security reasons, but that is only decoy. Internet bill will show you his home address."

"You really are devious, Phet."

"Not devious, but resourceful and knowledgeable how to leverage social engineering techniques against foolish mortals. I am Thai, Miss Marnie. Thais are excellent Phisherman. That's spelled with PH, so you know how clever is Phet."

"Yes, you are, and loveably so. Tell me then, why go through all that? Why can't I just contact your father through email?"

"Oh, I was showing off. That might work if you pretend you are needy tramp in want of his loins."

"Um, let's hold off on that idea for now," she said, "You'll tell me when you get a reply from Mr. Wichai?"

"Sure thing, Miss Marnie."

She left Phet in the lair with his guitar and the unread emails from his father.

CHAPTER 19

MONTHS HAD PASSED, and still there had been not a word from Ashad. Salome had spent her days working at the Foundation, and in her spare time she had honed her resume and reconnected with her favorite professor from her life at Georgetown University in Washington, D.C., John Vendetti. While she had kept in touch with her professor on a friendly and casual basis, it was the first time that she'd hit him up for a job. Once her father's bug had fully moved from her ear and settled into her brain, Salome began dreaming of a new life for herself. She imagined herself teaching at the university and working for the Center for Muslim-Christian Understanding. She began to feel the excitement again. Unfortunately, things did not happen as quickly as Salome would have liked, and she began to feel that Vendetti's promise to create a job for her was more lip service than any sort of guaranteed employment, although her constant follow up with him did return some glimmers of hope in his replies that read, "Patience, I'm working on it. I really am!"

Salome's excitement quickly festered into frustrated impatience. No longer waiting for Vendetti, she began approaching other universities that taught programs for which she was qualified. She contacted Columbia, Harvard, Stanford and several other universities that unanimously responded with polite form letters stating that there were no current openings but that they would keep her contact information and reach out to her should any opportunities arise.

While her father reminded her that he could easily arrange a position for her at one of the Foundation's offices in the States, he didn't push the issue. He just floated the idea every so often to remind her that she had a backup plan. He also encouraged her to keep applying and following up with the universities. Besides, Kahn knew full well that the more distance there was between Salome and the family business the better, regardless of the layers and shells that protected the Foundation's darker side from the unknowing public.

Then, it came. Oddly enough it was in the form of a phone call to the house on a Sunday morning. The home phone almost never rang, having been replaced by the convenience of mobile phones, but the Kahns kept the line for the mothers, servants, and Salome who hadn't quite caught up with the technology wave yet. The call was answered by Yaghoub, one of the male servant staff, who humbly informed Kahn that he had a telephone call from overseas. The conversation lasted for nearly an hour, and then Kahn came to tell Salome the news. He found her in her home office, firing off emails to universities across the United States.

"You may wish to stop sending those emails, Mooshi," he said after politely knocking so as to not startle her.

She gave her father a perplexed expression.

"I have just had the pleasure of a conversation with a most extraordinary young man," he said. "Your high opinion of Professor Vendetti is well founded. His manners are impeccable, and his Farsi is nearly so."

Salome bounced from her chair, her eyes brightened with hope. "What did he say, Father? What did he say?"

"Well, we spoke of Islam and how it is so misunderstood by so many—"

"Do not tease me, Father!" she interrupted.

"Okay, okay, I am sorry. I could not help myself. It is exceptionally good news. He said that you should expect to find a very acceptable job offer in your inbox before the end of his Monday. Apparently, he has been feverishly campaigning to create a position just for you. It has taken time for him to convince the right people that you were not someone to simply pass over—that you were in his words 'an extraordinary woman who should be considered a valuable asset to be attained at any expense.' You must have left quite an impression for him to go to such efforts and speak so highly of you. I am filled with pride."

"Tell me more!" she demanded.

"He has prepared all of the necessary paperwork as well for visa preparations, and he is sending them via overnight post. I believe he has indeed delivered on his promise. Are you ready to return to America, Mooshi?"

Salome squealed with delight and was jumping up and down, clapping her hands.

"Oh, you are wonderful, Father!" she said and wrapped her arms around him, squeezing him so tightly that he laughed, overcome by her aura of pure, innocent joy.

※ ※ ※

THE FOLLOWING DAYS DRAGGED ON with agonizing slowness for Salome. It seemed to her as if time itself had simply gone into slow motion. Her one respite from the drudgery of waiting was a trip to Istanbul, where she'd applied for her visa and would have to be interviewed in person. Due to the absence of a United States embassy or consulate in Iran, any visa processing for Iranians had to happen out of the country. Knowing that the time was drawing near and that Salome would be leaving him soon, Kahn accompanied her. They made a father-daughter trip of it, visiting the famous sites of Hagia Sophia and the Blue Mosque when they were not waiting in line or interviewing at the consulate.

While Kahn surely could have pulled some strings to smooth the process, he was determined to see that Salome's visa was as above board and as unrelated to his connections as possible. Of course he was her father and sponsor, but her credentials and paperwork prepared for her by Vendetti were certainly enough to qualify Salome without him becoming more involved than the situation required.

Salome was, as he rightly predicted, granted the necessary documents to enter the United States and begin her new life. Kahn told her that he would arrange for a sizable money transfer to occur once she'd got established and had opened her own bank account. In the meanwhile, she could use the ATM and credit cards he provided her. He assured her that they would never run dry.

During the final days before her departure, Salome was bubbling over with excitement. Though she was still concerned about Ashad, he'd been on her mind less often, as she was otherwise occupied with her new thoughts of a new life. Kahn promised that he would keep an eye out for Ashad and help him in any way he could if he were to reemerge from wherever he'd disappeared to. This helped sooth whatever guilt she may have had at leaving without knowing what had happened to him or not having being able to help him. Father would take care of him, she knew.

It was surprising for Salome to witness the change of attitude in her brothers since the news had become public of her leaving for America. She realized that this was probably because they knew they would be rid of her, and though the feeling was mutual, she was heartened by their apparent turn-around and their good wishes. She was equally surprised when the entire family, including the brothers and mothers, accompanied her to the airport. They formed a virtual motorcade as they drove across the city at midnight to Imam Khomeini International Airport.

After her check-in at the first class Lufthansa counter, the entire Kahn clan escorted her to immigration, beyond which they couldn't pass. She received a hug and a kiss on the cheek from each of her brothers and the mothers, which was not entirely uncomfortable considering that this had never happened before in her entire life. Nonetheless, she allowed the experience to settle warmly in her heart in hopes that it would become a memory of pleasantness that she could look back fondly upon instead of other memories she'd just as soon forget.

Her last goodbye was of course saved for Father, and here there was no hope in stemming the tears that flowed freely across her previously dry cheeks. They hugged and held each other with unspoken love as the others watched, silently knowing this was a bond they did not and would not ever share with the man.

"I will miss you, Mooshi," he said, patting the back of her head. "But I know that this is for the best for you. I know you will do well and continue to make me proud," said Kahn.

Salome said nothing, only burying her face deeper into her father's chest and wiping her tears on his shirt. Gathering herself, she finally took a deep breath and let out a loud sigh. "Oh, look at the mess I've made," she said, wiping at the mascara stains she'd left. "I love you, Father. Goodbye."

She went through immigration and turned back to see them all still standing there. Salome waved and put her hand over her heart. And then she walked away.

⌘ ⌘ ⌘

THE EIGHTEEN-HOUR JOURNEY from Tehran to Dulles with a four-hour layover in Frankfurt was grueling. Salome made the most of it by entertaining herself as best she could and even managing to get some sleep during the five-hour leg to Frankfurt. While Imam Khomeini International was conspicuously devoid of any Western reading material, Salome found a wealth of magazines and books to choose from in Frankfurt and gleefully stocked up on an armful of both to occupy herself on the last leg of her trip that would take her across the Atlantic.

Settling in after takeoff, she began to pore over her cache. She'd forgotten how brash, irreverent, and in your face some Western periodicals could be. She flipped through all of them in barely an hour, finding most of them filled with pedestrian articles about nothing she really found interesting. It was mostly the advertisements that oozed with brazen sexuality that kept her flicking through their pages. She then pulled a Sidney Sheldon novel, *Master of the Game,* from her carry-on bag. Salome had learned to love reading novels while in the States and found Sheldon to be a captivating writer. She was saddened to learn from the book's front matter that he had died at the age of ninety in January. It made her think of her father who was now in his seventies. "He will live to be to be a hundred and ten," she smiled to herself and dug into the novel, finishing it quickly. She'd have torn through it faster, but she found her English had rusted slightly after nearly a year of no practice.

Rather than another novel, Salome tried to sleep but gave up after a while, knowing her internal clock to be in a time zone far away. She checked the in-flight entertainment screen and viewed the miniature airplane icon as it arced across the globe. The screen changed and confirmed that it was 3:00pm in Tehran. "Ugh, five more hours," she thought, and reached in her bag for her Qur'an.

She leafed through the pages, letting them flip under her thumb while thinking of what she wanted to read. She had already begun to prepare a mental list of topics that she would structure part of her curriculum around. As she sifted through the Qur'an, something caught her eye. She flipped the pages backward and found a piece of notepaper carefully wedged within the chapter of Ibrahim. It took her a few seconds, but she then recognized what it was and pulled the folded sheet from its hiding place. "Fourteen eight," she thought, mentally picturing Ashad sitting at her desk. 14-8 was a chapter and verse number. He had given her an obscure clue that he thought would lead her to his missive. It was regrettably a bit too obscure, as it went right over Salome's head. She unfolded the note and began to read.

Dear Miss Kahn,

I am so very grateful for your caring and gracious generosity in trying to help me; however, I am afraid that in your doing so that I may have put you too in grave danger, and for that I am pained and regretful.

Admittedly, when I came to you, I had learned that you worked at the Martyr's Foundation. What I did not tell you is something that I had come to believe during my time in search of Javid. This was that there are ties between these recruitment organizations and a higher, unseen power.

While I had no proof of this, I truly believed that these connections existed. To my shock, this was confirmed in my mind when I saw your brother last night. Your brother, Firouz, I recognized as one of the leaders in the recruitment organization where I was first taken in. I believe he recognized me as well, although of this I am unsure.

There is no mistake; he is well connected in this organization and commands the respect of the leadership. I know that this does not happen for someone as young as Firouz naturally. It must come from an external influence. He is surely somehow closely linked to this shadow power to have achieved such a position of power himself.

My greatest fear is that he is not the only association your family has to this organization and that you now have become embroiled into this dangerous mess that I have brought upon you. I pray that I am wrong, but if I am right, you must protect yourself!

As I write these words, I feel that I am a dead man. I shall stay in this room that you have so kindly provided as shelter for this hopeless fool. If you find me still here in the morning, perhaps my theories are simply the ravings of a confused spirit, suffering from the loss of my family; however, if you find me gone, I do hope that you find this message and understand the warning that it brings.

You are a wonderful woman, Miss Kahn, like an angel sent from heaven who aids those in need. May Allah bless you and keep you safe from harm.

Ashad

Salome's entire body trembled with emotion after reading Ashad's message. "Was he saying that her family was in the business of recruiting terrorists?" she wondered. "Impossible! He must be mad to even think such things." She knew the Foundation worked very hard to help those who had been afflicted directly and indirectly by terrorism. While she admitted that her brothers, especially young Firouz, might be stupid and cruel enough to sympathize with these extremists, Father would never allow them to join ranks with such deviants. It was simply unthinkable.

She pored over the letter again and again, becoming increasingly disturbed, as a myriad of thoughts crossed her mind. "Why would he say these things? Why would he say that he would stay in his room and then not be there? Could he really be so fiendish to craft such a ruse so as to make her believe him? What purpose would that serve? Or was he telling the truth?" If what he said were true, it would rock Salome to the very foundations of her soul.

Chapter 20

"I DON'T THINK THAT THOMAS JEFFERSON, while writing Danbury Baptists Association in 1802, accidentally omitted a religion when he declared that the American legislature would 'make no law respecting an establishment of religion, or prohibiting the free exercise thereof,' thus building a wall of separation between church and state. I mean, really. Gee whiz, America. Thomas Jefferson forgot about the Muslims. I think we better change the constitution again!"

The audience laughed. John Xavier Vendetti commanded the stage like a seasoned performer, and Marnie was glad she was here. She'd left early on Thursday night for a change of clothes and drove to Georgetown University to attend a lecture at the Center for Muslim-Christian Understanding. Several speakers presented; however, Vendetti was the one she was here to see. Mark had put her onto Vendetti after she'd vented on him, expressing her confusion regarding what she now thought of as the bin Laden ultimatum. As usual, he knew precisely the medicine she needed, and of course, he knew John Vendetti personally. With a phone call Mark learned that tonight's lectures were scheduled spontaneously to address the hype surrounding the bin Laden video release. He also learned that the lecture had sold out, but he managed to procure Marnie a seat in the front row.

"It's funny to us, this notion," Vendetti continued. "But there are several countries now where the church and state are actually inseparable. For a great example, let's look at Lebanon. The Lebanese constitution, as it stands today, mandates that the elected president shall be Christian. It's written down, and it's in place to protect a minority, supposedly. But get this, the prime minister must be a Sunni Muslim and the speaker of the parliament must be a Shi'a Muslim. And just to round things out, the deputy prime minister and deputy speaker of the parliament must be Greek Orthodox. In other places, it's more fundamental. You simply wouldn't be considered as a candidate if you weren't a Muslim in Islamic states.

"Let's take a look at the American presidents, shall we? We've got a majority of Episcopalians, followed closely by a gaggle of Presbyterians, a smattering of Unitarians and Baptists, and a very unfortunate Roman Catholic—may God let him rest in peace. There are also a few Methodists, a Quaker or two, and allegedly a handful of Deists—though that's somewhat controversial. However, one thing is clear. They all were or are men of God with a capital G. Christians, one and all. And I doubt that will change in the years to come. In this light, we see that Christians and Muslims are not that different after all, and that is what I am talking about this evening: the commonalities of Christianity and Islam."

John X. Vendetti held a lot of titles. He currently held the honorifics of university professor at Georgetown as well as the title of founding director of the Prince Alwaleed bin Talal Center for Muslim-Christian Understanding, or ACMCU—another acronym Marnie had chalked up in her memory after a brief study of the man.

The ACMCU, Marnie learned by perusing their website, came into being in 1993 when Georgetown University and Geneva's *Foundation pour L'Entente entre Chretiens et Musulmans* agreed upon a mandate to facilitate understanding between Islam and the West. Its scope spanned the world's borders and the breadth of the Muslim world.

Marnie had discovered that Vendetti had devoted his life to the study of Islam. He was editor-in-chief of several notable works related to Islam, including dictionaries and encyclopedias of the Islamic world. He'd also written more than thirty books on the topic; many had been translated into several languages including Arabic, Turkish, Persian, Indonesian Bahasa, and Urdu. Mark could not have found a more perfect prescription for her troubled mind. He'd done it again.

Vendetti spoke from the stage. He was elucidating commentary from an article he'd recently had published in the *Washington Post.* He was upbeat, intense, and entertaining.

"Did you know that almost half of Americans view of Islam as a generally unfavorable religion?" he asked rhetorically. "This is according to a news poll from last year, and the numbers have been rising steadily since 9/11. This poses a dilemma, where it seems rather easy for us to lose sight of the forest for the tree—the forest being the majority of Muslims who abhor terrorism, and the tree, which represents Islamic extremism. The troubling side effect of this is that this very, very nasty tree is a barrier that prevents non-Muslims from getting to know and understand one of the world's great religions.

"How do we get to know Islam? Well, it's a good start for us to understand that all Muslims believe in the five pillars of Islam. The word Islam itself actually means to submit, and submitting to the will of God is what Islam is all about. To be a Muslim, one must submit to the knowledge of Islam's fundamental belief: There is no god but God, and Muhammad is the prophet of God. It is well worth noting here that God with a capital G is Allah, the one true God. And with this belief that there is one true God, comes the refutation of all other forms of worship including other gods (with a small g) and other more secular interests such as one's ego, money, *et cetera*. The Prophet Muhammad has conveyed all of this to the world, and Muslims *know* this to be true."

Vendetti paused for a moment and took in the audience. His eyes passed over Marnie without a trace of recognition.

He went on, "If we were somehow able to look beyond this 'tree' of terrorism, we would find some striking commonalities among other religions. For example, Christianity, Islam, and Judaism all were born in the Middle East. Not only do Muslims worship the same God as did Abraham, they also acknowledge the same prophets that we know from the Bible, including both Moses and Jesus. However, there is one key difference. Muslims believe that while Jesus was a prophet, he is not the Son of God.

"But guess what? Neither is Muhammad. And very much like Jesus, Muhammad is the ultimate role model for Muslims. It is my belief that by understanding just how revered Muhammad is, that we might be able to get an inkling of why all Muslims—and not just fanatics—become upset when they witness the denigration of the single most important person in their religion.

"All Muslims take this very personally, and as we all know, some go so far as to riot and even kill in retaliation for such acts. With this in mind, one might find it interesting that although you may see Muslims burning the American flag or effigies of western political leaders at times, you will never see a Muslim desecrating an image of Jesus Christ. For that would be sacrilege. Think about that for a moment."

Vendetti spoke for nearly forty minutes on several subjects, including the remaining pillars of Islam, the wildly diverse treatment of women in different Islamic states, and the age-old dispute between the Sunnis and the Shiites. His breadth of knowledge and uncanny stage presence allowed him to keep the entire auditorium in rapt attention. He took a moment to sip water from a glass upon the podium while his eyes surveyed the crowd.

"Okay, enough history. Let's talk about something that I think you're all interested in: terrorism." When he said this, he looked directly at Marnie.

"Interestingly, not all Muslims are in agreement over what some might call the sixth pillar of Islam. This is known as *jihad*. The Qur'an defines *jihad* to mean to strive or struggle. It also means to realize God's will and to lead a virtuous life. It means to create a just society. And it means to defend Islam and the Muslim community. To me that all sounds like some pretty honorable stuff; however, it's that last one that tends to give us pause. What we have seen through the eye of history is that some Muslim leaders have used *jihad* to justify war with the support of religious scholars. This is a potent combination of politics and religion that has facilitated the advancement of their realms. Today, we see a similar strategy with modern extremists, such as Osama bin Laden, who are asking for Islam to bless their acts of terrorism in the very same manner. And when we have Muslim clerics promoting terrorist attacks as the will of God, we have a very dangerous situation.

"I have spent several years of my life studying Islam. In my studies, I've come to realize that Muslim hostility toward the West is—for the most part—political in nature and not religious in spite of how extremists try to spin it that way. Having said that, what I believe all Muslims want—and deserve, I might add—is for non-Muslims to show a little more respect for their religion. It is distressingly unfair and unwise to persecute an entire faith based on the actions of a minority. After the attacks of September 11th, it is absolutely critical for us to have the ability to differentiate Islamic extremism from Islam itself, and I strongly believe that the only way to get there is through understanding. Only when we have this clarity can we see the forest of a great religion in spite of the tree of terrorism. We cannot afford to distance ourselves from the mainstream Muslims around the world, for this will only result in the marginalization of Muslim citizens at home and the alienation of Muslims abroad. The only way to approach the fight on global terrorism is from within Islam, and our allies in this battle must be Muslims."

A quiet followed in the wake of Vendetti's final words.

"Thank you," he concluded, and the crowd burst into applause. Someone turned the house lights on.

Marnie was impressed. In less than an hour, Vendetti had answered more questions than she'd ever asked herself on the troubling subject. However, she still harbored certain doubts— doubts that she thought might be reconciled if she were able to talk to Vendetti one on one. She felt somewhat out of her league but decided she might as well seize the moment and approach the man. Mark had never steered her wrong before, so she decided to see if she could have a chat with this professor of Islam.

The crowd was dispersing. It was nearly nine o'clock in the evening, and Vendetti was shaking hands with the few brave souls who wandered closer to bask a little more in the illumination of such a potent individual. Marnie stepped forward.

Vendetti must have sensed her presence, as he turned and with the grace of a classic gentleman said, "Miss McCloud, I presume?"

Marnie blinked at him. He was a strikingly handsome man. His eyes were a pale brown, almost golden, and they seemed to smile at her with an inner kindness. He reached out and shook her hand. His hand was smooth and soft. His grip was confident and pleasing to the touch.

"Come now, you don't think that Mark Harmann would have sent you all the way here without giving me a head's up, do you? I've cleared my schedule this evening. Let's have coffee together. There's a café nearby as earthy as anything. You attended

Marymount, didn't you? A superb little school, I must say." His smile had the charm of ages.

Marnie had no choice but to succumb once again to Mark's covert ministrations. It was fine, really it was, but for once—just once—she'd like to feel that she had some control over her destiny even if it was only a cup of coffee.

"Professor Vendetti," she said. "I would be delighted to join you."

"Please, call me John," he said and took her arm, leading her from the auditorium to the parking lot where he opened the door to an impeccably polished Ruby Black BMW Z4 Roadster convertible. Her Mustang was parked three stalls over. She hadn't washed it since forever. It was so filthy it looked colorless.

"Nice Donkey," she said to herself as she eased herself into the elegant machine.

"Pardon?" he asked.

"Oh, nothing," Marnie smiled.

Chapter 21

Miraculously, they arrived without incident at the Sign of the Whale, a bohemian watering hole on M Street NW just off Dupont Circle. The ride was over in what seemed the blink of an eye. Vendetti drove like a Formula 1 competitor, or at least he thought he did. With the top down, the open air along the path of their autumn evening drag race had tousled their hair with comic effect.

"Mmm, this is good coffee," Marnie said. She was sipping a pint of Pale Whale Ale, a micro-brewed beer with a resplendent bouquet. It was the house specialty.

"Indeed, though I find weather like this often calls for something with more body. Would you like a try my dopplebock?" He slid his glass across the table.

"Ooh, that's good too. You do know your beer, John." She was calling him John now. The beers had had some effect, but Vendetti had an uncanny ability to put her at ease. She felt comfortable, sitting there talking on a pleasant variety of topics from their backgrounds to the definition and interpretation of *jihad*. It was the most interesting date she'd been on in ages, but she continued to remind herself that she was here for information—not anything extracurricular.

She picked at the gigantic chicken Caesar salad they'd decided to share.

"I find you fascinating, Marnie. I hope I don't make you uncomfortable by saying this, but I've never met someone like you before. You're vastly intelligent, curious, and independent. You attended a Roman Catholic university, yet you are interested in Islam. A great majority of people these days tend to hide their head in the sand when faced today's challenges regarding Islam, mostly in reaction to their natural fear of terror. Too many have become conditioned to equate Islam with terror while you on the other hand seek to understand it. "

"Well, I think saying that all Muslims are terrorists is kinda like saying the Klu Klux Klan represents the whole of Christianity. We've all had our moments of fear, though I don't think many people in the States—you know, those who haven't travelled much—have experienced the reality behind the fear as have those who've actually been through something terrifying. Sure, there's the news that brings fear to us on a regular basis, but it's hardly instructional. I'd rather face my fear by at least minimizing my ignorance on the subject of the cause."

"I'm becoming infatuated now. This is simply marvelous!" Vendetti folded his hands into a temple and rested his chin on them. He beamed ardently at her. "You're involved in a highly secretive project, which—as you've said—you'd have to kill me if you told me anything about it. You work for one of the smartest men that I know, and he raves about you. However, you're not—how do you say—an item anymore."

"Let's talk about you, shall we?" Marnie deftly changed the subject.

"Well, I'm what some would call a helpless bachelor."

"I think helpless is hardly apropos."

"I tend to bore those that I'm attracted to, and I overcomplicate relationships rather than relying on simple emotion to carry my heart. Some have said that man's attraction to large-breasted blondes is a survival instinct stemming from our hunter-gatherer days. The sad fact is that smart girls generally don't want anything to do with me, and I often find myself seeking solace in the arms of a mindless twit. This is something I intend to rectify one day."

Marnie studied Vendetti over her pint glass and wondered just how much of what came out of his mouth was orchestrated to seduce her. "Who cares?" she thought to herself. She found herself becoming increasingly attracted to this man named John Vendetti.

"They say acknowledgement is the first step toward recovery," she said.

"I'll drink to that."

They clinked glasses.

"I'd like to ask you something, John," said Marnie.

"And what might that be?" he replied.

"Well, first I'd like to say that I found your speech to very enlightening."

"Why, thank you," he said, looking genuinely pleased by the compliment.

"But the thing is, I think everyone realizes that not all Muslims are terrorists. That's pretty obvious to me at least. The problem, as I see it, is that there is a minority of Muslims that have the ability to capture our attention more than the rest. These are the ones who keep blowing stuff up. This minority is a group of seriously bad people. They're so bad that I don't think America much cares about who's a good Muslim and who's a bad Muslim anymore. They just want it to stop. Then there are the rest of the Muslims; those who you call mainstream Muslims. To me it seems that quite a lot of them don't like us very much either. You don't have to be the Taliban to not like what America is doing. You know what I mean?"

"Do you have any Muslim friends, Marnie?" asked Vendetti.

"Um, well there was this guy in high-school—"

"Friends, Marnie, real friends."

"No, I guess not," she admitted.

"I think that's the key to everything. We, as Americans, are so disconnected from the rest of the world. We are a melting pot of culture, and yet we are still so compartmentalized. Our one commonality as Americans is democracy, but when faced with this specter of terrorism, we throw it out the window. Where is that line drawn between who is a real American and who is not? Who are we to decide—and *how* are we do decide—which Americans are more deserving of democracy than the rest? Is this religion?"

"Look, it's all well and good to play the Rodney King card and say, 'Can't we just get along?' but I think it's more complicated than that."

"But it isn't really, is it?"

"It is. Some people—the really bad ones—need to be stopped. And killing them seems to be the only way to stop them, because they aren't going to stop on their own. That's plain and simple. Trust me, I've got access to information that would put the fear of God into just about anyone. There are people living as American citizens here right now that are plotting various ways to kill other Americans—you and me. If they had nukes, they'd use them. Are we really expected to have the patience and understanding to sort through each and every Muslim on American soil when religious profiling is much more expedient?"

"Good Lord, you sound like a Nazi."

"And you're an idealist. There is no way to solve this problem by trusting first and hoping for the best."

"Reagan is famous for saying, 'Trust, but verify.'" Vendetti said somewhat smugly.

Marnie felt herself flush with anger. "Yes, while I doubt you've ever voted Republican, verify is the key point here. You can wail for peace and understanding from the top of your ivory minaret until you're blue in the face, but I don't think that's going to stop terrorism."

Vendetti sensed her annoyance, and ratcheted it down a bit.

"I do see your point," he said. "May I suggest that we try not to argue with each other? I don't think that we're about to solve the issue tonight. What we are dealing with here is a pernicious form of ideologically distorted Islamic fundamentalism. There aren't about to be any white flags waved on either side soon."

"So you don't think the war on terror can be won?" Marnie continued.

"I'm not a soldier. I'm an academic; however, I do think that in conventional wars that there is eventually a victor. So no, I don't quite see that happening."

"So, isn't it reasonable to think that the best we can do is create a sufficiently stable state in places like Iraq and Afghanistan so that they can take care of themselves—so they don't again become places where terrorists can set up shop? Don't we need to be vigilant right here at home to make sure Ali the taxi driver doesn't have some sort of *jihadi* postal episode? Someone needs to be there to stop him from setting off a dirty bomb or whatever's coming next. I realize that you can't defeat an idea, but I think you can whack the people who have the wrong ideas down before they pull another stunt like 9/11."

Vendetti thought for a moment. Marnie was challenging him, and while it did ruffle his feathers a bit—not many people had the gumption to go toe-to-toe with him, especially on the subject of Islam—her intelligence inflamed his attraction for her.

"Absolutely," he agreed. "But it's the way we go about it that defines what non-terrorist Muslims think about us."

"So you're saying it's not all that straightforward, right?" Marnie began to ease herself, not wanting this evening to end prematurely over some political dispute. She was liking Vendetti—liking having someone to talk to like this. She was mature enough to not let a little debate get in the way of a good time. And while she was not about to fall head over heals for the man, she was painfully aware of the fact that she hadn't been on a date in nearly a year.

"I concede," admitted Vendetti. "It is not straightforward at all. Shall we have another round?" He showed her his empty glass.

Marnie downed the remainder of her Whale Ale and said, "Bring it on." This made Vendetti laugh out loud. She laughed in return. She liked how he laughed. It was infectious.

Marnie and Vendetti carried their intellectual *tête-à-tête* into the wee hours of the night. Several beers later, last-call was announced, and they looked at each other, seeing a tinge of disappointment in the other's eyes.

"I believe they are giving us the boot, Miss McCloud."

"Infidels!" she snarled with mock contempt at which Vendetti obviously reveled.

"Two espressos please!" he called to the waiter, who nodded at him as he passed, hefting a tray of empty beer glasses.

"This will put some fuel in your jets. It's a bit of a drive for you from campus, isn't it?"

"Yes, an unconscionable three miles."

"Dear me! That seems terribly far. Will you make it in one piece?"

The espressos arrived with perfectly little flourish along with a remarkably long beer tab, which Vendetti promptly snatched up.

"Allow me," he said. "It's the least I can do to compensate you for putting up with my droll monologue."

"Be my guest, though we've both been drolling a little upon the corporal." Marnie swiped a lemon rind around the rim of her cup and sipped the intense, aromatic brew.

"You enchant me!" Vendetti beamed.

ON THE BARELY SUB-SONIC TRIP back to the Georgetown campus, Marnie proclaimed that she was unfit to drive home, citing inebriation. This had less to do with her inability to safely operate a vehicle than the potential embarrassment of being dropped off in a university parking lot by an acclaimed don where she would trade her carriage for a pumpkin.

Vendetti performed a sliding stop at the south entrance of the Georgetown quadrangle at her announcement. The campus was deserted at this late hour.

"I have just the solution." He seemed sober as a priest; his golden eyes sparkled under the sodium lights of the nearby parking lot. "I've a two-bedroom flat only a stone's throw away. Trust me, I am the consummate gentleman. Plus, it looks like you can defend yourself pretty well even if I turned masher on you. Please don't hurt me, or at least spare my nose. It's a family heirloom."

"Isn't tonight a school night?" Marnie asked.

"My Fridays are hardly what could be considered rigorous. The most challenging thing I have to do tomorrow is pick someone up at the airport in the evening."

"Okay then. Invitation accepted. Just don't kill us before we get there."

At this Vendetti, thrust the car into first gear and fishtailed the Beemer back onto Prospect Street. He then dropped down to the Canal Road and made for the Key Bridge. He was a mad pilot with the wind in his hair. All that was required to round off the image would be a pair of bomber goggles and a white, silk scarf flapping around his neck.

"Are you always a gentleman, John?" Marnie asked.

"That would depend entirely on you, m'lady."

"M'lady?" she asked. Marnie found this infinitely more appealing than being called Missy.

"I'm sorry, it's something I picked up at Oxford," he replied. "Shakespeare is food for the soul, don't you think?"

"It sounds good to me. Do you always drive this fast?"

"I went to the doctor, and the prognosis was a lead foot," he chortled and sped them through the night to Arlington.

Chapter 22

SALOME FRETTED OVER ASHAD'S LETTER for the remainder of the flight and was no closer to coming to terms with the message it carried than when she had first discovered it. Lost in thought, she absently took one of the trams from the terminal and passed through immigration with little hassle, politely answering questions and showing her passport and the docket of papers she'd prepared that detailed her employment arrangement with Georgetown University. As she'd given her fingerprints at the embassy in Istanbul, she was only subject to the minor inconvenience of having her photo taken, which she took in stride, being far too distracted to care that this was possibly the worst picture of her that she'd ever seen.

As she struggled to pull one of her two steamer trunks from the luggage carousel, a complete stranger came to her assistance and placed them on a luggage trolley for her. She thanked him, and he replied, "Not a problem, ma'am."

Salome finally pushed her trolley to customs. She saw the same raise of eyebrows that she'd seen from the immigration officer, which she ignored, and was waved through after being asked a few cursory questions.

She scanned the waiting area as passengers from her flight filtered through the exits and others milled about. It was 7:00pm on Friday, and Professor Vendetti was waiting for her as promised. When their eyes met, he smiled gallantly and trotted over to meet her.

"Let me help this weary traveler with her burden," he said and took her carry-on. He placed this atop her trunks and took control of the trolley.

"Professor, you are still as chivalrous as ever," she said, delighted to see him. "It is very kind of you to be picking me up like this. I am grateful."

"It is my honor to serve you, Salome Kahn," he said with a bow. "I am elated to be in your presence once again. Come, my chariot awaits, though I'm not sure how I'm going to be able to fit all of this luggage into it."

"Oh, I am sorry. I did not think. Is it an inconvenience?" Salome asked.

"Nonsense! This is why God invented the Bungee cord," he teased. "Where does Mohammed Kahn have his handsome daughter staying while she finds herself a place of her own?"

"I am at the Mandarin Oriental."

"Well, your father spares no expense, I see. The hotel is exquisite—definitely top-cabin. It's only half a mile from the Smithsonian. Perhaps I can bribe you into joining me to explore the calligraphy exhibit on display there tomorrow. I've been meaning to go, but all of my friends have turned me down. They are so vapid, or possibly I am the ultimate bore. Regardless, I cannot seem to spark even their remotest interest in the *Seven Thrones* by *Jami* or the Sultan Ahmad Jalayir's *Divan*, even if they are some of the most well preserved Persian manuscripts from the fifteenth century," he playfully sulked.

Salome couldn't help but be uplifted by Vendetti's infectious charm, but she had yet to shake off the tormenting effect that Ashad's letter was having on her.

"Are you all right, Salome?" he asked.

Salome wasn't all right, but she was surely not going to be dumping this revelation upon the professor only five minutes into their reunion. "I am just tired, Professor. That is all."

"Don't you worry about a thing, and please, none of this professor business. I insist that you call me John. We'll be working together, you know."

She smiled at the thought.

"Ah, here we are," he said as he aimed a keychain fob at his BMW, remotely opening its trunk with an electronic chirp. He fought with Salome's trunks for a bit and eventually did have to resort to a meshwork of well-placed Bungee cords to hug them securely in position as they hung out the back.

"There!" he said with an inflection of triumph. "Let us pray that they will not fly out and scatter your belongings across the highway. Within the hour, I shall have you safely deposited at your hotel where you can have a wonderful bath and be blissfully sandwiched between sheets of the highest thread count in Washington, except maybe the White House."

The smart comfort of Vendetti's Roadster and the warmth from the heater lulled Salome to sleep only minutes upon leaving the airport. Vendetti looked fondly at her and drove as if the Z4 was outfitted with a governor; full knowing the trip up to D.C. was riddled with speed traps. Despite this, they reached the Oriental in well under an hour.

Vendetti gently shook Salome awake, and it took her a moment to remember where she was. "Have we arrived?" she asked.

"Yes, and your luggage is fully intact. Let's get you checked into this palace," he said and told the doorman he'd be back in a short while.

"Kahn. Salome Kahn. I have a reservation," Salome told the receptionist.

"Yes, here it is," said the woman behind the broad marble counter after typing a few things on her keyboard. "Welcome to the Mandarin Oriental, Miss Kahn. May I see some identification please?" The woman was Asian, yet Salome noted she spoke English with a distinctly American accent. She was impressed but suspected one had to be raised in the United States to be able to speak like that.

Salome slid her passport across the counter.

"Thank you," said the woman, and she began to fill out the reservation form. "And how will you being paying for your stay with us," she asked.

"By credit card," said Salome and passed the receptionist the freshly minted American Express Platinum card that her father had given her.

"Thank you," she said running Salome's card. "It'll be just a sec—" the woman paused and ran the card again through her machine. "Hmm, there seems to be some issue with your credit card Miss Kahn."

"Oh dear, I just used it in Frankfurt. I am not sure what could be the problem."

"Salome, allow me to use my card until you can resolve this," Vendetti offered, reaching for his wallet.

"Are you sure about that, sir?" asked the receptionist.

"Er, why do you ask, Ms.—" He squinted at her nametag. "Wang?"

"Miss Kahn has booked an Executive Water View Suite. The nightly average rate is five hundred and seventy-nine dollars."

"Don't be silly. This is obviously some wrinkle that can be easily ironed out by talking to the credit card company. I'm happy to guarantee Miss Kahn with my card until this is resolved."

"You can use the house phone if you'd like to call them, ma'am," the receptionist politely offered.

"Yes, please let me do that. I am sorry for this inconvenience," said Salome.

Ms. Wang aimed her toward the phone, handing back Salome's card and passport. As Salome made the call, Vendetti stayed back and watched her, marveling at her elegant poise. He turned to Ms. Wang and pointed at the credit card machine. "Computers!" he said. "They can be such stupid things."

Salome returned with an uneasy look on her face. "They say that the card has been cancelled."

"They what?" cried Vendetti.

"Yes, and they wouldn't give me any further information because I could not properly identify myself. Apparently, Father has given them some secret password, which I do not know. Ms. Wang, may I use this phone to make a long distance call?"

"How long distance?" asked Ms. Wang.

"Tehran."

"That may be a problem," she said.

"Oh, what can be done?" asked Salome, mostly to herself.

"Salome, let me suggest an idea," Vendetti chimed in. "It's late. Allow me the pleasure of letting you be my guest. My place is quaint compared to this citadel, but I assure you that you will be comfortable, and you'll be able to get some much-needed rest. We can try to call your father from there. If that doesn't work, we can do it from my office tomorrow. That's how I called him before. It's a sure thing."

"This is so embarrassing," said Salome, averting eye contact by looking at the giant chandelier that hung from the lobby ceiling.

"Tut tut. There's nothing to be embarrassed about. It's a mix up, and it will be all fixed up pronto, I'm sure." Vendetti took Salome by the arm. "Ms. Wang, please be so kind as to hold the reservation until tomorrow, will you?"

"Of course, sir."

"You'll need clothes," said Vendetti. "Bellman, please return the trunks to my car." This resulted in a nonplussed look that promptly converted into a smile when Vendetti handed him a twenty-dollar bill. "I think that's the cheapest stay in the history of this hotel," he whispered to Salome as he walked her outside.

With the trunks strapped back into place, Vendetti sped off home. When their efforts to contact Salome's father failed with busy signals after repeated attempts, they agreed to try again from campus in the morning. Vendetti showed Salome his guest room and bade her goodnight.

CHAPTER 23

SALOME SLEPT IN and had somewhat recovered from the fatigue of her long journey. Upon awaking, her efforts to contact Kahn from Vendetti's home phone again proved futile. They attempted again to reach him at the Kahn residence from Vendetti's office and finally got a connection. It was 7:30pm in Tehran. As was usual, the phone was answered by Yaghoub. He informed Salome that the Master was out of town and would not return until tomorrow, which was Sunday. Determined to reach him, she decided to call her father's mobile phone. She tapped in the numbers as she read them from her personal organizer. It was a number she had rarely needed to use. Salome heard a few clicks, and then the line began to ring. After three rings, the line was disconnected. She tried again, only this time the line connected immediately, and a recorded message told her that the subscriber's phone was turned off and to try again later. She tried once more and got the same.

"This is most aggravating!" Salome was starting to smolder.

"Let's not let this get you down," Vendetti consoled. "Look outside. It is a spectacular day. On the bright side, we know your ATM card works." Salome had been able to retrieve five hundred dollars from the campus ATM.

"Yes, well, it is just so shameful to have become a nuisance on my very first day here. I am supposed to be an asset, not a vagabond."

"Salome, nothing could be further from the truth. It is to my absolute delight that you are here, and your allowing me to help you—especially if that means that we are temporary flat mates—is to my ultimate gratification."

Vendetti could put a silver lining on anything, Salome thought.

"I have an idea. Let's go have brunch," said Vendetti. "You must be famished. There is a superb bistro in McLean, just a hop, skip, and a jump from here. They serve the best Mediterranean food I've experienced anywhere this side of Lebanon. After that, we'll spend the day at the Smithsonian. I guarantee a complete distraction from these monetary trifles. Tomorrow, your father will be at home, and all your worries will be resolved. What do you say?"

Again, it was difficult for Salome to resist any idea once Vendetti had put his positive spin on it. As she mulled it over, her mind drifted back to Ashad's letter.

"Salome?"

"Excuse me, I was thinking," she said. "You are correct. I should not be dwelling. I am acting like a child. This is after all what Americans would refer to as small potatoes, is it not? Your remedy of distraction is a grand plan."

"Fantastic!" Vendetti was thrilled to see her come around. "Have you ever ridden topless Miss Kahn?"

"I beg your pardon, Professor?"

"It's John, remember. And forgive me; I was speaking of my chariot. It's a convertible you know, and the weather is perfect for it."

"Oh, well in that case, let us ride?" she said hesitantly, unsure of her English.

The day turned out to be just what Salome needed. They had a sensational time together. She reveled in the feeling of freedom as she let her hair fly in the wind while Vendetti raced them across roads that were flanked with trees, bursting with the fall colors of red, orange, and yellow. The brunch was indeed delectable, and each of them absorbed the exhibits at the Smithsonian with utter relish. They spent hours at the museum, and it was well past dark when they finally emerged into the crisp autumn night.

❈ ❈ ❈

GEORGETOWN UNIVERSITY

MARNIE'S FORAY INTO the library stacks was proving fruitless. She'd already spent part of the day in a plush chair at Barnes and Noble, sipping over-priced tea and pouring over whatever she could on Thailand from the travel section. She purchased Nancy Chandler's map of Bangkok after three hours of free research, though the tea compensated for much of that time. This had helped to distract her from the thoughts she'd been having about Vendetti. While nothing actually happened between them physically during their night together, something very well could have. And those types of thoughts could be very distracting. She'd not be having these feelings at all if Mark had ever just stepped up to the plate, but on that front, Marnie'd all but given up hope.

She was now ensconced in front of George, the library's electronic catalogue, in search of anything in print that might lift the shadow on Phet's father. For several hours she'd torn through books, periodicals, and microfiches. From her research, she'd gathered that the man had received a Master's degree and a PhD in computer sciences from the California Institute of Technology. He was a renowned expert in cryptology, and was heavily involved in the creation of the Strategic Defense Initiative until he abruptly left this post to become a vocal critic of the government. After that, *poof,* he was gone but not without leaving a trail of public ridicule in the newspapers.

As Marnie continued to dig, she kept coming to the same dead end. There was nothing that she could see that tied Lieutenant Colonel Andrew Milas to anything related to the NSA or whatever the source of Junior's bug might be. Whatever it was, she figured it must have been redacted and thus not in any public records. In contrast to this bug's elusiveness, there was one subject that seemed to fly off the pages, begging for recognition. A conversation she'd had with Mark back in March crystallized in her mind.

"Phoenix," he'd said. "You'll figure it out six months."

She was about a week late, but she'd made the connection. "Damn Mark and his mysteries!" she thought. "What did Phoenix have to do with anything?" Determined to know more, she had George show her every book available on the Phoenix Program of the Vietnam War. Vendetti was placed in the back seat of her thoughts as she delved into the past, absorbing what she could through total immersion.

What Marnie gleaned from her search was that the Phoenix Program was a highly contentious subject from the annals of recent history. Critics of the program referred to it as systemized assassination campaign, while its supporters described Phoenix as a counterterrorist program designed to neutralize the civilian infrastructure supporting the insurgency. To her, this smacked of the same rhetoric now used in the wars in Afghanistan and Iraq, but no matter how it was said, it sounded ominous. Marnie dug deeper.

She discovered that it was generally agreed upon that up until the mid-70's, the United States Central Intelligence Agency was involved in assassination attempts against certain political leaders, one of the most famous cases being Cuba's Fidel Castro; however, the scope was much broader than many people imagined. During the Vietnam War, the Phoenix Project involved the targeting of civilians known or those thought to be supporting the National Front for the Liberation of South Vietnam, otherwise known as the Viet Cong.

America had entered a war against an enemy where conventional tactics and strategy fell short. Faced with the overwhelming might of the American forces, the Viet Cong realized their annihilation would be near immediate in a traditional, knock-down drag-out fight and thus resorted to guerilla warfare, which proved to be highly effective in thwarting the American effort. In response to the Viet Cong's elusive hit-and-run tactics, America reached into its alternative arsenal of counterinsurgency and special activities to literally take the head off the enemy apparatus and its collaborators.

Elite forces of Green Berets and Navy SEALs were detached to carry out their orders. Working through their blacklists received from above, the teams systematically neutralized tens of thousands of targets, resulting in over twenty thousand deaths. Those who weren't killed were rounded up and placed in detention centers. It was not a new way to fight a war; and though Marnie was no closer to finding the bug-man, she couldn't help but see the parallels in the wars of today's world.

Marnie had exhausted her brain and her resources by the time the librarian finally resorted to flicking the lights to get her attention. It was well past closing time, and the librarian kindly let her overstay her welcome while she closed up, but it was time to leave. Her eyes were red and tired from reading, and her mind was grasping at the scattered straws of information, trying to weave them into some form of tangible storyline that would connect somehow to the bug man.

She couldn't think anymore. She craved a beer and the things that might come with it. Letting Phoenix fade from her immediate thoughts, she left the librarian to sort out the mess she'd made. Marnie made her way to the parking lot and paused a moment to gaze at the heavens, admiring the spangle of brilliant stars across the black canopy of the night sky. She did not notice the lone figure sitting in the car parked in a poorly lit corner of the lot. The man watched Marnie from the shadows as she got in her car and drove away.

Marnie headed for the Whale on the off chance Vendetti might be there; and if he wasn't, there was still a pint with her name on it. She needed to decompress. Finding a spot along M Street, she slipped her car against the curb and killed the engine. The car's low-throaty rumble gave out a final cry of defiance, belching out a small backfire. She entered the Whale and sidled up to the bar, trying not to look too obvious that she was looking for someone in particular. She ordered an ale and surreptitiously used the bar's mirrors to take in her surroundings. The beer was perfect: cool, hoppy, and bitter.

Marnie was politely fending off a barfly-cum-suitor when her eyes landed on the booth from her recent, memorable visit. There sat Vendetti in rapt conversation with one the most exotically beautiful woman she'd ever seen. She was stunning. Vendetti was facing away from Marnie, allowing her to study his companion from afar. She was elegant with broad facial features. Her hair was raven black. It shined with a luxuriant glossiness, and her eyes glimmered in the bar-light like gemstones in an exotic setting of burnt umber. Her makeup was flawless with the effect of being simultaneously mature, inviting, and seductive. The woman was majestic. Marnie thought she was perhaps Middle Eastern and had the looks and poise of a runway model. She dressed and conducted herself with certain classiness that only Western fashion might allow, which struck Marnie as a graceful blend of disparate cultures, combining old world class and new world chic.

TO ROUND THE EVENING OUT, Vendetti had taken Salome to one of his favorite haunts. It was a bit of a departure from the urbane; however, Vendetti knew from before that Salome was not one to shy away from new experiences. He was only slightly taken aback when Salome opted out of ordering one of the many beers on tap but then instead indulged herself by ordering a glass of Pinot Noir to accompany their light meal of appetizers.

"There is a woman at the bar, who has been staring at us," said Salome.

Vendetti turned to see Marnie, and his heart leapt. "Good God, she must be stalking me. How fabulous!" he said giddily. "Salome, that's a new friend of mine. I believe she might be feeling a little awkward right now. May I ask her to join us? I believe you will find she has a most refreshing viewpoint on things."

Vendetti turned again, saw Marnie leaving, and gave Salome an expectant look.

"Of course, I would be happy to make her acquaintance," she said, and Vendetti slid from the booth in a flash.

"THIS WOMAN IS SERIOUS COMPETITION," Marnie said to her beer, putting it away with a few rapid draughts.

She felt herself flush and thought of approaching the pair but caught herself in an instant, thinking better of it. Taming her reactionary burn, she signaled for the barman to give her the tab and left him a ten-dollar bill, not waiting for change. As she pulled the door open in an attempt to escape unnoticed, she heard Vendetti calling her name.

"Marnie! What are you doing here? What a wonderful surprise," he said, appearing by her side.

"Oh, I just came to fix my brain with a beer after a long day. I'm heading home now," she said, finding it impossible to not look over his shoulder at the magnificent woman he was here with. The woman smiled and offered a graceful wave to Marnie.

"I'm so glad you're here. I want you to meet my friend, Salome. She's spectacular, just like you are. Well, not exactly, but—oh goodness, what am I saying? Please, come and join us. I'm sure you'll get along smashingly."

"Er, I think I better not, John. I am really tired. Can we do this another time?"

"Come now, there's no reason to be that way," he pleaded and took her hand, which she reflexively pulled away from.

"No thanks; really, John. I'm gonna go." Marnie left Vendetti standing in the doorway. She turned back briefly to see his face a mix of confusion and disappointment.

"I'll call you!" she said as she spun into her car and slammed the door shut just a little too hard. She turned the ignition and gave out a groan of embarrassment as her Mustang barely sputtered to life. "This is ridiculous," she said aloud, mulling over her emotions. She pulled out onto M Street with a bit too much gas-pedal, leaving a little rubber in her wake. "God, I'm an idiot," she said, catching a glimpse of Vendetti still standing in front of the Whale in her side-view mirror. What she did not see was the unremarkable sedan that pulled from the curb and followed her.

❊ ❊ ❊

SALOME OBSERVED THEM FROM A DISTANCE and could tell from the woman's body language that she was not at all comfortable with the situation. When she saw Marnie look in her direction, Salome offered a courteous wave, but it was not returned. Their conversation was a short exchange, and the woman was out the door with Vendetti in pursuit. He returned a moment later alone and looking discouraged.

"I'm not sure what just happened," he said.

"If I may give a woman's opinion?" Salome asked.

"By all means."

"This woman—"

"Marnie. Marnie McCloud," he said sullenly.

"This Marnie McCloud is a jealous creature."

"You think?"

"Ah, it is amusing. Men are the same everywhere," she laughed. "You are all blind as babies. But do not worry; I can see that she is not ready to give up on you."

"So we've gone from me you telling you not to worry to the other way around."

"Refreshing, is it not? It may have something to do with this wine. I believe it may have medicinal value."

Vendetti raised his glass. "To a day of progress, Miss Kahn."

"Please, John. It is Salome," she smiled and touched her glass to his. "To progress."

CHAPTER 24

ON THE FOLLOWING DAY, progress made an abrupt turnaround for Salome. With the morning came the *Washington Post*. It arrived with a thump against the front door. The paperboy had a good arm. Vendetti retrieved the *Post* and returned to find Salome in the kitchen, waking up with a mug of coffee she'd brewed with his french press. He plopped down in his recliner, shook open the paper, and began to take in the news of the day.

"My word!" he exclaimed. "Salome, take a look at this. What is the name of your father's organization? It is the Martyr's Foundation, right?"

"Yes it is. Why do you ask?" she said and approached his chair from behind.

"This is shocking to say the least!" he uttered. "It says here that the U.S. Department of the Treasury, pursuant to Executive Order 13224, which is aimed at financially isolating terrorists and their support networks, has imposed financial sanctions against the Martyr's Foundation by freezing all of its U.S. based bank accounts."

"You must be mistaken!" she said, but a disturbing sense of confirmation was lurking in the back of her brain.

Vendetti read on, "The Martyr's Foundation is a parastatal organization that channels financial support from Iran to several terrorist organizations in the Levant, including Hezbollah, Hamas, and the Palestine Islamic Jihad. Also included in the designation is the Goodwill Charitable Organization (GCO) that has offices in Los Angeles and New York, which were established by the Martyr's Foundation. GCO has provided financial support to Hezbollah directly and through the Martyr's Foundation. Hezbollah leaders have instructed their members in the United States to send their contributions to the Martyr's Foundation via GCO." Vendetti gasped. "Salome, this is incredible!"

He whirled in his chair to face her and saw on her face a look of utter despair.

"Have I just employed the daughter of a terrorist funder?" he asked.

Salome opened her mouth to speak and nothing came out. She then swooned and collapsed onto the floor.

"Dear Lord, I think I have," he said aloud and leapt to where she'd fallen. "Salome? Salome!" He lightly tapped her on the cheek and didn't get a response. "I never could hit a woman," he muttered. He then carefully picked her up and laid her on the couch. Looking around, he saw a misting bottle used for watering his solitary houseplant. He grabbed it and gave Salome a good squirt in the face. She roused, but only slightly so he gave her another, and she came to. He could see she was frightened. "Salome, you fainted. It's me, John." Her eyes began to cross, and she started to fade again. He snapped his fingers in her ear. "Salome, please wake up!"

Her eyes opened and she bolted upright. Vendetti watched as her mouth formed a painful frown and she shook her head slowly side-to-side. Salome held her face in her hands, and began to wail, *"Nah, Nah, Nah!"* Reverting to Farsi, she was crying, "No, No, No!"

Vendetti remained quiet, not really knowing what to say or do. An occasional, "There, there," was all he could manage, though he mainly let her be and watched as her body shook under the influence of what he could only imagine was acute emotional distress—not that he really knew what that meant, but it sounded right to him in the moment. In time, her halted breathing became normal, and she slowly began to calm.

"Salome," he said. "I'm terribly sorry. I had no intention to upset you so."

She looked at him, her face streaked black with mascara and tears.

"And a little plant mist," he thought to himself. Vendetti went to the kitchen and returned with a clean dishtowel. He handed it to her and said, "Look, this article doesn't prove that your father is directly involved with this ballyhoo. There's nothing here that actually says that." He was trying to remain non-committal, though the article was rather black-and-white.

Salome got up from the couch and went to Vendetti's guest room. She returned with her Qur'an and sat beside him.

"All of this is happening for a reason," she sighed heavily. "My coming here was just a way for my family to be rid of me— to keep their terrible secrets hidden."

"You can't mean that," he said.

"I do, yes. Now I truly believe it," she said and opened the Qur'an, removing Ashad's letter. "You know that I worked at The Martyr's Foundation, but you must believe that I had no idea of these things. I would never be involved with such despicable, hateful people. You do believe me, John?"

Vendetti studied her face and determined that she was either the best actress to ever come out of Iran or she was speaking the truth. "Yes, I do," he said and looked at the folded paper she now held. "What is that in your hand?"

"This is all the proof I need to know that my father is a murderer."

⊠ ⊠ ⊠

AFTER HEARING SALOME'S STORY about Ashad and her father's idea for her to return to America, Vendetti was not fully convinced that Ashad's disappearance was altogether damning. When he read the letter, however, he felt a knot grow in his stomach.

"If this is true, do you know what it means?" he asked.

Salome only nodded her head.

"He did the poor boy in," Vendetti said to himself. "Salome, how is it possible that you've never realized that your father could be involved in such things?"

"I do not know. I was never interested in the family business. You must realize that I had only returned home just over a year ago. Father is into many things: banking, construction, oil, the Foundation, as well as other businesses. My brothers hold prominent positions in many of these organizations. I left for school before I could really understand what was going on around me, and when I returned, I was simply oblivious. He let me follow my whims, and I happily accepted his support. When I failed at my teaching job at the university, he gave me a job to keep me busy. My work for the Foundation was charitable. We really were helping people. I doubt my father had any idea that there would be someone like Ashad."

"Who would put two and two together and with nothing left to lose, spill the beans to you—possibly the only innocent of the bunch," Vendetti concluded. "Goodness! And I thought you had a lot of baggage when I picked you up at the airport."

"How can you possibly joke at a time like this," she practically hissed at him.

"I apologize," he said. "It's how I deal with insanely complicated women. Really, I am sorry, Salome. I can't pretend to know how you're feeling right now, but we are dealing with a very serious situation here. I'm surprised the FBI isn't knocking on the door."

"What am I going to do, John?"

"Your father loves you, Salome. I mean the way you've spoken about him and the way you described how he's treated you—even after learning about all this—he has to love you, right?"

"I…" she paused in thought. "Yes, nobody can fake the love we had for each other."

"It's 'have,' you see?" Vendetti said, enlightened now. "No matter what bad things he's apparently capable of, he loves you. And in order to keep you from harm's way, he has sent you here to live a life that is free from the danger you would be in if you had stayed in Tehran. I believe that Ashad was right in that his disappearance was a warning. You became a potential liability from the moment he contacted you, and if you were thought to have learned something you shouldn't have, I doubt you'd have ever made it out of Iran. In fact, you'd probably be sharing the same shallow grave as Ashad."

Salome shuddered and closed her eyes.

"But that's not the case," he continued. "I believe we should both thanking God that you did not find this letter sooner; otherwise, there's no telling how your father's hand might have been forced."

"And what does this all mean?" she asked.

"It means that you need to do what you were sent here to do. To start a new life."

"But how can I do that with no money?"

"By getting to work of course!" he said with a smile.

"You mean to tell me that you would hire me after all that you've just learned?"

"Absolutely! Terrorism is my bread and butter, you know. Well, not actually, but you know what I mean. Not only have I hired you, but I also have our first project for us to work on. We are going to quietly unravel the mystery behind The Foundation."

"Please, if I am to start a new life, I should leave this old life behind."

"If you can do that then, yes, you should," he said. "But I think you'll soon realize that you're going to need some closure. That letter you have is going to eat at you because, while it might be very convincing, it is not the rock-solid evidence you need to know for certain who or what your father is. This project will serve as a cathartic, and maybe—just maybe—we can discover something that will allow you to if not exonerate your father; at least you will be able to live your new life knowing you have the truth."

"You are a very wise man, John."

"Tell that to *my* father. He'd laugh in your face."

"I will when I meet him." She tried to smile and nearly succeeded.

"So that means you're on the bus?" he asked.

"Bus? To where?"

"To Georgetown, my dear woman!" Vendetti chuckled.

"Yes, I am on the bus, but I do enjoy riding topless." Salome finally smiled.

"There is definitely hope for you, Salome Kahn."

Chapter 25

MONDAY CAME. "Ah, blessed Monday," thought Marnie, "that special weekly reminder that I haven't yet won the lottery." She was sprinting along Marcey Road in a battle against the blustery gusts of a very chilly morning, heading uphill for the parking circle where she'd left her car. As she navigated a curb while passing the Nature Center, her legs were on autopilot, completely disconnected from a mind embroiled in thought. The past few miles were a green blur. She'd even unconsciously missed the small plank bridge at the Brown Creeper Connector Trail and wound up down along the Potomac on the Heritage Trail. This added another half mile to her run, which was fine with her, as she had a lot to think about as well as some pent up stress to release. The majestic view of the river was an added plus.

She'd made some headway on Saturday in her search for Major Ray's bug man. On Sunday, she broke the long-standing tradition of hers to never own a cell phone and visited an Apple store in Clarendon where she purchased an iPhone with a new voice and data plan that had international roaming. She had the store clerk set it up for her and give her a few tips, as she hadn't the slightest clue how to work a telephone without buttons. The clerk was quite helpful and set up the basics for Marnie along with a new email account at her request as well. He even helped her send a test message from the new account, though he said it would be queued for a few hours until the phone became active. The message was sent to Phet's personal email account, asking if he'd made any progress on locating his father. She paid with her company Amex. "Thanks, Mark," she thought to herself and smiled, also thanking the clerk for all his help.

Later that night she was lying in bed, her mind inevitably drawn of her run-in with Vendetti and the woman, Salome, when the phone emitted a tiny whooshing sound followed by an equally tiny bong tone within thirty seconds after that. She rolled over and lifted it from the nightstand. Thumbing the phone's slider, she found one new email message was waiting for her.

She opened it and read, "New secret exciting email! Miss Marnie come see Phet in lair on tomorrow. Give you low down on Daddy dumb-ass." She managed to awkwardly thumb the reply, "OK. C u then," which disappeared with another whoosh when she pressed the send button. Marnie had to admit, phones had come along way. She could get used to this kind of convenience. As long as Mark didn't get a hold of her number or new email address, she'd be fine.

Marnie started her warm-down and exited her weekend flashback as she approached her car. She kicked the tire and called it a tatty thing, admonishing it for embarrassing her. Then out of some odd feeling of guilt, she began to pet her Mustang. "There there, Rocinante, you know I didn't mean that," she consoled the car she'd named after Don Quixote's horse.

She was overcome suddenly by the sensation of being watched and glanced to her right to see a man sitting in the driver's seat of a non-descript sedan. He wore dark sunglasses that hid his eyes, which Marnie found odd as he was reading the newspaper, and there was not a spot of sun to be found in the overcast sky. She was unsure of whether to feel nettled at being ogled or self-conscious at having been seen petting and talking to her car. The man absently plucked something from his nose, examined it briefly, and flicked it out the car window. At this, Marnie looked down at what she was wearing and promptly slid behind the wheel. "Giddy up," she said, stroking the dashboard. "Let's go see Phet."

※ ※ ※

MARNIE ENTERED THE REFRIGERATED confines of the lair to find Hawk and Phet in yet another heated debate over something. They were so fixated on their verbal tussle that neither of them noticed her approach. She was still wearing her Nikes and sweats.

"Take that, you crusty crony! You are old enough to make dust fart," cried Phet.

"How in the world can someone make dust fart? You four-eyed, little freak," Hawk deftly parried Phet's barb.

"Are you not some shit-kicking cowboy? Don't cowboys know Spanish? Spanish and Thai same-same! First come adjective, then come noun."

"And if fart is a verb?" asked Hawk.

Phet pondered this for a moment before declaring, "You are fart!" He held his index finger in the air triumphantly, as if he'd achieved some moral victory.

"Wow," interrupted Marnie. "I never fully realized until now that you are both mentally still in kindergarten."

"Miss Marnie, it is good you are here!" exclaimed Phet. "This washed-up has-been is no help at all."

"What is he talking about, James?" asked Marnie.

"Well, believe it or not we were having a somewhat progressive discussion on the security aspects of hacking into the NCTC. This squeaking rodent here claims to have discovered a way to burrow around every firewall and encryption layer that guards the place, but he refuses to divulge his theory," explained Hawk.

"Phet?" asked Marnie.

"Miss Marnie. You know Phet is perfectionist. Phet will not reveal to this giant boob the glory of my genius until confident that my theory will work in real world," he said with an air of smugness.

"And what happens when you set off every intrusion detection alarm in the process of testing and proving your theory?" asked Hawk. "Marnie, the security systems are adaptive. Any vulnerability probe that is picked up by the intrusion detection system not only sets off alarms but causes the system to re-architect itself, making the initial probe worthless. The system also tar pits any connection it sees as a threat and launches a counter denial of service attack on the system doing the probe, rendering it useless. Even though we've been white-listed to perform vulnerability scans, which should prevent us from being brought down, I think we're still both tipping our hand and pissing into the wind here."

"Phet does not piss in wind, although I cannot speak for this ancient mariner," he said with defiance. "Phet can promise that there will be no detection. There will be no test until actual attack, which will work like magic spell."

"Watch out. He's going to break out his wand next," Hawk groused.

"Phet," said Marnie, "How long until you're ready."

"Three days, Miss Marnie, if left alone and not pestered by this over-curious daddy-longlegs."

"Good, that's settled. And when you are ready, you'll share your plan with the rest of us, right?"

"Of course Phet will share with Miss Marnie."

"And with James?"

Phet squinted at Hawk, looking him up and down as if he were examining a side of beef that had started to spoil. "Yes, Phet will share with mindless insect," he conceded.

"Hallelujah, I've been OK'd by the idiot savant!" Hawk got up from his chair. "I've had more enjoyable discussions with my proctologist. Parting is such sweet sorrow, but I must be off. I've got a meeting with Mark where I'll be able to tell him absolutely squat about the progress you're making. Thanks a million, Beanie Boy." He loped to the elevator on his stilt-like legs and then opted for the stairs, taking them three at a time to the ground level.

"He love me," smiled Phet.

"Ya, it does seem that way," Marnie said with an odd smirk. "So, Phet, what about your father?"

"Miss Marnie, we have received the address of the derelict from the cooperative yet oblivious Mr. Wichai; however, there is *pom-pem*."

"What kind of *pom-pem*?" she asked, realizing she'd just unconsciously mimicked Phet. He didn't seem to notice or care.

"This address is not home. It is business address. Actually it is bar, the Geronimo Bar in Bangkok. My mother is the owner. There is no guarantee that you would find him there. Polygamist Papa is rolling stone."

"So, what next?"

"Phet take liberty to send him email."

"I thought you weren't talking to him."

"Which is why Phet take liberty to send as you!" he beamed.

"And you did this how?"

"It's called spoofing, Ms. Marnie. You see, anybody can—"

"What exactly did you say in this email?" she interrupted.

"Check phone, message sent ten minutes ago and BCC you."

She groped around in her sweat pants and pulled out the phone. It took her a while, but she eventually found the email. It read:

> Dear Mr. Andrew Milas,
>
> My name Miss Marnie McCloud. I read your email on bathroom wall in Soi Cowboy. Are you handsome like your picture? If so, I want to meat you and jump on your bones.
>
> How can I find you, sexy man?
>
> Love Big Big,
>
> Miss Marnie

"Geez, Phet!" she groaned. "That is not how you spell meet."

At this Phet smiled from ear to ear and said, "This really will work like magic, Miss Marnie."

"It better," she said. "It just better."

⌘ ⌘ ⌘

MARNIE WAS TOWELING OFF after a long, hot shower in the subterranean facilities at the NCTC. She adored the privacy that a fingerprint scanner offered when it came to who could gain admittance to the locker room. She toweled her luxurious mop of hair, which when wet shone like dark, red wine. As Marnie moved from the showers toward her locker, she nearly walked straight into Rose who stood in wait, holding a clipboard. Though roughly a foot shorter than Marnie, Rose's severe features and smart-cut business attire were a formidable combination that demanded attention. Marnie quickly wrapped herself with her towel in a hurried flurry but not without noticing the slight hesitation of Rose's eyes that lingered on her nakedness before rising to meet hers. A rose-colored flush revealed that the woman was not a complete automaton.

"What can I do for you, Rose?" she offered.

Rose's initial response was inflected with a creak in her voice that she fought away with one of her demure *ahems*. "Major Ray would like to see you ASAP. He's waiting for you in Room 4-D."

"And this couldn't wait 'til I had my clothes on?"

"Major Ray said ASAP, Miss McCloud," Rose said and then performed an about-face. The swift, clicking echoes of her heels punctuated her departure.

❈ ❈ ❈

THE MAJOR WAS WAITING in room 4-D as expected when Marnie entered the room using her secure card. The air con had been set to a temperature that felt like she'd just entered a meat-locker, which seemed at odds with the weather on the other side of the shatterproof windows. Oblique rays of an autumn sun had broken through the cloud layer and glinted off the golden orb that sat atop the four-story flagpole in the NCTC's forecourt where a magnificently large American flag flew proudly in the late-morning breeze.

"Come, Marnie," said Ray. "Sit with me, please." He flipped shut the folder he was reading and placed it on the table before him along with two others. Marnie was able to glimpse a name written on the folder before he turned it over. Vendetti, John X., it read. She felt her ire rise.

Major Ray swiveled his chair around to face Marnie and crossed his legs. "How well do you know Professor John Vendetti?" he asked, casually patting the folder while looking Marnie directly in the eyes.

"How is that any of your business?" she asked, trying her damnedest to remain calm.

"Well, just about everything is my business these days, but it becomes a special concern when someone I work with is socializing with persons with known ties to Islamic extremists."

Marnie said nothing.

Ray reached for another folder and pulled an eight by ten black and white photograph from within, sliding it in front of her. Marnie fought back the onslaught of damning mental images she imagined the picture might show. Though she realized she really had nothing to hide, she could not for the life of her bring herself to look at it.

"Have you ever seen this woman?" asked Ray.

"Woman? I'm being paranoid," she thought with relief. She picked up the photo, and her heart skipped a beat.

"No. Should I know her?" she lied, battling to maintain her composure in spite of the mixed emotions that raced beneath her stoic façade.

"Her name is Salome Kahn," he offered. "Ring any bells?"

Marnie kept her eyes on the photo and shook her head.

"This picture was taken on Saturday night outside a bar on M Street. I think you know the place. The man with his arm around the woman is obviously someone you know, John Vendetti. Salome Kahn is the only daughter of Mohammed Kahn, an Iranian national who we believe with some certainty to be one of the largest financial backers of charitable organizations including the *Bonyad-e Shahid*, otherwise known as the Martyr's Foundation."

"That doesn't sound so bad," Marnie said somewhat sheepishly.

"While providing charitable funds to the families of suicide bombers might sound all warm and fuzzy to some, the fact that organizations like this funnel millions of dollars to pay for things like Hezbollah military and terrorist operations is not considered philanthropic by the U.S. government or its allies."

Marnie turned and looked at the flag that furled and unfurled in a strange dance as the wind bullied it about like a marionette at the mercy of a drunken puppeteer. She felt like that flag, neither in control nor understanding the forces that were surrounding her.

"I don't know what you want from me," Marnie said after a moment of contemplation.

"I want you to find out the details of why Salome Kahn is in this country visiting John Vendetti. She's come here for a teaching position at Georgetown, but we think there's more to it than that."

"I'm not going to spy for you. My job here is Junior," she said flatly.

Ray smiled. "Yes, and thanks to Junior we can cross-reference enough information to spy on most of the known world—at least the parts that matter—so I fail to see the line you're so righteously refusing to cross here."

"There's a difference between data mining and analysis for the protection of American citizens and the invasion of personal privacy."

"Is there?" he asked. "A whole lot of people see it differently."

"This is not what I signed up for. We should not be using Junior to spy on innocent people. This is a waste of time. We're trying to catch terrorists aren't we? Besides, he's still got the bug. You cannot allow decisions to be made on a flawed system."

"I think it's not up to you what purpose Junior will ultimately serve. Regardless, you might be interested in the fact that Salome Kahn was flagged at immigration—every Iranian is—but it was Junior, pouring over a new NSA feed, that connected her entry into the country and her relationship with Vendetti. There is a very high probability that neither of them is entirely innocent."

"So it's guilty until proven innocent. Is that it now?"

"I've asked for your help, Marnie, because I know that you know these people. I thought I was being rather nice about it, but if you're not up to the task, I'm sure the FBI will be more than happy to lend an interrogating hand."

"I cannot believe that you are this retarded. I mean we are talking about a system that has recommended the elimination of a religion, for God's sake!" Marnie was nearly shouting at him now.

"It's more for America's sake, and some people consider it as a means to an end," the major calmly retorted.

"You have got to be kidding me! Who could possibly be interested in entertaining this lunacy?"

"The interest, Marnie, is in national security." Ray's tone was sobering. "And whether you like it or not it determines whether you're a patriot or..." he let these last words hang in the air.

"Or what?" demanded Marnie.

"Or something else," he said.

"You're either with us or against us," Marnie muttered, shaking her head in disgust. She stood up, tossed the photo in his lap, and walked to the door. She opened it with her secure card and paused before leaving.

"Major?" she said.

"This conversation never happened," he replied.

"You can go fuck yourself," she told him. The door click shut behind her.

⌘ ⌘ ⌘

Marnie stormed out of the NCTC after gathering what few possessions she kept in her locker as well as her new phone, which along with all other electronic devices was held by security when entering the building. The fury of her dramatic departure was nothing compared to the tempest of anger that surrounded her as she stormed into Mark's office.

"She's here now, I'll ring you back," he said and quickly poked his phone off.

"Let me guess. Your buddy, the major?" she spat.

"Marnie, calm down," Mark pleaded as he came around his desk and put a hand on her shoulder.

"Don't touch me, Mark!" She was furious and spun away, taking up a defensive position with her back in the corner of the room. "Do you know what he's doing? He's using Junior, full well knowing that the system isn't ready yet. He says it's not up to me how the system is used."

"Well, he does have a point there. Remember we're contractors, Marnie. You may have built Junior. It's what we've been paid to do, but it's not yours."

"Ya, ya, I get it. But he's going to use it to kill people, Mark!"

"Oh, come on. Now, you're just talking crazy."

"No, he said it. He told me that people have already been killed because of the bug, and now he's acting like Junior's *fatwa* on Islam is just another bump in the road."

"Sorry, I'm not buying it, Marnie. This is too far fetched for me."

"Why would I be making this up?" she snapped. "He also said that John is associated with Islamic extremists!"

"John Vendetti studies Islamic extremists over breakfast."

"Believe me I know," she said.

At this, Mark intuitively tilted his head at a curious angle.

"Did I just say that?" she asked.

"Yes, but let's talk about it later. What else did Ray tell you?"

"He's using Junior to dig up information about John. And he's digging up stuff on this Salome Kahn woman, the daughter of some terrorist funder, who he wants me to spy on. And I think I'm being followed," she blurted this all out in rapid succession.

"What are you talking about?" Concern crept into Mark's voice.

"He had a picture, Mark. Someone took a picture of John at the bar where I saw him with Salome Kahn. And there was that guy in the park today."

"What guy?"

"Some guy reading the newspaper with sunglasses on."

"Marnie, you're sounding completely paranoid."

She'd thought the same just a short while ago. "He had a picture, Mark!" Now she was frustrated and scared.

"Look, there's probably a good explanation for the picture if Salome Khan is deemed a person of interest. And it doesn't mean that you're being followed. More likely, it's her that's being surveilled."

"Or John."

"Yes, or John, but not you. Here's what I'm going to do. I'm going to get in touch with Admiral Chase and get this sorted out. Here's what I want you to do: stay away from the NCTC and Major Ray for a while. Take a break from all this to clear your head. It's got you all frazzled, and that's no good for anyone."

"You know I can't just leave this alone," she said.

"You're going to have to for a while, and I mean it."

"Fine."

"That's not a word that I'm at all comfortable with coming from you." Mark put his hand on her shoulder again. She didn't pull away. "Seriously, let this be until I've spoken with the admiral."

"No, really. It's fine, I've got something I'm working on with Phet."

"Good. Stick with that. Hawk says he's made some sort of breakthrough."

"Ya, that's what we're working on," she said, looking at the floor.

She turned to leave.

"Marnie?"

"Yes, Mark?"

"Please don't do anything dumb, okay?"

"Oh, you know me," she said with unveiled sarcasm.

"That's what I'm worried about," he said.

Marnie stepped from Mark's office and walked straight over to Melanie's desk where she found her tidying an already immaculate workspace.

"Hello, Miss McCloud. How are you today?"

"I could be better, Melanie. But I think you can help me."

"Of course, how may I be of service?"

"I'd like you to book me a ticket to Bangkok, Thailand."

"Splendid city, Bangkok. The City of Angels! Does he know about this?" Melanie eyed Mark's door as she asked the question.

"No, but he will. And he won't be very happy about it."

"Well then, I guess I'll have to delay his signature until you've already boarded."

"You have my vote for sneaky secretary of the month."

"The pleasure is mine, Miss McCloud."

Melanie proficiently made all of Marnie's arrangements for her and handed her a folder containing her tickets and itinerary later in the day. The last thing Marnie did before leaving was send Phet's father an email. She explained Phet's prior message and apologized. She also noted where she'd be staying and said she'd like to meet with him to discuss some personal issues that involved his son. While it wasn't entirely the truth, she thought it better than showing up with him thinking she'd tracked him down from some toilet graffiti.

Chapter 26

MARNIE'S ARRIVAL INTO the Kingdom of Thailand was surprisingly uneventful and in sharp contrast to many of the horror stories she'd heard. This had much to do with the quick survival course Phet had given her, Melanie's expert coordination, and a forgettable number of glasses of a 1986 Bordeaux—compliments of the Royal First Class cabin crew. In fact, the trip had gone flawlessly from the landing and immigration process at Suvarnabhumi International Airport—Phet had taught her the correct pronunciation as *soo-wan-a-poom*—to the limousine service whose driver could have given Vendetti a run for his money on a racetrack with his Mercedes CL-600 Coupe. That extended to the swift and courteous, if not obsequious, attentions from the staff at the Oriental Hotel where she now found herself in the Siam Suite on a massage table being rubbed with oils scented with frankincense, lemon grass, and rosemary.

"I have died and gone to heaven," she said in a dreamy tone.

The female masseuse simply smiled and continued her ministrations, nearing the tail end of the two-hour, private spa treatment.

Marnie took in a deep, relaxing breath and sighed, drifting into a semi-conscious state induced by travel fatigue and the complete bliss of extreme pampering. An undeterminable time later, she awoke alone in her room covered with plush, white terry-cloth towels, having fallen asleep during her massage. A faint electronic *bong* she soon recognized as her iPhone had emanated from amid the stack of her neatly folded clothes placed on her suitcase. A note lay written on the table. It read, "You fall asleep. *Mai pen rai.* Enjoy your stay at the Oriental. Pim."

She smiled at the note and its intrinsic charm. She then spun herself around on the table and dropped her feet onto the supple, teakwood floor. It was warm on the soles of her feet. Marnie retrieved the phone and checked her messages with a few taps of the touch-screen. Standing in the nude, she stared at the phone and the singular message she'd just received. It read, "Nice digs. I bet you look good naked. Meet you tonight. Geronimo Bar, Patpong 1. 8:00pm Milas Out."

Suffering a moment of panic and vanity, Marnie looked about the room and found her image in a full-length mirror staring back at her. The muted incandescent lights reflected off her lithe, oiled body with a sensuous sheen. She saw her dark, coppery hair pulled back in a ponytail and furrows in her brow. She breathed to relax and put her shoulders back, twisting her torso slightly to enhance her curves. The lines between her eyebrows vanished and she smiled at herself. "I do look good naked," she thought and stepped into the spacious, on-suite bathroom for a shower to prep herself for whatever may happen in the night to come.

⌘ ⌘ ⌘

WHILE MARNIE'S INITIATION to the City of Angels involved the luxurious trappings and pampering at the Oriental, it had not prepared her for the city at night. She'd nearly forgotten Phet's warning until she was unceremoniously dumped off at the curb by one of Bankok's notorious *tuk tuk* drivers. He gave her a smile that was missing some teeth as he egregiously overcharged her for the ride. "You'll never find a more wretched hive of scum and villainy," Phet had said, pulling an old *Star Wars* quote from his mental vault. The thing was, Marnie soon realized, that he was not all that far off the mark. Patpong was a den of depravity.

Consisting of two parallel roads settled between the major thoroughfares of Silom and Surawong Roads, Patpong was divided into Patpong One and Patpong Two. It was along Patpong One where she was to find the Geronimo Bar according to the concierge who had faintly raised an eyebrow at the idea that Marnie would be seeking the whereabouts of such disreputable location. At 8:00pm, the Night Bazaar was coming into full swing and completely dominated what would be mostly empty road during the day. She stood at the outskirts, trying to get her bearings and take the scene in. Her senses were accosted by exotic and sometimes foul aromas that came at her from all directions, one of which turned out to be an Indian elephant grabbing at her handbag with a deft and greedy trunk. At this, she jumped and entered the fray where throngs of hawkers and tourists danced an ancient dance in the ritual of buy and sell.

Touts manned the sidelines of Patpong's playing field like cheerleaders, waving signs that harried Marnie's imagination. Sex show, frog show, ping-pong show, snake show, they touted. One sign read, "We have 50 beautiful girls and 2 fat ones!" Another buzzed in neon above her head. It simply read, "Super Pussy." Deafening music from every bar on the street poured out onto the sidewalks and swirled together into a cacophonous wave that washed over her. She did her best to defend herself against this onslaught, avoiding eye contact and clutching her purse, as she sidled and pressed her way through the crowd.

Five minutes passed, but it seemed much longer to Marnie when she finally arrived in front of the Geronimo Bar. Two girls in matching green flower-print outfits, wearing golf visors with "Geronimo" emblazoned upon them, welcomed her with smiles and the promise of a ninety-baht beer.

"I'm looking for Colonel Milas," she said.

The girls exchanged bemused looks and responded with a choreographed shrug of their shoulders.

"Colonel *Andrew* Milas?" said Marnie.

"Oh, you mean Khun Andy! He inside," one of the girls said.

Pulling back the heavy cloth drapes, the girls bowed their heads and motioned her inside.

As the drapes fell behind her, the street life was abruptly silenced. It was loud enough within to drown out the sounds just beyond the curtain, but it was a relief nonetheless as at least there was only one melody for her mind to focus on. AC/DC's *Highway to Hell* was the only thing she could hear now. The bar was nearly deserted, save two people hunched over what looked like a board game. There was smattering of dancers upon two stages, lazily grinding to the beat of the music. One of the door girls touched Marnie's arm gently and pointed to the man playing the game.

"Mr. Andy there!" she shouted above the din. "You like some drink?" she added.

"I'll have one of your ninety-baht beers, thank you," Marnie shouted back.

Marnie approached the table where the players were absorbed in their game, oblivious to their surroundings. She took an open chair and noticed they were playing *makruk*. It was the Siamese variant of chess descended from the sixth century Indian game of *chaturanga*, Marnie recalled, being the self-admitted chess nerd that she was. She studied the board and observed that Milas was defending himself from a vicious attack being waged by a fiercely beautiful woman wearing next to nothing but for a pair of nine-inch, hot pink stilettos and a mini-skirt bikini combo of an equally vibrant color of latex. Milas twirled the hairs of a massive beard with one hand and adjusted a pair of alarmingly thick eyeglasses with the index finger of the other. Marnie could see the man's mind at work behind the reflection of those glasses. She could also see a subtle but undeniable resemblance to Phet. The man looked much younger than she imagined this sixty-year-old would. She continued to watch those eyes, Phet's father's eyes, when suddenly she saw them change. A glint of revelation sparked within them and was followed by a wide smile, as the man reached to the board and moved his *met*, the queen piece, from one end of the board to the other and folded his hands in his lap.

"*Sha-mat!*" he cried, declaring checkmate in the ancient language of Persia.

His opponent shrieked then uttered a refrain of profane expletives that would have made Marnie feel more timid than the Catholic schoolgirl she was if she'd understood them. Milas grinned and drank it in, apparently reveling in both this woman's abuse and his victory. The moment was interrupted when Marnie's beer arrived.

"Miss Marnie McCloud, meet Joe, the best looking man in Bangkok," Milas said, assuming that the red-haired woman who had just joined the table was not just some tourist off the street.

"*Sawasdee kha.* My name Josephine," she greeted Marnie with the female inflection of the Thai salutation and extended her hand for deceivingly limp-wristed and delicate handshake.

"*Sawasdee kha,*" said Marnie, shaking Josephine's hand. She then immediately reached for her beer and downed the entire glass in a few rushed gulps.

"I'll have another, please," she said, motioning to a waitress.

"Don't mind Joe. He wouldn't hurt a fly," said Milas.

Josephine rolled her eyes and stood up, revealing a set of legs that runway models would binge and purge themselves bulimic for. "I go dance now," she said and ascended the stairs of the nearest stage. She writhed with a sexually charged grace rare seen atop such precarious heels.

"And you are Colonel Milas," said Marnie.

"Here I am," he grinned. "I see you made it here in one piece."

"I feel a bit like I've run the gauntlet, but I think I'll survive."

"Don't try to understand everything at once. Your head might explode."

"Thanks, I'll take that into consideration. And thank you for agreeing to meet me."

"Not much choice, seeing my son is the bait."

"Ya, well, I'm sorry about that."

"There's no need for you to be sorry. It's a family matter that I intend to put right any way possible, and if talking to you helps then that's okay by me."

The waitress arrived with Marnie's second beer and Milas's usual order after defeating Joe at *makruk*, a Mekong Coke. It was drink he recommended Marnie never to order unless she enjoyed the effects of low-octane petrol on her nervous system.

Marnie's eyes drifted to the stage where Josephine was performing an erotic pole dance. Marnie had never seen—let alone met—a transvestite before and was agog at the idea than a man could be so womanly and seductive. Milas caught her staring and asked if she was enjoying the show.

"I thought I looked good naked, but geez! She's um, he's um, on a different scale."

"Yes, that might not be a fair comparison. The third gender has its advantages. Besides, I think you'd dress up well."

Marnie looked down at her jeans, tugged at her sleeveless blouse, and shrugged. She severely doubted she could pull off a pink-mini as well as Josephine.

"Can I get one more of these?" she waggled her glass at Milas who promptly caught the eye of the nearest waitress and ordered by holding two fingers in the air.

"Best watch yourself. That draft elephant beer, or Chang as it's called, packs a wallop," Milas said, to which Marnie simply bounced her eyebrows at him.

"Brave girl. Care to play a game?" he asked gesturing with his hands palm-up at the game board.

"Sure, can you talk and play at the same time?"

"I can do a lot of things at the same time." Milas winked at her.

"Okay, rack 'em up," she said and began to set up her side of the board as black, though these pieces were actually red.

Marnie was a bit rusty at this variation of chess, but held her own against Milas even with the buzz of the hurriedly downed beers. Time passed quickly as they moved through the opening exchanges and middle game. Oddly, the alcohol seemed to help her focus, and she soon found that she could completely ignore everything beyond a meter radius of their table. She was in the zone, as Mark would say.

"Colonel Milas, have you ever heard of the Phoenix Project?" she asked and made a move.

"If you mean the Phoenix Project from the Vietnam War, then yes. That was some seriously bad karma. It was a long time ago. What of it?" he asked guardedly.

"I'm not sure, really. What does the name, Warden Islam, mean to you?"

At this, Milas turned to stone. He fell ashen and stopped dead still with his hand in mid-motion above the board. His eyes fixed like a mouse that sensed danger but could not see it. His whiskers then bristled, signaling a change somewhere in his mind. He then moved the piece that his fingers had hovered above, looked up, and met Marnie's eyes with a look of curiosity and fear.

"Where did you hear that name?" he asked.

"Junior told me. Am I hot or not?"

"Do you know how long it's been since I've even thought of that name? Have you any idea what you're even talking about?"

"Um, no on both counts, I'm afraid," she said.

"What in the hell are you doing even knowing that name? How in the hell? Who in the hell is Junior?"

Marnie interrupted him with a raised hand. "Don't panic. Slow down. Someone needs to go first here. I've got my story, and you have yours."

"It's your turn." He gestured at the board once again.

Marnie smiled and swiftly moved a knight onto a square of devastation for Milas.

"That's mate in two, and I think we both need a couple more drinks." Marnie waved at the waitress and signaled for another round with the peace sign.

"Do you remember what you were doing thirty years ago?" asked Milas.

"Can't say that I do. I wasn't even a year old. C'mon, I'll show you mine, if you show me yours."

"Don't even tempt me," he said.

The drinks arrived, and Marnie held out her beer for a ceremonious clink. Milas responded with a rattle of ice-cubes and earnest draft on his Mekong and Coke.

The waitress piped up, "Mr. Andy, you know that man over there?" She pointed with her chin at an unsmiling customer sitting alone in the far corner.

"No. Why?" he said.

"He's the only guy come in here and no talk to lady. He same you. I think maybe he know you. He been looking here all sneaky like."

"Well, I'm not gay. Go sic Joe on him."

"Ha, good idea!" the waitress chirped. She slapped Milas on the arm with a playful nature and skipped off in search of Joe, who could have been in either restroom.

"Okay, so where were we?" asked Milas.

"Warden Islam," said Marnie.

"Ya, I thought so. What a long, strange trip it's been," Milas sighed. "I tell you what. I have no idea what you're prodding at, but where you seem to be heading is a part of my life that I think is in my best interest if kept private. You go first, and I'll tell you everything I think you need to know based on what you tell me in your story. If I have an answer to your question, I promise I'll give it to you. After that, we talk about my son. Deal?"

"Fair enough, I guess." Marnie relented. "Here's what I got. Six months ago, I hadn't the faintest notion of what Islam was really about let alone who Colonel Andrew Milas—that being you—was, and I obviously had no clue that you were Phet's father. I never had any reason to think about it until just recently. The problem arose when I got started working on a project for the government."

"You're a spook?" Milas interjected.

"Hardly," she said. "But the system I'm working on is the spookiest I've ever seen. It acts like it's programmed to kill people."

"Kill people?" asked Milas.

"Murder by numbers, and next is a list is every Muslim leader as long as my arm."

"Holy crap!"

"Holy murder is more like it."

⌗ ⌗ ⌗

MARNIE BROUGHT MILAS UP TO SPEED on Project X under the confines of what she thought she could tell a fellow civilian who didn't possess any secret government clearance. She told him about Junior and the technology behind it. This was something that Milas was particularly interested in and asked several questions about. Marnie was amazed at his knowledge of programming concepts, and was thus able to talk in depth about the inner workings of Junior's brain with Milas. He pressed her on data sources specifically and asked her again just how she thought Phoenix was involved, which she admitted she really hadn't the foggiest idea how. He queried her on the specifics of Machiavellian mode and how it actually performed its chaining algorithms. She described the reaction of General Sharp when discussing Junior's *fatwa* on Islam at which Milas tittered with glee and rubbed his hands together. It was an odd reaction that she'd have to address later once she'd heard his side of the story. Finally, without naming names, she mentioned a certain major— though she did remark on his resemblance to a certain actor— who had given her the name Andrew Milas.

"When did this Junior give you the name Warden Islam?" Milas asked, looking seriously on edge now.

"About six months ago. Why?"

"And you're saying that Junior is knocking off people?"

"Well, he's suggesting that Uncle Sam do his bidding."

"And they're doing it?"

Marnie nodded.

"Well, crap! I mean, holy shit! I'm next! I got to get out of here and as far away from you as possible."

"Oh, come on, you're exaggerating."

Marnie sensed a dumb thump behind her followed by the tinkle of broken glass and turned to see Josephine standing above the lone customer in the far corner. His head rested face down on the table before him. Two bar maids scurried over armed with a broom and mop. She watched as Josephine lifted the guy's wallet and pulled a mobile phone out of his pants pocket with a show of dexterity and speed that would have left the Artful Dodger cooing in admiration. Joe sauntered over to Milas and dropped the wallet on the chessboard. She then thumbed the keys of the phone she'd filched and showed a text message to Marnie that read, "Warden Islam = Andrew Milas." Marnie checked her watch.

"This message was received twenty minutes ago," she said, handing Milas the phone.

Milas held the phone at arm's length. Peering over his spectacles, he read the backlit message. His eyes nearly bugged out of their sockets.

"You think I'm exaggerating now?" he hissed in a panicky whisper, looking over at the man collapsed on the table not but a few paces away.

"What did you do to him?" Marnie asked Josephine.

"I give him date-rape drug. He bad man. He think me stupid. Same all G.I. He say he want to fuck my ass, so I fuck his. *Salope salai leao.*"

"*Salope* means slut in French," Marnie said, looking puzzled.

"We have to leave. Now!" said Milas. He made a rapid series of gestures to the woman behind the bar, who nodded and gave him a concerned look. Milas then grabbed the wad of chits in the bill cup and handed them to Joe with a thousand baht note.

"Best you make yourself scarce as well," he told her. You don't want to be around here when he un-*salopes*, or that guy might fuck more than just your ass."

Milas stuffed the phone in his pocket, leaving the wallet on the table. Taking Marnie's arm, he marched her quickly out of Geronimo and into the street.

They ran into a wall of torrid Bangkok air and Marnie gasped. Milas broke left, and she hurried after him. He had a limp but moved at clip. Patpong intersected with Silom Road after a short sprint where traffic shot passed right-to-left. Milas ventured off the sidewalk, looking for a cab to flag down. There were none, and Marnie saw his panic as he tugged at his beard. From behind she heard a distinct clip-clop of high heels moving at a trot and turned to see Josephine running towards her. How she remained stable on those pins she did not know, but Marnie thought this must be another advantage of the third sex.

"Bad man coming!" Joe squealed while waving his arms in the air like a girl.

"Get in!" It was Milas. He'd hailed a cab that was not there a moment ago and had the car's back door open waiting for them.

Joe sailed past Marnie as she dove into the back seat. Marnie followed her without pause. Milas squeezed in and slammed the door behind him, locking it.

"Bai reo reo!" he said in Thai. Looking back at the entrance of Patpong, he saw Joe's G.I. emerge from the crowd. He was lethargic from the drugs but shaking it off quickly. He scanned the crowd and made eye contact with Milas through the glass of the car window. He stepped forward.

"Go! Go Go!" Milas shouted.

The cabbie pushed the meter button on the cab and said, "Where you go, go, go?" with an excited smile.

The man from the bar was nearly at the cab and reaching for something behind his back.

"Bai, Bai, Bai! Ya hai dtam taan. Dieo ni!" Joe screeched from the backseat.

The cabbie apparently got the point and stepped on the gas, quickly merging into the flow of traffic on Silom Road and leaving the man behind.

They all let out a collective sigh of relief and looked at each other in the aftermath of that crazed moment.

Marnie broke the silence. "What the fuck was that all about?" she said.

"It would seem that your Junior has done more than put two and two together," Milas said. He ran his hands through his hair in a stressed gesture.

"I think it's time you come clean, Colonel Milas," she said.

The cab stopped at a red light, and the driver looked back at them through the rearview mirror. "Where you go?" he asked again.

"We can go to my hotel," Marnie offered.

"Bad idea. Way too obvious. Besides, they'd never let Joe past the front door dressed as he is."

Joe let out a *hmpf* at that.

"Well?" said Marnie.

"We go my place. Can change clothes," Joe said, looking out the back window.

"Sukhumvit, Soi Ha," Milas told the driver.

"Where's that?" asked Marnie.

Milas eased a bit, and said, "It's the densest population of Muslims in Bangkok. You'll love it. The food is great, and besides our stalker back there won't be able to set foot anywhere near us without my network of hash-crazed assassins slicing him to pieces."

Marnie just stared at him.

"I'm joking, you know," said Milas. "About the assassin bit, I just made that up in the heat of the moment. The curry, however, is to die for."

The light turned green. They were moving again, safe for now, and Marnie managed not to laugh for about five seconds. She nearly burst a seam trying to hold it in, until it all came out at once in a contagious cackle of laughter. Milas and Joe joined in, both laughing until they were wiping tears from their eyes. Marnie caught the driver laughing with them and wondered if he even knew what they were talking about. She sighed and mellowed slightly then said, "I have to pee," starting another wave of laughter.

Tucked in the back of the Bangkok meter taxi between Milas and Joe, it dawned upon Marnie what a surreal situation she was now in. "How did it come to this? Who were these people? Just who was Andrew Milas, and how did he fit into this puzzle?" she wondered.

A phone rang. Everyone looked at each other. It was Milas. He didn't realize it at first because he didn't recognize the ring tone. Milas squirmed around in the seat and managed to get the phone out of his pocket after a brief battle with his oversized paunch. He looked at the small display on the phone and handed it to Marnie.

"It's for you," he said.

Marnie took the phone, read the screen, and said, "What the...?"

The phone's caller ID told her that the call was coming from Mark Harmann.

She thumbed the phone's green button, put it to her ear and said, "What are you up to, Mark?"

There was a short pause followed by, "Uh oh."

"Mark?"

"Marnie? What happened to my guy?"

"Your guy? What is your guy doing in Thailand hunting Andrew Milas?"

"The question is, what are you doing in Thailand at all, Missy?"

"Missy? Missy!" she shouted into the phone. She then said in tone as cold as dry ice, "I swear to God, Mark, if you don't tell me what's going on right now, I'll come back there and you will experience a wrath of mine so fierce that you will regret using the word, Missy, for the rest of your natural life."

"Marnie, you need to get back here now, and I mean it."

"I'm with Warden Islam right now."

"Christ on a bike!" cried Mark.

"And your guy, whoever he is, looked like he was about to take us all out."

"Look, you are way out of your depth here. You're in danger. You have to listen to me. You have to trust me."

"Trust you?" she yelled at the phone. "I'll trust you when you start telling me what's going on!"

"I can't tell you anything over the phone. Not right now. Get on a plane, get home, and I'll tell you what you need to know."

"Goodbye, Mark," she said and hung up on him.

Seconds later it began to ring again.

"Gimme that," said Milas. He rolled down the window, grabbed the phone from Marnie's hand, and tossed it out of the speeding cab.

It began to rain.

⌘ ⌘ ⌘

MARK GAPED AT THE SPEAKERPHONE in disbelief. It was still beeping after Marnie had disconnected the call. He silenced it with a frustrated stab of his finger, rubbed his face with both hands, and let out low, drawn-out whistle.

He gathered his thoughts for a moment and then looked up at the man seated across from him. "This is a fiasco!" he exclaimed. "What have you gotten her into?"

Major Ron Ray sat at quiet attention in spite of his relaxed civilian attire that consisted of a pair of neatly pressed khaki dungarees and a blue and white striped Tommy Hilfiger polo-shirt. He looked like a print-ad model out of *GQ* except for the grim slash that formed a mouth of a man that meant business.

"What happened to your guy?" asked Ray.

Chapter 27

SALOME AND VENDETTI got straight to work on their project. Salome now had the distinct feeling that that her calls were being intentionally ignored. Her father's mobile was always answered by the automated recording, and now even Yaghoub wasn't picking up anymore. She sent her father an email, asking her to please contact her and received a bounced message in reply. All her lines of communication to her father had been severed.

Vendetti in his ever-positive fashion explained that if Kahn were trying to protect her, then distancing himself—which included breaking all communications—did make sense. He also recommended that she stopped calling and to not send further emails. If Kahn wanted to find his daughter, he would.

For Vendetti, it seemed that Marnie was as elusive as Kahn. He'd left several messages and had heard nothing in return. He often found himself reaching for his mobile only to find that it wasn't actually vibrating in his pocket. Salome gave him reciprocal advice, telling him to not act so desperate and that Marnie would call him when she was ready.

They began their search to reveal the enigma that was Kahn by starting out with what they already had. Vendetti had amassed a considerable amount of data on terrorist organizations through his research work over the course of his career. They pored over this information together in the hopes that Salome might recognize some name, or company, or organization that might allow them to connect it back to the Foundation and ultimately Kahn.

Through the week, they'd scoured through all the information they could get their hands on. Vendetti's office looked like that of a crime investigator's as it became festooned with Xeroxed documents, photos, and newspaper clippings taped to the walls. They used different colored string and stickpins to link items that were related in varying degrees of importance and surety. What they created was a virtual web of connections, but to their dissatisfaction the only thing that they were able to conclude was that the entire thing was overwhelmingly complex and indeed very shadowy.

Vendetti studied the walls. It was maddening that nothing actually directly connected back to Tehran. Even the *Washington Post* article had only directly linked things back to the Martyr's Foundation offices in Lebanon. It was as if a shroud was pulled over the entire country of Iran. All connections seemed to stop at the border. Iran was a black hole that somehow prevented any information from leaving its pull. While Vendetti thought this might actually be a good sign, it just seemed a bit too tidy and that a higher power must be involved to maintain such a hermetic seal of secrecy.

"Well, we certainly are not the CIA," he said and got up to make himself another espresso with the machine he'd had just installed in his office. "You know, I bet Marnie could do this with her eyes closed."

"Why is that?" asked Salome.

"She's a contractor for some super-secret government project. Something to do with computers, but that's all I know. It's all very hush hush."

"Professor Vendetti?" a pretty young woman knocked on his open door.

Vendetti turned. "Yes, Safiya?"

"I have your mail, sir. Sorry, it's late," she said and brought him a bundle wrapped in rubber bands.

Safiya Barazani was the twenty-one year old daughter of Pakistani immigrants and about to start the final year of her baccalaureate at Georgetown. During school breaks, she earned extra money performing menial administrative work around campus. Vendetti had recognized her as a bright young spark and snatched her up for the summer. While he already had his own personal assistant, he knew he could secure a position for Salome and had been prepping Safiya to be her assistant.

"Hello, Professor Kahn," Safiya said with a bright smile.

"Hello to you, Safiya." Salome nodded politely.

"Wow, you guys have been really going at it in here," Safiya said, running her fingers across a few lines of string.

"Yes, and we are solving the mystery of a lifetime," Vendetti exaggerated. He always liked to keep the students interested in any way possible, and intrigue worked just as well as anything, even if he was spinning a yarn.

"Interesting! Maybe after I graduate, I'll get to work on this kind of stuff instead of delivering mail."

"I should hope so," said Salome with a smile.

"Just don't forget us when you hit the big time," said Vendetti.

Safiya began to ring. She reached into the back pocket of her blue jeans and pulled out a phone. She looked at the screen and said, "Gotta run! See you guys." They watched her as she left the office while typing a message, pushing the mail cart with her foot toward the next stop.

"Quite a prospect, that one," said Vendetti as he sifted through his mail. He tossed it all in the trash bin beside his desk. "Junk, all of it! A complete waste of a tree."

He then sat at his desk and checked his email. "Oh my, I have been neglecting my inbox. There are nearly two hundred messages in here!" he cried. "I can't be bothered reading these right now. Anyone important would use the phone wouldn't they?" He highlighted them all and pressed delete. "*Voilà,* the stain is gone!"

He stood up and paced the office with a caffeine-induced spring in his step. "So where were we?" Staring at their project, he plucked at the colored latticework of strings in thought.

Vendetti and Salome spent another five hours rehashing every morsel of information that they'd gathered. "I've had enough!" he said, rubbing his eyes. "I think I've found my limit for daily espresso intake." He held out his hand and watched it vibrate. "You know, I am loath to admit it, but we may have to put this project of ours on the back burner file for a while. The winter term is starting, and we've done nothing to prepare you for your course work. As you are—*qu'est-ce que c'est*—recently insolvent, it's in our best interests to ensure that you do a bang-up job with your first term."

"You forgot to mention homeless," Salome snapped.

"Come, come. We've only been living together a week, and we're fighting. And we're not even married!" he joked.

"Well, this might be amusing for you, but this research has proven nothing one way or the other."

"Agreed. We have bupkis."

Salome glared at him.

"Bupkis!" he cried. "Zero, zilch, nada, diddly-squat! It's a dead end. That's what I'm saying, Salome. We just may have to throw in the towel, or—you know—let it go for a while. The fact that your father hasn't made contact in over a week might be the biggest hint we have besides what's been written in the paper."

"You were right, though. Not knowing is tearing upon my insides. Look at me. I have become snappish."

"Well, I don't think you're going to just magically snap out of it. The only thing sensible to do now is bury yourself in your work. This file is not going away. I know what I said before, but frankly I thought we'd make better progress. Right now for you, dwelling on this without making any headway isn't going to be healthy either. We can come back to it, but I'm serious that you're going to need to prepare for this coming term. Eyes will be upon you, even more so in light of recent events. You're practically famous."

"Infamous is more like it," Salome sulked.

"All the more reason for you to prove what you are capable of. I know that you will absolutely blow the socks off people once you find your groove again. You are passionate, captivating, intelligent, and majestic; and I am going to push you to be all that you can be."

"You really do know how to talk to a woman, John Vendetti."

"Yes, I borrowed part of that from the U.S. Army, but I'll take the credit if it pleases you."

Salome finally succumbed to his unrelenting optimism and smiled.

"Let's call it a day, shall we?" He looked out the window and said, "Or maybe I should say night. I tell you what; we'll spend the weekend developing ideas for your curriculum. I started an outline, when you first contacted me. All we need to do is flesh it out and ensure that your classes will be the most popular on campus. No pressure at all."

※ ※ ※

WHEN SAFIYA BARAZANI RECEIVED the encrypted message on her BlackBerry, she'd sent back a reply, "They are still working on it."

The electronic conversation continued, "Did they receive our warnings?"

"Do not know. Could not check," she typed.

"Wait for them. Signal when they leave."

"OK."

Safiya finished her shift and then lounged around the office making small talk with some of the other staffers she'd become friendly with. When she saw Professor Vendetti and Salome Kahn walking toward the exit, she kept her conversation going and casually typed another message on her phone, "Leaving now."

※ ※ ※

"HERE, PUT THIS BETWEEN YOUR LEGS," said Vendetti, thrusting a bag at Salome as he leapt deftly into the driver's seat.

She examined the containers of take-out food she now held and gave and him a look that he found priceless.

"I swear, I'm starting to think you have a dirty mind," he said. "On the floor between your feet, so it doesn't spill. You smell that? That's Cornish hen kebab, filet mignon kebab, lamb *kudideh* kebab, and even a veggie kebab if you go that way. We are in kebab heaven tonight!"

"Mmm, it does smell heavenly," she said. "Now if you were only to work on your phrasing."

Vendetti grinned rakishly and pulled the Roadster out onto 28th Street NW. He swung a right on M Street NW and then made a left onto the Key Bridge. As he hit the bridge he found it devoid of traffic and punched it. The BMW accelerated with the grace of a thoroughbred. The driver of a yellow taxicab who had been tailing them at a careful distance saw the car streak away and jammed his foot on the gas pedal. He blindly fumbled for something in the passenger seat, keeping his eyes on his prey. The aged taxi he'd car-jacked was a pitiful match for Vendetti's Z4, but he only needed to maintain range he knew. He raised his sunglasses and stole a glance at the passenger seat. He grabbed the device from the seat beside him and pressed his foot to the floor.

As the end of the bridge neared, Vendetti let off speed and prepared to take the turn onto the George Washington Memorial Parkway. The taxi continued accelerating. Vendetti spotted the taxi bearing down on them and muttered under his breath, "Drag racing taxi driver. The man's a bloody lunatic."

He speed shifted, throwing the car down into second gear. The engine whined under high revs as he accelerated into the hard right turn. The taxi driver flicked a toggle switch on the radio transmitter he held and depressed the red button. Two muffled pops reported in rapid succession and the BMW immediately drifted left. With two tires blown, Vendetti lost all control over the vehicle and they slammed sideways into the curbside. Salome screamed as inertia launched the convertible into a roll. In the surreal slowdown of her adrenaline rush, she saw the flash of streetlights above her head replaced by grass and then the lights again. She looked to her left and saw an empty seat. The flying vehicle then broadsided the George Washington Memorial Parkway sign, obliterating its wooden section but connecting solidly with its stone protrusion that brought the car spinning to the ground. It careened forward carried by its momentum. Salome looked at the unmanned steering wheel, then straight ahead at the trunk of a massive oak tree. The next thing she saw was a flash of white as the airbags deployed and the car smashed to a halt.

Time decompressed as Salome sat in a momentary state of shock. She heard voices yelling, but was too dazed to answer their calls. The smell of burning car oil permeated the air as the engine bled out. Salome felt a warm sensation on her legs and panicked. She reached down expecting to find blood but found a handful of kebab instead. Sirens approached as she stared stupidly at her hand.

"Lady, are you all right?" asked a voice.

She turned and squinted into the beam of a flashlight.

"Hey Lady, are you all right?" the voice repeated.

"Where is John?" was all she could say.

Beyond the perimeter of the gathering crowd's attention, the yellow taxi pulled from the curb and crept away into the night.

Chapter 28

THE TWO SQUARED OFF across a flimsy plastic table. They were perched upon equally flimsy plastic chairs. Joe had left to dry off and change into her street clothes. Rain came down around them in sheets, cascading off the roof of the back street, open-air restaurant. It was like sitting in a cave behind a waterfall, but for Marnie it still felt like she was in a sauna. Determined not to crack a sweat in front of Milas, who sat smiling like the Cheshire cat, she stood up, caught a handful of rainwater that fell from the roof and rubbed it on her face and neck. Milas stood up, walked to the wall, and yanked the string of an oscillating fan on a nearby post. It started into a lazy spin and waved its head from side to side. The cooling breeze caught Marnie from behind. It felt wonderful.

"That should help," he said.

"Help with what?"

"To keep you from dying from heat prostration while I tell you my story."

"You know what else would help?"

"Behind you, in the fridge."

"Is that where you keep the truth?"

"No, that's where they keep the beer. The truth is in here." He tapped his temple with his finger. "It all started a long time ago, when I was a student. You know, I really didn't know what I wanted to be. I'm not sure if anyone really does at that age. But I did know what I didn't want to be. I didn't want to be anyone's possession. So I guess, in a way, I knew I wanted to be free. Free to do what I wanted, when I wanted, with who I wanted."

"You mean like hippie free?"

"More like American free. You know, that whole pursuit of happiness thing?" He smiled through his bush of a beard. "The problem was that I saw my freedom like a light at the end of a tunnel, and the tunnel through which I had to travel was dark. It was pretty scary too, considering it involved being drafted and used to kill people. You see, I had certain smarts that others didn't possess at the time and probably still don't. And it was these smarts that got the attention of a few folks in the military. Ironically, even they didn't know what I was capable of, but they knew I'd done something when I'd created a computer virus before computer viruses ever existed. In a way, that little event in my life—that decision to do something—has become both my savior and my captor."

"You know, either I'm extremely drunk or you're not making any sense. And there's no beer in here by the way."

"Possibly both. I forgot this is a Muslim restaurant. A Sprite would do me fine."

Marnie collected two Sprites and popped their tops on the bottle opener attached to the fridge. She moved back to the table and stepped over the plastic chair back, taking a seat while sliding Milas's drink to within his reach. She faced him squarely.

"Okay, pretend you're talking to a drunk person so that I'll understand."

"If you want the *Reader's Digest* version, here it is. In 1972, I wrote a computer program that virtually disappeared, although in reality it became a part of the computer system—or at least the files that were loaded on it for a period of time. Fortunately or unfortunately—depending how you look at it—this was one of many computer systems that the U.S. military used to run secret projects on. This got their attention and put me on their radar. In Saigon, they recruited me into intelligence operations and used me to develop algorithms that took intelligence information and turned it into black lists."

"Black lists?" Marnie asked, suddenly sobering a bit and giving her Sprite bottle a sideways glance.

"Ya, you know that deck of cards with Saddam Hussein as the ace of spades? Like that but with Vietnamese people instead of Iraqis, and there were many, many decks of cards. Anyhow, you mentioned the Phoenix project earlier. In short, Phoenix was about killing people. I came into Saigon at the tail end of that operation, but rather than shutting it down, I was involved in improving it, or at least its successor. Things like that do not simply go away. They just reappear later at a different time with a different name. From what I gather, Phoenix still is killing people. Only now, it's doing it under the guise of your so-called Junior."

"And just how is that even possible?"

"If I told you, I'd have to kill you."

"That's not the first time I've heard that in recent days."

"Let me guess. The major?"

Marnie nodded.

"Major Bacon, a pet name I've coined for obvious reasons, has been a thorn in my side for many years. The boy is clever. There's no doubt about it, but I have serious reservations with regards to his motives; and therefore, on principle I have refused to help him in any way."

"Help him with what?"

"He's wanted me to help him for years now to understand how my program works. The thing is that I retired a long time ago, and I really don't want to have anything to do with any of that business anymore. Besides, I have a theory that Major Bacon is a soldier who has become a full-blown neo-con blinded to all but one ambition. If given the chance, he would use my help to wage pre-emptive attacks on undeserving, innocent victims. In fact, I believe that he or someone like him is already doing just that."

"Do you really believe that?"

"People are dead, are they not? And more will die. Mark my words."

"Such as Warden Islam, a.k.a. Andrew Milas?"

"A fine example, yes. But that's been going on for years, I suspect. What Major Bacon really wants is to be able to control it."

"It being?"

"My program. My bug. The thing that got all of this started."

⌘ ⌘ ⌘

ANDREW C. MILAS WON the United States Selective Service System's lottery held on July 1st, 1970. He was unlucky on a few fronts. Being born on 9 July 1951, he was assigned a draft number of one, ensuring his induction. That was particularly bad luck. The fact that one of the lottery drums malfunctioned and only rotated for thirty minutes instead of an hour placed one of the two plastic capsules that would seal his fate in the worst spot possible—where it would be drawn first. This was not good either. From the age of nineteen, he prayed for the war to end before he finished his four-year degree, hoping his draft deferment would be his saving grace. His prayers were answered by the cease-fire in early 1973, but America's involvement was not yet over. This was the worst luck of all. In the summer of 1973, Andrew Milas reported for duty with the U.S. Army.

Military training did its best to beat the hippie out of Andy. The spirit of non-conformity and counter-culture did not bode well with a drill-sergeant who taught him very quickly how to march, salute, and stand at attention. He learned to make his bed, shine his boots, and the art of proper hygiene along with his fellow recruits. He learned how to shoot, maintain his M-16 rifle, and throw hand grenades, which he found both terrifying and exhilarating. He learned first aid to help those who unfortunately came up against the bad end of such weapons. The U.S. Army also schooled him in the Uniform Code of Military Justice, how to work a map and compass, and how to prepare meals with a can, a knife, and an open flame.

Above all, it was Milas's raw talent in mathematics and technology that caught the attention of superiors during his Advanced Individual Training following boot camp. Though that didn't save him from a final month of hell consisting of live-round firing exercises where he was drilled to aim and shoot his M-16 from the hip in a variety of treacherous scenarios.

Finally, after what he thought had been the worst experience of his life, he was stationed at the Defence Attaché Office in Saigon as a Data Communications Terminal Specialist. If there was one thing he learned in training aside from handling weapons, tolerating the verbal abuse of his drill-sergeant, and that it was not the worst experience of his life, it was how to run. This was a good thing because running was never far from his mind the moment he set foot in Vietnam.

What ate at Milas was not that he didn't necessarily believe in the reasons for the war. While he did not blindly embrace the domino theory as the gospel, he did have a sense of altruism. Milas believed that the powers that be must know more than he, and this fostered his sense of duty. What drove him near to tears when he dwelled on it was the futility of his presence in Saigon. He didn't need to be here. The Paris Peace Accords had already been signed, and Nixon had announced in January that offensive actions against North Vietnam were suspended; yet there was still a war going on. What made him livid was that working on data terminals gave him access to information, much of which was intelligence information. A good deal of this information was related to violations of the cease-fire. It was deliberate planning for military action as if the cease-fire had never been declared. As it would turn out, Milas was knee deep in the ashes of the Phoenix Project.

Chapter 29

THE DEFENCE ATTACHÉ OFFICE inhabited an organized sprawl of whitewashed, military structures adjacent to Tan Son Nhut Airport. Pentagon East, as it was known, had formerly housed the Military Assistance Command, but had been disbanded in March as a result of the Peace Accords. In a seamless transition, the DAO was open for business in Saigon before Mack-V ostensibly shuttered its operations. Less than ten years previously, U.S. pacification efforts in Vietnam came under the authority of Civil Operations and Revolutionary Development Support, or CORDS. In the mid-sixties, the Central Intelligence Agency already had counter-terror teams in play, hunting and killing cadres of the National Liberation Front who were hiding in villages across the south. In 1967, CORDS begat the Intelligence Coordination and Exploitation Program, later dubbed Phoenix, or *Phung Hoàng* in Vietnamese, named after the mythical bird whose presence, according to legend, was a portentous sign of luck and prosperity. This was somewhat ironic as the official purpose of Phoenix was the gathering of intelligence information regarding NLF insurgent operations and using it toward their ultimate neutralization through infiltration, capture, conversion, or assassination. It was gruesome wet-work and decidedly unpalatable; however, the Tet Offensive of 1968 was a major setback for the U.S. that came with its own set of atrocities. The Tet Offensive highlighted the influence and importance of the NLF infrastructure and served to galvanize support for continuing the Phoenix program. By 1970, there were a total of over seven hundred Americans serving as Phoenix advisors across South Vietnam, one of which was Lieutenant Colonel Robert F. Ray.

Andrew Milas first met Colonel Ray in the DAO library. He'd developed a routine of grabbing some fast chow at the mess hall and walking across the street to the library to play chess against himself on days when time permitted. Today, he found the colonel sitting at his table playing on his chessboard. He sat alone.

"Care to join me, Private Milas?" Colonel Ray's tone was friendly enough, and Milas took up a chair.

"It's your move," said Ray.

Milas took in the board in a matter of seconds. He knew this position. He'd seen it hundreds of times. It rarely left his mind. "Why would he set this up for me? How could Colonel Ray know?" he thought as his heart raced.

He moved a white knight, placing it on a square that threatened the Colonel's remaining black knight. Before he could remove his hand, the Colonel grabbed it in a vice-like clutch. "Don't play the fool, son. You know what to do," he said in a tone that belied the pressure he was applying to Milas's knuckles. He forced Milas's hand back to the knight's original square. "Let's try that again. Shall we?"

"Okay, okay," said Milas, shaking off the pain that lingered from the colonel's grip. He sighed and used his pawn to capture his opponent's king's pawn then sat there saying nothing, staring at the board.

"And?" asked Ray. His eyes were a piercing blue. His gaze was like that of a falcon with fresh prey in sight, and it bored straight through Milas like a laser.

"And that's mate in three, sir."

"I thought so. And now you know that I know something. Do you know what that is?"

"I believe so, sir. But I'm not quite sure what that means for me."

"It means, Private Milas, that you are now under my bailiwick."

⌗ ⌗ ⌗

To Colonel Ray and others, Phoenix was a patent achievement. Between the years of 1968 and 1972, it was directly responsible for the neutralization of over eighty thousand NLA insurgents, of which over twenty-five thousand met their ultimate demise by way of the bullet or some other method of killing. The success was not enough, however. In spite of the damage caused to the Viet Cong infrastructure, it was panning out that Phoenix was too little too late to change the course of the war in Vietnam.

Regardless, the project's effectiveness was undeniable, and Washington was all for turning lessons learned into future conflict strategy and thus continued support for honing Phoenix into a well-oiled machine.

Colonel Ray recruited Milas into stoking the still glowing embers of Phoenix. When the CIA finally realized that someone had somehow infiltrated the systems at Berkeley and compromised data, it got their attention. When they grasped the potential of the Milas Bug, it worked them into a lather. It took roughly a year to piece it all together; but in the end, they discovered that Milas had written a program that surreptitiously scoured files loaded into the system. It searched for names and placed them into position on a virtual chessboard and ran them through the rigors of a chess game, killing off the pieces one by one. As each piece was eliminated from play, Milas's program would cycle back through the source data and append the word, DECEASED, next to the name in the file. Certain people in the military quickly realized that if they could harness sophisticated algorithms toward surgical strikes—using a rifle shot as opposed to a shotgun approach—they could create the most efficient hunting and killing machine ever conceived.

Chapter 30

THE RAIN HAD STOPPED and empty plates were the only remains of one of the best meals Marnie could remember. They'd enjoyed dishes with exotic names she'd never heard of like *masaman nua*, *goong pat pong galee*, and *kao mok gai*. All were expertly chosen by Milas, who explained each order with the delight of a Thai food gourmand. The names she'd already forgotten, but the flavors lingered, as did the heat from one dish called *yam talay* that she was sure was somehow radioactive. She sucked on an ice cube to tame the burning on her tongue.

"And so you're telling me that you wrote the program that has Junior issuing assassination orders for all of Islam and, for some reason, yourself?" Marnie asked through the ice cube.

"In a word, sort of. Not that I'm necessarily proud of it," Milas replied.

"And this Colonel Ray is—"

"Major Bacon's dad, yes." He finished her thought.

"Wow," was all Marnie could muster as she pieced this all together in her mind.

The sound of a slow, deliberate applause caused Marnie and Milas to look a few tables over to see the man who'd chased them from the Geronimo Bar sitting casually and clapping. He'd obviously listened to their entire conversation. They tensed and poised to make tracks again, but the man raised both hands in a gesture of surrender and said, "Please don't run. I come in peace. I've been sent by Mark Harmann."

Marnie eased somewhat at the mention of Mark's name, while Milas remained on high alert. "Who are you, and how the hell did you find us?"

"Your son, Colonel," said the man.

"What the—?"

"—I found you through your son, Phet," said the man. "Sorry, I'm still a little groggy from having the whammy put on me. Luckily, I didn't finish my drink or I'd still be resting my eyes back at the Geronimo Bar. Here's the deal. I'll tell you who I am and why I'm here if you stay still long enough for me to explain." He slowly got up from his table, causing Milas to scoot his chair back in preparation for another quick exit.

"Look," said the man, his voice with an edge now. "I am not fooling around, and I'm not chasing you around for the fun of it, okay? You're both potentially in some real danger and not from me, so it would behoove you to sit your asses down on those chairs and listen to what I've got to say." He walked to the fridge, pulled out a bottle of water, and came to sit with them at their table. He popped the top the bottle with his finger and emptied half of it with a couple gulps. Rubbing his temples, he said, "My name is Christopher Dexter, and have I got a headache!" This brought a smirk to Marnie's face and somewhat eased their concern regarding his intentions.

"Let me see your phone," he said to Marnie. "C'mon, hand it over," he urged, snapping his fingers, while continuing to massage the pain in his head with his other hand. Marnie reluctantly gave him her phone.

"You see this lovely piece of design work? Well, this is how I found you. These things are like homing devices, you know, especially after leaving them with the security team at the NCTC. Finding you was as easy as following directions on a map. Getting your phone number wasn't all that hard either. Did you know that sending an email from one of these is a lot like sending a postcard? Just about anyone with the right equipment can read it. We could have run a query against all the collected Internet logs in Washington, but it was more efficient to work on Phet. He is not a tough nut to crack, by the way. Initially, we told him his father's life was in danger, but he didn't budge. When Mark threatened to ban his guitar from the lair, he crumbled." The remark elicited a raised eyebrow from Milas followed by a detectable frown.

"Whatever happened to privacy?" Marnie sighed.

"Privacy is dead. Get over it." Dexter pulled a small plastic kit of eyeglass screwdrivers from his front pocket and used one to remove the back of the phone. He held it at a distance and inspected the device's innards under the fluorescent lights. "Yep," he said and removed what looked like a small piece of plastic with two wires attached to it, which he slipped into his shirt pocket. He reattached the phone back and turned on the power. After thumbing the screen for a bit, he handed it back to Marnie. "There, I've turned off the 'How to find Marnie McCloud in a Muslim restaurant in Bangkok' feature. You've got 18 emails from Mark, and I just voided your warranty, although that's better than being bugged, I'd say."

"Well, aren't you handy!" said Milas.

"Now listen to me. Both of you are in trouble in different ways. I heard while eavesdropping on your conversation that you've managed to answer a lot of your own questions, but there's more going on than you know. Marnie, you've been taken off the project at the direction of Major Ray, who is citing a breach in contract, and Colonel, your program is recommending the extermination of you and every Muslim on the planet, and people are starting to listen."

"Give me a break!" Marnie spouted. "I mean telling people to go fuck themselves is not generally good manners, but how is that a breach of contract?"

"Aren't you the slightest bit interested in the fact that your creation is being used to start World War III?" asked Milas.

"My creation? It's your damn bug! If I were back home, I could be working to fix this mess."

"And therein lies our problem," added Dexter. "The two people that can actually do something about this situation aren't getting anywhere near Project X."

"That is possibly not entirely correct," said Milas.

They both gave him a quizzical look.

"Bugs," said Milas.

"Bugs?" Marnie asked.

"Yes, bugs, as in plural—more than one. I haven't really had a chance to think this through being chased around by Mr. Fixit here," Milas continued, giving Dexter an exasperated look. "But something just clicked. There's only one way that Junior would know the name Warden Islam, which as you know by now is an anagram of my name. That was something I coded into my original program way back when. It's a simple reenactment of famous chess match with a few bells and whistles, but the real magic—the prestige of the act, if you will—was its ability to disappear."

"Wait a minute," said Marnie. "What chess match specifically?"

"Spassky vs. Fischer. Reykjavik 1972."

"Damn," Marnie sighed. "Mark's been dropping hints like lead balloons, and I've been too stupid to see. Sorry, go on."

"The program's vanishing act is what got Colonel Ray's attention, and he basically forced me into developing systems to further the efforts of Phoenix. Now being the good soldier that I was—not that I was given any choice in the matter—I took the concept quite a bit further; however, the reckless hippie that lurked beneath my soldier's veneer had issues with what I was doing. And so I did what any bored and dissatisfied programmer who missed his psychedelics would do and riddled my work with backdoors, bugs, and Easter eggs to both entertain and distract myself. Now the only way for Junior to know the name Warden Islam is if it somehow has access to my original program. And if Junior is now calling for a holy war against all Muslims, it makes me think that Major Bacon has been feeding parts of my old work through Junior. If he's given Junior what I think he has, it's a doozie."

"Define doozie," Dexter and Marnie both said simultaneously.

Milas rubbed his hands together like a magician preparing for a slight of hand trick.

"Back in the seventies, I was a bit of a heavy thinker. I dabbled in all kinds of interesting topics to keep myself busy. You guys have heard of Nostradamus, right?"

They both nodded, each giving him their own look of skepticism.

"Yes, like I said, interesting things!" Milas gleamed with the delight of a child. "Well, Nostradamus is famous for predicting all sorts of stuff. Most notable have been his prophesies of war and the end of the days. I took to the stuff like a wino to Ripple. Being in Vietnam probably fueled my fatalistic slant on things, but for some reason, I was convinced that Vietnam was not a war to end all wars even though it was in many people's opinion a shit-fest of note. Still, I became more than a bit obsessed with the idea of Armageddon, and I became convinced that when it came, this would be a religious war fought against Islam." Milas paused for a moment and then recited a refrain.

In the fields of Media, Arabe, and Armenia
Two great armies shall assemble three times
Near the Arabic shore or Persian Gulf
The Israelites on land shall tumble

"That's old Nostro at his best," he explained.

"Colonel, what has this to do with anything?" Marnie asked.

"Patience, my dear. It gets better. There is the great camel that will not repent!"

Their furrowed brows spurred him on.

"Fight and slay the unbelievers wherever you find them, and seize them, beleaguer them, and lie in wait for them in every stratagem of war," he recited again. "That's from the Qur'an. Doesn't that sound delightfully ominous out of context? The Book of Revelation added even more fuel to the fire with its trumpets, horsemen, the Rapture, and all that. Anyhow, like I said, I was into some heavy thoughts, and I thought these thoughts would add a little spice to my programs."

"Colonel, I don't know what time it is, but I'm tired," groaned Marnie, now rubbing her face with her hands. "Please make some sense before I pass out."

"Okay, here you go. I baked various bits of the Bible, the Qur'an, Nostradamus and other delights into my Phoenix code. All of this stuff just sat in the background as the programs were used to do what they did for Colonel Ray & Co. As far as they were concerned, as long as they had their lists, they were happy. My guess is they simply never looked under the hood, and didn't much care as long as they had results, which they did, I might add.

"What's fascinating, while being pretty scary at the same time, is that Major Bacon has somehow gotten a hold of my work and is apparently trying to use it once again with the hope of similar results *a la* Junior. My best guess is that he's perpetuating Phoenix—or whatever it's called now—to achieve some goal. I'm really not sure what. But whatever it is, it can't be good.

"Now while I am sure that most of my buried treasure must have been discovered by those working for the major, it's evident that some of it's still there and is now being digested by Junior, who is in turn trying to fulfill a hodgepodge of prophesy and religious dogma with black and white determination. And I think it's trying to accomplish this by starting a war with Islam, which—if you ask me—is pretty much asking for Armageddon." Milas paused with dramatic effect. "Now, ain't that a doozie?" he finished with an uproarious laugh than ended with a coughing fit.

"Sorry, but this all sounds like something from a science fiction novel," said Dexter.

"Well, it would be if I didn't know how Junior worked," said Marnie. "The problem is that this is entirely possible. It's not like Junior's going to pull a HAL 9000 on us. That's science fiction. But if he's used to find an end game by people who don't care about the consequences—or worse yet, feel the ends justify the means—doozie doesn't quite cut it. Major Ray has already not so subtly hinted at the fact he's of that ilk. We're talking a seriously fucked-up situation here, people. Is that what you really think is happening, Colonel?"

"You don't want to know what I really think," he said.

"I think we do," said Dexter.

"Well, okay," he said hesitantly. "What do you fine citizens know of my inglorious departure from the military?"

"Only what I read in the papers from the eighties," Marnie said. "You retired and went on an anti-government speaking tour. After that, you pretty much disappeared."

"You've been studying me?" Milas said with delighted surprise.

"I've been doing my homework," she replied.

"I see that you have. Well, let me tell you a thing or two that you probably didn't find in the papers. I've already told you about my time in Vietnam. What I didn't tell you is that once I was there and in the thick of it all, I didn't want to leave. War is addictive, but I did leave on a C-130 when Saigon fell.

"When I finally returned home to the states and began to readjust to life there, it took a while to come to terms with what I'd been through. I realized that I was luckier than the many who were killed, maimed, and mentally ruined by their experience. I also realized that dropping bombs and killing people, including women and children, in a war that had nothing to do with national security, is just plain wrong.

"I'd say—and these are the types of crazy notions that eventually had people discounting me for a crack-pot—that all of America's wars going back to World War I and probably earlier were based on lies and motivated by money. General Smedly Butler called us out on this after World War I, when he made a damn good argument that war is a racket where profits are reckoned in dollars and loss of life. More than twenty thousand millionaires and billionaires were made in the United States during World War I, and the general public shouldered the bill. But the ones who really paid the price were those who died fighting in the trenches and the families they left behind. World War II? More death, more profits. Vietnam? The same.

"Vietnam was my war. I lived through it—thank God—but thousands didn't. The more I learned about the war, the more against I was about what we had done there. I became determined to do what I could to prevent such unnecessary killing. When I got to working on SDI, those of us on the project thought that we were protecting the world by preventing World War III. We learned, however, that there were people who went far beyond the original intent of preventing a ballistic missile attack; they were modeling offensive scenarios using the technology to seize military control of space and destroy targets on the surface of the earth. When the President Reagan ordered the Pentagon to prepare for and win a protracted nuclear war with the Soviet Union, I'd had enough and decided it was time for me to warn people about this lunacy.

"Unfortunately, it turned out that *I* was considered the loony, and it was easy for them to paint me as such in the media. They did their best to publically malign me. And when that wasn't enough, they began to threaten me. When I didn't listen, they gave me a warning. It was a warning that cost me my wife. At that point, I was completely gone, and I came here. I've remained here and have kept out of their sights for a very long time; but I'm not blind, and I still have my wits about me.

"With the Soviet Union and communism no longer a specter they could use to instill fear, they needed a new enemy to keep the war machine going. This is a machine that backs the financial interests of multi-national corporations that earn *their* dividends at the cost of innocent people's lives. The occupation of Afghanistan and Iraq provided a military staging ground to control the entire region not to mention tapping into the tens of billions of dollars' worth of oil and natural gas. The thing is that I don't think any of this would have ever been allowed to happen if it weren't for 9/11. September 11, 2001, was as big a catalyst as December 7th, 1941, and it paved the way for allowing the wars in Afghanistan and Iraq. They found an enemy in Saddam Hussein and took it from there. Lying is easy when not believing the lie is considered unpatriotic."

"Next you're going to say that the World Trade Center was a hoax," said Marnie, trying not to roll her eyes.

"Don't even go there," said Milas.

"What do these, er, theories have to do with the bugs you're talking about?" asked Dexter.

"That's a good question, and I think I have the answer," said Milas. "Whether you believe that war is a racket or not—and you probably should—some things you're going to have to figure out for yourself. There is a war happening right now within the government for the heart and soul of America. There are admirals and generals who are very much against these wars of aggression. I know these men, and *they* know that invading other countries is only alienating us more from our allies around the world. In fact, we're making new enemies and creating more recruits for al-Qaida and the like by the thousands. The battle is being waged by an administration that has pushed for these wars. If you ask me, people who have served in combat tend to make better presidents. They are less willing to send their sons and daughters off to be cannon fodder. The people making decisions about war in the White House today have never seen war first hand, but they are more than willing to reap the profits indirectly. Look at Halliburton and Unocal if you don't believe me.

"Regardless, there is an all-out effort to cull these sane and rational, long-time military men who are against unnecessary war. When you read the paper and see another retiree from the Pentagon, do a little research on them. Read between the lines for the real story. It's very disturbing to see the pattern of who goes and who stays.

"So now, along comes Junior. He claims to know it all, and he's giving the administration just what they want to hear—not that crazy 'not on my watch' lip they're used to hearing. He's giving them the information they've been longing for. They don't know or care that the system has ulterior motives, or that Major Bacon is fine-tuning Marnie's creation to spin these into songs of the Sirens. They're finally getting results, and no matter who steps up now to speak out against these wars, it'll be a waste of time. The oracle has spoken."

Marnie looked at Milas and couldn't help but admit he sounded more than a little crazy. "Are you sure, you've had all your pills today, Colonel?" she asked.

Dexter stepped in before Milas could respond and said, "Marnie, he's not all wrong in what he's a saying."

She sighed. "I'm sorry. I'm just really, really tired, and—"

"—What do you see as the options, Colonel?" asked Dexter.

"I can think of one. Pull the plug," offered Milas.

"But how? There's no way you're getting near that system," said Dexter.

"I might know a way," said Marnie. "Colonel, just how many bugs are we talking about?"

"Plenty, there's a toy surprise in every box, but I'm not sure how they'll work or how many have been found and fixed. Besides, I have no idea how he's feeding my stuff to Junior from a thirty plus year old system anyhow."

"I know who might," said Marnie. "But he's a bit stubborn when it comes to his father."

"Phet," said Milas. "I've got a secret weapon for that."

"Which is?" Marie asked.

"Not which, but who. Turn around."

Behind Marnie stood Joe. She was wearing jeans and a T-shirt that read, "Same same, but different." She looked ready to bring down a loaded Sprite bottle on Christopher Dexter's already aching skull, but settled for a venomous glare for the moment.

"Why bad man here?" Joe demanded.

"It's okay, Joe. He's not a bad man," said Milas. "Come have a seat."

Joe let out a *hmph* at this news and took the seat opposite Dexter, still giving him a bit of the stink-eye. Dexter looked wary as well. Even though Joe was wearing a comically thick pair of eyeglasses, she still looked like she could do some further damage to him.

"Marnie, Joe is Phet's brother," said Milas.

"Sister," pouted Joe.

"Whatever," said Milas. "Phet will do whatever you ask him to, Joe, so I need you to get him to talk to me."

"Why should I do that?"

"Because I'm your father, and I'm asking nicely?"

Joe delivered another *hmph*.

"Because I'll give you five thousand baht if you do?"

"Okay, no *pom-pem!*" Joe giggled and clapped her hands like a giddy princess.

"I'm glad that's settled. So Marnie, what's next?"

"I need to get back home."

❊ ❊ ❊

THEY PARTED WAYS AT THE RESTAURANT, having made plans to reconnect upon her arrival back in the states and sitting down with Phet. Dexter escorted Marnie back to the Oriental in a cab they caught out on Soi Nana. As the taxi raced among the other cars that sped along the rain-soaked streets of a city that didn't seem to sleep, Marnie stared absently out the window. Her eyes passed over people of the night who navigated the treacherous Bangkok sidewalks and sat at the ubiquitous curbside street restaurants, enjoying their late-night meals from steaming food carts that bore signage written in exotic Thai.

"Spassky vs. Fischer, Phoenix…" Marnie thought to herself. She couldn't wrap her head around why Mark was resorting to cryptic clues. Sure, he loved a good game, but why let her spin her wheels to this extent?"

Her purse began to vibrate, *brrr brrr brrr*, bringing her back to the here and now. She pulled the phone from her purse and recognized the number. "Hello, Mark. I was just thinking of you. I see you have my new number," she said and shot a withering look at Dexter, who responded with an apologetic shrug.

"Marnie, John's been in a car accident—a bad one," said Mark.

"Are you serious?" she said, shocked. "What happened? Is he okay?"

"He's unconscious. We don't know what happened. He's at Georgetown University Hospital now. I'm with a woman named Salome Kahn, who apparently has an interesting story to tell, but she says she'll only talk to you. How soon can you get back here?"

"I'm on tomorrow's, er, today's night-flight to JFK. With the time-zone time-warp, I'll be back in D.C. tomorrow night, I think."

Dexter nodded to her, confirming what she just said was correct.

"Okay, I'll check with Melanie and pick you up at Dulles when you land. We'll go straight to the hospital from the airport."

Mark waited for her reply, but only heard a vague static on the line.

"Marnie, are you okay?"

"No, I'm not, Mark."

"Marnie?"

"I left my car at the airport, so I'll just meet you at the hospital. I'll see you there," she said and hung up.

"Bad news?" Dexter asked. "Sorry, dumb question," he said a moment later when she didn't respond.

Her phone vibrated in her hand. She it passed to Dexter without looking.

"It looks like I'll be watching over you until your flight."

Marnie nodded in silence and continued staring out the window.

Chapter 31

Georgetown University Hospital

Marnie looked at Vendetti and wondered why she was so emotional. He really was a mess, but she didn't think their short encounter merited the butterflies she felt in her gut right now. Though well past visiting hours, Mark had somehow arranged access to John's room. John resembled a mummy laid out on the hospital bed covered in bandages from head to toe. He'd suffered a broken leg, a broken arm, several broken ribs, and a blunt force trauma to the head from which he'd yet to regain consciousness. It was a miracle that he was alive.

"Marnie, come on. The nurse is kicking us out." It was Mark by her side now.

Marnie felt numb. She rose from the chair she'd pulled to John's bedside and had sat for the better part of an hour just staring at him. She moved to touch his hand but thought better of it and simply turned and left. Mark followed behind her. Sitting in the hallway on a row of chairs was a uniformed police officer and Salome Kahn. Salome got up and walked over to Marnie.

"I am very sorry," she said.

"You should be," said Marnie with edge in her voice despite its hoarseness from the lump of emotion still in her throat. "It's your fault he's in here."

"Marnie, that's not fair," said Mark.

"No, I am afraid this is true," said Salome. "If I had not returned to America, I believe this would not have happened." She stole a quick glance at the police officer that was sitting comfortably and reading the *Washington Post* with a cup of coffee perched on the chair beside him. "Can we go someplace where we can talk?" she asked.

"What's with all the secrecy and the cop?" Marnie asked, now somewhat disarmed by Salome's admission. But she remained suspicious of this woman with Major Ray's words still ringing in her head—not that he was someone she exactly trusted either.

"Please, this is something that we should discuss in private. I am staying at John's apartment. It is not far from here."

"Oh, now that's just lovely." Marnie's eyes said otherwise. Her emotions were really starting to get the better of her.

"I am sorry. That was crude of me. It is not what you think. John and I are very old friends."

"Friends, Marnie," Mark said. "You hear that? Friends. Let me take you ladies to John's apartment."

They left the hospital together in Mark's Lexus, leaving Marnie's car at Georgetown. They made it to Vendetti's place in only a few minutes. During the short drive, Marnie tore into Mark like she never had before. She repeated much of what Colonel Milas had told her and added her own rant about the systematic subversion of civil liberties and how elements within the government were going to wind up starting World War III.

"Marnie, I realize that you're emotional right now, but you've got to see that this is a stretch. This is the kind of talk that got Milas laughed out of Washington in the first place."

"I'm not emotional! You're not listening to me!" she growled.

"Look, we're here," he said, pulling the car to a stop at the curb in front of Vendetti's townhouse. "This conversation is to be continued when you've got your head about you. Until then, I don't want to hear another word about it."

"Fine," she fumed.

Salome let them in with a set of keys John had given her. Marnie was first in. She flicked on the lights and patrolled the apartment, taking a mental inventory of things. She was more than a little relieved to see that there were signs that Salome was indeed staying in the guest bedroom. There was a telltale pink toothbrush in the guest bathroom as well. Satisfied at least for the moment that she'd not lost her chance with John to Salome, she made a B-line for the fridge from which after a moment of inspection she pulled a partially drunk bottle of wine. It looked to be one that she and John had shared on her last night here, which she considered to be another good sign. Marnie used her teeth to pull the cork from its neck, gave it a sniff, and took a swig straight from the bottle.

"Not bad," she said, smacking her lips.

"Make yourself at home, Marnie," Mark said with a look of surprise.

"I'm sorry. Where are my manners?" Marnie said offering them some wine by pointing the bottle at each of them.

"I will take a glass, thank you," said Salome.

"And you, Mr. Harmann?" Marnie asked.

"A glass will be fine, Miss McCloud."

"Fine. You two go sit over there." She waggled her finger at the living room just on the other side of the kitchen counter and began to rummage around for some wine glasses. She came up short not remembering how she and John had managed to drink the first part of the bottle, eventually opting for a pair of coffee mugs. She filled each halfway, which left a healthy four fingers for herself.

As she brought Mark and Salome their wine, she overheard Mark saying in a hushed voice, "I think she's marking her territory. I've seen her do this before."

"I heard that," Marnie said, coming around the corner. "And yes, I'm trying very hard to not act like a stupid, jealous girl right now. I also think I'm feeling a little loopy from jet lag and the Xanax I popped on the plane—not to mention the wine—so please just roll with it, people." She handed them each their mug, which they peered into with curiosity. Marnie slumped into John's La-Z-Boy that welcomed her with the caress and musky fragrance of leather. She tucked her legs beneath her and took an impressively long slug from the bottle, aiming it at Mark again. "You have some explaining to do, mister. But not before we hear from our terrorist friend here.

"You." She drew a bead on Salome with the bottle. "Start talking."

Mark threw up his hands and gestured to Salome. "After you."

"Very well," began Salome. "First let me say again how profoundly sorry I am for what has happened to John. He is a very dear friend, someone I've known for many years. He is a man who has done great work to help promote understanding and peace between the West and Islam. I am horrified to think that I may be a reason for someone to try and hurt John, but I believe this may be indeed true.

"You have called me a terrorist. This I can assure you is not true, in spite of what you may think of me. John has told me of your conversations regarding Islam. He says you have an open mind, so I hope you will listen and learn to trust me. Yes, my family—my father—is someone who I've recently learned is capable of great evil. I am not my father, and my family does not control me. I am not like my brothers or the multitudes of others who have been hypnotized by fanaticism. They have thrown their lives away, fighting holy wars that are in no way holy—not knowing how they have been manipulated in the name of God to serve the will of cruel and ruthless men. I have been called a whore and much worse because I will not bow to their twisted beliefs or follow their backward ways. But they dare not touch me for fear of the wrath of my father. In spite of the person he is, he still loves me. I am his only daughter. One cannot choose their family; however, I have been fortunate to be able to choose the life I lead, which is one of peace, and love, and the freedom to be who I want to be—"

Salome was interrupted by a loud snort that erupted from Marnie. She had miraculously polished off the remainder of wine and now cuddled the bottle in her arms. Marnie's mouth hung open and trail of drool had made it past her chin onto her shoulder. She was snoring with a deep, rhythmic tempo.

"I guess she wasn't kidding about the jet lag and Xanax," Mark offered. "I'll go get her bag from the car. She should probably sleep here tonight."

Salome nodded, giving Marnie a compassionate look.

Mark returned and placed Marnie's bag in the foyer.

"Should we put her in John's bed?" Salome asked.

"God, no. This is someone that you do not wish to wake when she's sleeping. I know this from experience; trust me. She'll be fine in the morning, and I'm sure that there will be plenty to discuss. I should probably be in on what you have to tell her, but I respect your desire to share this with Marnie first. If you really think that what's happened to John is in anyway underhanded, you need to be careful. The police are watching Vendetti, but they're not watching you here. Do you want me to sleep on the couch?"

"No, I do not think that will be necessary."

"Okay, just be careful. Lock the door and don't answer it for anyone. I'll ring Marnie's phone in the morning, and I'll catch up with you both then."

"Thank you, Mark. You have been very helpful and supportive. You are a kind man. John and Marnie are lucky to have a friend like you."

"Good night, Salome. And just so you know, Marnie tends to sleep walk and, um, sometimes more."

Salome dismissed this with an elegant, backward wave of her hand. "I believe I will be able to handle Miss McCloud. Good night, Mark."

"Okay, but consider yourself forewarned. And lock the door," he repeated and left the apartment. He stood on the front porch until he heard the click of the deadbolt then headed for his car.

Salome picked up a blanket from the couch and covered Marnie, leaving her holding the wine bottle like a teddy bear. She doused the lights and retired to the guest bedroom for the night.

❈ ❈ ❈

SALOME AWOKE SENSING the warm presence of someone beside her. It felt good, and she took pleasure in it. But she soon realized that she was not dreaming. She turned her head slowly to find Marnie in her bed asleep and spooning her through the covers. A golden ray of morning sunlight shone through a break the window curtain. It was just enough light for Salome to see that Marnie was completely naked on top of the bed. With one arm around Salome, Marnie let out a faint, feminine moan and snuggled her tightly. Before Salome had time to process what was happening, Marnie had her tongue in her ear. Salome was paralyzed by the shock of what Marnie was doing to her, but also uncontrollably aroused by the sensation she felt. Reeling from this sudden stimulation, Salome managed to spin around in bed to face Marnie, who proceeded to kiss her directly on the lips. Salome did not fight it, and not understanding or caring why, she kissed her back.

Marnie smiled in her sleep and said, "You're here. I missed you."

Coming to her senses somewhat, Salome could think of nothing but to blow in Marnie's face to wake her up. Marnie opened her eyes to find herself an inch away from Salome's face.

She looked around in a state of confusion, taking in what she could of the situation. "Was I just doing what I think I was doing?" she asked.

Salome nodded.

"Sleep kissing?"

Salome nodded.

"You're not going to kill me are you?"

Salome nodded again but couldn't hold back a smile that came to her lips. Marnie's faced flushed crimson. She rolled off of Salome, leapt from the bed, and sprinted from the room. Soon after, Salome heard the shower come on from John's bathroom. She took her time laying there, marveling at what had just occurred. Eventually she got up and donned a plush terry-cloth robe from the closet. She made her way into the kitchen and brewed a pot of coffee.

Marnie returned from her shower wearing a sweatshirt and a pair of faded blue jeans that were still a little ripe from Bangkok.

"I cannot believe that I just made out with a terrorist," she said.

Salome just looked at her.

"I'm sorry. That was a bad joke."

"Consider yourself lucky. We would be stoned in the streets for behavior such as that where I come from."

"Yes, well, God bless America," she said and laughed nervously, taking a cup of coffee offered by Salome. "Blech, I hate coffee," she said, taking a sip. "But you know, this isn't half bad."

"You are apparently opening up to new things." Salome smiled like an imp.

"Please, I'm embarrassed enough as it is. Do you think we can just rewind and go back to what you were saying last night before I passed out?"

"Where should I begin?" Salome asked.

"Right after the part where you said you weren't a terrorist."

Salome rehashed her brief soliloquy for Marnie, who seemed to be easing to the idea that she did not in fact just make out with a terrorist. The thought of what occurred in the bedroom, especially the being kissed back part, still had Marnie's stomach turning somersaults. That she was actually dreaming of kissing Mark had her thoroughly agitated, but she fought it off by asking Salome a series of questions while pushing the awkward emotions she was experiencing to the back of her mind.

Salome began her story.

CHAPTER 32

SALOME KHAN WAS BORN and raised in Shemiran, an affluent suburb of northern Tehran. She graduated at the top of her class at the University of Tehran with a Bachelor of Arts degree in theology and Islamic studies. Her coursework included Islamic philosophy that focused on the long-standing tradition in the compatibility of faith and reason, as well as the Islamic Kalam, a philosophical discipline that seeks theological principles through speech and debate. Upon graduation, she pleaded with her father to send her to study in the West. Her father, Mohammed Kahn, was only too happy to grant his only daughter's request—not only for the fact that she was a remarkable and deserving child but also because she possessed a fierce, independent spirit. Although he would never admit the fact except to himself, she was vastly more intelligent than all of her brothers. This was something that caused him to swell with pride at times, but Salome was a double-edged sword who also caused him and the family embarrassment when she decided to speak her mind in public.

Mohammed Khan's feelings for his daughter may have been different had Salome's mother, his first wife, not died during child birth; however, this tragic twist of fate served to form a bond between them that was stronger than either of them were able to control and was futile to rebel against. Regardless, Kahn knew his daughter's time away would provide a welcome relief from her incessant questions and continuous prodding into the family's affairs, which he'd thus far successfully sequestered her from.

She had spent a good part of her twenties studying under the sponsorship of her father in the United States. She received both her Master's degree in Islamic Studies and her PhD from Georgetown University.

Salome returned home to Iran only once over the years between her Master's and PhD due to the visa difficulties introduced for Iranian students after 9/11. During this brief visit home, she felt disconnected from her friends and family. Her time abroad had given her a sense of worldliness that she found lacking in those she reconnected with. They spoke of small-town gossip and topics that to Salome seemed largely petty. The exception, of course, was her father who projected an image of leadership and intellect that Salome held in the highest regard. Because of this, Salome spent most of her time at home with Mohammed Kahn, who indulged her need for heady discussions, spending as much time with her as possible while she was home before she returned to begin her PhD at Georgetown.

Upon completing her postgraduate work she returned home once again for good. To Salome's chagrin, her father began arranging introductions in preparation for her marriage. Though he was not entirely surprised, Kahn was disheartened as Salome perfunctorily sent away each in a steady stream of suitors. Not only did she find the idea of an arranged marriage archaic, she found that those whom her father had arranged introductions with to be repugnant and brutish in their views of how a woman should behave. They were very different from the men she'd met in the States. Perhaps, she thought, she had been poisoned by the West. This was one of the kinder demeaning slurs that had come back to her over the local gossip network. However, if this poison meant avoiding a life of oppressive servitude under the thumb of a thug of a husband, it was a poison she was willing to live with.

What Salome Kahn could not live with came as a revelation upon returning home. While her father had expertly sheltered Salome from the family business her entire life, her brothers were not as tight-lipped in their conversations that more often than not exposed their hatred for the West and all they felt it stood for. "Death to America, the Great Satan," was a phrase overheard far too often for Salome's liking. Her extensive education and experience of living abroad both had a profound influence on her perception of the world, which countered zealotry with understanding.

She saw her brothers as blinded and ensnared by their hateful mind-set and found their conversations inspired by ignorance as they echoed the anti-Western rhetoric they seemed to hold as gospel. These were not the teachings of Islam or any religion, for that matter. Salome knew these to be the words of men who bent the word of God to pervert the minds of those not only foolish enough to listen, but impressionable enough to embrace a fanatical understanding of *jihad* and strap explosives to themselves to die as martyrs. Too many were all too ready and willing to listen to these men instead of the true teachings of their faith. Sadly, whenever she tried to engage any of her bothers in even the most remotely of intellectual discussions, she was rudely dismissed. "Dog lover" became one of their favorite insults. This and others over time were crude and vicious enough to eventually make Salome give up trying to speak with them.

As dejected as she was over her brothers, she was compelled to do something to thwart what she saw as a cancer that was spreading through society. Inspired by her studies and research that promoted understanding and harmony among religions, Salome made it her mission to spread these same notions. With her impressive academic credentials and backed by her father's considerable influence, she was able to attain a position teaching at her alma mater, the University of Tehran. She was ecstatic over the idea that she would be able to debate and argue theology on a daily basis with her students. To Salome's dismay, however, her excitement was rapidly undermined by a faculty that condemned her teaching style as overly westernized and promoting American culture. Some went as far as calling her an American Trojan Horse, which she rejected quite vocally and publicly as utterly absurd.

Initially, Salome put up a fight, refusing to change her style and pouring even more passion into her lectures that were very popular among her students. However, as fiercely determined as she may have been, she was pragmatic enough to know that she was fighting a losing battle against the university system and made the decision to quit her teaching post after only one semester.

Kahn, sympathizing with his daughter's depression and frustration over the ordeal, offered Salome a position at one his many charitable organizations. It was a position that would allow her to counsel and provide support for families who had suffered the loss of a member to religious fanaticism. The charity was originally founded for the ostensible purpose of providing support for families who'd been affected by Iran-Iraq war. Currently, however, the families she counseled were those coping with sons—and more recently daughters—who were displaying radical behavior changes after the adoption of extremist beliefs. These changes were showing up as early as high school these days, and parents were seeking guidance with how to deal with a child who was too young to have fallen in love but was actively supporting the actions and values of Osama bin Laden and al-Qaida.

Sometimes Salome found that an intervention was effective, as she was able to speak and get through to these wayward youths with a voice of compassion and reason. She found the work fulfilling, yet she was well aware that many of the families she counseled ultimately lost their child to the powerful pull of fanaticism. What she was not aware of was that the charitable work that she had engaged in was merely a front for one of the largest sources of funding for terrorist activity in the world.

Chapter 33

MOHAMMED KAHN WAS A CLEVER, hard-working man who started from humble beginnings as a pistachio farmer. How he went from farmer to millionaire was a question that no one had dared to discuss in public in a very long time. Those that did had a tendency to quietly disappear, which proved very effective in quelling further inquiries.

The truth behind Kahn's rags to riches tale was that he was clever enough to align himself with factions led by the Ayatollah Khomeini during the 1960s and eventually earned his way to become a go-to guy for the millionaire mullahs after the revolution of 1979.

During the revolution, assets of Iran's wealthiest families as well as those of foreign investors were expropriated. Practically everything of value was seized by the mullahs and given to Islamic foundations, or *bonyads*, controlled by the clerics. The *bonyads* recycled this supposedly illegitimate wealth, rightly taken from apostates and blood-sucking capitalists and put it into funds used to build health clinics and low-income housing for the poor. However, after the death of Khomeini in 1989, the *bonyad's* interests turned more toward commercial activities than social welfare.

In Shiite tradition, devout businessmen are obliged by their faith to donate twenty percent of their profits to local mosques, where the money is used for charitable purposes to help the needy. Kahn, working for the mullahs as a strong arm for hire, assisted several *bonyads* to act as extortion rackets that targeted any successful entrepreneur who had more than a few riyals to rub together. Those who refused to pay were publicly accused of not being good Muslims. False witnesses hired by Kahn would show up out of the blue to claim they heard these business owners insult the prophet Muhammad—an offense that landed them in jail. It was the Cosa Nostra meets fundamentalism, and it worked like a charm.

Kahn made a name for himself as someone who got the job done and was rewarded handsomely for his efforts. He benefited greatly from privatization programs where as an insider he was able to secure exclusive properties, oil contracts, and ownership of companies previously held by the government. He used his connections and growing power to place his sons in key positions at banks, ministries, major construction companies, and other organizations that could be used to wield his influence.

Kahn turned his rapidly accumulating fortune into a gold mine through a remarkable run of less than above-board foreign trading. Through his connections he was able to obtain a currency import license, and by exploiting the subsidized import rate of less than two thousand riyals to the dollar, he capitalized by reselling them at a rate of eight thousand to the dollar on the black market. At the expense of the Iranian government, that lost anywhere from three to five billion dollars a year over the course of ten years from this exchange-rate fraud, Mohammed Khan along with fifty other insider families were virtually shoveling money into their coffers.

It is said of men that once money is no longer an object that power is what they crave. In the portentous words of Lord Acton, absolute power corrupts absolutely, and Kahn was no exception. Being a made-man with the mullahs—and eventually the higher-ups in the echelons of the secretive Iranian power circles—provided Kahn with a bounty of opportunity to expand his own power. He was tapped to be a key leader and organizer of the Hezbollah militia operating in Iran. He recruited young, bearded heavies from the countryside to subdue pro-democracy demonstrations and other activities deemed unsavory by a shadow organization. Although claiming to derive its legitimacy from Allah, it remained in power through intimidation, violence, and murder. Mohammed Kahn had become a kingpin of a shadow business empire, whose power was protected by an army of enforcers, while financing terrorist groups across the world supported by the foreign policy of a shadow government.

Chapter 34

As Salome shared the brief history of her life and the events leading up to the car accident, Marnie's attitude changed from cocksure to humble. When she came to realize the gravity of Salome's situation, she found herself in awe of the woman.

"Wow, if I ever complain about anything in front of you again, go ahead and slap me," said Marnie. "How do you do it? I mean, when I think about what you've been through—what you must be going through—I don't see how you're able to cope with it."

Salome thought before responding. "I cannot pretend that it has been easy for me, Marnie, but what choice do I have? Perhaps a woman of Islam grows accustomed to enduring. It is submission."

"Yes, but submission to God and submission to crazy people's interpretation of what God wants are two entirely different things. From everything you've just told me, all that's bad that has happened to you has been caused by people, not God."

"Succinctly put, yes," Salome smiled warmly at Marnie. "John was right about you. You have a very refreshing perspective on things. But as an outsider I am not sure you can appreciate how difficult it is to rebel against the influences of these forces. In Iran, the words of the Ayatollah Khomeini still reign even after his death, and there are many today who use religion as their tool for submission, while their ambitions remain quite secular. Americans do not know what it is like to have their beliefs dictated to them. You would not stand for it. I am sure that you have certain people here in America who use their influence over others to shape their beliefs, but I believe that the followers do have a choice."

"I'm not so sure about that," said Marnie, reflecting upon her last conversation with Major Ray and Colonel Milas's diatribe. "Since 9/11, I think that Americans have been forced to accept war as our religion. We've been forced to accept invasions of our privacy and giving up our civil liberties in the name of national security and the war on terror. There's been a thinly veiled threat that we've all been forced to live under. It's nuts! Anyone questioning the legitimacy of this new order is looked at with the suspicion of being unpatriotic. They're the new infidels. And while they may not be stoned to death, they are scrutinized, considered to be terrorist sympathizers, or possibly aiding terrorists in some way.

"My government has been surveilling its own citizens and has access to enough information that people actually don't even have to speak out. Their actions are monitored. Renting a library book or even Googling something is enough to set off a red flag. Once they've *been* flagged, there's a variety of stones to throw at them. If they're just noisemakers, scandal or humiliation in the media generally subdues them. If they do more than just touch a nerve, God help them. They're liable to wind up in Gitmo." Marnie let out a long, drawn-out sigh. "And what really makes me sick about all this is that I've actually helped them do it."

"John had said that you were working for the government," Salome said. "This is true?"

"Apparently, not anymore. I stood firm on an ethical issue and paid the price." She elected not to share the fact that the issue involved spying on Salome. "Not that I give a flying fuck at this point anyhow."

"I can only hypothesize what a flying fuck is. You Americans have quite a way with words," said Salome, blushing at the fact that such a phrase had just crossed her own lips. "May I assume this means you are not overly concerned?"

"Very perceptive. Yes, it means that I'm too pissed off to give a shit." Their conversation was interrupted by loud thump against the door, giving them both a start.

Salome said, "That would be—"

"—the paper," said Marnie. "Man, that kid's gonna be the next Joe Montana."

"Let me get it," offered Salome. She had made it a habit now of scanning the paper each day for any news relating to the

Martyr's Foundation and anything else that might provide her with information related to her father. The coffee table was littered with papers she'd collected over the past week as well as a backlog of issues that Vendetti had yet to recycle.

She returned to the couch armed with a pencil and a highlighter.

"When did Mark say he'd call?" asked Marnie, reaching into her bag for her phone.

"In the morning was all he had said."

"Damn, I should probably charge this thing if we're going to hear from him. Hand me the Sudoku, would you?"

Salome slid out a section of the paper and handed it to her with a pencil. She then began set to the task of highlighting various articles throughout the paper. Six minutes had passed when Marnie exclaimed, "Piece of cake!" and moved on to the Sunday Challenge crossword.

"What language do they speak in Pakistan?" she asked Salome.

"Urdu."

"That works. Thanks."

"What's a five letter word, beginning with U for an Eskimo's canoe?"

"You are asking the wrong person," said Salome, highlighting another article.

There was a knock at the door, and they looked at each other.

"I'll get it," said Marnie. She went to the foyer and looking through the peephole found Mark waiting at the door.

She opened it and said, "You could have called first."

"You might want to learn to turn on your phone," he replied, entering the apartment. "Good morning, ladies. I trust you've had a productive time together?"

Marnie shot Salome a look in a universal language that said, "Don't you dare tell him I kissed you."

"Yes, Mark. We've had quite an exchange," Salome smiled serenely.

"Excellent. I've just spoken to a contact of mine at Metro PD. He says that their investigators have found evidence suggesting that John's car was sabotaged, which means that you were right to suspect foul play. The FBI is now getting involved. I think it's time you let me in on what's happening with you,

Salome. It's only a matter of time before they will want to question you."

"She's not a terrorist," Marnie blurted out. "But her dad might be."

"Please, Marnie. I'd like to hear this from Salome."

Salome pulled a paper from a stack on the coffee table and showed Mark the article about the Martyr's Foundation. "This is my father's charity," she said. The word, charity, came out with a decidedly sour tone. She then gave Mark a very brief rundown of what happened with Ashad and her suspicion regarding his disappearance. She also described the cut in communications with her father and how she and Vendetti had begun to build the file.

"This file, where is it now?" Mark asked.

"In John's office at the university," said Salome.

"And this is what you two were working on the entire week before the crash?"

"Yes."

"I need to see this. John's office is right next door to the hospital. Are you ladies ready to go?"

"I think you should see this first," said Marnie who had been looking at the articles highlighted by Salome. She threw a stack of paper sections at Mark. "Do you believe me now? Recognize any of those names, Mr. I.B. Paranoid?"

There were three separate articles that had caught her attention. One described a mass arrest of several prominent members of the board of directors from the National Iranian American Council. Another told of a raid by American forces on the Iranian consulate in Arbil, Iraq, where five diplomats had been reportedly abducted. The last detailed a coordinated bombing attack along Iran's southeast frontier with Pakistan. Two attacks had left forty-two people dead and many others injured. Among them were seven high-ranking commanders from Iran's Islamic Revolutionary Guards Corp. The Guard's commander in chief had said that there was evidence that the American and British intelligence apparatus working with Pakistan was behind the bombings. Both American and British spokesmen claimed the accusations absurd, while condemning the senseless act of terrorism.

"Salome, you picked these out?" Mark asked.

Salome nodded in response. "I have been seeking information related to my father," she said.

"I'd say at first glance that this is your average, everyday news, but…" He paused.

"But what, Mark?" Marnie asked, leading him to the conclusion she'd already made.

"But with what we know about Junior's *fatwa*, I'd say it's actually being carried out. There are names here from Junior's list!" he said as if a light bulb had just switched on over his head.

"I'm sure that this is just the tip of the iceberg," Marnie said, pointing at the stack of newspaper Salome had collected. 'She's only circled articles regarding Iranians. There's bound to be more, and God knows what's happening that's not been effectively blacked out of the media. If it's not obvious to you now that the major is using Junior to work through his hit-list, you're not as smart as I thought."

"Who is Junior?" asked Salome.

"Marnie will tell you all about it," Mark said. Come on, I need to see this file."

❧ ❧ ❧

MARK, MARNIE, AND SALOME entered Vendetti's office to find Safiya Barazani sitting in front of John's computer. She looked up in surprise.

"What are you doing here, Safiya?" asked Salome.

"Busted!" cried Safiya, melodramatically throwing up her arms. "I'm sorry, Professor Kahn. I came in here today to deliver the mail and couldn't resist poking around. Professor Vendetti always has such nice things. And this new computer—my parents had told me they would help me buy one if I got good grades this semester. I was just checking it out." Safiya gave them a guilty look. "I hope I'm not in trouble."

"Please just leave," said Salome. "We will have to discuss personal boundaries another time."

"I'm really sorry, Professor Kahn. I won't do it again," she said and slinked out of the office, looking ashamed.

Marnie eyed Safiya as she left, then looked at Vendetti's computer.

"So this is the file?" asked Mark, motioning at the walls.

"Yes, in addition to what we have collected here." Salome went to a file cabinet and pulled out several file folders and plunked them on the table.

Mark opened a few of them, looking at their contents briefly. "But the meat of your findings are on the wall," he concluded. "And these strings represent the connections you've made between people, organizations, and events. Nice work."

As Mark scanned the walls, Marnie sat down at Vendetti's computer. She wiggled the mouse, interrupting the screen saver and got a login prompt. John's username was already filled in, so she tried guessing his password and received an error. She tried a second time. "Damn," she said, and scoured the desk and drawers in search of every computer system's single point of security failure, the yellow Post-it note with a scribbled password on it. "Salome, do you know John's password?" she asked.

"Perhaps I do." She walked to the bookshelf behind Marnie and pulled a book from the shelf. "He always opened this book before sitting down at this computer. Ah ha, here we are," she said, handing the book to Marnie. On the inside cover there was a yellow sticky that read, "M@rn!e123."

Marnie looked at it and said, "And he couldn't remember that?" She typed in the password and was granted access to his computer. She then checked a log to find that the computer had been accessed only fifteen minutes prior.

"I'm not sure John would appreciate you looking through his mail, Marnie," Mark said.

"And I'm not sure that girl was merely computer shopping," she replied. "Besides, since when is mail delivered on Sunday?" Salome and Mark looked at each other, then leaned over Marnie's shoulder. "You see that?" she said, pointing at the screen to a log entry. "She was reading his mail."

Marnie launched the mail program and perused John's inbox. Nothing seemed out of the ordinary, but she really had no idea what unordinary was in this case. Her eyes then fell upon a message with a subject line that was in a foreign language.

"Salome, can you read this?" asked Marnie, using the mouse to move the cursor over the words.

"Let me see," said Salome. It is written in Arabic. It says, "You have been warned."

Marnie clicked on the message to open it.

"How about this?" she asked Salome.

Salome read the message aloud in Arabic first, then in English. "The message reads, 'Our warnings to you, Mr. Vendetti, have gone unheeded. Let this be a lesson. Stop your research. It does not concern you.'"

"Son of a bitch!" Marnie cursed. She then performed a search upon John's mailbox for all messages from the sender. A list displayed upon the screen. Five of the messages had been deleted unread. She opened them chronologically. Salome interpreted them one by one. Each of the emails was a warning for Vendetti to 'cease and desist' all research pertaining to the Martyr's Foundation, and each of them threatened increasingly dire consequences if he did not.

"When did you arrive from Iran?" Marnie asked, looking at Salome.

"Friday last week. Why?"

"And when did you start investigating your father?"

"This past Monday."

"Look at the dates. These emails started to arrive on Monday. This last one was received yesterday."

"Who are they from?" asked Mark.

Marnie examined the messages more thoroughly by reading their internet header information. She then used Google to find information the on the sending server.

"It's impossible to tell," she said. "They've been sent through an anonymous mailer service that scrubs all sender information. The server's in Malaysia somewhere, but there's no way to trace these back to who actually sent them."

"Print these out," said Mark. "I want hardcopies. And forward them to Phet for good measure. Let's see what he can dig up."

Mark's phone rang. The conversation was short.

"John's awake," he said. Both women stirred with hope in hearing the news. "Before we go, I want this entire file taken down and packed up. We're going to hand it over to someone who can do something about this."

Chapter 35

"WELCOME BACK TO THE LIVING, JOHN. You had us all very worried. How are you feeling?" Mark said, entering Vendetti's hospital room after a quiet knock on the open door.

"Absolutely smashing," John groaned, clearly in severe discomfort. "The drugs they're pumping into me have me soaring high as a kite. Ah, I see you've brought my two favorite women with you."

Marnie and Salome approached John's bedside.

"Look at you, the cowgirl Catholic and the Persian scholar. What a pair you make!"

They regarded him with caring smiles that contradicted how they felt at seeing him as he was. He looked horrible, and they fawned on him, which he accepted with obvious enjoyment.

"Er, John, there's a third woman in your life apparently," said Mark. "We found your assistant rifling through your computer just now. Marnie's discovered some very disturbing emails that are definitely related to your car accident. And what I've learned from the police is that your accident was no accident."

Vendetti looked alarmed and he tried to rise. He winced in pain and collapsed back into the bed. He managed to utter, "Safiya?"

"Sorry, I probably shouldn't be telling you this right now in your condition, but I don't think her only job is delivering mail."

"You think this is related to the file?" Vendetti asked, looking at Salome.

"I've got it right here," said Mark. "It's going to the FBI first thing tomorrow morning."

"Unbelievable. Who can you trust these days?" Vendetti grumbled.

"You can trust us," said Marnie, and Salome nodded in agreement.

"I know that I can. And thank you for that. Mark, there are things in that file that might be of interest to your friends at the CIA. If someone's gone through the trouble of destroying... my car!" Vendetti looked at them expectantly. They all shook their heads in unison. "Hmm, I wonder if my insurance company would consider this an act of vandalism." His mind swirled for a moment as the I.V. regulator emitted a beep and shot a dose of morphine into his bloodstream. "Ah, that's better. What I was saying is that Salome and I must have been onto something for whoever to go to such drastic measures. I think someone with more resources may be able to connect the dots that we couldn't."

"You're probably right, but since the FBI is taking over the investigation regarding your accident, it's best they have everything they need to help them right now. I'll let them know what I'm giving them. If there's something there, it'll get to the right people."

"And Salome," said Vendetti, "these people had to have known you were in the car with me. This is a very bad sign. It could mean the situation has grown out of your father's control or that we've crossed a line that even he could not tolerate. You must be careful."

"John, I am much more concerned about you right now than myself," Salome said.

"I'm quite serious, Salome, and I'm not exaggerating. Marnie? Mark? You two need to make sure nothing happens to her."

"We will," said Marnie.

A nurse came in hauling a plastic bag filled with Styrofoam containers. She had a no nonsense air about her as she unfolded Vendetti's bed table and laid out the boxes before him. She then cracked open a Dr. Pepper and placed a straw in the can.

"Nurse Dana, you are an absolute miracle worker."

"I'm charmed," she said rolling her eyes at him.

"One of you is going to have to feed him," she said to the women, slapping down some silverware she'd pulled from her uniform. The nurse marched off without another word.

"It pays to have connections," said Vendetti. They were amazed that he could still manage his dashing smile though he looked like an ogre. "I mean I am quite a muck-a-muck around here, and there's no reason for my visitors to sit around and watch me try and eat hospital food. And more to the point, no one comes between me and my kabobs."

Marnie reached over and opened each of the containers. Salome recognized Friday night's take-out menu and gave John an appreciative look.

"Come on, there's plenty for all. Dig in," he urged.

"Well, I am practically starving," said Marnie and forked herself a bite.

Salome and Mark followed her example, providing audible sounds of approval. When Marnie offered to feed Vendetti, he balked. "No thank you. Frankly, I can't even think about eating right now, but having my friends here is definitely the best medicine I could possibly ask for."

Vendetti lay there watching them, grateful for their company. The food rapidly vanished, and by the time they were finished, John was asleep. Nurse Dana entered the room as if on a predetermined schedule and shooed them out the door. They left, quietly thanking her, and received a raised eyebrow in the return. The door was closed behind them.

Mark exchanged words with the policeman who was seated in the waiting area and returned to the women. "John has round-the-clock supervision. Now we just need to find out what to do with you," he said to Salome. "Marnie, she could stay at your place."

"One bed, sorry," said Marnie. "John's is better. I left my suitcase there. I just need my laptop. I have some ideas about this file."

"Do you think you might be able to see through this maze?" asked Mark.

"I might, but I won't know until I try."

⌘ ⌘ ⌘

BACK AT VENDETTI'S APARTMENT, Marnie was furiously typing data into her laptop, while shooting rapid-fire questions to Mark and Salome.

"Who were the men named in relation to that Goodwill Charitable Organization asset seizure?"

Salome answered her, and Marnie cross-referenced the names with the Omnimation account she'd opened online with her company credit card. Omnimation was a service that Marnie had learned about at the NCTC. It was one of the largest databases of consumer information anywhere, storing over twenty billion consumer records culled from public records, census data, tax records, and information supplied by corporations and credit card companies. Omnimation's data was only one source of information that Junior got to play with, but it was enough to tell those interested quite a bit about a person. The details Omnimation sold about people was enough to make Marnie's skin crawl, but she was only interested in a few key items, and plugged these into her system.

"What were the names of those board members from the NAIC?"

Mark searched around and found the paper, reading them off.

Marnie had been doing this for nearly four hours, when she finally said, "Salome, what're your credit and ATM card numbers?"

Salome went to her purse and read the numbers aloud, while Marnie typed them in.

"Okay, let's see what we have," Marnie said, cracking her knuckles and entering a few final commands. "Salome, each of your compatriots from the GCO holds credit cards that are—or were—being paid for with checks drawn from accounts at the same bank located in New Jersey. I bet their cards don't work either. Conversely, the poor boys of the NAIC are all over the place. There's AMEX, MasterCard, and Visa; they're all from differing banks, and their billing addresses are all unique. That all looks pretty clean to me, but if I were to have access to international wire transfers, I'd bet that we'd be seeing deposits to these GCO accounts from places like Dubai."

"You are speaking of *havaleh*," said Salome.

"Ya, except I've heard it called *hawala*. Tomato, to-*mah*-to, whatever. They would be using *havaleh* dealers to bring their money via a circuitous route into the United States so as to skirt around sanctions as well as making the transfers virtually untraceable."

"Marnie, how in the world do you know all this?" asked Mark.

"You learn a few things building inference rules that catch terrorists, Mark," she answered. "The *hawala* is a money transfer system that is hundreds of years old. It's recently been under some serious scrutiny by the Feds for being a conduit for funneling money to terrorist organizations."

Marnie tapped a few keys on her laptop. "You'll be happy to know, Salome, that your ATM card is linked to a savings account in your name located in Hong Kong. I'm guessing that Daddy's topped it up rather nicely and that it still works because it's totally unrelated to this GCO business."

"What else can you get out of that thing?" asked Mark.

"Not as much as I'd get if I had access to Junior. What I've got here is a severely malnourished version of Junior. The logic is the much same, but with hardly any data to work with there's only so many connections it has to chew on. Plus, I can't type *all* this stuff in. It'd take weeks."

"Well, accessing Junior is not going to happen."

"I know. Your friend Chris Dexter told me."

"What else did he say?"

"Something about a breach of contract," Marnie said sheepishly.

"No, that's been squared away. But you *are* off the project, and it's for your own good. They're using Hawk to work through the final hand-over."

"Oh, well that's nice." Marnie's sarcasm reared its head. "I think that both you and I know that's merely a formality. People on Junior's list—many of them surely innocent, I'll have you— wouldn't be being rounded up or blown to smithereens if the major hadn't already signed off in his own mind. Someone is knowingly asking Junior the wrong questions and passing the output upward as legitimate intelligence analysis. And it freaks me out when I think about how far they might go with this."

"I've got a one-on-one meeting with Admiral Chase tomorrow at ten."

"Good, tell him what I think of Major Ray."

"And I've got to drop this file of at the Bureau before that, so I better be heading home. I want you to go to the office tomorrow and see what Phet can do with those emails. Bring Salome with you. Don't leave her alone. I'll have Melanie arrange clearance and a visitor's badge."

Mark began gathering up the file that was scattered about the apartment.

"Mark, we have to stop him." Marnie's voice was unmistakably serious, and Mark knew that tone very well.

"Stop who, Marnie?"

"If not the major, it's gotta be Junior."

"I know you're right, but I think we're up against the impossible."

"Think about it. Think about where this is going. There's got to be something we can do."

"I will," he said. "You do the same. I'll see you both tomorrow afternoon. Good night you two."

"Good night," they replied.

"And lock the door," Mark said as he let himself out.

Marnie yawned. "Whose bed will I wind up in tonight?"

"Hmm, is there any wine left?" teased Salome.

The doorbell chimed.

Marnie looked around and said, "What did he forget?"

Salome shrugged and Marnie opened the door. Two men stood there, wearing identical dark blue windbreakers.

"Marnie McCloud, we're agents Jenkins and Short from the FBI." They each flashed their badge.

Marnie craned her head out the door, looking for Mark. She scratched her head and said, "Mark's just left. He said he was going to go see you tomorrow."

"We're not here for him, ma'am. We're here for Ms. Kahn."

"Isn't it a little late to be making house calls?" Marnie asked, trying to stall them while she thought this through.

"May we come in, Ms. McCloud?"

"Um, do you have a warrant?" she asked.

"We don't need a warrant, ma'am. And we are asking nicely."

"What? Are you going to go all Patriot Act on me now? Come back at a decent hour tomorrow," she said and tried to close the door. Agents Jenkins' boot kept it open.

"It is fine, Marnie," said Salome, having come up behind her. "I have nothing to hide from these men."

"Oh, Salome, you're awake," Marnie said lamely.

"May we come in, ma'am," asked Short.

Marnie let them in.

"Ms. Salome Kahn?" said Short.

"It is Miss Kahn. Yes?"

"Miss Kahn, we read the report you gave to the police regarding the car accident you were involved in with John Vendetti. You claim to have not seen anything."

"Yes, this is true. It all happened so very fast."

"It mentions that you heard Mr. Vendetti say something about a taxi, just before the crash. Did you see it?"

"No, but as I had told the police, I believe this is why John was speeding. He said that the taxi driver was a—" she thought for a moment, "A bloody, drag-racing lunatic, I think that is what he said."

Jenkins scratched something down on a small notepad.

"Miss Kahn, do you know of anyone who would wish to harm you or Mr. Vendetti?"

Salome looked at Marnie who said, "Tell 'em."

Salome described the threatening emails, Safiya, and the file the she and John had built.

"And why didn't you mention any of this to the police?"

"As I said, we just discovered these emails today. We had no idea we were in any danger."

"But you are the daughter of an Iranian national who you were researching in an effort to connect him to a terrorist network. You neglected to state that in your report."

"I didn't think it was relevant at the time."

"Well, it is very relevant." This was Jenkins. "We picked up the cab on a security camera from the parking lot at the Key Bridge Marriott. It's been found abandoned at a construction site off Dolly Madison Boulevard with the driver bound and gagged in the trunk. His throat was cut."

Salome put her hand to her mouth, appalled by the image that formed in her mind.

"We also know that the accident was caused by small explosive devices attached to the car's tires," Jenkins continued. "We found two of them still intact within the wreckage, and they are pretty high-tech. This was not amateur work."

"There is something that links you to whoever did this," Agent Short took over. "But the crime scene only gives us so much to work with. There's a motive, and it has to be related to something you uncovered with Mr. Vendetti."

"The fact is that we really hadn't come to any conclusions at all," Salome offered.

"This Safiya Barazani," said Jenkins. "How well do you know her?"

"She is a student that John hired for the summer and was training to become my assistant. I have only known her for a week."

"And she's never acted in any way out of the ordinary until today?"

"I have had no reason to even consider this, but no. She seemed quite normal. In fact, she is an above average student."

"Is she on a scholarship?"

"I am not sure of this."

Jenkins took some more notes.

"The emails on Mr. Vendetti's computer. You say they were anonymous, how so?"

Salome looked at Marnie, who described the process she went through to determine the source of the messages. Short raised his eyebrows, and Jenkins took more notes.

"Where is the file you put together with Mr. Vendetti now?" asked Short.

"Mark Harmann has it," Marnie told them.

Short glanced at his wristwatch and gave Jenkins a nod. "Miss Kahn, it's reasonable to assume that the contents of this file are of value to someone, enough so that you are probably still in considerable danger. There may be more attempts to stop whatever it is they believe you are working on. We already have Mr. Vendetti under watch at the hospital, and we're going to post someone outside for the night. Until we know more, we request that you do not leave the area. We may have more questions for you."

"I understand and thank you," Salome said.

When the agents left, Marnie was at her laptop again. After a few quick queries, she announced, "Safiya Barazani, daughter of Rahim and Malika Barazani who own and operate Exotic Fabrics in Georgetown." Marnie clicked through some more information. "Total gross revenue for Exotic Fabrics in 2006 was nearly seventy-five thousand dollars. Take off twenty-five percent for taxes, and that gives about fifty-six thousand net. Undergraduate tuition at Georgetown for a single year is roughly thirty-five thousand a year, leaving the Barazani's with twenty-one thousand dollars to live on. Divide that by twelve, and that's seventeen fifty a month."

"Is that good or bad," asked Salome, prompting Marnie to do another search.

"Considering that they own a home in Rose Hill that been appraised at just under a million dollars, I'd say it's impossible. Unless the Barazanis are declaring a lot less income than they actually earn, this money's coming from somewhere else."

"*Havaleh*," said Salome.

CHAPTER 36

MARK ARRIVED AT THE NCTC by 9:45am and was escorted by Rose to a waiting area outside of Admiral Chase's office. He'd been conflicted over Marnie's behavior ever since she stormed into his office the day before she left for Bangkok to meet with Colonel Milas. He knew of Milas, but he'd never met the man. His fall from grace occurred before Mark's time. There was no doubt the man had smarts; Milas was a *bona fide* genius. But the Milas was no longer one of the elite and was more of an obscurity when Mark had eventually become part of the Washington scene. The fact that the colonel was Phet's father was not lost on him. It was one of the reasons Mark had hired him. He saw that the apple had not fallen far from the Milas tree. That Phet had not spoken to or of his father for many years was a personal issue Mark felt best left alone.

When Mark confronted Major Ray about Marnie's claims, he rebutted the accusations entirely. No, Junior was not ready for production. No, there was no government-sponsored assassination program. No, he was not having Marnie followed. And no, he didn't ask her to spy on Salome Kahn.

Mark agreed with Ray when he said it was time to rein her in. He didn't think she was acting completely paranoid, but she was out of her depth and behaving far more erratically than was normal for her. The problem was that Marnie was like a pit bull; once she locked onto something, she didn't let go. And this could spell trouble, especially when dealing with a man such as Ray. Not wanting to test the major's patience and potentially stir things further, Mark did not let on that he knew Ray was lying. Phoenix did exist, only now its moves had evolved to incorporate targeted strikes with Hellfire missiles fired from Predator drones.

Mark had the foresight to understand that there was no way that the U.S. military would never act in a purely defensive mode.

Project X would eventually be evaluated for its offensive capabilities even if they weren't ostensibly part of its original conception. The dilemma was that unless one really understood how Junior worked—and few people did—there was nothing to prevent anyone from using the system to form an offensive strategy. The idea of modeling the future outcome of events was seductive regardless of the warning label it carried. If Ray was lying about Phoenix, Mark knew he was probably lying about the rest as well. The mystery that Mark could not solve was what Major Ray wanted with Colonel Milas, or why he'd told Marnie about him. It was somehow related to Phoenix. It related to a particular chess match. But he didn't know precisely how.

While Milas was an enigma, Mark also wondered who was giving Ray his orders. He now regretted dropping breadcrumbs for Marnie to follow. He'd thought that she would be able to see connections that he'd not been able to, but in hindsight, he'd unwittingly led her into a very tenuous and possibly dangerous situation.

Before he was able to talk to Marnie, she'd jumped on a plane to Thailand. That was when Major Ray called to tell Mark that Warden Islam was Andrew Milas. Worried sick over Marnie, he contacted the U.S. Embassy in Bangkok and eventually got in touch with Chris Dexter, who Mark had learned later got more than he'd bargained for in the form of a transvestite named Joe. Once Marnie was already on her way home, Dexter told him a great deal about Lieutenant Colonel Andrew Milas.

Dexter's report was considerably more succinct than Marnie's episodic rant in conveying their conversation with Milas and the revelations it entailed. Though Marnie was distraught, she wasn't that far off target. For Mark, the details Salome had picked from the newspapers were the condemnatory substantiation that he needed to realize that Junior was in fact being used far beyond its mandate. "But is it enough to convince others?" he asked himself. It didn't matter. Marnie was right. This needed to be stopped. But how to do it without winding up a laughing-stock like Milas or serving a considerable prison sentence he'd yet to figure out, unless he was somehow able to convince the admiral that Marnie's ideas about Major Ray were credible.

Mark heard the admiral's door open and saw Major Ray exiting the office.

"Mark," said Ray with a curt nod, not breaking stride.

"Major," Mark replied.

Rose appeared and ushered Mark in to see Admiral Chase.

"Mark Harmann, please sit down," said Chase.

"Thank you for making the time to see me, Admiral."

"Well, we are getting close to handing over this project, so I assumed that you wanted to discuss some final details. Major Ray has just briefed me on the schedule."

"About that, sir, you do remember the issues we discussed in our prior meeting?"

"Yes, of course. Major Ray has told me that these were identified as programming bugs. According to the report he just gave me, these have all been remediated. And I hate to say this, but he did not paint a very glowing picture of your star player, Miss McCloud. She apparently went AWOL last week, leaving the team to clean up her mess. I hope you can appreciate that this does not reflect very well on the relationship we've built with Burns and Lynch."

Mark was taken aback at the admiral's statement. "Sir, did the report provide any details leading up to her leaving?"

"No more than that things were moving along on schedule, and then she up and left."

It was clear to Mark that there was no sense in arguing this point. When it came down to it, it would be Marnie's word against the major's, and he knew how that would play out. He changed his approach.

"I believe there must have been a communication breakdown, sir. Miss McCloud had a family emergency that she had to attend to out of town. We'd have substituted someone in her place, but with time short we were told that James Hawk would suffice. I'm very sorry. I'm not sure how this wasn't included in Major Ray's report."

Chase frowned and looked over his eyeglasses at Mark. "Is she all right?" he asked.

"Er, yes. It was apparently a bit of a false alarm. She's back now. Everything is fine." Mark disliked lying to the man, but he wasn't the only one doing it today. Major Ray was playing games, and he wasn't going to be outmaneuvered.

"You didn't come here to talk about Miss McCloud." This was a statement, not a question.

"No, sir, I didn't. Not directly. Admiral, may I ask, how does intelligence flow from here to the White House? Does every piece of analysis cross your desk before it leaves here?"

"I am ultimately responsible, yes."

"But it is possible that some information could leave without you having read it, correct?"

"It's an inevitability, son. Do you know how much data we're sitting on here? The appetite for hard analysis is voracious."

"In fact I do, sir, and that brings me to my point. Who is responsible for clearing analysis for release?"

"That depends on who it's being packaged for," Chase explained. "We've a department dedicated to each audience, and each department has analysts that tailor the reports to match the information requirements of the audience. The Joint Chiefs have one set of requirements, while the president has another, and so on. What are you getting at with these questions? Come to the point."

Mark didn't know any other way to get to the point, so he just came out with it.

"I'm confident that—in your words—someone is shoveling shit into the president's briefs, and he's bought into it."

"What you are suggesting is outrageous." Chase bristled with annoyance.

"I would be thinking the same thing if Miss McCloud hadn't brought something to my attention." Mark reached into his valise and handed Admiral Chase a document. "You may remember a list of names that our system produced around the time Major Ray was introduced to the project."

"Yes, Junior's *fatwa*," acknowledged Chase as he leafed through it briefly.

"You may also recall that we determined that the only way to produce such a list is through backward chaining," Mark said.

"Vaguely, it was all that Machiavelli business, but that's why Major Ray was brought on board. To make sense of all the bits and bytes that fuel the engines."

"Yes, while you steer the ship, sir," Mark added. "I'd appreciate it if you noted the highlighted names on the list I've just given you, and then take a look at this."

Mark handed him a folder containing twenty articles he'd printed out. Inspired after watching Marnie's recent sleuth-work, he decided to take Salome's low-tech newspaper research to the Internet. "You can see, Admiral, that I have also highlighted several names within the articles. These names are all contained in the original list."

Chase scanned the file, confirming what Mark was telling him. "Is this a complete list?" he asked, his tone more harried now.

"That represents only an hour or so of me at my home PC, sir. Surely, there are more to be found," Mark told him.

"I recognize some of these. The GCO seizures were a major coup, but these others..." Chase's voice trailed off.

"Do you still think that these are programming bugs, sir?"

"You can do away with the lawyer act, son. I see your point."

"I'm sorry, sir. May I know what you're going to do about this?"

"No, you may not, but it will be handled. I can assure you of that."

"And, what of our involvement with the project?"

Admiral Chase thought for a moment before saying, "You just carry on as usual. I am not going to open my kimono until I talk to the right people about this. I do think it best that we leave the Miss McCloud situation as is. She strikes me as a bit of a loose cannon, and I don't need her firing any shots over the major's bow, if you know what I mean."

"Understood, sir."

A curt knock preceded Rose's entry into the admiral's office. She brushed past Mark and handed the Chase a slip of paper and then removed herself from the room like a diligent wraith.

Chase read the note, and Mark saw a look of surprise on his face.

"Excuse me," he said and picked up his phone, hitting a line button.

"This is Admiral Chase." His voice was sober and commanding.

His eyes tracked on Mark as he took in the other end of the conversation.

"Is there any confirmation as to the source?" he asked.

Mark watched as the admiral picked up the list Mark had given him and scanned it intently.

"I know the man, yes. Keep me posted on any developments. Thank you."

He hung up the phone and looked at Mark over his glasses again.

"Senator Barack Obama's apartment in D.C. is on fire. It looks like a gas explosion, but it's too early to tell."

"He's—" Mark began.

"—on his way from Kenwood now. He commutes between here and Chicago."

"He's—" Mark started again.

"—on the list, I know, and he's not even Muslim for Christ's sake."

"Admiral, I hope you see the magnitude of the problem we're dealing with."

"I'm beginning to," Chase admitted.

They both sat silent for a moment as they each contemplated what it was they were actually facing.

"Mark?"

"Yes, sir?"

"It took a great deal of balls to come to me and bring this to my attention. You did a good thing, and I appreciate that."

"Thank you, sir."

"As you can see, I have some serious shit to deal with here."

"I can only hope for the best and wish you luck, sir, for all our sakes."

"Yes, me too. That'll be all, Mark. I'll do my best to keep you in the loop." The admiral dismissed him.

❋ ❋ ❋

MARK FOUND HAWK and asked him to come to the office for a lunch meeting. He then raced there himself with the anticipation of telling Marnie how well he'd pulled off breaking her story to the admiral. He was still jittery from having laid it all out like he did but was elated by how Admiral Chase had handled the information. The news about the senator from Illinois was certainly alarming. He really did hope the admiral was in a position to do something about what was panning out; otherwise, Mark saw the next battle on the horizon would be reining in hell.

As he pulled onto Solutions Drive, he saw a crowd of people standing in front of the building; he headed for the commotion.

Two men were leading a woman through the crowd to an unmarked but still recognizable government issued sedan. Mark pulled alongside and got out of his car. The woman was Salome.

"Whoa, whoa, whoa," he called out, waving his arms in the air. "What's going on here?"

Marnie ran to Mark's side. "They just came in and demanded she leave with them. No charges or anything."

Mark knew better than to try to stop what was happening. "Agents, where are you taking Miss Kahn?" he asked.

"We can't tell you that, sir," said one of the agents while the other assisted Salome into the back of the vehicle. Salome looked calm, but Mark could tell she was intimidated.

Mark heard Phet shout, "Gestapo pigs!" from a well-hidden position within the crowd.

The other agent actually laughed out loud at this and approached Mark. He took out a pen and wrote something on the back of a card. "Call this number at the Bureau, Mr. Harmann," he said, handing him the card. He then got in the car and drove Salome away.

Chapter 37

Mark called Marnie and Phet into his office.

"I've just come from seeing Admiral Chase," he said. "Hawk's on his way over here right now. I'll wait 'till he gets here so that I can brief you as a team."

He took the card he'd been given by the FBI agent and dialed it into his speakerphone. "Agent Short or Jenkins, please," he said. "This is Mark Harmann with Burns and Lynch. Yes, I'll hold."

He looked at Phet and held his finger to his lips. He gave it a second thought and picked up the handset, disconnecting the speakerphone.

"Agent Jenkins, two of your agents just picked up Salome Kahn at our offices. What's the story?"

Mark listened to Jenkins on the other end of the line.

"Right, and what else can you tell me?" he asked.

"Is she a suspect?"

"How long before we can see her?"

"Okay, thanks. I'll be in touch," he said and hung up.

He looked at Marnie, "Salome's being taken to the Hoover building for questioning. Short and Jenkins paid me a visit last night. I gave them the file."

"They must have gone directly to your place after they left John's," she said.

"Apparently so. There was definitely something in that file that's got the hive riled."

Hawk walked in, leaving the door open behind him. "You guys gotta see something."

He stepped over to Mark's desk and picked up the remote for the flat-screen TV on the wall. He turned it on and clicked through the channels, stopping on CNN. The images on the television were showing firefighters hosing down the charred out remains of Senator Obama's one-bedroom apartment near Capitol Hill.

"I was with Admiral Chase when he got this news," said Mark.

"Not this. Hang on," said Hawk as he surfed through the channels.

"Here!" he exclaimed as he found what he was looking for. "This was all over the radio while I drove here. They were monitoring it in the pit when I left."

The TV screen depicted a scene of what looked to be thousands of demonstrators marching through the streets of a city. There were palm trees, and the scene could have been from several places but for the U.S. Bank Tower that figured prominently in the cameraman's composition. The news banner confirmed the location.

"This is happening in L.A.?" asked Mark.

"Yep," replied Hawk.

A news correspondent was reporting live from Tehrangeles, an area of Los Angeles, California between Beverly Hills and West L.A. Also known as Persian Square, it was home to the second largest population of Iranians outside of Iran. The camera panned a scene of throngs of demonstrators who had taken to the streets. Many held placards specifically condemning the arrest of NAIC board members while others used the opportunity to call for unity against what they saw as Islamaphobia. Police were on the scene, but the protestors were peaceful in spite of their numbers.

"Wait, that's not all," said Hawk, using the remote to scan through more channels.

He found another news program that showed a similar scene at the U.N. building in New York.

"This is happening all over," Hawk told them. "There's a demonstration in nearly every major U.S. city. There are also protests being staged across the Middle East in Iran, Pakistan, Afghanistan, and you-name-it-stan. The Indonesians are getting into the act as well. There's a lot of pissed off Muslims out there right now."

"And this all just happened overnight?" asked Marnie, nonplussed.

"Apparently, the planning for this has been in the works for a while. The word in the pit is that this is a coordinated worldwide condemnation by Muslims against what they're saying is Western aggression against their religion," Hawk explained.

"Think about it, Marnie," said Mark. "None of us here are tuned in to any Islamic wavelength. What we know about Muslims generally comes to us over news sources. Frankly, none of us hang in Islamic circles. It took someone like Salome to point out a trend to us that I'd say mainstream America is pretty much oblivious to. I know I was. And like you said, what she found was just the tip of the iceberg. I found plenty of examples that could be tied to Junior's *fatwa* for the admiral, but I knew what I was looking for."

"But how do we get from a few articles in the paper to something like this?" Marnie said, pointing at the TV. "We may think we know what's going on, but I think Obama's apartment fire is going to get more people's attention."

"Again, I don't think we were looking for it. Also, I think it's easy to become jaded by the continuous bombardment of news we are exposed to. You're right, I mean it takes bombs going off or gunmen to get our attention these days. News that could be important to any of us gets lost in the cloud of sensationalism. I think what we're looking at here is the result of resentment that has built up over time. Junior's *fatwa* is like the proverbial straw that broke the camel's back. Non-Muslims are just blind to the number of straws that have been piling up."

"Sorry," Hawk interjected. "This guy here is who the pit crew are thinking is the ringleader behind this. The word is that he's an American-born Muslim and prominent businessman living in New York. We should hear this." Hawk turned up the volume as one of the protest leaders was making a speech.

They all listened as the man spoke, eloquently condemning both terrorism and the treatment of Muslims who have been unfairly associated with terrorists. The crowd cheered him as he declared it was time for all Muslims to reclaim their religion that has been defiled by terrorists and to demand fair treatment that all Americans deserve. The newscast flashed back to the latest on the senator's apartment blaze.

"You see, I told ya. This makes better news," said Marnie. "Tell me truthfully, do you think the majority of Americans are going to care about these protests? I admit that the guy in the suit sure talks nice. He's definitely got a better chance of getting his message across because he's not standing dressed in robes like a cleric. I mean bin Laden would do well to take some notes here, but the thing is that someone's torching flags and pictures of the president somewhere. This happens all the time. We've almost come to expect this from Muslims, haven't we?

"Imagine if bin Laden were able to address the masses like this," Mark said soberly. "Seriously, look at the damage bin Laden has been capable of achieving with only a limited number of zealots. What if he were to rally over a billion people to his cause? This could be the start of something seriously big, people."

"Is that even a reality? You heard the guy just now," said Hawk. "The majority of Muslims want peace. They don't condone terrorism. They want to be rid of it as much as we do. I'd like to believe he's right."

"You know," said Marnie. "I'd like to believe he's right too—and I have had a conversation about this just recently—but I think Americans are just plain tired of this crap."

"Not crap!" said Phet in response to Marnie's last comment. "How long will Muslims endure the effects of the war on terrorism: the unfair treatment, the discrimination, harassment, interrogation, arrests, incarceration without trial, the wars that are brought to their land by foreign forces that consider the deaths of women, children, and innocents to be collateral damage?"

"Boy howdy! When did you start taking English lessons?" Hawk asked with mock surprise.

"I think he has eyes for Salome," answered Marnie.

"That would explain it," said Mark. "Phet makes a very good point though. If the president continues to allow this to happen, *we* are going to be seen as the terrorists and not just by the fanatics that already think we are. We'll be headed into a battle against the entire religion of Islam. These protests could be the seeds of World War III."

"This is what Colonel Milas said would happen," said Marnie.

Phet's eyes flashed at hearing the name of his father.

"And it looks like he could be right," said Mark. "I just hope the bomb I dropped in the admiral's lap has the effect I'm hoping for."

Mark told them of his meeting with Admiral Chase.

"So what am I supposed to do, just sit on my ass and twiddle my thumbs while the world goes to pot?" asked Marnie.

"Not exactly. Remember you have one friend recovering from a serious car accident in the hospital and another in the custody of the FBI. And in case the admiral is unsuccessful—which God I hope he isn't—I need you to be working on Plan B with Phet."

A voice boomed from the doorway, "Plan B! I like the sound of that. I am, however, allergic to car accidents."

Standing in the doorway was Lieutenant Colonel Andrew Milas. He was in full uniform, cleanly shaven, and looked like a completely different person than the man Marnie had met just a few days ago.

"I'm sorry, Mr. Harmann" said Melanie, squeezing past the Milas. "He's very persistent."

"Lieutenant Colonel Andrew Milas reporting for duty, sir!" he snapped.

Phet immediately rose from his chair and made for the door. Had Milas not stepped aside, there would have been some pushing. He watched the back of his son as he walked away.

Marnie approached Milas. "What in the world are you doing here?"

"Nice to see you too," he smiled. "I was paying my respects at the Wall over in D.C., and I thought I'd drop by to see how you were doing. Don't I dress up nice?" He blinked his eyes, hinting at the fact that he'd swapped his glasses for contact lenses. This apparently was supposed to make up for the fact that he looked like he needed a girdle if he was planning on keeping his dress buttons in place for much longer.

"Melanie, it's okay," said Mark. "You can leave him with us."

"Yes, sir," she said, giving Milas a stiff look as she left.

"Colonel Milas, I'm Mark Harmann." Mark offered his hand, which Milas shook with a grip of forged metal. "It's a pleasure to meet you, but really what *are* you doing here, sir?"

"Well, I got to thinking after this one had left." He tilted his head toward Marnie. "Your boy, Dexter, paid me a visit, telling me a bit more about the situation she was returning to. And as I'm partly responsible for that situation, it didn't sit with me too well. I figured she needed a little help, though I think she'd not be the kind to admit it. So, here I am. Oh, and I brought Joe who's probably slapping some sense into his brother right about now."

"You brought her here?" Marnie asked aghast, remembering the seductive image of Joe's pink-latex pole dance.

"Why not? It's a free country," Milas grinned. "Besides, the kid's got an American passport. He might as well use it."

Hawk shook his head in puzzlement over the ambiguous use of pronouns and decided he'd better go check on Phet.

"How do you think you can help?" asked Marnie.

"Remember those bugs we discussed?"

"Uh huh?" Marnie was skeptical, as she'd been hashing this through and hadn't seen a way to exploit them.

"I've got a feeling that none of those are going to work for us. Your Junior is an entirely new system on an entirely different platform. Whatever system or systems Major Bacon is using to affect Junior's thinking is where we'd need to be to fix this. If my hunch is correct, these systems are far removed and probably hiding somewhere within the impenetrable walls of the NSA. The only thing we'd be able to do to them, even if we did have access, is to get them to stop feeding Junior. I take it by what you've already told me and by what we're seeing in the news that Junior's already made his mind up a while back, so we either need to change it or give him a lobotomy. But even then, there's got to be backup systems in place that would make it easy to rebuild him. The problem is with people, not the machine. And people are just as buggy as computers—probably more so. Changing people's minds requires another strategy."

"What are you suggesting, Colonel?" asked Mark.

"The truth will set you free!" Milas beamed in response.

"I'm not following," said Marnie.

"Don't worry, neither am I," Milas grinned. "But that's normal for me. I do have a few ideas that I believe we can form into a plan. Plan B, if you will." He gestured to Mark. "We're going to need to tap into a few other resources as well if it's going to work."

"Such as?" asked Marnie.

"An inside man would definitely help. Barring that, we'll need some Russians."

"I'm going to pretend I didn't hear that last part," said Mark. "What do you mean, an inside man?"

"This admiral you spoke of, would that be Admiral Ephraim Chase?"

"Yes, it would," said Mark somewhat dubiously.

"That old squid and I go back a long way. As far as I know, Eph's not one who sits around dreaming up reasons to go to war for fun and profit; however, God help you if he sees you as a threat. He can be a formidable opponent.

"The problem as I see it is that he's working for people who have far less integrity than he does. The president and the cast of hawks who have his ear have invaded two countries during their administration. This is the same bunch of cronies that were trying to persuade Reagan to go to war with the Soviets. Luckily, I and a few of the sane people involved back then were able to convince him that nuclear war with anyone was a bad idea. The sane ones, however, have failed to prevent anything under the dust-cloud of 9/11. Eph now has to deal with threats from an opposition that is constantly growing due to this same administration's aggressive foreign policies. The world hates America more than ever, and as head of the NCTC, he has to see evidence of this on a daily basis.

"Eph was on my side back in the eighties with Reagan, and we're all still here to talk about it, though I took a stroll in the deep end as a result. I think we can still have him on our side, especially considering the backlash that's happening right now with the Muslim community."

"Colonel, what is your take on these protests?" Mark asked. "Marnie says you predicted this would happen."

"I wouldn't say I predicted anything, but I'm pretty sure I know what's happening now," said Milas. "I was admittedly caught off guard when Marnie decided to show up in Thailand. I've been a recluse for several years and wasn't quite prepared for the load she dumped on me with Junior and all that comes with it. I told her what I knew and what I thought, but now that I've had time to think things through, I believe we definitely have a situation on our hands. What if I were to suggest that these demonstrations are the precursors of a carefully laid plan?"

"Go on," said Mark.

"And what if these are only the first in a series of orchestrated social manipulations targeted to change the world's political landscape through wide-spread revolution?" Milas continued.

"You're saying that the people themselves are being used as weapons in a war," stated Mark. His tone was that of revelation.

"That's what I'm saying, yes. And they're not even aware that they're being used. They think they are fighting for their own principles—which indeed they are—but they can't possibly see the bigger picture because it's unfathomable."

"What about Junior?" Marnie asked.

"I think he's several moves ahead of everyone, and those that are using him to plan all this are being used as well."

"What is Junior's ultimate goal?" asked Mark.

"Only for the world to descend into total chaos and bring on the end of days," Marnie answered.

Mark blinked at her.

"Seriously, I'm not joking. You can ask him," she said pointing at Milas.

Milas nodded and did his best to look contrite.

"God almighty," muttered Mark. "This is bigger than any of us."

"How can we stop the major?" Marnie asked.

"Tell me something," said Milas, changing the subject. "What about this car accident you were talking about earlier?"

Marnie described Vendetti's car accident and the information she'd learned from Salome as well as Agents Short and Jenkins.

"Hmm," Milas said.

"Hmm, what?" asked Marnie.

"Just hmm for now," he said with intentional vagueness. "Did you people hear about the apartment fire?"

Mark and Marnie nodded.

"I'll have you know that the occupant of that apartment used his seven-minutes during the Senate hearing last week to harshly criticize the administration over the failures in Iraq. He got so caught up hearing himself talk that he left no time for General Petreaus to respond to his rant."

"And?" asked Marnie.

"And Miss Marnie, as my son likes to call you apparently, I believe your conspiracy—if you want to call it that—runs much higher than our friend Major Bacon. He's a pawn in a much larger game. Yes, he may be a bit overenthusiastic when it comes defining what makes a patriot, but that boy's just following orders. It's something he's damn good at. The real problem is with the people giving those orders, and that happens to be the folks who inhabit that large white building on Pennsylvania Avenue."

"You're saying that the White House firebombed Senator Obama's apartment?" Mark said with serious doubt.

"No, what I'm saying is that the office of the president is larger than any one man. And it's the obligation of that office to fulfill America's destiny, which depending on who's in office may involve the use of some very sordid tactics, including a little project called Phoenix. I am sure now that Phoenix is alive and well, and that the administration is using Junior to carry out some mandate via your aptly named Machiavellian mode. What they are unaware of are Junior's ulterior motives. In short, the gloves are off and Junior's calling the shots because some dumb ass has asked it how America can remain as the world's dominant superpower. The real problem is that they are following through with the plan.

"And this Armageddon stuff in your code?" asked Mark.

"Like I told Marnie, it's a doozie." Milas wasn't smiling now. The protests are just the first in a chain of events. Some very bad things will happen if the chain is not broken."

"Like what?" asked Marnie.

"Well, what are some of the worst scenarios that your team on Project X has imagined?"

"The worst?" Marnie thought aloud. "Attacks on the nation's supply chain could cripple the economy. Poisoning of water systems and food sources could lead to widespread illness and famine. There's the sabotage of nuclear plants, defense systems…"

"Excellent," Milas interjected. "All could be construed as signs of the apocalypse. Now imagine if my program were to run on a system that was actually able to act on its directives."

They stared at him dumbstruck as the horrific possibilities steeped in their minds.

"Computers control everything today." Marnie added. "Barriers that have prevented the intercommunication of computer systems have mostly been eliminated. Some of these barriers have been overcome through the advancement of technology, and quite a few have been bypassed in the name of national security. Junior is incredibly well connected through the Nexus, and I'd guess that whatever other systems the major may be hiding are equally so."

"And because of this, the Phoenix program has access to everything." Mark concluded.

"Maybe not everything, but enough to do some real damage." Milas answered, reaching to tug at his beard that was no longer there. "There's one more thing. History has shown that nations can recover from singular catastrophic events. My program knows this. When it launches its assault, it will be a combination of attacks. The result will be both overwhelming and devastating. Whoever is planning on seeing the course of action through that Junior has laid out for them is not preserving the American way of life. They are going to destroy it and a whole lot more."

"Colonel, even if you are right about this, how do we prove it?" asked Mark.

"I have an idea germinating at this very moment for that." Milas's smile returned.

Hawk knocked on the open door. "Excuse me, Mark?"

"What is it, Hawk?"

"Melanie just told me she received a call stating that I'm not needed anymore at the NCTC. According to the message, nobody from here is to enter the building for any reason until further notice."

Mark was stunned. "What the—"

"I believe the admiral's superiors have spoken," said Milas.

"I think it's time for Plan B," said Marnie.

"I'm with you there," said Milas. "I just need to do one thing before we get to that."

"What's that, Colonel?" asked Mark.

"I'm going to get my son back."

Chapter 38

AFTER CHANGING OUT OF HIS UNIFORM and into a pair of faded Levis, a flannel shirt, and some well-worn wallabies, Milas found Phet and Joe in the company canteen. They were eating. While Phet had grown accustomed to western food, having spent nearly half his life in the States, Joe had barely had a thing to eat since she'd arrived. Phet had a stash of instant noodles in his desk for just such an occasion. He'd nearly lived on these during his first year at school. Their distinctive Thai flavor fed his belly as well as helped to stave off homesickness.

Joe was eating her noodles loudly while talking even more loudly between slurps. Hawk was sitting there mesmerized, in an apparent state of enchantment and confusion.

Milas approached their table and sat opposite Phet, who looked at him calmly but distantly. "Ah, Mama noodles! Now where'd you get a hold of those?"

Joe simply pointed at Phet and kept on talking. The melody of her voice as she spoke Thai to her brother was like a tonal roller coaster. When she neared the bottom of her noodles, she picked up the bowl and downed the remainder in one big gulp.

"Ai, Phet!" she said, waving her hand in front of her mouth.

Hawk looked at Phet, who didn't answer.

"Phet means spicy in Thai," offered Milas.

"Ah, I get it. Um, hey, Joe... sephine," Hawk stumbled, "How would you like to give these two some time to talk. Do you like computers? I'll show you the lair."

"Josephine like computer," she said getting up, revealing a pierced navel on her taught, dark-skinned stomach. She was wearing a belly shirt and low-rider jeans that showed off more than just her abs.

Before Hawk made it to the door, Milas called out, "Boy?"

Hawk stopped in his tracks. "Yes, sir?" he asked.

"You do realize that's my *son*, right."

"And my brother," said Phet.

Hawk looked at Joe. She was gorgeous.

"I'll take good care of him, sirs," he said and led her from the room.

Milas watched them leave and shook his head, then turned to Phet. "I have missed you," he said.

Phet remained quiet, staring at Joe's empty noodle bowl. He then said, "You don't even know me."

"How much did your brother tell you?"

Milas watched his son struggle under a weight of pent up emotion.

"Enough," Phet finally said.

"Enough for what?"

"Enough to still hate you."

"Hate me for what?"

"For not telling me why you abandoned me and my mother."

Milas felt his throat begin to ache as he looked into his son's eyes and saw his pain.

❀ ❀ ❀

MILAS HAD GIVEN UP HOPE on Santana almost from the moment he'd left the orphanage. There was something about the man's tone that made him feel that there was some sort of grudge the pastor held against him. Perhaps he associated Milas with the vets whose careless actions resulted in the children that Santana now cared for. "Who knows?" he thought, and decided to once again put Fon out of his mind.

Still recovering from his bout of alcohol poisoning, Milas focused his will power on not becoming belligerently drunk again, rationing himself to two bottles of Singha per night. He found a gym where he could work out during the days, and spent a good deal of time reading novels he picked up at the used bookstores on Ko Sahn Road.

Milas was just starting to feel as if his head was screwed on straight. The exercise and abstinence from Bangkok's nightlife were having a positive effect. He lay on the floor of his room under the wash of the air-con with his feet propped up on the edge of the bed. He was nearing the climax of Clive Cussler's *Night Probe!* when he heard a faint tapping on his door. He didn't need the housekeeper interrupting his read so he hollered, *"Mai dong tam!"* loud enough for the maid to hear and move along her business. There was another light tap on the door. Milas groaned and folded the corner of the page he was on and got up. He was ready to explain the meaning of *mai dong tam* to the housekeeper though he knew perfectly well she already did. As he yanked open the door, he said, "I said, I don't need—"

Fon was standing before him. They stared at one another, each at sea in a storm of rekindled emotions. She stepped forward and put her arms around him. After a prolonged moment, Fon stepped back. Her eyes glistened with tears. She pointed to her chest, then her chin, and then at Milas. It was the sign for, "I miss you." Whatever anger he'd held in his heart melted away. Milas began to cry as Fon fell back into his arms.

❀ ❀ ❀

HE ACCOMPANIED FON back to the orphanage where he was reintroduced to Father Santana. Milas was furious when Fon had explained that the school had forced her to cut off communications with him. She'd pleaded for him to come back to the orphanage so that Father Santana could explain.

They sat in Santana's modestly appointed office. Though its furnishings were austere, the room's walls were covered with photographs of the pastor with several notable people, including one with President Jimmy Carter. He noted another where Santana was receiving some type of gift from Her Royal Highness Princess Maha Chakri Sirindhorn of Thailand. Nearly all of the photos included smiling children.

"Colonel Milas, I can understand your anger with this situation," said Santana. "But this mission established a strict policy early on that forbids written contact with foreigners for those under our care. We have seen all too often how these communiqués wind up creating false hopes and unnecessary heartache on both sides of the equation. Both of which, we have learned, undermine the process of progress toward a more positive outlook on life, which is necessary for moving on."

"Who do you think you are?" Milas seethed. "What do you know about my side of the equation?"

"I only know that you are here now in person. This is a lot more than I can say for the fathers of the children who have passed through these halls. Our Fon here is a very special young woman; however, I sincerely believe that had she not come to me to explain the circumstances that she found herself in seven years ago that she would not be sitting here as an educated young member of our organization. She would more than likely be working in a bar or brothel like the countless others who have fallen to the same fate. I personally have the highest admiration for her and her courage to overcome her handicap and excel as she has in spite of the tribulations she's endured."

"You make it sound as if I was somehow wrong for loving her—that I would have somehow prevented her from becoming who she is. I can't say I'm not offended by what you're suggesting," Milas said soberly.

"It's time for you to know something, Colonel," said Santana, rising from behind his desk. He walked to the door of his office. "I'll ask that you refrain from speaking unless spoken to. The child does not know his father, and I'm the closest thing he has to one." Santana opened the door and beckoned a young boy to enter his office. The boy ran to Fon and hugged her. They exchanged a few signs, and the boy looked at Milas.

"Hello, Mister," said the boy.

"Hello, young man," Milas said, "And that's colonel to you." He gave the boy a salute, which the boy mimicked in return, smiling shyly.

Fon tapped the boy on his shoulder so that he would see what she had to say. They exchanged another series of gestures and the boy left them, giving Milas another salute and a smile.

Santana returned to sit at his desk. He gave Milas a look that seemed to convey regret. "Colonel Milas, that boy is your son."

Milas was leveled at hearing this news from Santana. He turned to Fon, who only nodded in confirmation. All at once, he saw her in a different light. She was the mother of his child. His heart swelled and sank simultaneously. To have had a son and to have missed the golden years of his childhood without knowing he even existed seemed a cruel punishment. "If I'd only known," he said. His voice was a distant murmur.

"If you had known, Colonel, what would you have done?" asked Santana. "Would you have left your life and your career to be the father of this boy? I am not going to say that you are like the other fathers who did learn that they had children and knowingly left them behind as they returned to their life back home, but I will say that the track record of U.S. soldiers in this regard is deplorable. It is the reason of our mission here and the reason we were willing to help Fon raise the child and become an independent woman without pining her life away over someone who would never return."

"But, I'm here now," said Milas, humbled.

"Indeed you are, which poses a certain dilemma for us," said Santana. "Are you here for Fon, or are you here to become a father, Colonel Milas?"

Milas couldn't answer immediately.

"I want you to rest assured that the child has been well cared for," added Santana. He's a very well loved boy, as I am sure that you can imagine with Fon as his mother. He will continue to be cared for as long as he stays within our walls. With all our other children, we are very selective when it comes to prospective parents, for we do not wish to see our work cast to the wind. Parents must be competent and willing to sacrifice in order to raise a child properly."

"Are you saying that I cannot be a father to my own son?" asked Milas.

"I am saying that you have a choice to make. I have discussed this in great detail with Fon, and I expect that you will come to a decision with her. Every child deserves and needs a father; however, when you arrived here the other day I was compelled to run a background check on you. This is standard procedure for all would-be parents. Regardless, you can imagine my alarm when I discovered that you are considered an anti-government activist. If I may be frank, the circumstances surrounding your abrupt departure from the United States and coming here to Thailand give me pause. I cannot say in good faith that I believe the child will be better off under your care than ours."

Santana's words stung him. "What can I do to earn your trust, Father," asked Milas.

Santana sighed. "It's not just my trust you'll need to earn, but if it were up to me, I would ask that you stay away from the child and from Fon until you can get your priorities straight and your life back on track. I'll leave you two alone to discuss this." Santana got up and walked from the room.

Although Santana's words cut sharply, Milas was reluctant to dispute the truth behind them. He knew he was a wreck, and the last thing he wanted was to derail Fon's life even if that meant staying away from his newly discovered son. Santana was right. Though he wanted to prove him wrong, Milas wasn't sure how he'd provide a better life for his son or for Fon in his current condition.

"I think I should leave," he told Fon with sadness in his voice.

Fon pointed at him then extended her pinky and thumb horizontally, bouncing it twice in the air. "You stay," she said.

"I can't take care of you. I can't take care of myself."

Fon rolled her eyes at him. She pointed at herself, and then extended the first and second fingers of each hand. She then stacked these atop each other at an angle and made a churning motion. She finished the phrase by pointing at him. "I'll take care of you," she'd signed.

"You're going to do my laundry?" he asked, knowing this was probably not what she meant.

She hit her forehead with the front of her fist, "Stupid!" Fon got up and pulled a book from Santana's collection. She then wrote a note on a piece of paper and handed both to him. The book was a dictionary of sign language. The note read, "Class starts tomorrow at noon. Don't be late, Colonel."

⌘ ⌘ ⌘

THEY TOOK THINGS SLOWLY. When Milas shared the tragedy of losing Daphne, Fon could not help but feel an initial pang of jealousy. She realized that she could not blame him for moving on with his life after she had stopped writing, and she became more concerned by how deeply affected he was from his wife's traumatic death. He was in a state of mind that could only be healed with time and love, and she would give him both.

Milas was coming to the orphanage five days a week. Fon taught him sign language over her lunch breaks, and then he'd leave her to her classes. She was remarkable with the kids, and they loved her. Both Milas and Fon had decided not to tell their son the nature of their relationship, until after they both knew that things were going to work out.

And work out things did. Eighteen months after Milas had reunited with Fon she became pregnant with their second child. Father Santana, who had grown to respect Milas in spite of his initial failings, insisted that he preside over their Christian wedding ceremony. The Thai ceremony would be held up-country in Chiang Mai, where Fon's family lived.

They both hoped for a girl.

Chapter 39

MILAS GOT UP FROM THE TABLE and ventured over to the soda machine. He scanned the offerings and said, "What, no red Fanta?" He bought two A&Ws and returned to Phet, cracking his own can open and enjoying the acidic bite of the root beer.

"So you see, son, there's more to this story than you know. I loved your mother, and I still do. And we both love you. As time went on, we didn't think it necessary to tell you I was your real father. You and Joe were happy kids. And I *was* your father. It wasn't until you were leaving for college that you got a bug up your ass about who your *real* father was. And when we told you, we had no idea you'd react the way you did. We didn't hide anything from you to hurt you, Phet."

Phet was quiet and avoided talking by opening his soda and taking a sip.

"But boy, do you know how to hold a grudge," he told his son. "You came out here almost fifteen years ago, and you haven't been home since. Your mom misses you, Phet. Joe misses you. I miss you."

"Why am I so stupid?" Phet scowled.

"You'll have to ask your mother, I'm sure she'll say you got that from me."

Phet couldn't help but smile, though still obviously pained.

"We're proud of you, Phet. Both your mother and I are enormously proud of the man you have become. You've done good, kid. I'd at least like to be in your life to be able to tell you that every once in a while. But at this point, I'd even settle if you'd just be my friend on Facebook."

Phet sniffed and ran his nose along his shirtsleeve. He then uttered one of the longest discourses of self-abusing profanity his father had ever heard. Milas waited.

Marnie walked in. "Um, Colonel, are you two ready for Plan B?"

Milas looked at his son, and used his hands to sign, "Are we good?"

Phet made a fist and bounced it twice palm down in the air, "Yes." He then took his fist and moved it in a circular motion over his heart, "I'm sorry." His face said the same.

"Yes, Miss Marnie, I believe we are ready to conquer the beast," said Milas as he reached over and tousled his son's hair for the first time in what seemed an eternity.

❈ ❈ ❈

They gathered in a meeting room adjacent to Mark's office.

"Colonel, she probably shouldn't be here for this," said Marnie, looking at Joe.

Milas nodded. "Joe, are you still hungry?" he asked.

"Joe is starving!" she snapped.

"I'll take her to get something," offered Hawk.

"We need you here," said Mark. He then used the speakerphone to dial Melanie. "Melanie, I need you to take the colonel's, er, daughter to lunch."

"I'll be right there, sir."

"Have her take you to Pasa Thai," Phet told his brother in Thai. "And tell Janya, the chef, that Phet sent you. You'll get real food."

Melanie arrived. "Bring something back for all of us, would you?" Mark said.

"Of course, sir," she said. "Shall I take your orders?"

"Let him choose," said Milas, implying Joe.

"Very well," she said, "Come along Ms. Josephine."

Mark called the attention back to the table. "I've just spoken with Admiral Chase over a secured line. The news is not good. The order to have us removed from the premises came directly from the White House. His hands are tied. I mentioned that Colonel Milas was in town, and that piqued his interest. He said to say, 'Hello,' sir. He also said that he was rustling up the Old Guard and that you would know what that meant, but he added for us not to hold our breath."

"He's a crafty old seadog, that Eph," said Milas. "What he meant is that he's garnering support for his own attack, but if we have a plan of our own, we should not hesitate to use it."

"So, just what is our plan?" said Marnie.

Milas turned to Phet and asked, "You wouldn't happen to know how to get a hold of a bot-net would you, son?"

"I might," he said charily.

"Out with it, Phet," said Marnie.

"I've used them before. I know how to gain access to more than one."

"What exactly is a bot-net?" asked Mark.

"A bot-net is a collection of computers," said Milas. "They are linked together by the commonality that they have all been compromised by some kind of computer virus. Russian mafia types are somewhat infamous for designing these viruses and propagating them out across the Internet. It's a very lucrative business. Once a machine is infected, it can be controlled remotely to perform a variety of tasks under the nose of their unwitting users. These machines send out tons of spam and infect as many other computers as they can, but that's not what we're really looking for. What we want is a—"

"Denial of service attack!" said Phet. "That is my plan!"

"Great minds think alike, my boy," he said, smiling at Phet. He then addressed the others. "A bot-net can consist of thousands of computers. The more the merrier. When enough machines focus an attack on a single target, it can be rendered completely inoperable. You may have heard of Web War 1 back in April, where the websites of Estonia's banks, ministries, parliament, and the media were overwhelmed and taken down. And then there was Titan Rain, where it's thought that the Chinese had coordinated a series of cyber-attacks against the United States. Both of these attacks used bot-nets to carry out their cyber-warfare."

"The NCTC has some of the most sophisticated firewall and intrusion protection systems I've ever seen," said Hawk.

"I would imagine so," said Milas. "However, we're not looking to take the place down. I think we already know that's impossible. What we can do is get them to look in the other direction while we make off with the gold."

"Are you saying what I think you're saying?" asked Mark.

"That depends on what you think I'm saying," Milas smiled. "Do you really want to know?"

"Yes, because if you're planning on breaking into one of the most highly guarded information centers in the world, it better not damn well be from here."

"Not to worry. If there's one thing I've learned, it's to cover my tracks, or better yet, not to leave any at all."

"And you two are going to make sure of this?" Mark looked at Marnie and Phet.

Phet nodded. Marnie was staring out the window.

"Marnie?" Mark asked.

"I'm thinking, Mark." Marnie grabbed two handfuls of her hair and pulled tightly. What Milas was proposing was a heist of phenomenal proportion. Hacking a bank was one thing. Marnie had read about the Russian computer geek, Vladimir Levin, who electronically lifted ten million dollars from Citibank in 1994. He'd bought the information that allowed him to pull it off for a hundred dollars.

Hacking the NCTC was incredibly dangerous. There was zero margin for error. It could be considered treason if they were caught. Marnie thought of the Major Ray. She thought of Salome's news clippings, the threats leading up to Vendetti's car accident, and the fire at the senator's apartment. She thought of the Muslim protests and all of the scenarios that Milas predicted would follow.

"There will be more if something's not done about this, but is it really up to us?" she thought to herself. Finally, after a lengthy moment of inner contemplation, she let out a deep sigh. "We have to," she said. "We have to do it." Her voice and the look in her eyes conveyed her determination.

"Okay, I want to review the plan before it's enacted," said Mark. "All of this is off the record. No emails, no files stored on the network, pencil and paper only. Got it?"

They all nodded.

"I'm not much help here, so I'm going to go find out what's happening with Salome. I'll check on John as well. You know how to find me, Marnie, if you need me." Mark left them to it.

"People, I'm going need your help in knowing as much about Junior as I can," said Milas. "I'm guessing you're running a Cray supercomputer, is that right?

"It's a state of the art Cray XMT," said Hawk. "The model has not been released to the public yet. We're the first group to be working on it other than Cray themselves. The operating system is Cray's own as well."

"How about interfaces? I understand that Junior is fed data from a multitude of sources," said Milas.

"There's an API we use to do this," said Marnie, referring to the application programming interface she built upon to create the Nexus. "It's basically BSD with extensions from Cray. We then developed upon that to create our own interfaces to support differing types of data flows."

"Berkeley Software Distribution. I like it!" said Milas. "Would you believe I used the first Berkeley Unix system on their DEC PDP-11?"

"You're really old," said Phet.

"Hey, don't knock it. It's where my bug began, before you were even a glimmer in my eye," Milas remarked. "What about the programming language for the data-mining application itself?"

"We defaulted to a message passing interface to allow programmers to write code in C++. This gets tweaked for the parallel processing environment then re-compiled to run natively on the Cray," Marnie explained.

"So, if I were to write something in C++, it could conceivably run on Junior?"

"With some tweaks, yes."

"Interesting," said Milas. His eyes twinkled.

"Mr. Hawk, we're going to need you to map out the infrastructure and security elements within the NCTC. We'll need subnets, gateways, firewall placements, and details on their intrusion detection and prevention systems."

Hawk went to the whiteboard and began sketching things out. Milas watched intently as the NCTC network took shape before their eyes.

"Colonel, how do you plan on getting a program onto Junior?" Marnie inquired.

"If I'm right, I believe Phet's been planning a phishing expedition," he said. "It looks we're finally going to have that father-son trip after all."

BY 5:00PM THEY'D HASHED OUT A PLAN that was ready for Mark's review. Marnie retrieved him from his office, and he joined them in the conference room. Mark sat down and saw a lone container of food.

"Ah, you saved me some," he said. "Thanks, guys. I haven't eaten all day. Go ahead. I can munch on this and listen at the same time." He opened the container and attacked it with a plastic spork.

Marnie began. "Plan B consists of a multi-phased—"

"Holy mother of God!" Mark exclaimed. They looked at him with knowing smiles. He punched the speakerphone. "Melanie! Ice water! Stat!" He looked at his team and said, "This is the hottest thing I've ever had in my life. You people are evil." Mark closed the container and pushed it away to a safe distance. Melanie arrived with a pitcher of ice water and glasses for everyone.

"Just wait till you see what we've cooked up for Major Bacon," Milas smirked.

Mark waved his hands in the air, motioning for them to continue as he filled his mouth with water in an attempt to quell the fire that burned there.

Marnie outlined the attack for Mark. She skipped over much of the technical details and focused mainly on the strategic and tactical elements of the plan. Mark absorbed it all, asking a few key questions along the way. His vast knowledge of war strategy allowed him to make a few suggestions of his own.

"So phase one is the phishing attack," he began to summarize. "This lays the ground work for a zero-day attack on the internal systems. When that attack commences, we enter phase two. This is the denial of service attack launched from distributed zombie computers across the Internet. This gets them looking in the wrong direction. The *coup de grâce* is the Trojan horse."

"That's it in a nutshell, yes," said Marnie.

"Colonel, you and Phet proceed with phase one," said Mark.

"Already underway," said Phet.

"He's crafted several rather seductive looking emails that are spectacularly authentic," Milas added. "If we're successful in poisoning their upstream DNS servers, this attack will be more effective; however, it's not entirely necessary. All we need is a few clicks on the right emails to bring the payload onto an NCTC workstation. After that, the worm should spread unnoticed. We wrote it from scratch so there's no fingerprint patterns for the security systems to act on. It'll remain dormant until Z-Day. According to Mr. Hawk, they're not running differential file comparisons on the workstations so unless the worm spreads to a server—which it shouldn't—we're good."

"Denial of service attack?" asked Mark.

"A twelve-thousand node bot-net is rentable for two-hundred dollars per day, according to Phet," said Milas. "We'll be launching the phishing attacks I just mentioned from one of these. It will generate emails to virtually every known combination of English names that match the naming conventions of their email system. It's first name, dot, last initial. Some email is bound to get through, and someone's bound to click on one of Phet's emails, which as I said will bring in the virus. For the DoS attack, we're going to aim another bot-net at their edge firewall to get their attention focused externally and away from what we're actually doing."

"Isn't the payment for these bot-nets traceable?" asked Mark.

"I pay cash long time ago to stranger. I have credit. No tracing," said Phet.

"I do not want to know why, Phet, but okay," said Mark. "The Trojan?"

"That's something I still need to write, and it's our weak point," said Milas. "It still needs someone to get it onto Junior. This is going to require some psychological finesse that preys upon the young major's ambitions." Milas outlined his plan for Mark.

"I was wrong," said Mark. "You people are not evil. You're diabolical."

"Can we start the phish?" asked Marnie.

"What do you need to do?" asked Mark.

"Press one button," said Phet.

"Make it so," said Mark. They all watched as Phet clicked a button on his laptop screen labeled, 'Let's Go Phishing!'"

"What do we do now?" asked Mark.

Together, Milas and Phet said, "We wait."

Chapter 40

MARK HAD GOTTEN WORD from Agent Short that Salome had been released from questioning. Short mentioned that he and Jenkins had uncovered some further evidence that they wanted to share in private, and he asked that they come to the Bureau headquarters. He and Marnie left the team to keep working; it was more than likely they'd continue into the evening at the hotel room Milas had taken at the Sheraton National in Arlington. Hawk offered to join the Milas duo so as to offer technical assistance, though it was obvious that he would be serving to keep Joe occupied while they worked on the Trojan code.

The J. Edgar Hoover building was well lit when Mark and Marnie arrived. The structure's brutalist architectural design and the exterior constructed from poured concrete gave it the appearance of a modern castle that glowed from within. They were escorted to a briefing room where they were met by Agent Short.

"Where's Salome?" asked Marnie immediately upon seeing Short.

"Don't worry. Miss Kahn has been very cooperative," said Short. "I must say that she's a dignified and highly-intelligent woman. Right now she's having something to eat. You can see her in a short while. She's free to go.

"Safiya Barazani, on the other hand, has been less cooperative. We picked her up on campus earlier this afternoon. She had a chance to fire off a message from her BlackBerry, but we think we managed to shut it off before a remote wipe could be executed on the device. We've got copies of the emails she's sent and received, but they're encrypted. The device is with our white-coats now. They're pulling what they can off the handset. Barazani is still being interrogated, but she's not doing much talking."

"You should check on how her tuition is being paid," said Marnie.

"We're looking into that already, thanks," said Short, looking somewhat impressed by Marnie.

"Is this the new evidence you wanted to share with us?" asked Mark.

"Partially, Mr. Harmann," said Short. "Miss Kahn was particularly helpful with regards to the emails that you found on Mr. Vendetti's computer. She told us that while they did make sense, they were grammatically incorrect. She's of the opinion that whoever wrote them was not a native Arabic speaker."

"That's odd," said Mark.

"Yes, odd enough to get our interest. As you may know, there is a shortage of Arabic resources in the U.S. security community, and those that we have onboard are in high demand. Many of us rely on computer-based translation programs to perform initial subject matter analysis; however, we need true native speakers be able to understand subtle nuances and deeper meaning. What it looks like is that these emails were generated by one of these translation programs. In fact, we believe that they were created by a specific language software that is not available to the general public and is only used by U.S. government agencies."

"Woah," said Marnie. "The government is behind these emails?"

"Or an organization that is working for the government," replied Short. "Now take a look at these." He slid a folder that contained some photographs across the table. "We were able to pull more video feeds from the Key Bridge traffic cameras. That black blur is Mr. Vendetti's BMW leaving the frame. The taxi in the other shot is the one we saw from the Marriott video. The driver is clearly visible. Do you notice anything about this picture that's odd?"

"Well," said Mark. "They're kind of blurry. The driver's wearing sunglasses, and it looks like it's already dark out."

"Look closer," said Short. Marnie leaned over to get a better look. What she saw chilled her to the marrow.

"Mark, remember when I told you I thought I was being followed? That's the guy!"

"Are you sure? You can hardly see his face," said Mark. "Wait a minute. I *can* see his face. His glasses are up on his forehead. He's got raccoon eyes like a skier."

"Correct," said Short. "I want you to also note that the driver is Caucasian. Those white rings around his eyes suggest that he's either very tan or he's wearing make-up to darken his skin. We suspect the latter based on trace residue of make-up foundation our forensics team picked up in the taxi." Short turned to Marnie. "What is this about being followed, Miss McCloud?"

Marnie gave him a brief run-down of her feeling of being watched at the park. "Mark, I could swear that's him."

"We're running the images through facial recognition software, but there have been no hits yet. Even with image enhancement, we're not sure we'll get a match."

"What does all this mean?" asked Mark.

"The evidence seems to be telling a different story from what we originally thought after investigating the crime scenes of the accident and the abandoned taxi. We're beginning to believe that whoever is behind this went to great lengths to make it appear that the act was perpetrated by foreign nationals, specifically a Middle-Eastern man."

"For what possible reason?" asked Marnie.

"We don't know," said Short. "To antagonize someone maybe? Hate? We understand through our investigation and having spoken with Miss Kahn that Professor Vendetti and his work represents a significant positive effort toward the peaceful resolution of differences between Christians and Muslims. He's a symbol that personifies understanding between these two religions, and there are some bad people on both sides of the fence." Short paused for a moment, studying the pair before him. "I understand you've been in contact with Colonel Andrew Milas," he said.

Mark and Marnie looked at each other.

"How could you possibly know that?" asked Marnie.

"We're the FBI," Short said matter-of-factly. "I only mention this because Colonel Milas had a similar car accident that remains an open case to this day." Short described what he knew of Milas's accident and the death of his wife.

"Are these accidents connected?" asked Mark.

"Only in that they were not accidents," said Short. "I just thought you should know that Colonel Milas's accident is what led to his supposed instability. Right now, what's important and what's really got some folks roused is evidence we've found in the aftermath of the apartment fire at Senator Obama's. There are clues of a false evidence plant similar to Mr. Vendetti's car accident. Whoever's behind this is doing their best to pin this on Islamic radicals."

"Can I tell you something off the record, Agent Short?" asked Mark.

"In confidence? Certainly." Short nodded.

Mark told him of their work on Project X and how in building Junior, they had given the government a valuable and dangerous tool. It was a tool that could possibly be behind the events that had unfolded in recent days. However, the idea that anyone was acting out Junior's directives—against innocent civilians on the streets of Washington D.C. no less—was unthinkable. He did not mention Milas's theory that the administration was behind it or that Junior was trying to bring about Armageddon at the risk of sounding like he'd completely lost his marbles.

"And just how and who do you say are being targeted by this system?" asked Short.

"We can't say, but it's apparent that Junior isn't squeamish about who, and he definitely fights dirty," said Mark.

"Mr. Harmann, that is one of the wildest stories I have heard in a very long time."

Mark looked at Marnie. "It does sound pretty far fetched, I admit."

"Well, I too will admit that crazier stories have been investigated by the FBI, and some of them have turned out to be true," said Short. "And I'm not talking X-Files crazy either. I'm talking seriously scary stuff here. If who's behind the story is some whack-job at the Puzzle Palace or our Christian cousins from Foggy Bottom, anything is possible. While it might appear we work together these days, they still play some very dangerous games on their own. If some of the things I've heard about were ever to become known to the public, we'd be dealing with a nation of very upset citizens. I sincerely hope you are not right about this Junior business, but if you are, may God, Allah, or whoever help us all."

Chapter 41

VENDETTI WAS LOOKING VASTLY IMPROVED since their last visit. His facial swelling had diminished considerably, and the bandages around his head had been removed. Marnie and Salome each took a position on opposite sides of the bed and Mark helped himself to the room's refrigerator.

"They serve wine here?" Mark asked.

"It's medicinal," said Vendetti, winking at Salome. "Good for the heart they say. By all means, help yourself."

"Ladies?" Mark asked, presenting a split of California Zinfandel in one hand and an Australian Shiraz in the other. "You've had a long day, haven't you?" Mark cracked the Shiraz first and poured them each a serving into cone shaped paper cups.

"So tell me," said Vendetti. "What *is* going on? I'm comatose for a couple days and the Muslim world is in a frenzy. With the only thing keeping me company being television news commentary from blithering idiots, I'm about to go stark raving mad! They should be interviewing *me* for God's sake, not these pundits who act as if they know what they're talking about. Islam is crying out for justice and the media is rattling sabers. They're making Americans look like a bunch of ignorant jingoists."

"John," said Mark. "We just picked up Salome from the FBI."

"The FBI?" he cried.

"It is fine, John," assured Salome. "They had some questions for me about the file and my father. They were respectful and seemed genuinely concerned for my well being as well as yours. I was treated well, and I cooperated with them. It was not at all like they show on TV," she smiled.

"And we learned some very distressing facts regarding your car accident," added Mark. "Agent Short has some photographs of the taxi driver, who they are confident is responsible."

"And he's white," said Marnie.

"Intriguing," said Vendetti. "What of Safiya? Is she still suspected of foul play?"

"She's in on it," confirmed Mark. "But she may have been an accomplice of someone who was pandering to her extremist tendencies. Safiya was used—not that it makes up in any way for her involvement. What's more troubling is what Salome discovered regarding the emails we found in your inbox."

Salome told Vendetti of her opinion on them and how Agent Short determined the nature of their origin.

"A government conspiracy?" he exclaimed. "Against me? Whatever for?"

"Agent Short said it could be the work of someone working for the government," said Mark. "He said the whole thing smacks of a setup to make it look like you were the target of a *jihadi* assassination attempt."

"Well, they've done a good job of it," said Vendetti. "Check out page three of the newspaper. Page three! I deserve better coverage than that."

Mark picked the paper from the table beside the bed. He looked at Vendetti and said, "How do you read with your arm in a cast?"

"Nurse Dana. She's actually rather pleasant when no one's looking."

Mark found an article on page three with a headline that read, "Islam Professor in Terrorist Taxi Crash."

"Isn't that the most wretched headline?" said Vendetti in disgust.

Mark read the article aloud for Marnie and Salome. It laid out several aspects of the accident that Mark had assumed were confidential to the investigation. All the facts were interwoven with the innuendo that Vendetti was a victim of a terrorist attack by Islamic fundamentalists operating on American soil. They did not forget to mention that his passenger was Salome, who they portrayed as an Iranian national who had recently entered the country. She was described as a person with a questionable past who was known to have ties with the Martyr's Foundation."

"What utter rubbish!" exclaimed Vendetti. "Does the FBI know who really did this?" He looked at each of their faces.

"We may have just given them a juicy lead," said Marnie.

"I don't think they're going to get very far with it, though," said Mark.

"Salome, what *are* they talking about?" Vendetti was becoming exasperated.

"I think it best they tell you themselves, John," Salome said.

Marnie went through the same spiel that Mark had just delivered to Agent Short.

"Good Lord, what kind of work are you people involved in? Why haven't you told me any of this before?"

"Because it would have voided my security clearance and probably have me sitting in jail cell," answered Marnie.

"You don't seem so tight lipped about it now," said Vendetti.

"Things have changed," said Mark. "But John, you cannot talk about this to anyone."

"I've a right mind to hold a press conference first thing in the morning!" Vendetti's morphine drip kicked in with a beep, giving him a cool rush that calmed him for the moment.

"I have an idea," said Marnie. "Mark, come here for a second." They walked just outside the hospital room's door to talk in private.

When they returned, Marnie said, "We think you should have a press conference, but you need to wait a bit."

"And John," said Mark. "You can't let these people suck you into their game. If you go against them, they might even try to finish the job they started."

"At this moment people need to hear a voice of reason," added Salome. "You need to do what you do best. Be a role model and promote understanding."

"I'm not going to take this lying down," said John.

"Right now you don't have much of a choice," said Mark, prompting a glare from Vendetti. "Sorry, that wasn't meant as a joke. Without any evidence, they'll tear you apart if you start spouting what we just told you."

"You're my evidence," said Vendetti.

"We'd be just as easy targets for the derision of the media if we came out with what we know," said Mark. "We'd also get into some serious trouble. There is no evidence, John."

"Not yet," added Marnie, and she told him about Plan B.

Nurse Dana entered the room and scowled at each of them, jabbing her thumb in the direction of the door.

"I guess that's our cue," said Marnie. "So you'll wait on the press conference?"

"Yes, I'll wait," said Vendetti. "But if your Plan B goes tits up, I may change my mind and go to war with these people."

"That would be extremely unwise, John," said Mark. "You'd be putting yourself right back in their sights."

"I'll take my chances with Nurse Dana anytime," said Vendetti, at which Nurse Dana revealed the faintest trace of a smile.

Chapter 42

MILAS APPROACHED RAY from behind and stood beside him.

Major Ray stared straight ahead and responded to his presence with silence. It was early morning and cold at Arlington National Cemetery. They stood alone along the path that led between the Tomb of the Unknown and the gravesite of President John F. Kennedy. Milas maintained the silence as he read the words upon the copper plaque of the memorial before them.

The block of granite was miniscule in comparison to other memorials of the cemetery. It stood like an islet upon the sea of frosty dew that blanketed the hallowed grounds. It may never have existed at all except for a handful of Americans who had pushed for the recognition of those who had died in the secret Lao theatre of operations during the Vietnam War. Not until 1997 did the United States officially acknowledge the Secret War through the dedication of this memorial to the U.S. Secret Army in the Kingdom of Laos.

"What are you doing, Ronnie?" Milas broke the silence.

"I'm looking at a rock that is the last remaining memory of my father," Ray replied in a flat tone. Milas could sense the anger hidden behind the major's deadpan expression. He knew that Ray's answer was a deflection, but Milas played along out of respect for the man's loss.

"He loved you, you know," Milas told him.

"That doesn't really help when he's dead now, does it?"

Milas sighed. The reality was that Colonel Ray had spent more time in Southeast Asia than he had with his only son. Milas had grown to know the colonel while under his command. Colonel Ray would have made a great father, Milas thought. He often felt a paternal connection with the man, having lost his own father while in his teens. There were many times when Colonel

Ray had spoken of little Ronnie, but he never made it home to be his dad.

"I'm sorry," said Milas. "I don't know what to tell you other than that."

"Then why did you ask me to meet you here, Colonel?" asked Ray. He looked at his watch and said, "You've got five minutes."

"I want to know what you're doing with Phoenix. I think you've started something that you're not going to be able to stop."

"Why would I want to stop it?"

"Because I don't think you know what it's capable of."

At this, Ray turned to face Milas. "I don't think you know what *I'm* capable of," he snapped.

"Oh, I've got an idea," Milas replied as calmly as he could.

"Just what is that supposed to mean?" Ray's voice now revealed his hostility.

"For starters, it means that I know you pretended to befriend Marnie McCloud in order to manipulate her. And I know that you provided her with enough information to cause her to seek me out and bring me back into the game."

"And here you are," Ray said with a dry smirk.

"I also know that you've arranged to have the team that developed Junior removed from the project so that you can operate without any interference."

"Are you ready to help yet?"

"The only thing I'm prepared to help with is preventing you and anyone else from using my system to kill any more innocent people."

"Collateral damage. It's a necessary price we must pay when fighting a war."

"Look around you, Ronnie. Almost every tombstone here is the price of war."

Ray did look around in response to Milas's words, but they did not appear to sway his resolve. "When the War on Terror is won, there will be fewer soldiers to be buried here," he said.

"I'm not here to argue about that."

"Then what? Are you here to tell me about the great conspiracies of the New World Order you're so fond of parroting?" Ray asked with a humorless laugh. He was trying to aggravate Milas, who didn't need to see the antagonizing look in the major's eyes to know he was being needled.

"Ronnie, I know that you're following orders, but I also know you have your own agenda. What you need to realize is that Phoenix also has an agenda, and its scope is far greater than you imagine."

"I've been working with your code for years. I'm pretty sure I know what it does."

"Then why are innocent people still being targeted for murder?"

"I said I know what it does. I didn't say it was perfect. While my system, not yours, does have a near flawless success rate when its plans are carried out to the letter, any variance to a plan dramatically undermines the chance of success. The campaigns that lead to victory are the essential steps to achieve it."

"No matter who dies in the process?"

"Basic chess tactics. That's something you know a little about, isn't it? Spassky vs. Fischer? Sacrificing lesser pieces for the sake of a larger strategy? There is no price too great for the scalp of the enemy king."

"If you're still running my code, your system is going to be responsible for bringing about hell on earth. And I mean that literally."

"Right. And aliens are secretly running the government." Ray rolled his eyes at Milas. "Maybe it's a good thing that you don't want to help me. You're still not playing with a full deck are you?"

Ray reflexively put his hand to his chest and pulled a vibrating BlackBerry from his shirt pocket. "Yep," he answered and turned around to spot a black SUV that was idling up on Roosevelt Drive. "Be right there," he said and returned the phone to his pocket.

"I'm serious, Ronnie," said Milas. "Check the code. It's not as simple as it looks. I wrote it to—"

"—I've heard enough, old man." Ray held up his hand, stopping Milas in mid-sentence. "I've got work to do. You and McCloud best just walk away, and I'm serious about that."

Colonel Ray turned away from Milas and set into a jog toward the SUV.

"Ronnie!" Milas called out after him. "Ronnie!"

Ray never looked back.

Chapter 43

OVER THE NIGHT, the Muslim protests around the world had intensified. America awoke to continued news coverage of the largest publicly-staged vilification the world had ever seen. At home, the protests also continued; however, opposition groups were now joining the fray. Each demonstration site had become a tinderbox, stoked and ready to ignite. Local law enforcement was in place and doing their best to maintain public order. They refrained from arrests for fear the situation would deteriorate, leading to full-scale riots, but it was evident that police action was imminent. In other parts of the world, the protests were far less than civil. Demonstrators from both sides were increasing in numbers, and the riffraff had come out of the woodwork, adding vitriol and the incitement of violence to the already tenuous situation. What began as peaceful demonstrations had now spiraled out of control.

The screens of the NCTC displayed live footage of the swelling crowds of demonstrators as the situation was being closely monitored from war room. Major Ray was on a super-secure line with the Vice President of the United States, while Admiral Chase was attending an emergency meeting at the Pentagon.

"What are our options, Major?" asked the vice president.

"I believe the plan to bring in the National Guard is our best bet, sir," Ray replied.

"What you're talking about is akin to declaring martial law." The vice president's voice was surly, bordering on angry.

"With respect to marital law, the system has put forth that the president is authorized to use the National Guard to restore public order under section 1076 of the John Warner Defense Appropriation Act."

"This goes directly against Admiral Chase's recommendation."

"Respectfully, sir, the admiral is not here right now. And as you know, his nose is rather bent out of shape after he discovered that I've been directly providing you information under the president's order."

"That's understood; however, it could be construed that your information is what's gotten us into this mess."

"Sir, my orders were to provide you with information."

"What was provided was supposed to be a game plan: a beginning, middle, and an end. There's an end game in all of this, and we're stuck in a muskeg. We need actionable strategy at this point, not just information."

"My recommendation is to follow through with the plan you've been given, sir," said Ray. He enunciated these words with a robot-like quality. "At your request, you were provided a course of action that would result in a desired outcome. The system has analyzed all possible permutations to arrive at this course of action. The steps taken thus far are crucial toward achieving the end result. Again, sir, my recommendation is to continue forward. The system hasn't proven to be wrong yet."

"Some may argue with that after they see the National Guard on their streets, Major, and I am not going to mention just how insanely over the line things were with the senator from Illinois. We need to see some forward momentum soon, or we're going to pull it."

It was not hard for Ray to imagine the vice president frothing at the mouth like a rabid wolf from the sound of his voice.

At that moment, all screens in the war room flickered to black.

"Major, are you there?" asked the vice president.

Ray looked around the war room at the baffled crew. A moment later, the screens came back to life.

"I'm here, sir, but I need to go. My recommendation stands."

"I'll be back in touch, Major. Think of something better." The VP cut the line.

Ray sought out the war room's chief engineer. "What was that?" he asked.

"We don't know yet," the man answered nervously.

"Find out," he said and marched back to his office. He sat down and logged into his computer. He checked his email, and after reading the most recent entry, he picked up his phone and dialed the extension of his lead analyst.

"What is this email about Milas?" asked Ray.

"Sir, you've requested that all correspondence sent from Colonel Milas be sniffed."

"Correct."

"We intercepted a series of emails from him to Marnie McCloud," explained the analyst. "They contain encrypted code fragments, but when decrypted and pieced together they form a program."

"How was it encrypted?"

"AES-256, sir."

"How'd you crack it?"

"We didn't. We pulled Ms. McCloud's private key from her workstation and brute forced her password. It took all of about thirty minutes using the Cray."

"Outstanding," said Ray. He knew that Milas would never have sent the mails unencrypted, but his blunder was trusting that Marnie understood security well enough to protect her private key adequately. Ray felt the tide turning his way.

"What does the program do?" he asked his analyst.

"It's remarkable, really; it's a full re-write of Junior's backward-chaining algorithm. It uses techniques we've never even thought of. If Milas wrote this, he's a genius, sir."

"I know that. And stop calling the system Junior."

"Yes, sir."

"Are you sure that's all it does?" demanded Ray.

"That's what it looks like. He uses some strange loops in his coding-style, but from what the team sees it's meant to be a vast improvement over the original code. We've run it in the sandbox, and it works well, sir."

"What could Milas gain by sending this to her?" Ray muttered aloud.

"Excuse me, sir?"

Ray went over the conversation he'd had with Milas earlier in the morning. Milas may be a genius, he thought, but he was still crazy with a head full of wild ideas. Ray couldn't see how the old man could possibly be a threat.

"Send me the code," said Ray. "I want to read it."

"Yes, sir."

"WE GOT PING!" This was Phet, squinting into the screen of his laptop computer. The team had joined forces in Milas's room at the Sheraton National. Mark insisted that everyone be as far away from Burns & Lynch when things went down. They needed every layer of insulation they could to prevent the discovery of their involvement in what was about to happen. He and Marnie were gazing out the windows overlooking the Air Force Memorial. The Pentagon was just beyond, at the bottom of the slope. And off to their left, they could see the graves of fallen soldiers who lay at the southern edge of Arlington National Cemetery.

They turned away from their thoughts at Phet's announcement. Milas, who was wearing a white terry-cloth robe and black socks, began to sing, "We're in the money! We're in the money!" His enthusiasm was overriding the fatigue of his and Phet's all night programming session. "Phase One of Plan B complete!" he chirped.

"What's next?" asked Mark.

"More coffee!" said Milas, picking up the phone and calling room service.

"Phet?" asked Mark.

"The ping means that at least one computer is infected at NCTC."

Milas hung up. "We wrote the virus to send a solitary ping at random intervals within a sixty minute period after time of infection," he said. "These are sent to a server in Malaysia. They should be sparse enough to fly under the radar at least for a while. They should keep trickling in as more machines are infected." Milas gestured with finger quotes in the air. "Should being the optimal word here," he added.

"We have trickling," said Phet, his eyes still glued to the screen.

"Hee hee!" Milas tittered mischievously. "When they stop, it means that someone's picked up on it, which they would be idiots not to, especially when the screen blanker I added to the mix gets them scrambling. That's when we should launch the denial of service decoy attack."

"Malaysia," said Marnie. "Nice touch."

"We got the idea from the Vendetti emails you sent Phet," said Milas. "It does add a certain mystique. Wouldn't you say?"

"How long until Major Ray lets in the Trojan horse?" Mark asked.

"That depends on if he actually bites and whether he can bypass protocol," said Milas. "Any normal human being would test the bejesus out something before putting it into production on a system this vital. I believe our major, however, has his back against the wall with the Muslim situation having deteriorated as it has. He's got two choices, back out or push forward. My bet is that the recipient of his scheme has got him looking to pull a rabbit out of his hat to save the day as well as a few asses."

"But will he do it?" asked Marnie.

"After our little chat this morning, I'm pretty sure that he's dismissed me as a tottering old fool. Your idea of sending the virus disguised as encrypted code fragments for Junior's Machiavellian mode was brilliant. Hopefully, he'll be cocky enough after decrypting the emails to not see that we've served him his head on a platter. I've hidden things very well within Junior's code, and as long as nobody looks too closely, we may actually have a shot at this. If he does load the program on Junior, the Trojan's payload will activate immediately after he runs the next Machiavellian scenario."

There was a knock at the door. "Room service," said a voice on the other side.

"Coffee!" said Milas and scooted across the floor in his socks. He opened the door to find a group of five men standing in a V formation. At the point of the V was a grey-haired man holding a room service tray.

"You haven't changed a bit." Chase smiled, taking in Milas's choice of wardrobe. "I brought some old friends. If you don't mind," he said, eyeing the tray he held. "Your coffee's getting cold."

MAJOR RAY'S FINGERS RACED across the keyboard of his workstation. Milas's work was genius, he thought, as he absorbed it. He'd gone through the code and was now running some preliminary checks on the Muslim scenario in the sandbox. His glimmer of hope grew brighter.

His phone rang. "Yes," he said, reading the extension number of the caller.

"Sir, we've discovered some, er, interesting network activity occurring after the blip."

"I'll be right there," he said and headed for the pit.

"What is it?" he asked curtly as he found his engineer and cut through the cluster of computer geeks hovering around his desk.

"It's something the intrusion detection system flagged. What we're seeing is random data packets being sent outbound. They're meant to look like normal network traffic, but they're not."

"Sent from where?" Ray asked.

"Here, sir," said the engineer. "Several workstations in the building have sent a single ping. The destination address is a server in Malaysia." He paused, then said, "Uh oh."

"Spit it out, man!" barked the major.

"Our edge firewall is shutting down. It's getting hit by something."

"From where?" Ray demanded.

"Hang on, sir," said the flustered engineer, his fingers typed commands in rapid bursts. "Brazil, Russia, China, the United States," he said, scanning the information on his screen. "It's coming from everywhere."

"Lock it down!" Ray growled. "Not a bit of data comes into or leaves this place. You got that?"

"Yes, sir," he said and picked up the phone.

⌘ ⌘ ⌘

"THEIR SHIELDS ARE UP," announced Phet.

"I can't believe I'm watching a Thai hacker give the NCTC a run for its money," said Chase as he sat on the corner of the bed.

His team had taken up similar positions around the now crowded hotel room.

"With a little help from Maybelline," said Milas, batting his eyelashes at his old friend, Chase.

"You know, I'm really glad after all that's happened to you, Andy, you've still managed to keep your sense of humor," he said.

"Thanks, Eph. It's helped keep me sane," said Milas, which resulted in sideways looks from nearly everyone in the room. "Well, mostly sane," he added. They all laughed together at this.

"And this is the guy we didn't allow on the Project?" Chase asked Mark, pointing at Phet.

"That's right, sir." Mark replied.

"Unbelievable," Chase said, shaking his head. "So, where are we at with this thing?"

Marnie spoke up. "At this point, it's another waiting game. It all depends on if Ray takes the bait or not."

"That little prick will do anything if it means crawling further up the administration's sphincter. He's like a power-hungry gerbil, that one. It's a shame he didn't turn out more like his old man," said Chase looking at Milas, who nodded thoughtfully.

"What ever happened to Colonel Ray?" Marnie asked.

Milas gave a questioning look to the admiral who responded with a nod of consent.

"Out that window there in Arlington Cemetery is a tiny little monument known as the Laos Memorial. It's there to honor the American advisors and the Hmong and Lao who took part in the Secret War that ran parallel with Vietnam.

"Soon after Saigon fell, Laos was a lost cause and America began to pull out. The problem was that there were thousands of Hmong leaders and their families that needed to be evacuated or they would face execution. Colonel Ray—fresh out of Vietnam—stayed back and helped scramble a couple C-64's and a C-130 out of Thailand with the help of General Aderholt. He oversaw the operation under the direction of the CIA.

"The mission saved a lot of lives, but Colonel Ray's chopper went down in the mountains of the Golden Triangle at the tail end of the evacuation. The rescue teams never found him. He's considered M.I.A. to this day, but I'd say that if he was captured, we'd have know about it long ago."

"The man's a hero," said Mark.

"Yes," said Milas. "Yes, he was. Be that as it may, I think he left his son with some serious unresolved daddy issues."

"Such as?" asked Marnie.

"Well, for one, he resents the fact that I had a better relationship with his father than he was ever able to. But what's worse is I think he feels betrayed that his father gave his life to save a bunch of Hmong rather than stay alive and be there for him. Not that I'm Sigmund Freud or anything, but I think that somewhat fuels his xenophobia, making him the über-patriot that he is."

"It's ironic," said Chase. "He questions his father's allegiance, while being completely blinded by his own. The boy's in the thick of things for the moment, but once the president's done with him, he'll be cut loose and set adrift. I tried to tell him, but he's got a head like a rock, that one."

"Admiral," said Mark. "What *is* happening on your side?"

"Yes, well, enough about Major Ray." Chase shook the thoughts from his head, and said, "I brought the posse. Let's talk turkey."

❋ ❋ ❋

MAJOR RAY APPROACHED his chief engineer. "Status?" he asked.

"It's gone, sir," said the engineer with a tinge of perplexity in his voice. "There was a constant wave of attacks on the firewall for about twenty minutes. Then it stopped, just like that. It was obviously a denial of service attack, but it seems pretty much pointless. It's more like harassment than anything else. All it did was cause us to turtle for a while. Maybe they, whoever *they* are, were just testing the fences, seeing what effect their attack would have."

"And there's no way to trace it?"

"No sir, not that I know of. It was a distributed attack. There were thousands of machines pounding at the door. It had to be a bot-net."

Rose appeared. "Major, the vice president is on the red line."

Ray nodded and picked up the phone, selecting the blinking extension. "Yes, Mr. Vice President?"

"I need a progress report, Major. The president is preparing to give a televised speech, addressing the nation on the Muslim crisis."

"When will that be, sir?"

"Hopefully, the moment I get some better ideas from that infernal machine of yours."

"We've just made some modifications to some of the algorithms," said Ray, stretching the truth somewhat through omission. "We're re-running the scenario again. It may give us some other options, but you should be prepared to go with the original plan if there's no change in the result."

"When will you know?" asked the vice president.

Ray cupped the mouthpiece with his hand. "How soon to bring us back online?" he asked the engineer.

"Do you really want to do that? We don't know who just hit us?"

"How soon?" he repeated.

"Ten minutes, maybe." The engineer shrugged.

"I can get you that in less than an hour, sir."

"Make it happen," said the vice president, and the line clicked dead.

"Do a final systems check," he ordered the engineer. "I'll wait."

"Already underway, sir. Nothing seems outwardly wrong. Malware checks are all green. Systems are all operational. Everything's normal. There's nothing happening except a backup in the mail queues as far as I can see, but that's normal. Still, we should continue investigating what really happened before we bring the links back up."

"I need the links up and everyone in this place focused on this," Ray commanded, pointing at the big screens. "Got it?"

"Got it, sir."

Ray rushed back to his office. He would carry out his orders. More than that, he'd worked his whole life for the opportunity to actually have the power to help his country secure its future. Milas had unwittingly given him the final piece that he needed to complete the game his father had started so many years ago. Phoenix was back in action, and the White House was running with it. America was going to win the war on terror. If they just didn't stray from the plan, all would work out. He was sure of it.

Picking up his phone, he dialed his lead analyst. "Milas's program, run it," he said. Run it now."

"Sir, this really should be tested further. We've only just scratched the surface of what the code entails."

"Run it. Don't make me say it again."

Chapter 44

A PODIUM STOOD ALONE upon the dais while television crews set up their cameras. Spotlights flicked on and off in the rigging above as different gel-films were tested for finding the ideal lighting conditions for the speaker. The final preparations were hurried as the audience began to fill the room. The auditorium rustled with the sounds of murmurs and scuffling while nearly four hundred people filled the seats and eventually spilled over into the aisles. The event had become standing room only.

House lights were dimmed, and the crowd's attention focused toward the front of the room. Two stagehands scurried over to the podium and quickly removed it from sight. A voice came over the PA system and said, "Ladies and Gentlemen, please welcome Professor John Vendetti."

The audience packed into the Intercultural Center Auditorium at Georgetown University offered a polite yet subdued applause as they watched Vendetti pushed to the middle of the stage in a wheelchair by a comely woman with Middle Eastern looks.

Vendetti said, "Thank you, Salome," which was echoed over the PA system. He tapped the lapel microphone with his good hand and said, "I guess I'm already on," smiling at the crowd. A few chuckles emanated from the audience, and he began.

"Ladies and gentlemen, Christians and Muslims, brothers and sisters. I am saddened and disappointed. You may ask why, and it's not because I'm here today in a wheelchair. I am sorry that I have not been able to speak sooner on this subject, but I was indisposed, recovering from an unfortunate accident. An accident, which I can assure you, was not the work of Islamic terrorists regardless of what you may have read in the newspapers.

"Each of you, I'm sure, is acutely aware of what is occurring around the world with regard to the Muslim protests. We are experiencing a backlash, a global reprimand for decidedly unjust discrimination against one of the world's most populous religions. And what is our response? What I see and what the world sees from the media is not balanced or objective commentary. What we see are commentators with undeniable political agendas. They present their preconceived ideological and political perceptions as if they are fact, when indeed they are not. This, people, is why I am disappointed and saddened. It is because a country as great as ours continues to allow itself to be influenced by these agendas, which are decidedly not in America's best interest. They are not in our best interest, and it is not in the world's best interest for us to continue to widen the gap that divides us.

"Religion is not our enemy. Terrorism is. There is no doubt in my mind that terrorism is a threat to the entire world. It is a fact that there are religious extremists who would like to impose a medieval, intolerant, and tyrannical way of life if they could, but it is also a fact that the religion of Muhammad is not the religion of al-Qaida, Osama bin Laden, or suicide bombers regardless of what those who have hijacked Islam to serve their own agendas would like you to believe. Again, it is terrorism that is our enemy, not religion."

Vendetti's speech was being televised live. A hastily arranged team was deployed to spread the word to as many demonstration sites as possible, alerting them that Professor Vendetti would be speaking. Some camps were able to prepare for the video feed to be shown on large screens on site, while others now listened to Vendetti's broadcast over loudspeakers. By the time he neared the end of his speech, he had undivided attention of thousands of people across the country.

"We cannot permit a clash of cultures to distract us from this truth, yet we have. Ordinary citizens have become polarized. Today we see mainstream people under siege. We find ourselves accepting and even advocating our government's military options that only a short time ago we would have abhorred. And how does this serve us? I'll tell you. It serves to further alienate us from those who could be our friends. It serves to support the great divide that stands between us and prevents us from understanding one another. It serves to provoke increased radicalization that undermines any efforts to promote strong ties with those we should consider to be our allies in this war against terrorism.

"But how do we fight terrorism without a global clash of culture? We do not do this by turning on each other. We do this by addressing the conditions that create breeding grounds for extremists and radicals, not by establishing an aggressive stance against entire countries and religions. We do this by addressing the issues of foreign policy, not by heading down the path of a religion-based conflict. The further we are polarized, the further apart we are from understanding each other. It is through misunderstanding and ignorance that hate garners its power. As both sides become more isolated, we will continue to see opposing sides turn to extremism. We will continue to see friends become adversaries, joining an opposition that perhaps they would not have even considered unless it was felt there were no other options.

"There are other options, my friends, but they are hard to see when our very own government is promoting its own agenda. Options are hard to see when we are bombarded by an irresponsible media. If you want to see your options, look around you. You are the options…"

❀ ❀ ❀

RAY TAPPED THE SPACEBAR to stop the screen saver and entered his password. A message read, "Scenario analysis complete."

"This is it," he thought, "Do or die time." He hit the enter key. The machine processed for a moment, and another message was displayed. Major Ron Ray's heart nearly flat-lined as he read the words on the screen. With each letter the message cycled through the colors of the rainbow from red to violet and back to red. He gaped at his monitor in shock. Centered neatly between a peace symbol and a smiley face was the phrase, "Make Love Not War."

As Ray stared at the screen, thousands of emails were leaving the NCTC at the speed of light through fiber optic cables. The Milas Trojan horse had effectively parsed a large chunk of

Junior's database and had relayed it through the infected workstations of the NCTC to the email servers. When the engineer reopened the firewall, a torrent of information flowed from the email servers destined for a variety of organizations who would take great interest in the information it carried.

Ray thought about running to the pit and demanding that the firewall be shut down again, but he knew better. It was too late. He reached into his desk drawer and removed his BlackBerry. Rank had its privileges. It was one very few mobile devices allowed in the building. He consulted the updated list that Junior had prepared prior to the latest scenario run. Ray tapped a coded message into the BlackBerry and pressed the send button.

⌗ ⌗ ⌗

MILAS WALKED ONTO THE STAGE and approached Vendetti. He bent down and whispered into his ear. Vendetti nodded and watched him walk off to rejoin the small group of supporters off stage. Milas had just given him the news that Plan B had worked. Vendetti smiled at Marnie, Mark, Milas, and Salome who silently cheered him on from the wings. He also noted that Agent Short of the FBI was present among them. Vendetti knew that Short's partner, Jenkins, was positioned somewhere nearby, presumably in another strategic locale to ensure his security. They were here serving as sentinels. As part of his protective detail, they would be continuously scanning the auditorium for potential threats. Though he deemed their presence entirely unnecessary, he found it reassuring all the same.

"Options," he continued. "We are all options and opportunities to promote understanding between each other and those we come into contact with every day, and that is a good beginning, but we must follow through. We must not be intimidated from opening our hearts. We must not let fear or hate blind us to the beauty of another's culture or religion. We must not let extremists limit us in our ability to love one another, nor can we allow our reaction to extremism drive us further apart—for that will only make our true enemy, terrorism, stronger.

"I ask each of you here in the audience, at the demonstration sites, or wherever you may be to think about this. Think about how your every action is an opportunity to promote understanding. Think about how only through understanding one another we can stand together, united against our common foe. You may remember Aesop's four oxen that were able to turn away the lion when they stood together, but fell prey when they were distracted by quarreling amongst themselves. The moral of the story rang true over two millennia ago, it became a national motto when this country was born, and it is still relevant today. United we stand, divided we fall."

A smattering of applause followed as Vendetti paused in his speech. It quickly gained momentum, evolving into a standing ovation. Vendetti had touched them at their core, and they cheered him for it. He raised his good arm and waved to the crowd. His attempts to speak further were drowned out by the uproarious applause. He smiled, waiting for the ovation to subside.

A split second later, Vendetti's head vaporized into a cloud of red mist.

Short reacted immediately, drawing his gun and seeking the source of the shot that had just decapitated the Professor. It took only another second for the others in the room to realize what had happened. Marnie lunged past Mark in an attempt to reach Vendetti, but Mark grabbed her firmly by the arm.

"Let go of me!" she cried.

"You stay here!" he commanded and thrust her toward Milas, who pushed both Marnie and Salome behind him, putting himself between them and the stage. Mark ran out into the open and slipped on the slick remains that had pooled upon the dais. What was left of his friend was unrecognizable. The scene was horrific. Mark wretched, uncontrollably vomiting at the gruesome sight.

As the scarlet splatter upon the stage's backdrop and the headless torso slumped in the wheelchair registered in the collective mind of the audience, survival instincts kicked in and pandemonium broke out in the hall. There were screams, and people clambered over each other as a mad scramble for the exits ensued.

Mark did his best to compose himself and rushed off stage. Salome stood there alone.

"Where the hell is she?" he asked in a panic.

"They all left through that door," she said, clearly shaken.

"Come on!" he said, grabbing her hand a pulling her along.

Outside the auditorium, sirens could be heard in the distance. The audience was still pouring out through the doors. They formed a confused mob through which Mark fought as he desperately sought out Marnie with Salome in tow.

"Mark! Over here!" It was Milas.

They pushed through the crowd and reached him at a clearing near the Jesuit cemetery adjacent to the building's forecourt. Agent Short was moving people back to a distance as Jenkins stood with his boot on the neck of a handcuffed man who was laid out prone on the concrete. Jenkins turned as he saw Mark approaching.

"Where's Marnie McCloud," Jenkins snapped.

"That's what I was about to ask you," said Mark.

Jenkins held up the BlackBerry phone he'd pulled from the man on the ground so that Mark could read the screen. There were two names listed. Vendetti's was one. Marnie's was the other.

Mark spun around and called out for her, searching the throng of onlookers that surrounded them. He looked to Milas.

"She was here just a second ago!" Milas told him.

A loud pop came from the parking lot. Everyone standing outside the auditorium reflexively flinched.

"That wasn't a gunshot," said Milas.

"I'd know that sound anywhere. That's Marnie's car!" Mark exclaimed and sprinted after her.

❈ ❈ ❈

MARNIE PUSHED ROCINANTE and her driving skills to their limits as she tore over the Key Bridge. She flew down Lee Highway, passing cars and crossing the centerline to face oncoming traffic with reckless abandon. The grisly image of John's head exploding was all she could see now. Her mind was shot.

"He's dead because of me!" she cried aloud, wiping the steady stream of tears from her eyes.

When she'd seen Short and Jenkins apprehend John's killer outside the auditorium, she'd had the instinctive feeling that this was the man who'd been following her. As the agents wrestled him to the ground and cuffed him, the man's face was turned toward Marnie. She didn't recognize him, but she saw the recognition in his eyes.

He gave her a baleful smile and mouthed the words, "You're next."

She broke down. All she could think to do was run. And she did.

CHAPTER 45

THE POLICE AND THE MEDIA arrived near simultaneously at the Intercultural Center. Agents Short and Jenkins had remanded the shooter into custody and the search was on for Mark and Marnie who'd both abruptly fled the scene. Short had given his card to Milas and told him to call if they heard word from either of them. Members of the press were interviewing the traumatized individuals who'd remained. There was no shortage of witnesses to the murder of the university's famous professor of Islam, and the TV cameras weren't being shy about broadcasting the graphic descriptions of the event onto the airwaves.

Milas and Salome grew furious at seeing the spectacle this had become. The press seemed more interested in depicting the horror and sorrow of the crowd than focusing on the man who'd just been slain—a man who'd just given one of the most profound speeches on compassion and human understanding that either of them had ever heard. Compelled by his anger, Milas marched over to the nearest camera and pushed himself in front of the lens.

"Follow me," he said to the cameraman.

Milas then stepped up onto the cement ring that surrounded a nearby elm tree. It gave him a good two feet over the crowd.

"Attention everyone! Attention!" Milas shouted. "If you want to know what really happened here, come this way and listen!"

The horde followed his lead, and the television cameras focused on Milas.

Milas felt a familiar feeling wash over him. He was back on a stage, and it felt oddly good despite the circumstances.

He spoke to the crowd. "United we stand, divided we fall. Those are the last words of Professor John Vendetti, and they are potent words. These are words that should fill us with pride at the courage and dignity that symbolizes our great nation. But do they?

"Professor Vendetti was murdered here today by terrorists. Not Muslim terrorists, but American terrorists. I'm here to tell you that the atrocity we have just witnessed is not an isolated event. It is not random, and it is part of a larger more insidious conspiracy perpetrated by Americans upon Americans."

Milas took in his audience and noticed more than a few dubious expressions.

"Some of you look skeptical. Well, I am going to ask you to re-think that position once you've heard what I am about to share with you. Just a short while ago, several news organizations across the nation began reporting the receipt of an information database from an anonymous source. While the messengers who delivered this information have yet to be identified, the information itself appears to be highly classified material stolen from computer systems owned and operated by the United States Government. The content of this database is some of the most alarming evidence to have ever come to light regarding our government's blatant violation of the privacy of its own citizens. The database contains very sensitive information about millions of Americans who I am sure would be appalled and outraged to learn that their elected government has not only allowed this information to be collected about them but is also using it to secretly investigate them.

"That's not so bad, you might be thinking. Well, it gets worse, a lot worse." Milas paused for dramatic effect. "The information in this database provides details of a heinous series of crimes involving political assassination perpetuated by the United States Government that has gone on for decades. And I am deeply saddened to say that Professor Vendetti is our nation's latest victim."

Milas saw he'd now seized the crowd's interest and decided to go for the jugular.

"There are names on this list that will shock you. They will shock the nation, and they will shock the world. As analysts begin to sift through this windfall of data, I am certain that this body of information will make J. Edgar Hoover look like a mere dilettante. This information leak corroborates evidence that we've all heard before but that we don't want to believe—that these assassinations are in fact murders performed at the hands of people working under the orders of the United States Government. President John F. Kennedy, his brother Robert Kennedy, Martin Luther King Jr., and yes, even John Vendetti. These are but a few men whose names are found on this list. Their crimes? Standing firm in their beliefs. The price they paid? Their lives. And how do I know this? Because I wrote the program behind it all…"

❇ ❇ ❇

MARK'S LEXUS SKIDDED around the corner as he approached Vendetti's apartment. Marnie's car was nowhere to be seen. He'd already circled the block once as he'd done around Marnie's apartment just a few minutes ago.

"Where in God's name did she go!" he shouted, slamming his fists against the steering wheel in frustration. She was now officially targeted. He could only assume that this was the work of the major, and Mark was genuinely terrified at the prospects of that. He'd seen what they'd just done to Vendetti. Mark looked at his hands. They were covered with dried blood. He knew he had to find Marnie before it was too late.

Mark pressed a button on his car stereo and said, "Call Marnie, mobile."

The car's speakers responded with, "Calling Marnie, mobile," followed by the sound of a phone line ringing. There was no answer. He slammed the accelerator to the floor and sped off toward Burns & Lynch.

Chapter 46

MARNIE DID NOT HEAR HER PHONE RINGING. She'd left it back in her car. She'd driven in her distressed state somehow on automated pilot to her special place by the Potomac. She now sat alone upon a large rock in a secluded niche formed by sycamore trees, trying to make sense of all that had happened.

Calico clouds were painted in delicate shades of pink across a massive canvas of gradient blue. Everything around her turned to gold as it was bathed in the magical glow of twilight. Stars appeared one by one, twinkling into existence above her, yet all she felt was sadness.

Marnie sensed the presence of someone nearby, and her hackles rose.

"I gotta say, you're not making this much of a challenge," said a voice behind her.

Marnie rose and whirled to face the voice, already knowing whom she would see. He wore no sunglasses now and held a pistol casually at his side. The gun was equipped with a long, black sound suppressor that Marnie equated with a weapon of a trained killer. She knew she was as good as dead.

"Why don't you give me a head start then," she managed to utter. In her anger over the senselessness of John's murder, she found a bravery she did not know she had.

"Heck, why not?" said the man who'd come to kill her. "I'll give you a ten second head start. This oughta be interesting."

He started counting.

Marnie lost nearly five seconds not grasping that he actually meant it. She then came to her senses and bolted for the nearby edge of the forest. The killer finished his count and started after her.

Within the trees it was black as pitch, yet Marnie's legs flew beneath her as if they knew this patch of forest by feel alone. She could hear the crunch of leaves behind her as her pursuer increased his pace. He was moving now to catch her. She sprinted for her life.

At a crossroads well known to her, Marnie leapt down an embankment and nimbly skipped over the tops of smooth river stones as she crossed Donaldson Creek. Its gelid waters glimmered in the moonlight under a break in the forest canopy. She picked up a stone the size of a grapefruit and ran up the other side of the stream basin. Hiding just within the shadows of the tree line, she waited.

Marnie watched as the man scuttled down the bank to the creek's edge, clearly unfamiliar with the terrain. She remained in place as he navigated the river stones. He lost his footing halfway across, nearly falling into the creek. He whirled his arms to regain his balance and then stood perfectly still. She felt his eyes scanning the tree line in search of her.

Marnie looked at the stone she held. She then kissed it, stepped from behind the tree, and let it fly with all her might in a windmill softball pitch. The stone flew silently. Its aim was true. It connected with a meaty thud, hitting her stalker directly in the chest. He grunted in pain and fell to his knees in the creek. Marnie looked around for another rock, but there were none at hand. The man fired his gun blindly into the tree line with a series of muffled cracks. Bullets buzzed like deadly, lead wasps as they tore through the air around her head. She bolted down the trail away from her hunter, not looking back.

Marnie ran as fast as she could along the darkened path. Her endorphine-high had ebbed, and she was now thinking how she could to circle back safely to get to her car or to where there might be some people. She had no way of knowing if she was still being chased, but she wasn't going to turn back or slow down. Marnie hoped that the man might be injured enough from her stone throw to have given up, but she wasn't taking any chances. She did the one thing she knew would work. She kept running.

❇ ❇ ❇

MILAS AND SALOME WERE DELIVERED from Georgetown to the Sheraton in a police squad car. As they entered the suite, they found the mood of the room was somber. All eyes were riveted upon the television. The National Guard had been deployed to several large demonstration sites in response to the potential clashes that seemed imminent only hours ago. The news being reported was nothing short of remarkable.

Milas walked through the open connecting door into the adjacent room where the admiral's crew had set up shop, leaving Salome with Hawk, Phet, and Joe who were sprawled out on the bed eating room service cheeseburgers and freedom fries. Chase had returned to the NCTC to retake the helm.

"What's happening?" Milas asked Chase's team.

"You're watching the successful defusing of what could have been Kent State times about a hundred," said one of the admiral's men. "After what just happened to Professor Vendetti and that bombshell of a database leak, we've got a incredible twist unraveling."

Milas looked out the window said, "I see the Pentagon hasn't levitated, turned purple, and disappeared yet."

"Hey, remember we're the good guys here," said another of Chase's crew.

"Yes, you are," said Milas. "The Old Guard comes through in the end again."

"Who are these good guys?" whispered Salome, having appeared at Milas's side.

Each of the men recited one after the other, raising a hand, "Army, Navy, Air Force, Marines." Then they said in unison, "And that's all you need to know." Milas knew more, but he wasn't about to let Salome in on the fact that she was standing in a hotel room with the Joint Chiefs of Staff.

"Are those flowers?" Milas asked, squinting at the TV.

"Yep, and copies of the Constitution. They're passing them out to the Guardsmen."

"It's a love-in!" exclaimed Milas.

"Pretty much," replied the man. "I just wish it hadn't required a public assassination to have stopped this whole mess."

The Air Force guy spoke up, "The Guard is standing down. We had a word with the chief of the National Guard Bureau. We gave him a little reminder about the oath of enlistment."

"To support and defend the Constitution of the United States against all enemies, foreign *and* domestic," said Milas. "You think we can convince anyone that the administration is the enemy?"

"Everyone can dream, Andy," said Army Guy. "But right now, we should be thanking Professor Vendetti. All sides seem to have taken his message to heart."

"Killing him was stupid and pointless," said Milas.

"Yes, it was. And it may have even had the opposite effect than intended. Add that to the wounds you've reopened with your Phoenix disclosure, and I'm imagining the mob will brandish pitchforks and start hunting monsters in the rose garden soon."

"People deserve to know the truth about just how far the government will go to protect its interests," Milas retorted.

"After today, I'm not sure that there's anyone who'd be willing to argue against that. I know I'm not going to, but I'm not sure you're going about it the right way."

"Someone needs to kick the hornet's nest every once in a while if just to remember those who've been stung. The media can flay me for all I care. If this somehow puts the kibosh on Phoenix even if for a while, at least we've accomplished something and Professor Vendetti will not have died in vain."

"You're liable to be the next American martyr if you're not careful, amigo."

"I realize that, but thanks for the warning. Say, what is the backlash from the White House on all this?" asked Milas.

"Oh boy," said Navy Guy. "While the turmoil on the streets is abating, the database leak has got you know who seeing red. Your impromptu press conference was like gasoline on a fire. The staff medical team is standing by to treat a mass case of apoplexy. Admiral Chase is keelhauling Major Ray right about now just to appease the chief."

"Any word on the mysterious perpetrators who performed this treasonous act?" asked Milas with a mock look of innocence.

"Not yet," said Marine Guy. "Admiral Chase has vowed to find out who's responsible for the breach and bring them to justice. He believes there may be Russians involved." He winked. "I very much doubt that Major Ray will be telling anyone that he loaded the Trojan horse responsible for the leak onto the systems of the NCTC. I don't think he'll be doing much talking to anyone where he's headed either. But if he does, these hackers have covered their tracks well, haven't they?"

"I believe they have," Milas said with a small prayer to himself.

"Should we check in with the FBI agent to see if they have been found?" Salome asked Milas.

Milas nodded.

"Excuse me gentlemen, we need to check on our friends."

They placed a call to the number on Short's card from the phone in the adjacent room. It was answered by voice mail. Hawk and Phet gave them expectant looks, hoping to hear that Mark and Marnie had been found and were safe. After having heard the news of the shooting at Georgetown they both feared the worst.

Milas shook his head. "Nothing yet," he said. "Let's hope that's a good thing."

CHAPTER 47

IT TOOK HER NEARLY THIRTY MINUTES to circle back. She stopped to catch her breath at the forest's edge. Marnie had navigated her way through the woods to reach the road from the opposite side of where she'd left her car. There was no sign of the shooter, and she breathed a sigh of relief. Now all she had to do was get out of there. Marnie carefully inched her way out from the protection of the trees and saw Mark's car parked in front of hers. Mark was pacing back and forth in a quandary.

"Mark!" she whispered as loudly as she could. He didn't hear her. "Mark!" she tried again, but he was out of earshot. If she was still being hunted, Mark was a sitting duck. Knowing she had to do something, Marnie burst from the trees and ran toward him.

Mark saw her and called out, "Marnie! Thank God you're all right!" His relief was unmistakable.

She'd reached the painted yellow line in the road when a menacing voice spoke from the opposing tree line, "Don't you fucking move."

The killer emerged from the forest's shadows with his pistol trained on Marnie's chest.

She thought of running and took a step backward.

"If you run, I'll put a bullet in his head."

The threat induced its intended effect. Marnie froze in the middle of the road. She was vulnerable and helpless.

Mark stepped toward her.

"You," he said to Mark. Sit on the ground on your hands. Now!"

Mark defied the order and said, "If you hurt her, you're dead." His voice simmered with rage.

The gunman's response was simple. He shot Mark in the arm.

"Shut up," he said as Mark staggered and fell to the ground.

Marnie screamed.

"I'm okay," Mark managed. He held his arm and grimaced in pain.

"Why are you doing this?" Marnie demanded, mustering her courage once again and buying whatever time she could.

The man walked around the back of her car and leaned on the trunk. He winced, and Marnie could see that he was still in pain from the blow to his chest.

"Someone wants you dead," he said plainly. "I'm just doing my job." He pushed himself off the Mustang. "Actually, I lie. I *was* just doing my job, but now I'm pissed off."

He rubbed his rib cage and moved between Marnie and Mark, leveling his gun once again at her. "So what I'm going to do is shoot your boyfriend again and let you watch him die. Then I'm going to shoot you. How does that sound?"

Marnie was unable to move or say a word and could only watch impotently as the man swung his arm with deliberate slowness away from her and aimed his gun at Mark. The second he had his back to her, she imagined leaping upon him, doing whatever she could to stop him. But she remained fixed, as if the road were made of flypaper. In her moment of indecision the gunshot rang out followed quickly by another round that echoed through the night.

"Mark!" she cried out. She cast aside her fear and sprinted forward, skirting around the killer to reach Mark. As she did, the gunman toppled over sideways. His pistol clattered upon the pavement. Marnie stopped dead and blinked her eyes at the nightmarish scene. Two dark stains seeped across the man's chest and what remained of his life flowed out in thick rivulets of blood. She broke from her horrible study of the dying man and turned to Mark. He was alive.

"Christ, that hurt!" he said. His lopsided smile said he was glad they were both alive. She rushed to him as he struggled to get to his feet.

"Are you two all right?" Agent Short materialized from the tree line, followed by Jenkins who was carrying a shotgun. Short holstered his weapon and retrieved the fallen man's firearm. Kneeling upstream of the blood, he placed his fingers upon the man's neck and checked for a pulse. He found none. His second shot had found the heart. "Miss McCloud, are you all right?" he repeated, looking up to meet her eyes.

"Mark's been shot," her voice was a hollow whisper.

Jenkins stepped over to Mark and inspected his wound. "Nothing major," he said. "He just got winged."

"It's a damn good thing you called us, Mr. Harmann," said Short. He then reached beneath his jacket to retrieve a portable radio. He depressed the talk button, and said, "Packages are secure. Threat eliminated. Bring the team around to the end of North Marcey Road."

"Who was he?" asked Marnie, her eyes drifting back to the corpse.

"Mercenary," said Short. "Same goes for the man who shot Vendetti. They're both from a private security firm. One that will soon have holy hell rained upon it by all the fury the FBI can muster." He searched the man's pockets and fished out a BlackBerry mobile phone. "This one was also Safiya Barazani's pen pal," he said, showing it to Marnie.

An unmarked sedan approached from down the road. It was followed by a large black Chevy van. The vehicles stopped, and a team of agents poured from the van. Short called one of the men over to tend to Mark's arm. It was cleaned and expertly bandaged within minutes.

"You're lucky," said the medic. "You don't even need stitches."

Short looked at Mark and said, "I don't think it's a good idea for either you to drive. Why don't you two let us ride you back to the Sheraton? There are some very worried people over there that are eager to see you. We'll make sure your cars get there as well."

They nodded as Jenkins opened the car door and helped Mark get in the back seat. Marnie got in on the other side.

Jenkins leaned through the driver's side window. "We'll be back in a minute," he hold them.

Sitting beside Mark, Marnie gently placed her head on his good shoulder.

"You're okay, right?" she asked him.

"I'm damaged goods," he told her, trying to make light of his injury. "The question is whether or not you're okay."

"Not really."

"I'm not sure what would have happened if the FBI hadn't have come when they did."

"We'd have ended up like John," she said.

"I'm so sorry, Marnie."

"He was your friend too."

"I know. What I meant was that I really thought I was going to lose you back there."

"You and me both," she sighed.

"No, listen. All of this has made me realize that I've made a terrible mistake."

"What are you talking about, Mark?"

"I'm sorry that I've not been as good a person that I could have been. I've taken you for granted."

Marnie lifted her head from Mark's shoulder and looked into his eyes.

He smiled at her. "I'm sorry that it's taken me so long to realize this. You're the most important thing in my life. I love you, Marnie. I always have. I can only hope that you still love me."

They each saw in the other's eyes a dormant longing that had been reborn.

"I—" Mark started to speak, but she put her finger to his lips.

Marnie was overcome. After all they'd just been through, she could barely process the tumult of emotions that washed over her. The only thing she was sure of in that moment was that she loved him, and that was all that really mattered.

"You don't need to say another word."

Chapter 48

Jenkins and Short returned Mark and Marnie to the Sheraton National. They arrived at just after 8:30pm. The agents brought them to the rooms on the 11th floor. Milas answered the door and exclaimed, "They're here!" Everyone rushed to see them.

"Get inside," Milas beckoned. "Agents, I can't thank you enough for bringing them back safely." He shook both of their hands with sincere appreciation.

Phet wrapped his arms around Marnie and gave her hug that hurt her ribs. "Oh, Miss Marnie, Phet so glad you not dead," he said and squeezed her harder.

Hawk gave Mark pat on the shoulder, carefully avoiding the arm with the large bloodstain on the sleeve. "You had us worried there, boss."

"Ya, that was a pretty wild ride. It could have gone either way."

"We're really glad you made it."

"Me too, Hawk," he said, looking at Marnie. "Me too."

Milas pried his son off Marnie and led her and Mark into the Admiral's war room. Chase was back. He and the Joint Chiefs were in hushed conversations on their mobile phones. Jenkins and Short stood lost for words, knowing full well that the hotel's floor was barely supporting the weight of the accumulated brass that filled the room.

Chase clicked off his phone first, followed shortly by the others.

"Admiral?" asked Mark.

"It looks like you've earned yourself a battle scar, Mr. Harmann."

"It could have been much worse, sir."

"Yes, I heard about Professor Vendetti. I'm very sorry. His death is all our loss. America owes that man a debt of gratitude. His was an exceptional message delivered today. It got people thinking like humans again."

"Thank you, sir. What's the situation with the demonstrations?"

"Well, we may have avoided a catastrophe here at home, but we may not be so lucky abroad," he replied. "We've just confirmed that the president has ordered the launch of predator attacks within the Iranian border."

"Iran?" exclaimed Milas.

"Yes, Iran," Chase replied. "The administration has declared the data leak an act of cyber-warfare, and they're using it as an excuse to launch what they're calling retaliatory strikes against known Islamic terrorist training camps. They are, of course, conveniently using the leak to their advantage since it's as impossible to disprove as it is to prove who was behind it."

"Is Major Ray behind this?" asked Marnie.

"He won't be bothering anyone for a very long time, Miss McCloud," said Chase. He glanced at Agent Short when he said this, giving him a barely perceptible nod.

"I think we all know who's really pulling the strings here," said Milas.

"You're right, Andy," Chase said. "Even with Major Ray out of the picture, it looks like the administration is still running with the same game plan. The CIA controls the drones, and they're taking orders straight from the top. It doesn't seem that any of what's happened over the last forty-eight hours has made even a dent in their thick skulls. They're attempting to deflect attention away from the media buzz and continuing their offensive."

"The fools!" said Mark. "We've done all this for what?"

"Don't give up," said Chase. "Look, all of you did some great things today. You should be proud of yourselves. Now it's time for you to stand down. Stay here and stay safe. This is out of your hands now." The admiral signaled to his team. "Come on, people, we've done all we can from here. Now we need to go prevent idiot boy from starting a fucking war with Iran."

Chase and the Joint Chiefs filed out of the room.

When they left, Mark proclaimed, "If I don't lie down, I may pass out." Short and Jenkins helped him onto the bed. Marnie sat beside him and propped him up with some oversized pillows behind his head.

"She took his hand, kissed him on the cheek, and said, "My hero!"

Salome entered the room, carrying Phet's laptop. She sat down in the reading chair in the corner of the suite and said, "My father is dead." Her voice was monotone, devoid of emotion.

"Salome, how do you know that?" asked Marnie with obvious concern.

"I received this email," she said, placing the laptop on the ottoman before her.

Milas dropped to one knee and viewed the screen. "Salome, I can't read this. I'm guessing it's Persian," he said.

"I am sorry. Yes, it is." she said. "I shall read it aloud."

"Are you sure?" said Mark. "You really don't have to."

"I must," said Salome. "I need to share this."

My Dear Mooshi,

By now you have learned that I have led two lives. For many years I have kept my identities separate, and in doing so I have done my best to protect you from the secrets our family keeps.

While I have been able to maintain this masquerade, this is something that I cannot do forever. If you are reading this message, I am no longer able to protect you. I have asked a trusted source to deliver this message in the event of my death. And so, my Mooshi, if you are reading this, that day has come.

For whatever wounds you will carry in your heart because of me, I am sorry. I will not attempt to justify to you what I have done in my other life, the one I have hidden from you. I have done what I have done for my reasons. You have your own mind, and you will determine for yourself what kind of man does such things.

My one last hope, inshalla, is that someday you may come to understand that part of me was a father who loved his daughter more than anything he could ever imagine. This is the man who can say he has given something remarkable to the world, by having you as a child.

I have managed one last gift for you. When it arrives, treat it well and know that I will always love you.

All were respectfully quiet after Salome finished reading Mohammed Khan's letter. They were all still reeling from Vendetti's murder, and none of them could find the right words to say. Salome got up and went to the washroom, closing the door behind her. They heard the tap come on and sobbing through the door.

"I think we'll be going," said Agent Short. "We've got some work of our own to do."

"Do you think we have anything to worry about?" asked Marnie. "I mean are any of us still targets?"

"We can't be sure," said Jenkins. "We do think there's just too much visibility on all of this right now, which should put a halt on any other operations that might still be in play. Admiral Chase has assured us that he'll be fully supporting our investigation into the Major and his mercenaries. We've got the shooter from Georgetown, and we're going to squeeze him until he pops."

"I hope you water-board the shit out him before he gets the electric chair," said Marnie.

"He'll get what's coming to him. All we can promise is that we'll be doing what we can to protect you and others like you. That's our job. Your job is to remain vigilant."

"I'd also say your job is to get back to fixing that system of yours," added Short. "I don't know how, but you're going to need to make it impossible for bad seeds to be using it again against the wrong people."

"Thank you, gentlemen," said Mark. "That's something we intend to do if we're allowed to."

"We'll be in touch," said Short, and the agents let themselves out.

"So what *are* we going to do?" asked Marnie.

"I think what we've achieved today is a Pyrrhic victory," said Mark. "We have won the battle, but as what cost? John is dead, and if the president carries out the attacks on Iran, this may actually provide just the excuse needed to allow Junior's quest for the end of days."

"Seriously, what kind of maniac would actually write a program that tries to bring about Armageddon anyhow?" Marnie gave Milas a look that could easily have burned a hole through the ozone layer.

"What can I say?" Milas cringed under her gaze. "I can tell you what I'm going to do though," he said. "I'm going to hit the road again with my traveling freak show. There is too much at stake here, and we've lost too much for me to remain a recluse. I'll be damned if I'm going to let the professor's death be for nothing. Remember, we've just gotten away with probably the most beautifully executed hack in history. Their pants are down, and I intend to kick 'em wear it counts while the opportunity is ripe."

"You know we can't help you with that," said Mark.

"And you're making yourself a huge target again," added Marnie.

"Ya, I know. Don't you worry about me. Our little secret will remain our little secret. You just need to keep Junior off the world's back. Believe me, I've got enough material to work with. That database makes the Hoover files look like a peanut operation. The info is out there now, and I'm not the only one who is going to be talking about it. I doubt they're going to send a team of mechanics to take us all out."

"You got amnesia or something?" snapped Marnie.

"Sorry, no. But it doesn't really work like that. I'm reluctant to say this, but if the guy who came after you tonight were a real pro, we wouldn't be having this conversation. I mean no disrespect for Professor Vendetti, but the fact that his killer was caught and the other was taken out before he got to you makes me pretty sure that we were dealing with amateur mercenaries."

"It's possible, Marnie," added Mark. "The government's use of private security companies is certainly on the rise in recent years, and the people they hire aren't bound by the same principles as are U.S. military personnel. The quality of their training and leadership has come under scrutiny on more than one occasion."

"That's right," said Milas. "But using these private firms provides a convenient buffer for deniability. Using them for domestic wet work, however, is a big no-no. Your would-be assassin wasn't any company hit man or a Manchurian Candidate for that matter. He was being run by the major—highly illegally I might add—not that killing people is legal, mind you.

"Major Bacon is going down for this. He'll be the administration's fall guy, but life will go on. He is going to quietly disappear from the scene, and the security firm he had working for him will more than likely continue to operate under a different name after the FBI's investigation. The fire at the senator's will be explained away as accidental, and the administration will continue with its agenda. But I think, for you at least, it's over."

"Colonel, aren't you going against your own advice by going back on the road with this?" asked Mark. "The FBI told us of what happened to your wife."

"Ya, well, again, if they wanted me dead, I'm pretty sure I wouldn't have made it out of the forest that night." Milas paused, remembering the crash in the blizzard and the car idling up on the road. "They wanted to send me a message, which I received loud and clear. I could have been killed, but losing Daphne had all the effect required to marginalize me completely." He paused again. Mark and Marnie saw the distant look in his eyes. It was a look of sad remembrance. They waited for him to return from his thoughts.

"But that was a long time ago." Milas came back to the present. "More than likely the response to my anti-Phoenix campaign will be character assassination, which I can live with. It helps that I'm a little crazy too. It makes me easy to dismiss, but I still hope to get this story out to as many people as possible— some of which might actually be sane and able to do something with it. Besides, I truly have some hope again, and that's also something worth sticking my neck out for. Daphne would have wanted me to. I believe the professor would have too. I think Americans will finally stand up and say they've had enough once they've grasped the scope of this thing. If the true nature of that information becomes public knowledge, I don't see how we're not going to see some inkling of real change back to a government of the people, by the people, and for the people."

"Lincoln's Gettysburg Address," said Mark.

"The truth will set you free," added Marnie.

"Let us hope," said Milas. "And let's not forget the final words of the professor."

Salome emerged from the washroom, looking somewhat recovered.

She said, "United we stand, divided we fall."

Marnie looked at Salome. Her tears were gone—replaced by an expression that exuded confidence and resolve. Marnie regarded the woman who stood before her and marveled at her courage. She thought of those responsible for John's death and how, while there were people in the world who were so full of hate that they would never find understanding, here was Salome, the polar opposite of such fanatics. It didn't matter that she was Iranian. It didn't matter that she was a Muslim. It didn't even matter what her father had been. Salome was a good thing in this world. Marnie felt that in her heart. She rose from the bed and took Salome by the hand.

"We'll stand with you," she told her.

Epilogue

THE NOVEMBER ELECTIONS in the United States reflected a marked turnabout in public sentiment. Polls showed the president's approval index at an all-time low and those candidates who remained defiant, towing the line of the war on terrorism and defending the need for continued intelligence surveillance on the citizenry, were exorcised from office without sentiment by the voting public. The elections of 2008 loomed on the horizon with the promise of real change.

The televised slaying of John Vendetti and revelations of the Phoenix project had set off a firestorm that had Americans in a fervor and catapulted Milas into the national spotlight. This time around he was wise enough to hire a marketing manager and an image consultant. Though he often strayed from their advice, he was armed with the magic sword of Junior's database that acted as his weapon of truth. His entourage of bodyguards was also armed just in case.

Milas gained instant notoriety by publically elaborating upon the Phoenix exposé. As expected, he was faced with ridicule when it came down to what continued to be seen as merely conspiracy theories. There was just too much history and too few people that wanted to believe that their government was culpable in a plot to assassinate its own citizens. Even Vendetti's murder had been expertly spun in the media as the work of a rogue private security firm operating without proper oversight. Based on a partial truth, this was enough to satisfy the majority of the people, but Milas didn't let up.

He toured the United States on a relentless speaking campaign that lambasted the current administration and sounded off against the flagrant violation of American constitutional rights and the erosion of civil liberties under the Patriot Act. Milas appeared on talk shows, including Leno and Letterman, as well as Oprah, the Today Show, and several others on his *tour de force* of truth. He'd honed his message to a fine art, demonstrating just how invasive Phoenix was by revealing salacious tidbits of personal information about the hosts and their celebrity guests to astonished audiences who, in spite of their shock, lapped up the dirt like greedy gossip hounds.

The press, while well-tempered in providing any praise for Milas, could not deny that his message had found the hearts of Americans who felt violated by their own government. He'd given them a voice and the courage to use it without the fear of being marked with the stigma of being unpatriotic.

The evidence Milas exposed coupled with the compelling message he delivered were enough to not only get the attention of the American public but also to get people to begin questioning things again. And this, he felt, was a healthy change that was just what the country needed.

⌘ ⌘ ⌘

WITH THE TURMOIL OF Junior's *fatwa* having passed, the major out of their hair, and with the Admiral Chase's support, Marnie and her team were able to return to their work at the NCTC. In an ironic twist, Phet was granted clearance directly by the admiral and was put in charge of a team to make sure that a security breach like that which had occurred under Major Ray's watch could never happen again.

Mark and Marnie had been charged with the task of refining Junior's safeguards to eliminate the possibility that the system would ever be able to be used again to target innocent civilians. The temptation of some men to shape the future was too great, the admiral had told them. The Old Guard could only do so much to keep these ambitions in check. They were successful in averting a war with Iran by convincing the president of the disastrous consequences that would have resulted if he'd gone through with the air strikes. There was already too much going on in Iraq and Afghanistan, they'd argued. That and the fact that they were able to prove, with the help of Marnie's team, that the remnants of Milas's original Phoenix code had perverted their game plan was enough to get the administration to reevaluate their reliance on using the technology for decision making—at least for the interim. Mark and Marnie's own experiences were all the proof they needed to know that the ambitions of some men could lead to ruin; they felt it was their duty to never let their creation be a part of that again.

❋ ❋ ❋

THE PASSING OF SALOME'S FATHER together with being witness to the appalling murder of John Vendetti packed an emotional blow from which few could have recovered. She could have crumbled. Instead, Salome immersed herself into preparing for the role that she had come to Georgetown University to perform. It's what she believed that both men would have wanted for her. And it was what she wanted.

As the winter term began, she was honored to serve as Vendetti's replacement for a number of his classes. Though many students expressed their requisite sadness and an initial disappointment that they would not be taught by the great Professor Vendetti, everyone quickly came to appreciate Salome's captivating teaching style, passion, and expertise. Word soon spread around campus about this outstanding new professor, and she quickly became a favorite among both the student body and faculty. She'd gotten her groove back, as Vendetti had told her she would. She was in her element, and she was absolutely delighted to be doing what she was doing. She was poised to find her happiness once again.

❋ ❋ ❋

IT WAS CHRISTMAS EVE. Mark, Marnie, and Salome were spending it together at Mark's palatial home in Chesterbrook Woods.

"Where's the food?" cried Mark.

Salome was studying the pieces of a chess game in progress beside the hearth. "It should be here any moment," she said and knelt down to tend to the logs in the fireplace.

They basked in the fire's comforting warmth that kept the blizzard at bay just beyond the windows of the house.

The doorbell rang as if on cue. "I will get it," said Salome.

Marnie leaned over and whispered into Mark's ear, "Say it again."

"I love you," he said without hesitation.

Marnie planted a passionate kiss upon his lips.

Salome returned with the delivery boy in tow from the foyer and announced, "Madame and Monsieur, it is my honor to present Mr. Ashad Alizadeh and his soon to be famous Christmas turkey kabobs!"

Mark and Marnie applauded and rose to greet him. Salome beamed dotingly at Ashad and touched his cheek with unabashed fondness. She relieved him of his food packages and beckoned, "Come with me to the kitchen."

Mohamed Kahn's final gift to his daughter followed her command. He would for all eternity, thought Ashad, as she manhandled him into the other room and plied him with further affections.

"It's amazing how those two have been brought together," said Marnie. "I still can't believe her father snuck him out of Iran."

"A terrorist with a soft-spot," he replied. "I know. It's hard to believe, but they sure do seem to like each other."

"Oh! What time is it?" asked Marnie.

"It's nine o'clock," replied Mark.

"Time for our call!" she said.

Marnie got her laptop and placed it on the dining room table. After she clicked a few things, a distinctive tone was followed by a ringing signal as she placed the call on Skype. After three rings, the call was answered, and Phet's face appeared on the screen.

"Can you hear me?" Phet asked.

"Loud and clear," said Mark. "We can see you too!"

"Where are the rest of you?" asked Marnie.

"Moment, Miss Marnie," Phet replied as he called everyone behind his web-cam.

Salome and Ashad returned to the room carrying plates overflowing with a fantastic array of Middle Eastern cuisine. They placed these on the table and joined the others at an angle where they could see and be seen by the Milas family in Thailand.

"Where's Hawk?" asked Mark.

"I'm here!" Hawk's face entered the screen from the side with Joe's chin upon his shoulder.

"So how do you like Bangkok, Cowboy?" asked Mark.

"It's amazing. I'm not sure I'll be coming back, boss," he beamed at Joe.

"Don't be disgusting," Phet said with a grimace. "It's bad enough to have lecherous geezer for future brother in law. Let's not get it on film."

Joe let out one of her *hmphs*, and the woman in the center of screen gestured at Phet in sign language.

"I'm sorry mother," said Phet. "I will not insult nauseating, old pervert in front of our guests."

Milas entered the screen laughing. "Merry Christmas everyone," he said. He wore a Santa cap, and his beard had begun to fill out again. "I trust America is doing well without me?"

"It's the Age of Aquarius over here," said Mark.

"Is that Mrs. Milas?" asked Salome. This prompted a smile and a wave from Fon.

"She's beautiful," said Marnie.

Fon touched her fingers to her mouth and extended a flat hand backward toward the camera, signing, "Thank you."

"Hey, it looks like your dinner's on the table," said Milas. "Don't let it get cold on our account. We can do this anytime."

Marnie said, "I wish you guys were here to join us."

"Maybe next year," said Milas. "We'll all come there to celebrate the holidays with Phet and the rest of you."

"That sounds great!" said Mark. "Okay, everyone. Merry Christmas!"

"Merry Christmas!" said the Milas family.

They all waved and smiled at their respective cameras until Marnie cut the connection and removed the laptop from the table.

"Wow, this is some spread," said Mark. "I guess we're kinda lucky that Marnie can't cook."

"Yes, we are also fortunate that Ashad is learning to be a chef at one of the finest Persian restaurants in town," said Salome.

"I prepared each dish personally," said Ashad with pride. "I hope that you all enjoy."

They took their seats at the dining table. Settings had been placed for five people. At the head of the table, a chair remained empty. It was there for Vendetti.

"I'd like to propose a toast," said Salome, passing a bottle down the table.

"I see we are abstaining from alcohol, which is probably for the best," said Mark with a smirk as he poured sparkling cider into Marnie's champagne flute.

Marnie jabbed him in the ribs with her elbow.

Salome raised her glass and spoke. "To our friend John, a true martyr. While those we have lost may not be with us tonight in body, they will surely be with us forever in spirit. We are blessed enough to have shared our lives with them. Let this be a reminder for us to cherish our time with those we still can. Love them now, love them well, and may peace prevail on Earth."

❆ ❆ ❆

THE MAN SAT WITH HIS BACK TO THE WINDOW, indifferent to the snow that fell in turbulent flurries behind him. The house was asleep but for the embers of a hearty fire that had run its course. They still glowed hot as the great log finally cracked in half in the final stages of its burn. Red sparks spiraled upward into the flue. He reclined in his chair with reading glasses perched on his nose and his feet atop the old desk handcrafted from the timbers of the HMS Resolute. His mind was elsewhere as his eyes scanned the pages of the report he held in his lap. The package had arrived earlier in the day by courier in an unmarked parcel, and he knew just where it had come from.

He thought of the Founding Fathers who had seen their fledgling nation as Hercules in a cradle—powerful, yet special in a moral sense. Empowered by its core beliefs that liberated human potential, making transcendent greatness a possibility rather than a dream. He thought of Washington, who had predicted that the country would acquire the power to enable, with just cause, the ability to bid defiance to any power on earth. He thought of Jefferson, who foresaw the vast expansion of an empire of liberty. He thought of John Quincy Adams, who considered the United States destined by God and nature to be the most populous and powerful people ever under one social contract. He shared these beliefs, beliefs that were enshrined in the Declaration of Independence, which in the words of Alexander Hamilton was a document written as a sunbeam in the whole volume of human nature by the hand of divinity itself.

He thought of the men who had shared this station before him—how it was their obligation and now his to share with the rest of mankind this most precious gift of democracy. The day that Hamilton had envisioned in the 1790s had come. America was now powerful enough to assist peoples in the gloomy regions of despotism and to rise up against the tyrants that oppressed them. This battle between liberty and despotism was what James Madison saw as the great struggle of the Epoch, and America's role in the battle was inescapable.

He remembered the words of Woodrow Wilson who proclaimed that democracy is the right more precious than peace. He remembered how Harry Truman had said that it was the duty of the United States to support free peoples who resisted subjection and to assist them to work out their destinies in their own way. Then there was Kennedy, who proclaimed America's determination to pay any price, bear any burden, meet any hardship, support any friend, and oppose any foe in order to assure the survival and the success of liberty. And there was Reagan, who in citing the words of Thomas Paine promised to begin the world anew by vanquishing an evil empire and leading the world into a new era of freedom.

The great weight of the nation's fate rested palpably upon his shoulders. His legacy would be remembered by the hard decisions he had made over the course of his two terms in office. Yet history was a fickle thing, only remembering what was convenient and shrouded by a veil of secrecy that prevented so many things from becoming public knowledge. Perhaps, he thought, the Freedom of Information Act would eventually reveal things over time, but he knew better. Some things would never leave the safe house of knowledge that only a very select group of men were privy to.

The report he held added to this burden of leadership, but it was also his mandate. It was he who would continue to lead the nation into the new era of freedom, and his successors would be charged with the same. There was no escaping America's destiny, and while so much of what had been done and was still yet to be done would be remembered as isolated events that would mar his image, he saw the bigger picture, the end game. He shared the same vision as the great men who begat this nation and who have commanded it from the Oval Office.

America, to him, was a beacon of democracy that would never fade in its magnificence or as a symbol of hope for the rest of the world. And if keeping that beacon alight meant war upon those who challenged America's resolve in striving for its ideals, then so be it. War was a necessary evil, he knew, but it was a means to an end. The steps had been laid out. The course was clear. The plan was right on track, exactly as it was predicted to be.

"I will lead this great nation," he said aloud. "So help me God."

❀ ❀ ❀

DEEP WITHIN THE HEART of the NSA, the seductive eye of the computer system blinked. Behind the machine's soulless stare was an unfathomable amount of information recently updated by its temporary nexus with Junior. The system perpetually processed data with one objective. Though the inputs changed from moment to moment as time continuously passed, the system's output never wavered from a course it had first been set upon decades ago by men who wanted one thing. Another report would be generated in a matter of hours and each day ever after. It would be delivered around the world as it had for years to the select few who were capable of executing the plans it entailed. The recipients of these reports were pawns, bishops, knights, rooks, queens, and kings in the great game. They were tactical players on a global chessboard dedicated to their role in the bigger picture. The plans they received were a means to an end—part of a strategy broader than their ability to comprehend, but something each knew was their destiny to carry out.

There was no denying the oracle.

Author's Note

I started writing FALSE POSITIVES in 2007. A lot has happened since then. On the world stage, some interesting events have come to pass such as Arab Spring, Stuxnet, and the capture and killing of Osama bin Laden. While I could have changed the direction of the book as a result of more current world events, I decided to keep the story in 2007. Any similarities with the plot or occurrences within the book to more modern events are the result of educated (and lucky) guesses more than anything else.

The idea for this book was born from the concept that the world runs on bad code. The software crisis is a term that was discussed as early as 1968 during the first NATO Software Engineering Conference. On this subject, Edsger Djikstra has said:

> "The major cause of the software crisis is that the machines have become several orders of magnitude more powerful! To put it quite bluntly: as long as there were no machines, programming was no problem at all; when we had a few weak computers, programming became a mild problem, and now we have gigantic computers, programming has become an equally gigantic problem."

Things may have gotten better since then, but they have also gotten worse. At the heart of the matter is that technology has become pervasive regardless of the fact that very few people really know how much of this technology works. This becomes potentially dangerous when systems run out of control. When I say this, I don't mean that SkyNet has become omniscient; I mean that the system's operators don't understand the impact of what it is they're doing all the time, and that the receivers of data from these systems may be over relying on information that has not been adequately vetted by the necessary human element.

It would be pretty bad if the government were running around killing people based on the decisions of computer system riddled with bad code. Thankfully, FALSE POSITIVES is make-believe, although that doesn't mean that certain concepts within the book aren't plausible.

Though this is a work of fiction, I felt compelled to use certain real-world people and organizations as characters and locales within my book. For example, I could have come up with a pseudonym for President George W. Bush, but I just couldn't bring myself to do it. The same goes for the National Counterterrorism Center and the ACMCU. What's key to remember here is that this is a work of fiction, and as such, all characters and organizations are used fictitiously. I'd like to be clear that have the utmost respect those (in uniform and civilian) who serve, work, and risk their lives to protect others and their freedoms. I mean no personal disrespect toward any person or organization mentioned directly or indirectly (or even omitted) within the book.

It's impossible to write a story like this and avoid politics and religion. Any reader will obviously view the material with his or her own slant. None of the characters in the book represent my personal political and religious viewpoints in total; however, I believe that each of them represents a good variety of positions that were prevalent during the story's timeline as well as today. While it may be naïve optimism on my part, I still like to think that everyone has the ability to overcome their differences with others and to transcend these obstacles and live together in harmony. It's whether or not we do that really counts.

Acknowledgements

Writing a novel can be a lonely process, and getting it published can be daunting. I've been lucky enough to have the help of a group of strong supporters along this journey. A big thanks goes those listed below in no particular order:

Unkle Roy, for being an early beta reader and providing excellent feedback regarding security clearances and government contract workers.

Mellissa, whose feedback convinced me that I really should hire an editor.

Len Sherman, who gave some great advice on how to make the first draft of FALSE POSITIVES and its characters better.

Bob MeCoy, who wrote me the best rejection letter I've ever received from an agent.

Chris Allen, who tirelessly draft after draft of FP and still wonders why it isn't for sale in airports everywhere.

Kristin Lindstrom, my editor at Flying Pig Media.

Farshid, who gave me "Mooshi."

Jenifer Todd Arsenault, who took my early concept for a cover design and turned it into something cool.

Madee James at xuni.com, who took Jen's cover and polished it to perfection.

Ben Goode at bengoode.com, for letting me use his fantastic flame picture that is the backdrop of the book's cover.

PB Crichton, for creating the "bug" symbol and making it open source.

Viquar, for long nights discussing Islam in Banphai and for giving me my first and only copy of The Qur'an.

About The Author

Kim Aleksander has worked with computer technology for over twenty-five years, and holds a Master's degree in Information Systems Management from the University of Liverpool. He was raised in California, spent his twenties in Hawaii, and moved to Asia in 1999. Presently, he lives in a jungle in Thailand with his wife, two sons, a Jack Russell terrier, and a few ducks.

More can be found here: http://kimaleksander.com.

REFERENCES

While FALSE POSITIVES is a work of fiction, this book owes its inspiration to real world events and things that have made the author go, "Hmm." The below represents a non-exhaustive list of references for information unearthed while researching this project. Any or all of the below found within the pages of this work has been fictionalized and a heavy dose of artistic license has been taken. Please refer to the copyright page at the front of this book before brandishing any pitchforks or hiring any lawyers.

ACLU. 2006. *Eavesdropping 101: What Can The NSA Do?* [Online]. American Civil Liberties Union. Available: http://www.aclu.org/files/pdfs/eavesdropping101.pdf.

ACLU. 2010. *Spy Files* [Online]. The American Civil Liberties Union. Available: http://www.aclu.org/spy-files. The ACLU maintains a blog about illegal domestic spying on Americans and related topics.

ACMCU. 2011. *Prince Alwaleed Bin Talal Center for Christian-Muslim Understanding* [Online]. Georgetown University. Available: http://cmcu.georgetown.edu/. The ACMCU is a real organization. It's mission is to improve relations between the Muslim world and the West and enhance understanding of Muslims in the West.

AYRES, I. 2007. *Super Crunchers : why thinking-by-numbers is the new way to be smart,* New York, Bantam Books. A good source on data mining and the impact it has on our lives.

BBC NEWS. 2006. *Thousands join pro-Islam protest* [Online]. BBC News. Available: http://news.bbc.co.uk/2/hi/uk_news/4700482.stm. There are lots of protests, but a quote from this one got me thinking: "We have the right to be angry." 1.3 billion angry people can be a very formidable force.

BUTLER, S. D. 1935. *War is a racket,* New York, Round Table Press, inc. This is U.S. Marine Major General, Smedley D.

Butler's publication on how business interests commercially benefit from warfare.

COWELL, A. 2006. *West Beginning to See Islamic Protests as Sign of Deep Gulf* [Online]. The New York Times. Available: http://www.nytimes.com/2006/02/08/international/europe /08islam.html. A good article that describes suspicion and miscomprehension with which we (or at least many Americans) regard Islam and *vice versa.*

DIJKSTRA, E. 1972. *The Humble Programmer* [Online]. Available: http://www.cs.utexas.edu/~EWD/ewd03xx/EWD340.PDF

ESPOSITO, J. L. 2002. *Unholy war : terror in the name of Islam,* New York, Oxford University Press. While John X. Vendetti is fictional, John L. Esposito is not. This book answered a lot of questions about why Americans are hated by certain Islamic groups.

ESPOSITO, J. L. 2007. *Want to Know About Islam? Start Here* [Online]. The Washington Post. Available: http://www.washingtonpost.com/wp-dyn/content/article/2007/07/20/AR2007072002137.html. A fantastic primer on Islam for the uninitiated and the inspriation for the creation of John X. Vendetti.

KAGAN, R. 2008. *Neocon Nation: Neoconservatism, c. 1776* [Online]. World Affiars Journal, Spring. Available: http://www.carnegieendowment.org/2008/05/29/neocon% 2Dnation%2Dneoconservatism%2Dc%2E%2D1776/889. A great article that inspired the final scene in the Oval Office.

KLEBNIKOV, P. 2003. Millionaire Mullahs. [Online]. *Forbes.* Available: http://www.forbes.com/forbes/2003/0721/056.html. Mohammed Kahn was a millionaire mullah.

KPFA. 2010. *Guns and Butter - "Vietnam, Star Wars, and 9/11" with Dr. Robert Bowman* [Online]. KPFA & Pacifica. Available: http://www.kpfa.org/archive/id/63529. A radio interview filled with some wonderful conspiracy theory, much of which sparked the creation of Lt.Col. Andrew Milas. But not all of it. The "real" Andy lives in Thailand last I heard from him.

LERNER, K. L. & LERNER, B. W. 2004. *Encyclopedia of espionage, intelligence, and security,* Detroit, Thomson/Gale. This is a great all-around reference for just what the title says. In here are some seeds on war games and computer simulation that bore the fruit for Mark's penchant for computer games and the birth of Project X.

NAVARRO, J. 2009. *Unmasking Terrorists - Two Critical Characteristics!* [Online]. Psychology Today. Available: http://www.psychologytoday.com/blog/spycatcher/200912/ unmasking-terrorists-two-critical-characteristics. Keen phychological insight on how terrorists begin their decent and ultimately reach the point of no return.

NPR. 2011. *Looking Back 10 Years: President Bush's Address to the Nation* [Online]. National Publich Radio. Available: http://www.npr.org/blogs/thetwo-way/2011/09/11/140374567/looking-back-10-years-president-bushs-address-to-the-nation. "None of us will ever forget this day."

PAVYAND IRAN NEWS. 2007. *US Imposes Financial Sanctions Against Iran's Martyrs Foundation* [Online]. NetNative. Available: http://payvand.com/news/07/jul/1278.html.

PRATCHETT, T. 1998. *Carpe Jugulum,* London, HarperCollins. Terry Pratchett is one of my favorite writers. "I've seen more meat on a butcher's pencil," is his.

PRICE, D. H. 2003. *Prosrate to the Patriot Act: Librarians as FBI Extension Agents* [Online]. counterpunch.org. Available: http://www.counterpunch.org/price03062003.html. Yes, your reading habits are known by the F.B.I. via your local librarian.

PRINCE, B. 2009. *FBI Director Nearly Hooked in Phishing Scam, Swears Off Online Banking* [Online]. Ziff Davis Enterprise Holdings Inc. Available: http://www.eweek.com/c/a/Security/FBI-Director-Nearly-Hooked-in-Phishing-Scam-Swears-Off-Online-Banking-616671/.

REDD, J. S. 2007. *Yes, We Do Have a Clue* [Online]. The Washington Post. Available: http://www.washingtonpost.com/wp-dyn/content/article/2007/07/12/AR2007071201199.html.

SCHNEIER, B. 2009. *Data Mining for Terrorists* [Online]. Schneier.com. Available: http://www.schneier.com/blog/archives/2006/03/data_min ing_for.html. This is what got me thinking about technology going seriously wrong. The idea is where Junior was born and inspriation for the title, FALSE POSITIVES.

SLAVIN, B. 2008. *Mullah, Money, and Militias: How Iran Exerts Influence in the Middle East* [Online]. United States Institute of Peace. Available: http://www.usip.org/files/resources/sr206.pdf.

SYMONDS, P. 2007. *Is the Bush administration behind the bombings in Iran?* [Online]. World Socialist Web Site. Available: http://www.wsws.org/articles/2007/feb2007/bomb-f17.shtml. An article regarding alleged, covert activities by the U.S. in Iran.

USC. 2011. *Institue for Creative Technologies* [Online]. University of Southern California. Available: http://ict.usc.edu/. Great things being done here with interactive digital media.

WAR ONLINE. n.d. *The Mechanics of a Living Bomb* [Online]. War Online. Available: http://www.waronline.org/en/terror/suicide.htm.

WIRED. 2007. *Pentagon Forecast: Cloudy, 80% Chance of Riots* [Online]. Condé Nast Digital. Available: http://www.wired.com/dangerroom/2007/11/lockheed-peers. Wired's Danger Room has some great articles related to technology and national security. This one in particular describes how the Pentagon uses computer modeling technology in hopes to predict world events.

www.ingramcontent.com/pod-product-compliance
Lightning Source LLC
Chambersburg PA
CBHW020339180626
46812CB00001B/264